A Crown Without Mercy

Crowns of Darkness | Book One

J.L. Weir

Trigger Warnings

A Crown Without Mercy contains content which may trigger some readers. If you are bothered by torture, kidnapping, self harm, or mentions of rape, please consider carefully before reading this book.

Chapter 1

It was ominously silent as Sylvana walked through the unfamiliarity of the forest, and it appeared as if all the wildlife had long ago disappeared. She knew she was being followed and froze when the snapping of a twig off in the distance startled her; her canines slid from her gums, she turned in the noise's direction, and squinted her eyes, trying to see who, or what, had been following her. After taking a few cautious steps back, she sprinted deeper into the woods. A rush of wind blew over her body and her legs flew out from beneath her when something crossed her throat; the air exploded from her lungs when she landed on her back. She fought back against her attacker, but whomever, whatever it was, lifted her off the ground and slammed her face down. She heard numerous males speaking however, their words were unintelligible, and she could not see through the strange material covering her head as they pinned her down and bound her wrists and ankles.

"Why are you doing this?" she bellowed.

The heavy weight of their bodies disappeared, and she lay there doing her best to hear anything that would indicate who had taken her, or why they had taken her.

They picked her up and placed her face down on what she assumed was a wood floor, based solely on the smell of the aged wood. Although they removed the binds from her wrists and ankles, she could not move. There was an ethereal energy pinning her down. They pulled the bag from her head and as she looked out of her peripheral vision; a large piece of wood obscured the attackers and the energy holding her down dissipated. She hastily rolled over, only to realize she was being sealed in a wooden box.

Sylvana pounded her fists on the smooth planks which did nothing more than cause trickles of dirt to cascade down on her face, causing her to choke on the dust and debris. Her sight was blurry and her eyes were watering having been coated in a layer of dirt. It wasn't long before the sounds of the dirt thumping against the top of the coffin became muffled and the last trickle of light shining between the planks from the lanterns above disappeared.

When the claustrophobic confines of the small structure consumed her, her breathing became labored, and she was panic-stricken. "Why are you doing this?" she screamed.

She continued pounding her fists against the planks over and over which did nothing more than drain what little energy she had left. She closed her eyes to let them heal, and held her breath to calm the erratic hammering of her heart.

After a moment, she opened her eye and used her keen sense of sight, seeking any means of escape. She slid her fingers over the planks, took a deep breath, and waved her hand across the lid. A yellowish-orange glow grew in intensity, and symbols and writing in a language she did not know morphed and twisted above her body.

"Powers of the Faye," she said aloud. The tears spilled from her eyes. "No one is coming. No one is going to save me."

"Sylvana, wake up," Calista said. After a moment, she gently shook her shoulder. "Sylvana, wake up."

Sylvana gasped for a breath and sat up in a cold sweat. "Calista?"

"Yes. I heard you scream. Are you okay?"

She tossed the covers to the side, and draped her legs over the edge of the bed. "I had had a terrible dream, is all."

Kadric sat at the table with his head resting on his cupped fists, dreading having to leave his family. He heard the scrape of the door and turned to see Alaric appear.

"Sit. Have a drink with me, son."

Alaric picked up a wood pitcher, filled a cup, and took a seat across the table. "What's on your mind, Father? You look troubled."

"I'm tired is all. What did you find out?"

Alaric reached into his pocket, pulled out a piece of cloth, and tossed it on the table. "It's as you suspected. There are Lycans in the area."

Kadric picked up the cloth, rubbed it between his fingers, and smelled it. "Fuck." He mumbled under his breath.

"How bad is it?" Alaric asked.

Kadric tossed the piece of cloth into the slowly, burning embers within the hearth. "There's much you are unaware of. If the Lycans are crossing our lands, the Acherons will soon follow."

"Why is it a problem? We're members of the Legion, you're a warrior for the Cynfadel clan, and the Acherons' respect them. They shouldn't have reason to suspect we have anything to do with it."

"You know them as well as I do. I won't allow my daughters to become their whores."

"Father, I know your animosity for their clan runs deep, but you worry too much."

"And you don't worry enough."

Alaric leaned back and studied the look of concern on his father's face. "What else is on your mind?"

"I need you to stay here and attend to your sisters. I have to leave, and I need you to give me your word that you will protect them by any means necessary."

"You're leaving? Why?"

"It's better if you don't know; any information you have can and will be extracted should Riordan become suspicious."

"It sounds like treason. What are you doing?"

"It's not treason, son, it's Cynfadel clan business."

"Does this have something to do with the dissidence of the Lycans against the Acherons?"

"Yes, and I'll say no more."

Alaric took a drink and peered at his father from over the rim of his cup, knowing there was more to this than *clan business*. When are you leaving?"

"Tonight."

"Tonight? You are going to disappear in the middle of the night? Are you at least going to tell your daughters?"

"No. They will have an incessant number of questions I am not prepared to answer." He finished his ale, pushed his chair back, and stood.

Alaric stood and walked to his father. "When will you return?"

Kadric pulled him in for a tight embrace and patted his back. "Do I have your word?"

Alaric hugged him tightly, feeling as if it was the last time he was going to see his father. "Father, you have my word. I will protect my sisters, and I need you to give me your word that you will return."

"Son, I have every intention of returning."

Alaric and his sisters, Sylvana, Calista, and Mira were sitting in the parlor drinking ale, and playing a game of dice called Angon.

Alaric filled his cup and nodded toward Sylvana. "Your shot."

Sylvana picked up the dice and shook them in her hands before tossing them onto the table. Once the dice stopped rolling, she looked at Alaric and smirked. "Beat that."

"Looks like you're losing again, Brother," Calista chuckled.

Calista grabbed the dice and Sylvana picked up on a subtle scent of smoke. She looked at the hearth and then out of the window and noticed an eerie red glow coming from the top of the barn. "Shit—fire!"

"What?" Alaric shoved his chair back and by the time they ran out of the door toward the barn, swirls of black smoke and forked flames were already crawling across the wood planks. The girls filled buckets of water from the well and handed them to Alaric, who leapt onto the roof. The smoke and the sounds of hissing steam consumed him when the negligible amount of water splashed into the growing flames.

Calista ripped the barn doors open and she and Mira ushered the horses out. "Out—go!" Calista yelled, as she opened each of the stalls and slapped the horses on their hindquarters.

"The water, it will never be enough!" Sylvana waved her hand and an icy-blue mist enveloped Alaric and the scorching flames.

He felt a bitter chill and a haze of ghost-gray smoke surrounded him. He spun around and looked down. "Sylvana! What the fuck are you doing?"

Calista grabbed her wrist. "If anyone saw you and word gets out—"

Sylvana wrenched her wrist free. "What was I to do? Stand here and let the barn burn to the ground?"

Alaric leapt off the roof and grabbed Sylvana's arm. "And if someone saw you, what then? We will never see this place again. They might as well burn it all down! How many times have you been told not to use your powers?"

She wrapped her hand around his fist and pulled his fingers loose. "Alaric, let go."

"That was fucking careless," Calista snapped.

Sylvana held her arms out to her side and walked in a slow circle. "Who's here? The nearest manor is a mile away, and it's pitch black out!"

Mira was standing with her arms across her chest, not understanding what was occurring all around her. She looked across the field to see if any of the horses were there when she noticed something in the tree line. She narrowed her eyes, sharpening her acute sense of sight, and thought she saw a silhouette leaning against a tree. Whatever, whomever it was slipped back into the shadows. Her pulse quickened, and she stepped backward toward her brother. "Alaric," she said.

"Not now, Mira," he snapped.

"You will not do it again. Do you understand me?" he bellowed.

Mira tugged on his shirt. "Alaric!"

"Mira, stop," he demanded.

Calista gently grabbed the back of Mira's night shirt and pulled her away. "Leave them alone."

"But, Calista—"

Calista interrupted her and nuzzled her forward. "Go open the gate to the stable. Let us deal with this."

Mira stood momentarily and looked at her siblings. "Fine, I won't tell you at all," she snarked.

Calista rolled her eyes and turned her attention back to her siblings.

"All of our kind possess powers, Alaric. What makes you think anyone is interested in us? No one so much as speaks about the war that took place. We've been living here for over one hundred and twenty-three years and in all that time, no one has ever looked at us twice."

Alaric grabbed her wrist and held her hand up. "They do not wield powers like you do. Do not think the Acherons, or The Guild of Entente have forgotten. If they get wind of this, they will come."

Sylvana pulled her hand back. "How do you know?"

Alaric cocked his head, and squinted his eyes. "I am a member of the Legion. It is my business to know."

She rolled her eyes and walked away, but Calista stepped in front of her. "Where are you going?"

"To fetch the horses. Where else?" she snarked.

After they sequestered their horses and secured them in the outer stable, they went back to the manor. Calista snatched her cup off of a table and took one large drink, followed by another.

Alaric placed his palm on the edge of the window, the other on his hip, and stared at the barn. He then turned and looked at Sylvana. "I need you to understand. I know there are whispers in the castle—they have not forgotten. This is serious, and your lack of judgement puts us all in peril."

Sylvana stared at Alaric and then looked at Calista, who was scowling at her. "Riordan and his brothers have never so much as whispered our names."

Alaric rubbed his face, feeling exasperated with his sisters' continued defiance. "Have you ever asked yourself why Riordan and his brothers have never taken a mate?"

"What does it have to do with us? Do you think they would ever consider me as a suitable mate?"

"Your naivety is not becoming. You are smarter than this," Alaric scolded.

"What do you and father know you are not revealing?"

Alaric took another drink and stared at her.

"Well?" Sylvana asked.

"There's nothing to tell. Father asked me to look after you and our sisters, and it's exactly what I am doing."

Sylvana furrowed her brows. "Does this have something to do with the Lycan I smelled in the fields a few days ago?"

"Leave it alone, Sylvana."

Calista reached for Mira's hand and smiled. "Let's get you to bed." She then addressed Sylvana and Alaric. "I don't know about the two of you, but I've had enough for one night."

Sylvana followed her sisters before glancing back at Alaric. "At some point, you're going to have to tell us the truth, whether you like it or not."

As they headed up the stairs, they heard the door slam shut behind them. Calista looked at Sylvana. "You sure have a way of stoking his temper."

Sylvana shrugged her shoulders. "He'll get over it."

Riordan and Kieran were sitting on a large, ornate settee five steps above the main floor, watching the games. When Riordan noticed Nicolai entering through the doors, he nodded in his direction. "Nicolai has returned."

"Good, the games are just beginning," Kieran replied.

Nicolai glided up the marble stairs and took a seat next to Kieran. "What have I missed?"

"Nothing," Kieran replied.

"Don't keep us in suspense. How did it go tonight?" Riordan asked.

"Sylvana, the eldest sister, put the flames out."

"Where the hell was her brother? Our scouts led us to believe they were all there," Riordan replied.

"They were there. Alaric was on the roof tossing meager buckets of water over the flames."

"Was Sylvana on the roof as well?" Kieran asked.

"No," Nicolai replied.

"I want a straight answer," Riordan stated adamantly.

"She was standing in front of the barn, and when she waved her hand a wash of energy put the flames out."

"What are you saying?" Kieran asked.

Nicolai looked over and nodded at the servant, who handed him a silver goblet. "It seems she yields powers only an original can conjure."

"Well, hell, it appears the mystery is ever growing," Riordan replied.

The Guild of Entente, which was comprised of thirty-members, each of whom was the eldest Lord of their clan, were sitting around a long table discussing the recent events transpiring throughout the lands.

Astaroth, the highest ranking member, was sitting at the head of the table. "The Faye are suffering from ill-begotten delusions, and their compulsions are a threat to all. We cannot, will not, allow them to cross into our world. This will do nothing more than spring old wars into life."

"The Barouqe Warriors seized another Faye two nights ago and have secured confirmation they are planning to launch an attack," Rhazien stated.

Marque placed his forearms on the table, and looked at the large map that was spread out. "Not only do we need to secure the edge of the veil, we need to deal with the Lycans, who have been scouting the surrounding territories."

"Inbred Lycans have also been spotted crossing the Black Moor and are hunting again," Norix added.

"I don't believe they are hunting. I suspect Ranan is sending them over as a distraction," Astaroth said.

"Yes, milord. The Lycans in the surrounding territories are not inbred," Rhazien agreed.

"Riordan believes they are looking for a purebred Ascelin," Leon added.

"Punitive actions against the Faye will continue as ordered. As for the Lycans, we should allow them to continue without interference. If they are indeed looking for an Ascelin, we can use the information we gather to our benefit," Theron suggested.

"Agreed," Astaroth replied.

"We should pit the Faye and the Lycans against one another. Allow another Faye to cross the veil. We will seize it, take it to the edge of the Black Moor, and make it appear as if an inbred killed it. The treaty will dissolve into suspicion and bitterness on both sides," Norix suggested.

Astaroth sat back momentarily, contemplating what he was suggesting. "Do all members agree?"

"Aye," they stated, along with a nod.

"If an Ascelin does indeed exist, what are your intensions where she is concerned?" another asked.

Astaroth cocked his head and glared at him. "The Acherons will take her as their mate. Why do you ask a fool's question?"

Kirnan tipped his cup at Astaroth. "And if there is more than one, what will we do with them?"

"The Acherons will decide," Astaroth replied.

Kirnan gave a slight nod of agreement.

Chapter 2

Sylvana and Calista loaded up a small cart with fresh vegetables for Sylvana's latest delivery.

Calista tossed the burlap cover over the load and secured her side. "I don't know why you insist on going. Get a Helot to do it."

Sylvana pulled the ropes and stepped around the wagon. "I don't want them on our land. You know they bring discord wherever they go, not to mention they can't be trusted any more than a shifter's whisper."

"There's talk of another uprising. You need to be careful," Calista stated.

Sylvana mounted her mare and looked down at Calista. "Always. I'll be back before dark."

"Wait!" Mira shouted as she ran across the pasture. "Sylvana, take me with you."

Sylvana and Calista looked at her and scowled. "You're not going, Mira. How many times do we have to tell you?"

"That's bullshit! I need new things and I want to go with you."

Calista grabbed her arm and spun her around. "Mira! Watch your mouth."

Mira grabbed the reins and looked up at Sylvana. "Why do you always get to go while I'm stuck sitting around here all the damn time?"

"Mira, you're too young and I am not taking you. Now let go." Sylvana wrenched the reins from her hand while Calista pulled her back.

Mira crossed her arms and stomped her foot. "I'll tell father!"

"Tell him what you will." Sylvana shrugged.

Calista wrapped an arm around Mira's chest and looked up at Sylvana. "Go. I'll deal with her spoiled ass."

Sylvana pulled the reins and Calista took Mira's hand and walked her back to the manor. "You need to stop threatening to tell secrets whenever you don't get your way."

"I'm not a bairn anymore."

"Ohh, Mira," Calista replied with a heavy sigh.

"One day, I'll be the one going to the Castle and Sylvie will be the one stuck here," she snarked.

"You need to stop hating on your sister. She's good to you."

"No, she's not. She treats me like I'm a bairn."

"Then stop acting like it!" Calista demanded.

"You're just as mean! When I mate an Acheron, I'll leave both of you."

Calista fisted the back of Mira's cloak, and pulled her back. She then grabbed her jaw in her hand, meeting her face to face. "If you ever speak in such a manner again, I will wipe the words from your mouth."

Mira swung her arm over Calistas and hit her forearm. "Let go!"

Calista let go and watched her run across the field. *That girl is going to get into some serious trouble*, she thought. *Father or Alaric had better do something.*

Sylvana reveled in the warmth of the morning sun as she crossed the fields and headed into the forest. The nut-brown trees closed behind her like a cloak of armor, while their knotted branches rose upwards like a thicket of upstretched arms. The boughs, gnarled with age, dropped their trove of nuts onto the path while briars and brambles bordered the road. She listened to the sounds of the crows calling, the chirping of chipmunks as they rushed up the trunks of the trees, and the rustling of small animals scurrying beneath the dense brush. Although the dirt road was cast into shadows by the labyrinth of tall trees on either side, soft rays of sunlight filtered their way through the thick canopy, dotting the forest floor around her. The sweet fragrance being carried with the gentle breeze washed over her in a comforting embrace.

It wasn't long before she heard the muffled voices of the Helots tending to the fields off in the distance. The forest became brighter, and the trees gave way to fields of fertile land. She followed the rough gravel path leading toward the large, gated entrance. Per usual, Helots begging for handouts approached her.

"I have nothing for you," she stated adamantly.

"Just a scrap is all I ask for," another begged.

Another grabbed Rana's reins and pulled the wagon to a stop; a dozen Helots then rushed over surrounding the wagon.

She "turned," bared her canines, leapt from her mare toward the one who was holding the reins, and seized his throat in a tight grip. "Remove your hand or I'll remove it for you," she snarled.

He gave a slight bow and released his grip just as Sylvana raised her knee and thrust her foot forward, sending him spiraling backwards. The rest of the group took heed and backed away.

Fucking scant, I would've ripped his throat out if their blood wasn't so rotten, she thought, as she mounted Rana, again.

She passed rows of guards and numerous warriors before being stopped, two of whom held her mare's reins, while two more approached and flipped open the burlap.

"More food for the mortals?" one of them asked.

"Yes," Sylvana replied.

"You're always in danger out there. Why do you insist on doing something so beneath you?" another asked.

Another looked at her as if in disgust. "I don't understand why someone of your status would bother doing a Helots job?"

"It's a wage, is it not?" However, it was information she was seeking, not a wage.

"There are better ways for someone like you to earn denarius."

Sylvana rolled her eyes and looked at the gate. "May I pass?"

He nodded at the guards, and they stood back, motioning her forward.

The noise of the outer courtyard became a sea of sounds, and the shadows being cast on the ground from the towers and turrets looked ominous and uninviting. She made it to the market, where tables and baskets of goods were being sold in a mess of confusion. She continued past the market and followed the cobblestone road until she rounded the corner, pulled Rana to a halt, and waited patiently at the back door of the kitchen for Muriel.

Sylvana was untying the burlap when she heard the clank of the lock. Muriel opened the door and pulled Sylvana in for a friendly hug.

"How was your ride? The fields are full of beggars today."

"Yes, they are." Sylvana chuckled.

"What happened?"

"Same as usual, only this time one of them grabbed Rana's reins."

"Scant is what they are. I don't know why the Acherons allow it."

"I have a feeling it's more about listening to their whispers."

Muriel smiled and led Sylvana into the expansive kitchen. "True, they chatter—a lot."

Muriel turned to the staff and motioned toward the door. "Fetch the goods from the wagon."

"Come, let's talk in private," Muriel suggested.

"First things first." Muriel walked to the other side of the kitchen, collected two cups and an amber hued bottle filled with fresh ale.

They walked along a small hallway before they reached the main hall where the blue-gray walls rose like a fortress of stone. The light from the sun shone through the small, asymmetrical windows adorning every wall in perfect symmetry. Enormous statues and large oriental carpets decorated the main hall, while gigantic, black iron chandeliers filled with hundreds of candles hung from the cathedral ceilings.

"It's beauty always catches me off guard," Sylvana said.

"The Acherons would accept nothing less than regality in its finest," Muriel replied.

"It defies their reputations," Sylvana joked.

"It sure does." Muriel chuckled.

They entered the courtyard and followed the gray, stone path toward the well-kept gardens where fragrant flowers, pruned trees, and hedges lined the expansive pathway. Sylvana looked to one segment which contained large trees whose branches sagged beneath the weight of its heavy fruit. *Fruit trees for those who don't eat, and none for those who do,* she thought.

Riordan and his brothers stood on the parapet walk near the main tower, watching over the gardens.

"Sylvana makes a lot of deliveries here, but I've never seen her sell anything in the market," Kieran stated.

Nicolai rested his forearms on the stone battlements, feeling as curious as his brothers. "She sells to the kitchen staff and spends most of her time with Muriel."

"Some guards refer to Muriel as having inquisitive eyes and ears," Kieran added.

"Why would a female of Sylvanas's status sell goods for Helots and Mortals?" Riordan asked.

"Your guess is as good as mine. From what I've witnessed, she loathes both races," Kieran replied.

"Riordan, what's with your sudden interest in the female?" Nicolai asked.

"Lycans were seen in the forest around her manor, and I've received word her father Kadric snuck out in the middle of the night. No one seems to know of his whereabouts," Riordan answered.

"I'm curious why the Lycans are scurrying around his land like rats?" Kieran questioned.

Nicolai stood up and leaned against the tower with his arms crossed. "Kadric and the Cynfadel clan have always been loyal. He and his son, Alaric, are also well-respected members of the Legion. It would make sense Kadric would leave on clan business for periods of time, especially if he knows about them. He may be hunting them down?"

"Since you want to defend her family, I want you to make her acquaintance," Riordan stated. Nicolai nodded and the three of them stared down at the two females.

Kieran rested his forearms on the stone wall. "I would like to make her acquaintance as well."

"This private enough?" Muriel suggested.

They took a seat on a stone bench that sat beneath an ancient Anker-wycke Yew in the center of the garden and Muriel filled their cups.

"How are your sisters?" Muriel asked as she handed Sylvana a cup.

"Calista is good, but Mira is becoming something else to deal with, and yours?"

"Bothersome," Muriel joked.

Sylvana took a sip of her ale and smiled coyly at Muriel. "You going to ask about Alaric?"

Muriel smiled back and shrugged her shoulders. "No, but since you brought him up, how is he?"

"Other than spending most of his time with the Legion, he's great. He asked about you the last time I made a delivery. You should come to the manor for a visit."

"I might take you up on the offer. If I tell you something, will you keep it between us?"

"Of course I will."

"I really like Alaric, but I've also met someone."

"Really? Who? When did that happen?"

"Not too long ago. But we aren't compatible, status wise."

"Is his status above or below yours?"

"Below." Muriel sighed.

"That will be a problem. However, situations tend to work themselves out."

"I hope so. Not to change the subject, but I have a little gossip for you."

"Go on."

"The uprising, there is more to it if what hushed voices say is true."

"Like what?"

"It is said that the Lycans are holding a female purebred as a breeder."

Sylvana was taken aback. "Seriously? Do you know where?"

"No. No one seems to know for sure. The information is broken at best."

Sylvana looked at the ground and sighed. "Do you think my mother could be with them?"

"I don't believe so, but my advice to you is to never speak of it aloud. We all know your mother was—" she stated gently, without needing to finish her sentence. "What makes you think she's alive?"

"Honestly, I'm just keeping the faith alive.It's better than accepting the cruel truth."

"That was so many years ago, Sylvie. I wouldn't get your hopes up. If she were alive, your father would have found her by now."

"Maybe. But what if she's the purebred female?" Sylvana questioned.

"I suppose, it's possible? Have you told your father or Alaric you have been looking for information on her?"

"No, and I would appreciate it if you didn't bring it up to Alaric."

"I won't. The two of us, even speaking about this matter, could get us both thrown into the bowels of hell."

"Riordan and his brothers are cruel and unforgiving. I have no intention of mentioning this to anyone," Sylvana replied.

"Sylvie, I have another bit of salacious gossip for you."

"Well, that sounds interesting."

Muriel leaned forward and whispered in her ear. "The other night, I heard two warriors talking, and they mentioned the name Ranan."

Sylvana's eyes widened, and she raised her cup to her mouth, trying to hide her reaction. *"Shhh.* holy hell if anyone heard you."

"I know, but I had to tell you. How could I keep it to myself?"

"Ranan?" Sylvana mouthed.

Muriel nodded and looked around, feeling nervous having spoken the name, even if in a whisper.

"Speak of this to no one," Sylvana demanded.

"I'm done speaking of it at all now that I got it off my chest. By the way Lenora's here, want to go see her?"

"Yes. We need to put this conversation to bed."

Tobias is also a purebred Acheron and a progeny of Riordan, Nicolai, and Kieran's uncle, while Lenora is the progeny of a purebred clan known as the Phelans.

Muriel and Sylvana made their way to Lenora's' bed chamber and knocked on the door. "Come in," she answered.

"I have a friend here to see you," Muriel stated.

"Sylvie!" Lenora exclaimed. "I haven't seen you in months. Come—sit." She reached for her hand and pulled her over to the table and chairs in her chamber. "So tell me, how have you been?"

"Busy with the manor. When did you return?"

"Last night. Seeing how I'm mating Tobias during the next full moon, I'm here for good."

"I'm so happy for you," Sylvana offered.

"You should come to the ceremony. I'll get you an invitation."

"I'd love to."

Sylvana looked out the window and stared at the ember-red colors of the setting sun. "I should head home. It will be dark in a few hours."

"You have plenty of time, lets sneak out and have an ale," Lenora suggested.

"Sneak out?" Sylvana questioned.

"Yes. Tobias is ridiculous. He won't allow me to go anywhere alone. We can sneak out the back passageway."

"I don't think it's a good idea, and I don't want to be in the woods at night."

"I'll get you an escort or you can sleep at my place tonight," Muriel offered.

"Sylvie, come on, have fun for once. All you ever do is work." Lenora chuckled.

"Fine, why not?" she replied.

Lenora, Muriel, and Sylvana entered the tavern through the large wood door and a feeling of discomfort crept over Sylvana when they were welcomed with watchful eyes. It was crowded and the conversations being told with raised voices seemed to compete with one another for superiority. Marble pillars supported the upper floor, and the ambient light came from the gentle flames flickering within the numerous lanterns hanging from the ceiling and the sconces attached to the walls. Long, stained wood tables lined the center, while smaller tables placed along the interior walls allowed for some privacy. Various weapons, shields, and other clan décor hung from the stone walls while aged barrels of ale were stacked behind the bar. Other than the mortal females who served as blood hosts, lords and warriors made up most of the patrons.

Sylvana wasn't sure they should be there based on the casual glances and curious looks they were getting. "I'm uncomfortable," she whispered as she glanced at the unwelcoming crowd.

"Don't worry about them. They all know Lenora is mating Tobias. I'm sure they weren't expecting to see a purebred female tonight," Muriel offered.

"They won't bother us," Lenora added as she sat next to Muriel.

"We're safer here than anywhere else. They would all protect a mate," Muriel replied.

Soon after they took a seat in the back corner, one barkeep made his way over. "What can I get you and your friends, milady?"

"Three ales," Lenora answered.

After the barkeep handed out the drinks, he looked at Lenora. "You shouldn't be here, milady."

Lenora waved her hand dismissively and tossed three silver coins on the table. "We would like a pitcher of the fresh ale."

He collected the coins and nodded. "If it pleases you."

Alaric returned home and noticed Rana wasn't in the stable. He immediately headed into the manor. "Calista, Mira?" he called out.

"Alaric, is something wrong?" Calista asked, as she headed down the stairs with Mira in tow.

"Where is Sylvana? She should have been home hours ago."

"I don't know. I'm sure she's fine. She has mentioned she has a friend she likes to visit," Calista offered, covering for her sister. *What is she up to now?* Calista wondered.

"A friend? And what's this friend's name?" Alaric demanded.

"She never said, but in case you're worried, it's another female."

"It will be dark in an hour. I'm going to fetch her."

"Alaric, relax. You and father can be extremely overbearing. Let your sister enjoy herself with a friend."

"I don't have a problem with her having a friend. I am concerned because it's going to be dark soon."

"Leave her be," Calista demanded.

"Who gave you the authority to decide?"

"Don't be an ass. She's not a bairn anymore." She filled a cup and shoved it in his direction. "Relax."

Alaric picked up the cup and headed for the door.

"Alaric!" Calista shouted, as he shut the door behind him.

"Is Sylvana really with a female?" Mira asked.

"Yes, and you don't need to concern yourself with your sister's business."

"It is his duty to protect us while father is gone," Mira replied snarkily.

Calista turned and walked away.

A loud roar erupted from the crowd, startling the girls. They looked to see what the uproar was about and realized it was regarding Kieran Acheron, who had entered the tavern.

"Shit," Sylvana mumbled as she and the girls looked at each other nervously. Lenora took a large sip and sunk into her seat as if trying to hide. "If Tobias doesn't know I'm here now, he will sooner than later."

Sylvana studied Kieran as he greeted a group of warriors who were following him to the bar. He was wearing brown leather trousers and matching leather boots which laced up the front. His white tunic was unbuttoned, untucked, and partially hanging off one of his shoulders, revealing his solid chest, which was covered with intricate tattoos and multiple battle scars; even the thin black hair that adorned his chest and stomach couldn't hide his toned pecs and chiseled abs. A single black leather strap, encrusted with colorful gems, rested between his pecs and held a sheath firmly attached to his back.

Sylvana studied every feature; his broad shoulders, the way his muscles stretched the fabric of his sleeves when he moved, and how the hair on his stomach followed the V that disappeared beneath the waistband of his trousers. It mortified her when she looked up and realized he was staring at her. "Fuck me," she said as she diverted her eyes and fumbled for her cup.

"Sylvana, what's wrong?" Muriel asked.

"He's looking right at me," she replied nervously.

"Who?" Lenora asked as she looked around.

"Kieran Acheron," she stated.

Muriel and Lenora glanced at the bar and Kieran was now making his way through the crowd, and heading in their direction.

Muriel leaned forward and whispered, "Dammit, he's heading over here."

"Please tell me he isn't," Lenora replied as she looked down at her cup.

"Ladies," Kieran said as he pulled the strap over his head and plopped the heavy sheath on the table.

"Milord," Muriel and Lenora said in unison.

Sylvana looked at the handle of the sword rather than make eye contact with him as she greeted him. "Milord."

"Mind if I take a seat?" he asked, as he slid onto the bench next to Sylvana.

Sylvana glanced at Lenora and Muriel and scooted over as far as she could get. "Not at all."

"What brings you here tonight? I didn't realize the tavern was a place for the ladies?"

"I—we were having an ale, milord. I only arrived last night, and I thought—well, we thought we would have a drink is all," Lenora replied.

"Does Tobias know you are here?"

"No, milord."

"Well, hell, this evening has taken an unexpected turn of events. I'm curious to see what his reaction will be.I believe his is on his way."

Fuck me, Lenora thought as she leaned back, and her hands fell into her lap.

"I assume you are Sylvana Orfaedo and Muriel Guston?"

"Yes," Sylvana replied, feeling the claustrophobic confines of the booth along with Kieran's menacing presence.

"It was nice to meet you, but I think it's time for us to be on our way," Sylvana stated.

Sylvana felt his knee touch hers when he adjusted his body and a jolt of nervous energy seared through her very core. "Leaving so soon?"

Sylvana casually adjusted herself and moved her knee away from his, hoping he wouldn't notice as she spoke. "Yes, milord. I should head home. It's late."

Kieran glanced down and then looked at Sylvana. "Do I make you nervous?"

"No, milord."

He reached down and squeezed her thigh. "Stay. We should get to know each other better," he said, genuinely curious about the undeniable pull he felt toward her.

Sylvana, Muriel, and Lenora looked at each other, not knowing what to say or how to respond.

"The two of you are as quiet as the dead," he joked. *Speaking of which, I feel as though her energy is pulling me from the grave. What the hell is it?* He wondered.

Alaric would kill me if he found out about any of this, Sylvana thought before answering. "It's late is all and we were about to leave."

Kieran picked up her cup and set it back down. "Leaving a cup full of ale on the table?"

"Yes. I've had enough."

"Who's Alaric?" Kieran asked.

Sylvana did all she could to keep her facial expressions in check, realizing how easily he had read her mind; it was as if he had simply looked at a page in a book. "My brother."

"Tell him you were my guest. It should settle the matter."

The girls became came increasingly uncomfortable as their gaze shifted absently to each other.

"We really should go," Muriel said.

"Sylvana, you make enough deliveries for the castle. Have you met my brothers?"

"No, milord."

"You will soon enough," he said before taking a drink from his silver goblet.

The girls noticed the abrupt silence and hushed whispers coming from the once boisterous crowd. They looked toward the door and Tobias had entered with Nicolai Acheron and was looking around the tavern before setting his sights on Lenora.

Shit! Lenora thought.

They walked over, and Tobias placed his hand on Kieran's shoulder. "Milord." He nodded.

"Tobias, good to see you. I'm curious. Why are you here?" he asked with a half-cocked grin.

Tobias tugged at Kieran's tunic in a joking manner. "I see you've dressed up," he joked back. He then placed his palms on the table and leaned towards Lenora. "What the hell are you doing in this place?"

Lenora placed her hand on his forearm. "I was having a drink with my friends. I meant to tell you, but I didn't know where you were," she lied.

"This is not a place for your friends, much less my mate."

"Tobias, I didn't know. I only arrived last night."

"Now you know. Get up Len, you're leaving."

She stood, and he wrapped his arm around her body, lifted her chin with his fist and stole a heated kiss, after which he pulled back and brushed the back of his hand down her cheek. "If you ever venture out on your own without my permission, I will carry your ass home every time." He then playfully flung her body over his shoulder and smacked her ass.

"Owe! Dammit, Tobias. Put me down." She chuckled.

"Nope. Never," he replied as he carried her out.

A flash of amusement crossed Sylvana and Muriel's faces when they looked at each other. However, it only lasted momentarily. Sylvana turned her attention back to Nicolai and subtly looked him over. His tunic, leather trousers, and boots had been fashioned from materials only those sired by a purebred could afford, and he reeked of wealth and power. His pleated tunic was partially opened, revealing a scar on his chest which looked like someone had carved it into his smooth, chestnut colored skin with hatred and malice. His raven black hair was shaved on the sides of his head just above his ears, while the rest was perfectly coifed on the top. His demeanor, his stoic expression and the way he stared at her were nothing short of menacing; the waves of warning she felt were like nothing she had ever experienced.

Nicolai studied her as much as she was studying him. *Who are you? There's an underlying scent that speaks to me. Its familiarity is—centuries old?* "Brother, what brings you here?" Nicolai asked.

"Making new acquaintances," Kieran replied as he stood.

Muriel and Sylvana slid from the benches to leave, but Nicolai put a hand on Sylvana's shoulder and held her in place. She inhaled deeply and stood motionless.

"Muriel, I assume you know the way home?" Kieran asked.

"Yes, milord." She curtsied and gave Sylvana an apologetic smile.

"I'm curious why you're in a place like this. You should know better—yes?" Nicolai asked.

"Milord," was all Sylvana managed to say.

He then looked at Kieran. "She can speak, can't she?"

"A little." Kieran chuckled.

"Milord, I did not know Lenora would get into trouble or I would never have asked her here."

Nicolai raised his eyebrows and cocked his head. "You want us to believe you suggested this?"

"Yes, milord."

Nicolai filled his cup, and Kieran picked up Sylvana's and handed it to her. "I know it's not the truth. At least you're loyal to your friends. I can respect that," Nicolai replied.

Sylvana looked up at Nicolai, and then at the door.

"Shall we?" he stated as he and Kieran looked at each other. "Brother, I'll meet you for a drink later."

"You know where to find me," Kieran replied.

Sylvana nodded politely toward Kieran. "Milord."

"We will see each other again." Kieran winked.

Once she and Nicolai were out of the tavern, they heard the bellows of laughter echo from the door as it slowly closed behind them.

Nicolai looked down at Sylvana. "They will talk about this for some time."

"I'm sure they will," Sylvana replied.

"Do you have an escort to see you back to your manor?"

"No, milord."

"You're not thinking you can travel alone, are you?"

"I can stay with Muriel. It's down the road from the market."

"I don't think staying with Muriel is an option. I'm sure her father has received word of her whereabouts by now."

"I assume he wouldn't care. According to Muriel, he spends most of his time drinking and gambling."

"And you're comfortable putting yourself in the home of a besotted male?"

"No. I was hoping I could stay with Lenora. Obviously, it's not an option. Honestly, I don't know what I was thinking."

"I will see you get home safely."

"Milord, I appreciate the offer, but I will be fine."

"Milord is so formal. Call me Nicolai."

"Yes, milord."

Nicolai looked down at her and raised an eyebrow.

Sylvana looked up at the intimidating warrior towering over her. "Yes—Nicolai."

"Much better. Since we have that settled, what brings you here? Other than drinking where you shouldn't."

"I deliver goods to the kitchen."

"Why would they need you? It's beneath you, is it not?"

"Everyone tells me so, but it pays well."

"I didn't realize your family was in need."

"We're not—" she began.

"Then why do a Helot's job?"

It's not like I can tell him the truth about my mother. She thought, having cloaked it from Nicolai. "I like to earn my own wage."

"Respectable, I suppose. Although, if you were to take a mate, you wouldn't have to."

"They will not mate me off so I can go from relying on my father to relying on a mate."

"What does your father think?"

"A lot." She chuckled.

"I'm sure he does. I heard you had a bit of trouble in the fields today."

"It was nothing more than a couple of beggars. I'm used to it."

"I also heard you sent one head over heels. Why didn't you drain him?"

"I have no desire to get their blood in my mouth, much less drink from the filth," she stated, before taking a sip.

"There are other ways to kill without getting their blood in your mouth."

She choked on her ale. "I'm—sure there is." She wiped her mouth, feeling embarrassed by the uncouth behavior.

Nicolai stepped in front of her and ran his thumb down the corner of her mouth. "No need to be abashed."

After a short time Sylvana pointed at Rana, who was in the visitors stable. "That's my mare."

Nicolai picked her up, sat her on Rana, and placed the bit in her mouth he had removed from the wall.

"What are you doing? I need my saddle."

"I will escort you home."

"What? You?"

"Yes," he replied sternly, as he mounted Rana and adjusted himself behind her.

"There's no need to put yourself out. I'm sure someone else would see me home," she suggested.

"No." He pulled Rana's reins and gently kicked her hindquarters. He then wrapped one arm around her waist and scooted closer. She reluctantly placed her hand on his forearm and held Rana's mane with the other.

He leaned down and whispered in her ear. "I can hear the erratic hammering of your heart. I have no ill intentions."

"I never expected to being heading home like this is all," she replied.

Rana leisurely walked down the road leading into the forest. Sylvana glanced at the shadows waning amongst the outstretched branches, and the burnt-orange rays of the moon cleaving their way through the thick canopy. She then noticed one shadow in particular that appeared to be the silhouette of a man, gently swaying beneath a large branch from where he hung. His arms and legs were awkwardly contorted as if he were a jester hanging from uneven ropes. The lifeless corpse was suspended above a dark pool of depravity which had cascaded down his body onto the forest floor. The dampness lingered in the night air and wrapped within it was the stench of death and a familiar scent. Sylvana looked at the body, and then glanced back at Nicolai, who pulled Rana to a halt, just shy of the body.

They have no mercy, she thought. She placed her hand over her churning stomach. "Is he the beggar who stopped me earlier?" she asked.

"Yes," Nicolai replied unemotionally.

"Did you do this?"

"He is a victim of his own circumstances and choices," he replied cryptically.

"I hope you didn't get his blood in your mouth?"

Nicolai chuckled and gently kicked Rana's hindquarters. "Have you ever take a life, Sylvana?"

"Once. It was a long time ago."

"What happened?" Nicolai asked.

"I don't enjoy talking about it. It's not a pleasant memory."

"Tell me. I'm genuinely curious," he urged.

The memory flooded her mind, and for reasons she did not understand, she wanted to tell him. She took a slow, deep breath and began. "My sisters and I were home alone, and we heard the horses in the barn whinny, as if in distress. My sister, Calista and I looked out the window but we couldn't see through the heavy downpour, so we ran to the barn. The door was slightly open and the moment we entered, we felt someone's presence. We didn't notice anyone right away, so we walked toward the stalls. I then heard what sounded like Calista's muffled voice, and a struggle. When I turned around, she was gone; the next thing I knew, someone hit me over the head and then grabbed me. I tried to fight back, but the blow all but knocked me out; he dragged me to where Calista was and forced me onto my knees and bound my wrists behind my back."

Nicolai listened intently, and a small seed of anger and the desire to protect her sprouted deep within.

"The Helot who had ahold of Calista, dragged her over, threw her onto her back, and ripped her night shirt open while the one who had me, grabbed a fistful of my hair, and forced me to watch. I still remember the look in his soulless eyes, and how they had taken root in mine the entire time he was assaulting my sister and I knew I was next."

"I'm sorry, Sylvana. Had I known this was such a horrific experience, I would not have pushed you."

"It's fine. Really. It's sort of cathartic telling you about it. I have never told anyone."

"If you're comfortable, I would like to hear the rest."

"The one who was holding me felt his around way around my body while the one who had Calista shoved her legs apart and untied the laces on his trousers. I will never forget the look in Calista's eyes and how she cried without making a sound. When I think about the incident, I still smell the way they reeked of body odor and cheap ale, their soiled, tattered clothing, and the sounds of the rain pounding on the roof. I don't know what came over me, but I broke the binds. The next thing I remember, Calista and I were standing over their dead bodies."

"They didn't force themselves on you then?"

"No. Thankfully, he didn't get the chance. Unfortunately, I didn't act soon enough to save Calista."

"I am truly sorry, Sylvana. I don't remember this being brought before the Guild? Their clan would have been hunted down."

It is not like my father could bring two frozen corpses before the Guild, she thought. "The last thing Calista and I wanted, or needed was to go into detail in front of the Guild and be forced to recount the incident. Our father never questioned our decision, and he and our brother disposed of their bodies."

"Your father is Kadric Orfaedo?"

"Yes. You know of him?"

"Only by reputation. He is a well-respected warrior."

"Off the subject. Why did you decide to escort me home?" she asked curiously.

"I'm intrigued."

"*Intrigued*?" she repeated.

"Yes. You have captured my interest," he admitted lightheartedly.

It took twice as long as it normally did to reach the edge of her manor. It was obvious he was not in a rush to get her home.

Sylvana motioned for Nicolai to stop. "This is it."

"I assume you would like to head the rest of the way alone?" he asked.

"Yes. I don't want to wake anyone. They have to be up early." *Hell, the last thing I need is for Alaric to see Nicolai.*

"As you wish." He dismounted Rana and stood next to her.

"Thank you for seeing me home."

"Until we meet again." Nicolai winked, gently squeezed her thigh, and then disappeared into the darkness.

Chapter 3

Alaric paced back and forth, awaiting Sylvana's return for what seemed like hours, when a shadow appeared from the tree line. *It's about damn time,* he thought. He mounted his stallion and met her midway. "Where have you been?"

"Damn, Alaric. You know where I was."

"I don't want you traveling alone again at night. You should have sent word. I would have come for you. Not to mention you have rarely been this late. Did something happen?"

Sylvana squinted her eyes. "No. Now stop."

"Then why are you so late?"

"It was busy there today."

"I'm curious why you rode home without your saddle?

Shit. "There wasn't anyone in the stable, and I just didn't have time to look for it in the dark."

"So, who's this friend of yours?"

"What friend?"

"Calista told me there's another female whose company you hold."

"I'm allowed to have a life outside of this manor. Not everything is your business."

"You and your sisters are my business. What's her name?"

Sylvana glared at him, refusing to reply.

"I want a name."

"Enough! I don't need to tolerate you intruding on every aspect of my life. My god, you are as bad as father."

Alaric looked around and realized the cart wasn't with her, either. "Where's the cart?"

Shit! Think, think, she told herself. "I left it with Muriel. I'll fetch it tomorrow."

"Muriel?"

"Yes, the same Muriel you have a thing for."

Alaric dismissed the snarky remark. "At least I know your *'friend's'* name now, but why did you leave it?"

"Alaric, this is the last question I will answer. The staff was busy preparing for Tobias's mating ceremony, and they didn't have time to unload it. It was getting so late I decided it would be better to leave it."

After a few moments of silence, Alaric spoke up. "We fare well and the amount you make isn't worth the time or effort. I don't want you making any more deliveries."

"A few extra denarius in one's pocket is never a bad thing. And since you're in the mood for questions, why don't you tell me what father is really doing?"

"I already explained as much as you need to know," he stated firmly.

"Suit yourself. I'll ask around next time I make a delivery."

"You'll do no such thing. It's clan business, and you'll keep your nose out of it and your mouth shut."

"And I expect you to *keep your nose* out of my personal business."

Sylvana awoke the following morning just as the sun had risen, feeling as if she had not slept at all. She sat up, reached for her emerald-green, satin robe, and loosely tied it around her waist before getting out of bed and walking to the other side of her chamber. She stood on the varicolored, hand sewn, cotton rug and swirled her hands over the copper tub her mother had commissioned. As the hot water rose from the bottom, she reached for a jar sitting on top of a large washstand heavy with ornamentation, and a black marble top. She then poured the fresh petals into the water, stepped into the tub, and slid her body down the curved back. With each deep breath, she smelled the calming aroma of lavender, being carried by the steam moving serenely around her upper body.

The entire world seemed to be ablaze under the rays of the mid-morning sun and, despite the heat, a large crowd had gathered in the market. Sylvana stopped to look at a basket filled with an assortment of fresh flowers and then looked up at her mother, Myrine, who was protectively holding her hand to keep from being dragged into the bustling crowd. Her long, auburn locks glistened in the sun and flowed over her shoulders, and her crisp green eyes were gleaming with an unearthly quality above her concave cheekbones when she smiled back.

"Come, love. If you dally any longer, we will be here until the sun goes down," Myrine said.

As they continued down the dirt road, an old man stepped before them. "I have something special for the bairn."

Sylvana stared back at the stranger; his face was timeworn and wrinkled and he struggled to kneel, as if life had gotten the better of him. His clothes were ragged, soiled, and torn along the seams in places and his face was wrinkled and scarred, and partially obscured behind his long, gray, unkempt hair. However, his time-worn, brown eyes and smile were soft and friendly, in contrast to the rest of his appearance. He held out his hand and a sun-kissed pinkish-yellow ball, covered in a layer of fuzz, sat in his palm, resting gently against his gnarled fingers and knotted joints.

"Would you like one? I picked it from the Acherons orchard myself," he said with a crooked smile.

Sylvana cocked her small head to the side as if amused, and let out a giddy chuckle.

"I'm Laster. What is your name?" he asked as he pushed the peach toward her.

"Sylvana Asc—" Before she could finish her sentence, she felt the sting of her tooth as it stabbed her bottom lip when her mother hastily cupped her palm over her mouth.

Sylvana looked up, and her mother's eyes were ablaze with warning, and she looked panic stricken. Her heart drummed against her small chest, and even though she was only seven years old, she understood the gravity of her careless words.

"My daughter shouldn't be speaking to strangers." She nodded to the old man and hurriedly walked away, pulling Sylvana with.

"Sylvana, how many times do I have to tell you? You can never speak your sired name," she scolded in a harsh, hushed tone.

She could taste the blood on her lip and feel the tears running down her cheeks as she tried to keep up with her mother's long strides. Once they rounded a corner, her mother placed her hand over her stomach, leaned against one of the stable walls and took a deep breath, before she kneeled down.

"Sylvie, I'm sorry. I didn't mean to hurt you." She cupped her cheeks in her hand and wiped away her tears. "We must remain diligent. Do you understand?"

"Yes, Mother. I'm sorry."

Myrine lifted her chin after having pricked her finger with one of her canines. She then gently slid it across her lip and healed the small gash. "How about we pick out one of those beautiful flowers? How does that sound, my darling?" Her words were once again as gentle as a kitten's caress.

Sylvana's arm slid off the edge of the copper tub and splashed into the water, pulling her from the memory. She reached for a rag and washed her face, desiring nothing more than to be wrapped in the protection and comfort of her mother's arms again.

Sylvana scowled as she brushed the knots from her freshly washed hair before braiding it along the sides and top. She then walked across the chamber and pulled a clean pair of black, wool trousers from a drawer in her armoire along with a gray, cotton shirt. It was not customary for a female of her status to dress in trousers, but she had little choice. Her father kept them relatively secluded, which left most of the labor for Sylvana and her siblings. Had Sylvana been mated, she would be sitting on satin cushions, adorned in jewels, and waited on hand and foot; her life, however, resided within the muck of the fields and stables.

Once she finished getting ready, she headed downstairs only to run into Mira.

"Alaric is mad at you," she offered with a sneer.

"He'll get over it. Don't you have work to do? You should be with Calista, feeding the animals."

"You want sis and I to work while you can sleep in like someone's mate?"

"Mira, enough."

"You should be nicer to me. One day I'll be mated, and I'd be happy to leave you here."

"It would be a welcomed relief." Sylvana chuckled.

"So be it," Mira snarked as she slammed the front door behind her.

What she needs is a hard hand, Sylvana thought. She wandered around the manor looking for Calista. "Calista?" When she did not get an answer, she went outside to find her and headed toward the stables when out of the corner of her eye noticed the cart was sitting beside the barn. *What the hell?*

She walked into the barn looking for Calista and Mira, who were nowhere to be found.

"Good morning Sylvana," a deep, velvety voice said.

She jumped back and turned around, only to see Nicolai appear from the shadows in the back of the barn. "Nicolai?"

He slowly approached her. "You remembered my name?" he joked.

"What are you doing here?" she asked nervously.

"I came to see you."

"The cart's back. Did you bring it?"

"No, I had the stable boy do it earlier."

"You shouldn't be here."

"Why not?"

She did not know how to answer. After all, he had the right to go anywhere he pleased without an invitation.

"Well?" he questioned again.

"I didn't tell my brother you escorted me home last night," she admitted.

"Why not?"

"I would've had to explain what else happened."

"Ahh, I assume it would displease him finding out you were in a tavern?"

"Yes." *At least that's the truth.*

"Very well. It shall remain our secret." He then pulled her tightly against his body.

She placed her hands on his chest, not having expected his advances. However, before she could protest further, his mouth was on hers. After a heated kiss, he pulled away ever so slightly. "I'll send for you tonight."

"Wait—what? I can't see you tonight."

"Why not?"

"I don't have another delivery, and Alaric will never allow me to go back so soon."

"I'll handle it." He pulled away and left her standing in stunned silence.

Does he think he can just demand I see him? Shit! What if he wants to bed me?

"Where were you last night?" Calista asked.

Sylvana yelped and placed her hand across her heart. "What are you doing?"

"Looking for you. What's wrong?"

"Nothing, you scared me is all. I called for you earlier, so I didn't think anyone was here."

"Where were you last night? I had to cover for you with Alaric."

"I know, and thank you. He was waiting for me in the fields when I returned."

"What were you doing?"

"I ran late. The staff were too busy to unload the cart with the mating ceremony taking place."

"You seem nervous. Are you sure you are okay?" Calista questioned.

"Really, I'm fine. Where is everyone?"

"Alaric left early, and I let Mira go to the Marques manor a few minutes ago."

"That girl is something else," Sylvana said.

"I'm not sure we should continue letting her associate with him. His mother puts big ideas in her head," Calista said.

"I'm not sure who is putting ideas in whose head." Sylvana leaned against the wall of the barn and placed her hands on her hips. "She should be here working, not running off to play whenever she sees fit."

"Would you rather deal with her, or should I say fight with her every step of the way?"

"You got me there, but at some point, she has to know what work is. She has this crazy idea stuck in her head she is going to be mated to a high-ranking lord and live in the castle."

Calista let out a belly laugh. "Can you imagine what it would be like to deal with her if it happened?"

Sylvana laughed aloud. "She threatened to leave me here this morning."

Calista leaned against the wall next to Sylvana. "Mother would never have allowed her to be there."

"I know. She loathed Enatta."

"She always came back from their soirées in a huff," Calista agreed.

Sylvana smiled at the memory. "Mother always said Enatta would go to any extent to help her mate Cadell climb the ranks."

"He's done pretty well for himself over the years. I'm sure Enatta's siting on a gilded throne right now."

"Cadell is nice enough, from what father and Alaric say. I wonder how he's put up with her?"

"Who knows, but I bet that's what Mira will be like should she ever find a mate worth a shit," Sylvana joked.

"Maybe we should pull in her reins ourselves. Their son, Laurent, has sure taken a liking to her."

"I believe she's smitten. He's going to be her first broken heart," Sylvana replied. "I feel like we're betraying Mother by letting her spend so much time with their clan."

Calista looked at Sylvana and raised her eyebrows. "Are you going to tell Mira she can't see Laurent anymore?"

Sylvana shook her head. "I'll leave it to father or Alaric."

Calista shifted her stance, and her face became solemn. "Ever since mother disappeared, father and Alaric have done nothing but coddle her."

"I can understand why, as she was so young, but I'm afraid they've created a monster."

"I still remember how angry father was with her when she disappeared for a few days last spring and she said she was with Laurent."

"I remember," Sylvana replied.

Calista turned her body and leaned on her shoulder so she could face Sylvana. "Enough about Mira. What were you really doing last night?"

The last thing I need is someone else prying into my life. "I was with Muriel." Sylvana pushed herself off the wall and walked to the feed buckets. "We have work to do. We should get to it."

"You're being evasive," Calista said.

Sylvana bent over and picked up the buckets. "No more than usual."

Laurent was waiting by the stables for Mira when he heard her mare trotting down the road. Once she pulled Prada to a halt, Laurent reached his arms up and helped her down. She turned around, and Laurent wrapped his arms around her. She nuzzled her head against his chest. "I missed you," she said.

"It's only been two days." Laurent pulled away and smiled at her.

"I know. But I still missed you."

Laurent took her hand in his. "I missed you too, Mira." He then stepped away and ran toward the barn, pulling her along.

She squealed in delight and once they entered the barn Laurent shut the door. "I have our favorite spot ready. Are you thirsty?"

"Yes." Mira smiled as she took a seat on the blanket he had laid out.

"It's fresh, curor. Mother took it from a feeder just this morning," Laurent said, as he handed her a goblet.

Mira took a drink and placed the goblet in the hay. "It's very good. Thank you."

Laurent got comfortable and set his goblet down as well. "Do that thing again," he suggested.

"Okay. But promise me you won't tell anyone."

Laurent rolled his eyes. "I've already promised you ten times."

"I know, but we could both get into trouble. And father would kill me."

"It's fine, Mira. Do it."

"Okay. What would you like to see?"

"Umm? How about a black spider?"

"Ew, no! They are so gross." Mira laughed. "I have something else." She closed her eyes, cupped her hand together and when she opened them, there was a little bat hovering above her palm.

"Wow! How do you do it?" Laurent reached out and stroked its little back. "It feels like the leather on my stallion's reins?"

"You ask me every time," she said, sounding giddy. "I just do it. I don't know how."

"You're incredible, Mira. One day we will be mated and maybe you can teach me?"

"I will try. But I don't think you can?"

After, a short time and a few more creatures, Mira got bored. "Let's do something else."

"Let's go inside. We can play a game or something," Laurent suggested.

Enatta was sitting in the parlor when Mira walked in with Laurent. "Hello, Mira."

Mira gave her a slight courtesy, and then politely cupped her hands in front of her. "Good morning, milady."

"What brings you here so early?"

"Calista said I could come over. They are working."

"Your sisters are going to work themselves into rags."

"Not I," Mira stated proudly as she lifted her chin.

Enatta grinned, took a sip of her dark cherry wine and stared at Mira. *She looks more and more like her mother and certainly has her attitude. She is a beautiful, petite little thing with high cheekbones and striking features for a bairn so young.* Enatta glanced over the soft waves of hair tumbling over her shoulders and peered into her deep, umber-brown eyes.

After briefly admiring Mira, Enatta spoke. "Would you like to join Laurent for an afternoon drink, dear child?"

"Yes, milady. I don't like our feeders. They taste dirty."

Enatta laughed aloud. *The look of disgust on her face says more than her blatant honesty.* "Laurent, take Mira to the gardens."

"Yes, Mother." He nodded at Mira and walked her out.

Laurent nudged her shoulder. "I'll make sure you have a proper feeder."

Mira smiled from ear to ear. "Thank you."

"What did you find out?" Riordan asked.

"Her father has yet to return. The fields are unattended, and I didn't notice any servants. I find it odd for such a large manor," Nicolai replied.

Riordan leaned back in his chair and thought momentarily. "There are two reasons one would be short on servants and/or field hands—either they don't have the means, or they don't want prying eyes."

"I assume it's the latter. They certainly have the means," Kieran stated.

Nicolai took a drink and tilted his cup towards Riordan. "Their youngest sister, Mira, has been spending a lot of time with the Marques son, Laurent. She headed there again this morning."

Riordan raised an eyebrow, curious what Enatta was up to. "Enatta never invites guests without reason. She's Nosferatu scant as far as I'm concerned. She is always scurrying around, looking to claw her way up."

"Enatta won't allow her son to mate anyone not of pure blood. Why would she allow Mira to spend so much time with him?" Kieran questioned.

Riordan rested his forearm on the arm of the chair and spun his cup in circles. "I'm more concerned about the secrets running deep within Kadric Orfaedo."

"We should find out more about Enatta's attachment to Mira," Nicolai suggested.

"Maybe it's time one of us pays Enatta a visit," Kieran suggested.

Nicolai finished his drink and set his cup down. "I'll stop by the Marques manor today." He then looked at Kieran. "By the way, did you feel the pull toward Sylvana the other night?"

"I did. Obviously you felt it as well?"

"What pull?" Riordan asked.

"I can't explain it, but her energy felt centuries old," Nicolai said.

"I agree. It is as if I was being pulled by the energy of a mate," Kieran admitted.

Riordan laughed aloud. "The pull of a mate? What the fuck did the two of you have to drink?"

Nicolai stood up, walked to the window, and stared into the courtyard. "It is true Riordan, I felt it as well."

"Only those with Ascelin blood running through their veins have that kind of a pull on another purebred—" Riordan stopped mid-sentence and looked at Nicolai and Kieran. "I want to meet her tonight."

"I'll go to her after I've finished with Enatta. I've already invited her," Nicolai replied.

"If I feel the slightest pull, we will send two of our Barouqe Warriors to keep their eyes on her until we figure out what the hell is going on with her and her family," Riordan said.

Kadric came to the edge of The Black Moor, pulled his stallion to a halt and stared at the churning waves of vaporous mist swirling over the abysmally dark river rolling over large boulders and rotting trunks. The sounds of the creatures had long ago disappeared, and he had seen neither man nor beast for hours. And an ominous silence hung heavy in the air, as if salivating over its prey. Clumps of wet moss hung from the spotted, black boughs of the contorted trees, and he could taste the pungent aroma oozing from the foliage and brackish mud. His horse dug at the dirt with his front hooves and became increasingly agitated.

Kadric reached out and ran his hand beneath his horse's wavy, charcoal mane and spoke gently. "Shhh, it's okay, Kesaro. Calm boy," he urged.

He dismounted Kesaro and led him to the edge of the river. "Drink boy." He placed his hand on the dagger hanging from his hip and scanned the immediate area.

This is no place for the living, he told himself. He kneeled down, cupped the water in his hands, and splashed it on his face. After he felt Kesaro had enough, he walked him back to the tree and tied him up. He then sat down, removed his sword from the sheath on his back and laid it across his lap. With a wave of his hand, he cloaked himself and Kesaro and leaned his back against the tree, heavy in thought. He listened to the slapping of the waves against the bank, and the rumbling of stones being confined within the depths of the water as they were carried downstream.

He had not realized he dozed off until the single snap of a branch off in the distance startled him. He wrapped his fist tightly around the hilt of his sword, placed his other hand on the damp ground, feeling its vibrations, and listened intently before he caught sight of the creature.

It had a bestial look in its eyes; its heavy breathing and snorting sounded as lifeless as the groans from an ancient grave. Its knotty hands shoved the brush aside with each slow step it took in his direction as if beckoning him to raise his blade. He knew the creature could not see him, but it was clear by how it pointed its ears and lifted its nose to the air it had caught the scent of its prey.

An inbred Lycan, he thought.

Kadric remained frozen in place with his eyes locked on the creature. Its hair was knotted with mud and small bits of debris, while its pointed ears sprouted out from either side of its head. Its skin was covered in large, spiny hairs similar to that of a boar. Its face had a distorted wolf like appearance, and a long jaw line while rows of colossal, gray teeth glinted from beneath its curled lips. A single loin cloth made from the skins of its victims hung from its waist, revealing its upper body, which was marred with wounds from countless battles; some of which appeared to be recent, while others looked old. The scent of the creature was a heady mixture of the decaying forest, festering wounds, and dried blood.

Kadric slowly rose to his feet, as the creature stared at the trunk of the tree and scanned it from top to bottom, while its blackened tongue slid across its long, leathery lips. Its head moved from side to side, and the hackles raised along its back and neck as it took one cautious step forward. A low snarl rose from deep within its chest and drips of saliva lingered from its mouth before falling onto the ground at its feet.

Let's do this, big guy, Kadric said to himself as he adjusted his body into a defensive stance.

The creature took one cautious step, followed by another, and then another; without warning, it swung its wide hand and outstretched claws with unearthly power in Kadric's direction.

Kadric ducked and fluently leapt to the side, evading the blow before he brought his blade across the creature's midsection. It let out a thunderous roar and violently spun its massive body in his direction without cause or reason, as if he had gone mad with determination to spill Kadric's blood.

Kadric recoiled his blade and swung again. However, the beast lunged and flung one arm toward Kadric's sword, knocking it to the side, while it's other hand crossed Kadric's forearm where its curved claws tore through his sleeve and into his flesh.

Kadric gathered his sword off the ground, leap into the air, and his blade seared through the flesh on its back as he landed behind the creature. It let out a roar of pain, spun around, dropped to all fours, leapt over Kadric, and ran through the tree line, as if it was not willing to stay and fight what it could not see. Kadric gave chase and followed the sound of breaking branches and the crunching of the brush, and it was not long before the sounds became muted against the agony of the raging river. He stood at the edge of the ravine and looked down for any sight of the creature. He took a step back, turned, and walked around using slow, choreographed movements, He then lifted his chin and took a deep breath through his nostrils and caught its scent. He grasped his sword with both hands and cautiously moved forward.

Shit! They are not supposed to be hunting on this side of the river.

He noticed a piece of material hanging from a bush; he stuck it with the tip of his sword and lifted it into the air before him. After studying it momentarily, he tossed it into the ravine, kneeled down, and stared at the pool of blood.

Ranan had better have some answers. As Kadric walked back to his stallion, he looked at his torn sleeve and pulled the material apart, noticing the deep laceration was now mostly superficial. *It looks like we both survived to fight another day.*

Chapter 4

Enatta made her way to the gardens, looking for Laurent and Mira. "Laurent?" she called out. When she did not get a response, she walked further into the gardens and could hear their voices coming from somewhere in the orchard. "Laurent?"

"Over here, mother," Laurent answered.

She wandered between the rows of pruned bushes and found Laurent and Mira lying on their backs on a woven blanket. "What are the two of you doing?"

Laurent pointed to the sky. "We're watching the clouds make shapes."

Enatta took a seat on the stone bench and placed her hands in her lap. "What shapes have they made so far?"

"We saw a bat and a crow," Mira offered.

"And a warrior on a horse," Laurent said.

"Mira, would you like to stay the night? We're having quite the soirée."

"Really? I would love to."

"Of course, a young lady of your status would do well to immerse herself with lords and ladies. I don't think your pigs and chickens are suitable company."

"Laurent, would you like me to stay?"

"Yes, I will be your escort."

"Then we need to get the two of you bathed and dressed. Up—up, quickly now."

Two of Enatta's chamber maids led Mira into a large guest chamber where they had placed a beautiful gown on the end of the bed, along with a pair of matching leather flats. Colorful pieces of silk cut into the shapes of various flowers covered the long bouffant skirt, while the constricted bodice and tapered wrist length sleeves were fashioned with a myriad of glass beads that had been meticulously sewn into the fabric.

The chamber maids were seeing to Mira who was now sitting in a large marble tub with her arms wrapped around her knees while they scrubbed her hair and back when Enatta walked in and motioned for them to leave. She walked over to the large, ornate bureau, pulled the crystal stopper from the bottle and filled her flute. She then took a seat on the settee across from the tub.

"What is that, milady?" Mira asked inquisitively.

"It's honey gin."

"What does it taste like?"

"Has your father ever let you have a sip of his drink?"

"No—well, only on special occasions."

"Would you like a sip?"

Mira placed her palms together and filled them with the hot water and poured it over her shoulder. "No thank you, milady. It makes me sleepy."

Enatta tilted her head, feeling curious. "It makes you sleepy?"

"Yes, father, says it's because I am too young to drink." She chuckled.

"What special occasions does he let you have a sip?" Enatta questioned.

Makes her sleepy? That's odd.

"During the Wolf Bane Moon. Father has a poem for it." Mira smiled sweetly and stared at Enatta. "Would you like to hear it?"

"Of course, my dear." Enatta took another sip and nodded for her to continue.

"On a cold winter's night,
the Wolf's Bane Moon will rise high into the dark night sky
and part the clouds with blood blossomed blooms.
Don't listen to the tales like a trembling fool.
Be still like the wolf or the wolf will come calling for you."

Enatta took another sip and was taken aback. She had not expected to hear such a deep deliverance of what they all knew to be true, especially haven been told by a child like it was nothing more than a storybook tale.

Enatta stared at Mira, whose smile was irresistibly radiant and innocent. "Why, it—it's beautiful. Does your father recite it to you during every Wolf's Bane Moon?"

"Yes. I sit in his lap by the fire, and he lets me have a drink while he tells me it. It's my favorite thing to do with him."

"You and your sisters are quite special."

"Father thinks so too," Mira agreed.

"I bet you have a lot of special gifts."

"No, just one."

"What is it?"

Mira looked down into the water and swirled the petals around the bubbles but didn't speak.

"You spend a lot of time here, Mira. I know you miss your mother, as do I. She was a dear friend of mine. If you would like to tell me about it, I will keep it between us."

"Really?"

"Of course, darling. Now come, I want to hear all about it, but first things first." Enatta winked at Mira and called out. "Ema?"

Ema opened the door and gave a slight courtesy. "Milady?"

"I would like my glass re-filled."

"Yes, milady." She re-filled the glass and without haste she saw herself out.

Enatta leaned back and motioned her hand towards Mira. "Go on, child, tell me."

Mira looked at Enatta and smiled. "It's something I can do, not say." She closed her eyes, shook the water off her hands and cupped them together. She then looked at Enatta with a smirk, separated her hands and held out one fist over the edge of the tub.

As she raised her hand, Enatta sat with bated breath. *Whatever is she doing?*

"Ready?" Mira asked.

Enatta nodded.

Mira opened her fist and there sat a large, glacier-water, blue butterfly in her palm with velvety wings. Mira ran her finger gently down its back and smiled radiantly at Enatta.

Enatta placed her hand over her stomach and sat transfixed with the little creature, whose wings slowly rose and fell in the palm of Mira's hand. *My god, it is not possible? She can create life? Other than the Acherons, the Ascelins are the only other breed who wield this kind of power—is she—are they?*

The sound of Mira's voice pulled her from her thoughts. "Do you like her?"

"Yes, she's beautiful. May I?" Enatta slid off the settee, reached out and ran her finger down the back of the butterfly, needing to make sure what she was seeing was real and not some sort of trickery. It fluttered its wings and floated above Enatta's and Mira's hands, to her shock and bewilderment.

"Her name is Nime," Mira said as she reached up, grabbed the butterfly in her hand, and squeezed her fist shut.

Enatta gasped under her breath and watched in horror as minuscule pieces of velvety dust floated to the floor. "Why did you kill it?"

"It's mine, and if it flies away, it won't belong to me anymore. I didn't kill her, not really. I can bring her back whenever I want."

Enatta slid back into the settee and did her best to quell the spike of adrenaline, as the possibility of whom the girls may be settled in. She took a large drink and looked out the window, trying to quell the look of shock and excitement she felt radiate across her face.

Mira leaned against the back of the tub and looked out the window. "What are you looking at, milady?"

"Nothing, dear. I can hear the wagons coming down the road. I think it's time to get you out of the tub and dressed."

"Okay," Mira replied.

"Ema?" Enatta called.

Ema opened the door and walked in. "Milady?"

"It is time for Mira to dress."

"Yes, milady." She motioned toward the door and another chamber maid walked in.

Ema picked up a large cotton towel off the bureau and the two of them walked to the edge of the tub and held the towel open so Mira could discretely stand up. They wrapped the towel around her body and helped her step out of the high tub. Mira stood on the black, bearskin rug and turned to Enatta. "Did you like my butterfly?"

"Very much so," she said, before ushering the girls out of the room. "I'll dress Mira myself."

"Yes, milady," they replied.

"Mira, what you did was incredible, and I agree. We should never speak of this to anyone, not even Laurent."

"He knows. I've shown him already," she replied bluntly.

If she is indeed a purebred Ascelin and I play my cards right where she and Laurent are concerned—I will rule the court. Enatta stood statuesque, trying to figure out her next move as well as what to say. Instead of speaking, she walked over to the bed and held up Mira's dress. "What do you think, darling?"

"Oh, it is beautiful," Mira exclaimed.

"How would you feel if I called you Miriam rather than Mira?"

"It's fine, but why?"

"Mira is a child's name, and you are a young lady now."

"Okay. I like it better than Mira as well."

"Enough said, Miriam it is."

Sylvana and Calista sat at the edge of the pond with their backs against a tree after another long day. "It's going to be dark in a few hours. We should fetch Mira," Sylvana suggested.

Calista stood and wiped the dirt from her butt. "Well, let's go. Hopefully, Mira won't put up much of a fight with us both there."

Sylvana chuckled and rolled her eyes; they mounted their mares and headed down the dirt path and it was not long before they crossed the green pastures surrounding the large estate of the Marques.

They tied their horses to one of the barn railings and as they walked up the stone path toward the expansive door; they had to weave their way through a large crowd, all of whom were busy cleaning, hanging lanterns, setting up torches, and designing enormous bouquets of flowers. Sylvana lifted the large brass ring and knocked it against the heavy, ornate door twice. "It's busy, she must be having another party,"

"Obviously. She loves nothing more than to flaunt their wealth," Calista replied.

The door opened and a well-dressed lady stood before them. "Miladies," she replied.

"We're here for Mira," Calista stated.

"I'll fetch the lady of the manor for you," she stated as she shut the door.

"What a warm welcome." Sylvana chuckled.

The door opened again, and Enatta's cold eyes greeted them and she looked at them as if they were no better than serfs. "What can I do for you?"

"We've come for Mira, milady," Calista said.

"Oh, didn't you get word? I've asked Miriam to stay. We are entertaining tonight, as you can see."

"That's generous of you to invite her, but we would like her to come home," Sylvana said.

"You would rather she sit at home with the pigs and cows than mingle with royalty?"

Sylvana coughed under her breath and side eyed Calista. "I didn't know you belonged to the Acheron's court."

Calista raised an eyebrow. "When did that happen?"

"I'm sure your father would allow her to stay, but I've heard he has disappeared—again," Enatta snarked back.

"She's not your bairn. Please fetch her," Sylvana said sternly.

"Someone needs to look after her. Your father is missing, your mother is dead, and the way the two of you fail to look after her properly is simply shameful."

Sylvana stepped forward, but Calista grabbed her forearm and squeezed. "Milady, we need you to fetch Mira," Calista stated.

"I will do no such thing."

"Sylvana," a smooth voice said from behind.

Sylvana's and Calista's heads spun towards the voice, and Enatta's eyes widened when Nicolai appeared behind the girls.

"Milord," the three of them stated in unison, along with a courtesy.

Enatta stepped to the side and opened the door fully. "Milord, will you be joining us tonight?"

Nicolai stepped between Sylvana and Calista and walked into the expansive parlor. Sylvana's pulse quickened, and she held her breath when she noticed how Calista looked at her when she saw Nicolai slide his hand across her lower back.

Sylvana and Calista were still standing at the entrance when Nicolai looked back. He then looked at Enatta. "Are you going to invite the girls in, or don't they suit you?"

Enatta motioned to the girls and smiled. "Please, girls, do come in."

Nicolai wandered through the parlor, slid his hand across the back of the large chaise lounge, and studied his surroundings. They all turned when they heard the sounds of Mira's and Laurent's voices coming down the hall. Laurent stopped mid-stride when he saw Nicolai and Mira ran into his back, causing the two of them to stumble. They glanced between Enatta, Sylvana, Calista, and Nicolai before Laurent spoke up. "Milord," he stated politely.

Mira stood at Laurent's side and curtsied. "Milord," she stated with a larger-than-life smile.

Nicolai looked at Laurent and Mira before addressing Enatta. "I heard part of your conversation earlier. It seems you have over stepped you place where the child is concerned."

"Milord, I was simply inviting the girl to stay and enjoy herself for the evening."

Cadell walked in and was a taken-a-back to see Nicolai Acheron standing in his parlor. "Milord," he stated, as he crossed one arm over his chest, placed his fist over his heart, and nodded. "What brings you here?"

"Are you the lord of your manor?" Nicolai asked.

Cadell tilted his head to the side. "Yes," he replied, sounding confused.

Nicolai nodded his head in Mira's direction. "It seems your mate is making decisions for the young girl which are not hers to make."

Cadell looked at Enatta and furrowed his brows. "What seems to be the problem?" he asked, as he looked at Sylvana and Calista. "Is everything okay, girls?"

"Yes, milord. We came to fetch Mira," Sylvana replied.

Mira looked at Sylvana and Calista with pleading eyes and motioned with her hand for one of them to come to her. Sylvana walked over and kneeled before her. "Please, Sylvie, let me stay."

"I don't think it's a good idea, Mira."

"But Enatta gave me a beautiful dress." She walked in a slow circle and held out the sides of her dress. "Please, everyone is going to be here," she pleaded.

Sylvana looked at Calista, who gave her a slight shrug of her shoulders, wanting nothing more than to get out of the parlor. "Fine. You can stay, but you need to be home first thing in the morning."

"Thank you!"

Sylvana walked back to Calista. "She can stay, but we would like her home first thing in the morning."

"I'll see to it," Cadell agreed, before addressing Nicolai. "Milord, is there a reason you are here?"

"No, I came to pay Sylvana a visit and was told she came here."

"I didn't know the girls had staff at their manor?" Enatta questioned.

"They don't," Nicolai replied coldly.

Sylvana did all she could to ignore the curiosity written all over Enatta's and Cadell's faces when they looked between her and Nicolai.

"We should go." Sylvana grabbed Calista's hand and pulled her toward the door.

"You have some explaining to do," Calista whispered.

Nicolai nodded to Cadell and followed the girls.

"What the hell is going on?" Calista demanded softly.

Before she could answer, Nicolai called her name. "Sylvana."

They stopped and turned to face Nicolai. "Milord?" Sylvana replied.

"I'll escort you home." He then looked at Calista. "I would like to speak to Sylvana privately."

"Yes, milord," she replied as she mounted her mare.

Cadell grabbed Enatta's forearm and led her to another room and shut the doors. "What the hell is going on?" he demanded.

"Nothing. I simply invited Miriam to stay, but there is something you need to know about the girls."

"Whatever it is, you will mind your own. Is this *something* the reason Nicolai was here?"

"I don't think so?"

"You *don't think so?*" Cadell questioned.

"I don't know what it was about, but the girls—I think they are Ascelins?"

Cadell glared at Enatta. "What the hell gave you such a crazy idea?"

"Miriam, she showed me something today—"

Cadell cut her off mid-sentence. "Whatever is spinning in that head of yours now is going to get someone killed.Kadric is my friend and a well-respected member of the Legion.I will not allow you to spread such rumors."

"It is not a rumor. Miriam can create life. If that's not Ascelin blood, I don't know what is?"

"Enatta, enough! You will speak of this to no one. Do you understand me?"

"Cadell, if they are Ascelins, it would be in your best interest to take the matter seriously."

The thoughts swirled in his mind. He did not know what to say, what to think, or what to do. After contemplating the situation momentarily, he chuckled. "Ohh, now I see. You want Mira to become Laurent's mate when she comes of age? Is this your grand scheme?"

"It would benefit you as well."

"How in the hell would it benefit me?"

"Once they are mated, the bond cannot be broken. The Acherons would have to provide us our own quarters in the Castle."

Cadell walked to his desk and filled his glass with a tapered decanter. He felt the chill of the liquid as it flowed down his throat and the heat of his anger as it settled in his head. "I have never understood how you can so easily dismiss the consequences to yourself and those around you when you get something stuck in your fucking head."

"And what consequences do you speak of?" Enatta asked angrily.

"If she is an Ascelin, and if you somehow manage to have them mated, Riordan might see fit to kill Laurent. That will put an end to the bond," he bellowed. "Did you ever once consider the fact you are risking my son's life?"

"They will not harm Laurent! And it's the only explanation for his sudden interest in Sylvana."

"All the more reason for you to stay the hell out of this. They will possess whomever, whatever, they want and will not hesitate to put anyone standing in their way to the blade."

"I will not—" Enatta began.

Cadell stormed over and grabbed her arm. "I will speak to Kadric when he returns. Until then, you will do exactly as I say. I will also escort Mira home in the morning, and you will keep your distance from here on out."

Nicolai took Rana's reins and walked toward Sylvana's manor. "Why did you give in to Enatta instead of standing your ground?"

"I had no intention of backing down, but you showing up unannounced was a bit much for my sister."

"She should be grateful."

"*Grateful*?"

"Yes. I don't believe Enatta will cause you any more problems."

"You don't know Enatta well enough." Sylvana chuckled.

"I asked you to join me tonight, but you didn't answer me this morning."

Sylvana stopped, turned to face Nicolai, and crossed her arms. "What is it you want with me?"

"I thought it was obvious?"

"Well, it's not."

"I enjoy your company and I would appreciate if you would join me for a drink."

"A drink? Just a drink?"

"Yes," Nicolai replied as he looked down at Sylvana and held her gaze.

Sylvana rolled her eyes. "I know of your reputation, and I will not be one of your whores."

Nicolai let out a belly laugh and began walking again. "The *whores* you speak of have their own agendas. They choose to crawl into the beds of whomever might secure their status. You didn't make a move toward Kieran the other night, and you haven't given me any reason to believe you are interested in joining the ladies at court. You, my dear, are a breath of fresh air in a stagnant marsh."

Sylvana laughed with a mocking tone. "I don't believe you. First, we could never be more than bedmates. Second, how am I to believe you don't have a hidden agenda?"

"*First*," Nicolai repeated in a mocking tone. "If I wanted a *bedmate*, I would have one. *Second*, what hidden agenda would I have?"

"I haven't figured it out yet."

"If you join me tonight, maybe you can *figure it out*."

"I'll join you on one condition."

"What is your *condition*?" he replied as he looked at her curiously.

"Stop repeating me." Sylvana smiled.

"Done."

The guests were arriving by the dozens, each looking as refined and dignified as one would expect. The ladies wore long gowns with fitted corsets fashioned from the finest of fabrics, while their mates wore tailored vests, pleated shirts, leather trousers, and matching boots. Scores of servants offered greetings to the arriving guests along the road; some of whom greeted them at the garden's entrance while carrying silver trays and handing out goblets of fine wine. The flickering glow from the torches' flames, along with the melody from the harpists, violinists, and flutists, drifting from the expansive parlor created an exotic atmosphere of wealth and nobility.

Cadell, Enatta, and Laurent stood at the entrance of their manor greeting each guest as they arrived, while Mira weaved her way through the growing crowd, feeling elated. She took in every detail; for as much as the Marques soirées were discussed, they remained a mystery to the villagers. However, they all knew the Marques didn't invite just anyone, and they also knew the status required to receive an invitation.

Mira moved from the crowd, stood with her back against a marble pillar, and looked out the door. In between the scores of guests wandering about, she caught glimpses of Laurent as he stood like his father, with one arm bent behind his back and the other resting at his side. He nodded to each guest as they passed, while his mother kissed the females on either cheek, and his father grasped hands and/or a patted the males on the shoulder with warm greetings.

One day I will stand with Laurent, greeting our guests, Mira thought, as she carefully studied how they carried themselves.

Calista placed a pillow over her lap as she sat on Sylvana's bed, watching her getting ready to meet Nicolai. "You need to be careful. I don't understand why he is showing such an interest in you."

"That's rude! I'm not a Helot," Sylvana protested..

"You know what I mean. Father leaves, suddenly Enatta takes an interest in Mira, and now Nicolai is all over you. There is something more to this than meets the eye."

Sylvana stepped into her emerald-green dress and as she pulled the corset up, a curtain of pleated silk cascaded down from her waist to the floor. The silhouette of her body was barely visible through the fine linen drifting across the dark stone floor as she walked toward the bed. "It will be fine. I don't believe he has any ill intentions. At least that's what he told me."

Calista rolled her eyes and laughed. "A man would say anything in order to get between a girl's legs." She slid from the bed and turned Sylvana around to secure her corset.

"He's an Acheron. If he wanted to *get between my legs* as you so eloquently put it, he wouldn't have to say anything."

"True, but I'm still concerned. I know something is up. What if they have somehow figured out who we are?" she asked as she tugged the laces.

"Damn, not so tight! I'm not used to wearing this shit. I can barely breathe as it is."

"Do not avoid the subject."

Sylvana grabbed onto the large bedpost to steady herself. "How would they figure anything out? Our ancestors went into hiding long ago, and we have never revealed our lineage to anyone."

"I don't trust Enatta any more than a rat trusts a cold snake."

"Neither do I, but what you are saying is nearly impossible."

Calista stepped back, and Sylvana walked to the dresser and draped a gold necklace around her neck. As she stared at it in the mirror, she rubbed the triangular shaped, emerald pendant between her fingers. Calista appeared in the mirror behind her and slid Sylvana's hair off of her shoulders. "You are stunning, you always have been. Dressing up suits you well."

Even though Sylvana smiled, her sister's words of warning cut through her thin layer of self-confidence. "Should I dress more casually?"

"No. You can't show up for a royal invite looking like a field hand."

"A royal invite? I hadn't thought about it like that."

"What did you think it was?" Calista chuckled.

"I don't know? I guess I hadn't really thought this through."

"Again, I need you to promise me you'll be on your guard. The Acherons are dangerous."

"Stop. I'm nervous enough as it is and you're not helping the situation."

Calista walked away, sat on the bed and leaned back on her hands. "At least Alaric has been called to order by the Legion. Can you imagine what he would say right now?"

Sylvana laughed aloud. "He would lose his shit, and I believe Nicolai had something to do with the Legion's meeting."

"I wouldn't put anything past the Acherons," Calista replied.

The sounds of the heavy metal door knocker echoing from downstairs startled them both. "Shit, your escort is here." Calista jumped from the bed and headed toward the partially opened chamber door.

Sylvana reluctantly followed, all the while second guessing her decision to go. *Maybe Calista is right. This suddenly feels like a bad idea.* She reached out and grabbed Calista's shoulder. "Wait, maybe there is some truth to what you have been saying. What if any of it is true?"

"I'm sure it will be fine. I'm just nervous for you is all. I never expected one of us to get a royal invite."

"You're back stepping on your words and it's not comforting."

"Sylvana, it will be fine. Just don't fall head over heels in love with him tonight," she joked.

"Falling in love with him is the furthest thing from my mind. Honestly, I really don't know what I'm doing?" Sylvana chuckled.

Chapter 5

The ladies were meandering through the gardens, each angling for a bit of salacious gossip, boasting about their wealth, their mates' newly gained titles, and assassinating the reputations of those who had crossed them.

Calantha was sitting on one of the marble benches beneath an old wisteria vine with a group of ladies and noticed Enatta headed in their direction. "Here she comes."

Orenda Cynfadel smiled and nodded. "Good evening, Enatta."

"Orenda, I hope you're enjoying yourself," Enatta replied.

Orenda nodded and smiled. "It has been a wonderful evening. Please, join us."

They adjusted themselves, allowing enough room for Enatta and her friends to take a seat. "How's Jorin?" Enatta asked. "I heard he's taken a position as a royal guard?"

"Tis true," she said. "In no time at all, we shall belong to the court," Orenda replied.

"That's wonderful news," Lavine replied.

Calantha glanced around the large group and then tipped her goblet toward Enatta. "Enatta, how's Laurent? I noticed he and Miriam Orfae-do are enjoying each other's company this evening."

"Yes, they spend a great deal of time together."

"I'm surprised you allow it? We didn't know you were fond of the Orfaedos? When did that happen?" Lavine questioned.

"She's quite the young lady," Enatta replied with a coy smile.

"Aren't you concerned she will damage Laurent's reputation amongst the elite?" Calantha asked.

Oh, they have no idea, Enatta chuckled to herself before responding. "No, quite the opposite. I think you will all be surprised."

"Surprised? Well, do tell," Orenda said.

"In due course, all will be revealed."

"You must tell us? The Orfaedo girl's reputations have been soiled since their mother's disappearance. What has changed?"

Just as Enatta spoke, Cadell approached her from behind and placed a firm hand on her shoulder. "Ladies," he said as he acknowledged them with a slight nod and kissed Enatta's cheek.

She placed her hand over his and smiled at him. "Is there something you need?"

"No. I wanted to make sure you and your ladies are enjoying your evening."

"We are. Thank you, my love."

Cadell looked at Enatta and spoke telepathically. *"I hope you remember what I said to you about Mira?"*

"I haven't revealed a thing," she replied.

"Good. Make sure you keep it that way," he said sternly, before acknowledging the ladies with another nod as he walked away.

"Is everything okay?" Lavine inquired, knowing they were speaking telepathically.

"Of course," Enatta replied.

"I heard a rumor. Is it true Nicolai Acheron paid you a visit?" Orenda asked.

The rest of the group looked at Enatta with wide eyes and a few hushed gasps.

Enatta smiled proudly and motioned for her goblet to be filled. "It is true."

"Don't keep us in suspense. What did he want?" Calantha asked.

"He came by to personally decline our invitation," Enatta boasted proudly.

"He *personally* came by to decline an invitation? I don't believe it." Lavine chuckled.

"What you heard is true. It seems he has taken an interest in Cadell."

Enatta has always told larger tales than a bairn whose imagination has run wild, Orenda thought. "What has Cadell done to deserve such an honor?"

"We can't reveal everything, now can we?" Enatta stated.

"I don't believe any of our mates have mentioned this?" The ladies looked amongst each other, all of whom agreed with Calantha in way or another.

"Why would they? No one would dare to reveal information when the Acherons are involved."

Calista opened the door and stepped aside. "Good evening."

"Good evening miss, my name is Klyn. I've come for Sylvana Orfae-do."

Sylvana took a deep breath and nervously ran her hand down the front of her stomach, as if smoothing out the satin material. "Good evening, I'm Sylvana."

"Shall we?" Klyn stepped aside and as Sylvana and Calista took a few steps out of the door they stared at the gilded, open roof, carriage and four regal, black stallions.

Sylvana awkwardly pointed between the carriage and the parlor and then stepped back. "One moment, please." She then grabbed Calista's hand, pulled her back into the manor, and shut the door.

"What is wrong with you?" Calista chuckled as she stumbled over Sylvana's foot.

"A carriage? I thought we would ride on horseback?"

"What difference does it make?" Calista replied.

"Calista! I'm being serious. It's a royal carriage and I am not a member of court. Can you imagine what everyone who sees me sitting in that thing will think?"

"Who cares what they think?"

"I care. They will whisper about me for weeks, and I can only imagine the rumors they will spread."

"Sylvana, relax. You're nervous and making something out of nothing."

"First, you didn't want me to go at all, and now you've changed your mind?"

"Yes. He sent a carriage for you. It says something about Nicolai. Honestly, I thought you would ride Rana."

"What do you mean?"

"I think it's safe to assume he wouldn't send a royal carriage to fetch a bedmate." She then opened the door and motioned for Sylvana to leave.

Sylvana reluctantly walked out of the door. "I'll be home later."

"I'll wait up, or not," Calista joked.

Lagar hung from the chains binding his wrists, unable to stay conscious for more than a few fleeting moments. He glanced around the cell and watched his shadow being cast onto the damp, tinged wall before him. The gentle, flickering flames could barely alleviate the darkness, however, each time he moved, as did his shadow, like a phantom of death mimicking him.

Riordan, Kieran, and Nicolai walked down the spiraling, stone staircase leading to the dungeons below.

"He will not talk. We've tortured him for weeks now," Nicolai offered.

"He'll talk—eventually," Kieran replied.

"Do you think the rumor amongst them has any validity?" Nicolai asked.

"I'm not sure? I assume his mate would say anything to save his life," Kieran replied.

"We'll find out momentarily." Riordan looked to the guards as they approached the door and nodded.

As they entered the cell, Kieran looked at Riordan and Nicolai and pinched the bridge of his nose. "I can't stand the fucking stench of them."

Nicolai stepped over a dank puddle as he walked to a wood table having been lined with various instruments of torture; he picked up a few of the objects and tossed them back down.

Lagar gasped and clenched his teeth together, doing his best to not cry out when the blow from Kieran's foot radiated across his torso. "He's still with the living," Kieran offered.

Riordan walked in a slow circle around his listless body, listening to each shallow, raspy breath. "I want answers, Lagar. What do you know?"

"I—will give you—nothing, Nosferatu scant," he replied, his words barely audible.

Riordan let out a nefarious chuckle. "*Scant?* How torturous of you."

"You ma-may as well kill me," Lagar mumbled.

"That would be too easy for you. We want answers." Nicolai chose a long dagger and spun it around.

Riordan grabbed a fistful of Lagar's hair and wrenched his head back. "We found out some interesting news. It seems you have been searching for a purebred Ascelin, and Ranan has been communicating with the Faye."

Unable to control his innate reaction, Lagar's eyes met Riordan's, and it was clear he had struck a nerve.

"It seems the rumors are true," Riordan stated.

Nicolai walked up behind him and stared at his partially skinned back. He then slid the flat side of the blade across the bloody, exposed layers of tissue which forced Lagar's body to lurch.

"I will skin you alive, should you choose to keep your mouth shut," Nicolai threatened.

Riordan nodded to Nicolai who slowly cut another layer of skin, what little of it remained, from his lower back.

Lagar let out a throaty, pain-filled roar, and wrapped the chains in his fists, trying to control his reaction.

"Tell me, and I will put you out of your misery," Riordan offered.

Nicolai tossed the piece of skin to the side and looked at Riordan. "Maybe we need up our game?"

"Bring her," Riordan shouted, in the door's direction.

Lagar looked up with blurred vision as the door made a loud clank; its metal bottom scraping across the floor as it opened. The guards shoved another Lycan into the cell and closed the door.

Riordan grabbed the female and tossed her to the floor at Lagar's feet. "I believe you will talk now."

Lagar refused to acknowledge the female. "Who is she?" he mumbled.

Kieran wrenched her to her feet, drug his blade up her chest, and across her throat. "Speak or I will do to her what my brother is doing to you."

Lagar lowered his head and took a shallow breath. They had his mate, and he knew full well their threats were not idle. *Either I tell them what they want to hear, or I'll watch them torture her to death.*

Riordan nodded to his brothers. They lifted her arms and fastened the iron shackles around her wrist's. Her wool shirt parted and fell open when Riordan's blade effortlessly slid through the material.

Kieran shoved her body and a look of defeat crossed Lagar's face as he watched his mate swinging back and forth, while the tips of her toes drug across the begrimed stones.

"Stop!" Lagar demanded.

"Stop? We have yet to begin," Nicolai threatened.

"Lagar, do not tell them anything!" she screamed.

Her head snapped to the side from the force of the blow and she felt the warmth of the blood as it ran down her cheek. Kieran then grasped her jaw in his hand and stood face to face with her. "Speak again and I will cut your fucking tongue out."

Lagar couldn't stand watching the swirling mixture of blood and tears run down his mate's face. "Leave her be! I'll rev-reveal what I know," he stammered.

"No Lagar!" she wailed.

She could almost taste the steel when Kieran shoved the tip of his dagger into the soft flesh beneath her chin. "Shut. The. Fuck. Up," he snarled.

Nicolai walked over, placed his hand on Kieran's shoulder, and gently pulled him back. He then dragged his blade across her throat. She tried to stifle her screams when her skin parted and the blood flowed from the gaping wound. "My brother's words of warning weren't enough?" Nicolai asked.

"Stop! I will—it's true," Lagar shouted.

Nicolai stopped just shy of killing her. He then struck her temple with the butt, knocking her unconscious.

"Speak," Riordan demanded.

"We don't," he paused. "Know who—but she exists," he mumbled.

"Must I spell it out? *Where the fuck is she?*" Riordan demanded, enunciating his words.

Lagar looked at his mate and, not having any other choice, he told them all he knew. "She—she crossed Kadric Orfaedo's fields."

"Kadric?" Nicolai repeated.

Riordan rubbed his face and stared blankly at Lagar. "Crossed or is being hidden?"

"We don't think they are hiding. I know no more." After speaking the words, his head slumped forward. *Now death comes for me. At least my mate won't suffer beneath them,* Lagar thought.

Nicolai stood before Lagar and lifted his head. "Soon you will be nothing more than a shadow of yourself."

"I think we have all we need," Riordan offered. He then pounded his fist on the door a few times, while Nicolai and Kieran tossed the daggers onto the table.

"Milord," the guard replied, as he stood aside and held the door open.

"A swift death for both," Riordan ordered.

"You sa-said you would spare her!" Lagar bellowed.

Riordan turned to face Lagar. "I've changed my mind."

"Milord." The guards nodded to the brothers as they left and shut the door behind them.

They walked up the winding stairs, listening to Lagar's bellows echoing behind them, as they silently contemplated Ranan's involvement.

Riordan glimpsed a torch hanging from the stone wall which was partially askew, so he reached over and straightened it out as they passed. *Is there no one here than can pay attention to fucking details?*

Nicolai and Kieran side-eyed each other and a hint of a smile crept across their faces.

Riordan then looked at Nicolai as they continued up the stairs. "You've been around his daughter a few times. Have you picked up on anything suspicious?"

"No," Nicolai answered.

"She will be here tonight, yes?"

"She accepted my invite, reluctantly," Nicolai replied.

Riordan patted his shoulder. "Don't let her leave without my permission. I believe we are chasing a dragon so to speak."

Riordan, Nicolai, and Kieran walked through the courtyard and into the bathhouse, and undressed.

Riordan tossed his shirt onto the stone bench and looked down at Kieran's feet. "You have blood on your boot."

Kieran pulled it off and tossed it at Riordan. "Since you noticed, you can clean it."

Riordan tossed it to the side and removed his trousers. "I should put it up your ass."

"The only thing going up my ass is the tongue of a whore," Kieran joked, causing Riordan and Nicolai to laugh aloud as they sunk their bodies into the heat of the pool and leaned back.

Riordan cupped the water in his palms and let it run down his face. "It always feels good to wash the stench of the Lycans off."

"What does The Guild of Entente have to say about all of this?" Nicolai asked.

"If it is true, they want the Ascelin as much as we do," Riordan answered.

Kieran motioned for his cup to be filled. "Is there anyone on the Guild that would betray us?"

"I have eyes and ears in every corner. Our enemies do not pose the biggest threat of treachery. It is those vying for power," Riordan replied.

"They have been loyal for centuries. Why would you question them?" Nicolai asked.

Kieran shrugged his shoulders. "I'm being cautious, is all."

"Cynical is more like it." Riordan chuckled.

A handful of young ladies wearing sheer, silk gowns walked into the bathhouse and stood at the edge of the pool. Their gowns fell into soft, folded piles at their feet, and they seductively walked down the steps and swam over to the brothers.

Riordan reached around, took one of them by the back of her neck, pulled her head to the side and sunk his canines into her flesh.

For as much as the carriage wheels fell in and out of the ruts in the road and rolled over rocks, it was a relatively smooth ride, seeing how the springs beneath the padded, velvet seat absorbed most of the bumps.

Sylvana looked down at her nails, and after picking at a rough edge, she held up her hands with outstretched fingers studying their appearance. *At least they're clean,* she thought.

She placed them back into her lap and stared into the darkness of the forest, contemplating the entire situation with Nicolai. All the while listening to the chorus of sounds coming from the nocturnal creatures, which became muted only when the noise from the horses' hooves and the rumbling of the carriage approached.

I've been down this road many times, but never like this. Everything looks so different. Just as the thought crossed her mind, she grabbed onto the side of the carriage with one hand and placed her other on the seat when the lunging of the carriage startled her.

"My apologies, milady. The heavy rains a few nights ago created some deep ruts."

"No need to apologize. It's fine."

"It's a full moon tonight," Klyn added when he heard wolves howling in the distance.

"Yes. It's beautiful. I've been down this road many times, but I've never been able to sit back and enjoy it."

"You've never ridden in a carriage?"

"No, sir."

"There's always a first for everything."

"Yes—" Just as she replied, she noticed a form beyond the tree darting in and out of the shadows which appeared to be following them. She watched intently and could see the snow white color of the creature when it crossed through the silvery rays of the moon cleaving their way through the dense canopy.

Klyn turned his body and looked at her. "Is everything okay?"

"Would you mind stopping for a moment?"

He looked at her inquisitively and caulked his head to the side. "Stop?"

"Yes, please."

He turned back around and pulled on the reins. "Whoa, easy boys." Once the carriage stopped, he leapt from the seat and walked to the door. "Are you okay?" he questioned again.

Sylvana kept her eyes on the creature and watched as it leapt into a tree and crouched down on a thick branch. Klyn opened the door and took a hold of her hand as she stepped down from the carriage. She stopped at the edge of the road and Klyn stood so close to her she could feel the warmth of his body on her back.

"Sylvana, I need to know what you are doing?" he asked sternly.

"I need a minute alone." She collected the sides of her dress and walked into the forest.

Klyn placed a firm hand on her shoulder. "I cannot let you head into the forest alone. I don't know what you are doing, and I insist you get back into the carriage."

The wolf leapt from the branch and landed with a thud on the ground. Klyn let go of Sylvana, pulled the sword from the sheath on his back, and moved in front of her. "Sylvana, stay there," he whispered sternly.

Sylvana stepped to his side and placed her hands on his forearm arm. "Stop. He's not looking to hurt us."

"What the hell is going on?"

"It's Amarok. The villagers refer to him as the Mystic White Wolf."

"They haven't been spotted in hundreds of years. It's a fucking Faye Shifter," he stated.

"He's not a Faye Shifter. You need to trust me," Sylvana replied as she stepped further into the forest.

"Ahh, fuck," Klyn rumbled as he reluctantly followed her.

After a short walk, Sylvana stopped and held up her hand. "Shh, don't say or do anything."

Amarok's hazel eyes were aglow in the dark as he stepped from the shadows. "Wait here."

She walked toward Amarok, kneeled down, and held out her hand. "Amarok, it's okay," she whispered.

Amarok nervously paced back and forth and then took one cautious step after the other in her direction. He looked over her shoulder and he and Klyn held each other's gaze with a mutual look of distrust and malice. The hackles slowly rose along the nape of Amarok's neck, along with a low, guttural snarl and curled lips which revealed his enormous ivory canines.

Sylvana ran her hand over his head and along his back. "Amarok, he won't hurt you."

After a moment, Amarok looked at Sylvana, rubbed his head against her chest, licked her face and nipped at her chin. *"What are you doing along the road?"* she asked telepathically.

"Watching you."

"Where is your pack?"

Amarok sat on his butt and curled his thick tail around his body. *"They're waiting out of sight."*

"You shouldn't be out here. It's not safe," Sylvana said.

"You're not safe either. Do you trust the one who stands behind you?"

She turned ever so slightly and glanced at Klyn. *"I do."*

"I don't," Amarok replied.

"I know," Sylvana smiled.

Amarok rose on all fours and walked in a small circle and then sat again. *"I have news for you."*

"Did you find my father?"

"Yes, he headed for the Black Moor."

"Shit! Really?" This is not good. Why would he go there? she asked herself.

"I tracked him as far as I could. The Lycans have changed, and it's become dangerous for our kind. They've been hunting on the other side of the river."

She leaned forward and kissed the top of his head. *"I don't know what I will do if something happens to you."*

"I haven't survived for as long as I have without keeping my wits about me."

"How have they've changed?"

"I'm not sure. They are volatile, without their innate abilities, and appear to be rabid."

"Do you have any idea why my father would travel there, of all places?"

"I have an idea. My pack chased two of their scouts from your lands a week ago. He might be hunting?" Amarok rubbed his head against her chest, trying to provide a bit of comfort.

Sylvana sighed and sunk her fingers into his thick, soft fur. *"Thank you for doing that. They've been sneaking around for some time now."*

"A word of warning. I believe they suspect one, or all of you, may be a purebred Ascelin."

Sylvana placed her hand across her stomach and stared blankly at Amarok. *"How the hell would the Lycans know?"*

"I have the same questions."

"You're not the only one who has warned me about this lately."

Amarok flicked the tip of his tail. *"Again, be careful and call to me if you need. I'll always be listening."*

"Thank you, as will I."

His eyelids slowly rose and fell, and he tilted his head. *"I owe you my life."*

Sylvana grabbed his face and playfully shook his head. *"You don't owe me a thing."*

Amarok rose to all fours and shook his entire body and looked at Klyn. *"Your friend appears to be nervous."*

"He thinks you're a Faye shifter." She winked.

"A Faye?"

"Yes, it seems we have both gained ill-fitting reputations."

"It's a shame."

"That it is," Sylvana agreed.

"Did you tell him I'm a Lupine Changeing?"

"No."

"Thank you."

Sylvana stood. *"Of course. I should go. He won't stand there much longer."*

Amarok took a few steps back. *"Be careful Sylvana, he's been listening. I cloaked our conversation as best as I could."*

"As did I. Nicolai and Kieran Acheron have read my thoughts already."

"Take caution where they are concerned. I can't protect you from them."

"I'll be fine, and I need you to watch out for yourself as well."

Sylvana made her way back to Klyn, and the silence between them was awkward as they walked to the carriage. He reached for the door but before he opened it; he looked down at Sylvana. "Care to explain?"

"I found Amarok when he was a pup and I nursed him back to health. He still visits me from time to time."

After another uncomfortable moment of silence, he spoke the words she was afraid to hear most of all. "I'm smelling bullshit. I don't believe you, Sylvana."

The way in which his words rolled off his tongue scared her more than she cared to admit. *Dammit, what the hell was I thinking?* "I'm not lying."

"I know you were communicating with the wolf. When did they learn to speak telepathically?"

"I've always been able to communicate with animals." She chuckled nervously.

"The simplicity of your answer speaks volumes."

"I don't suppose you would keep this between us?"

Klyn adjusted his stance and stared down at her. "I will not lie to the Acherons. That will be on you. Now, I suggest you do your best to get the dirt off your dress. Should you run into Riordan, he will notice anything which appears out of place."

Sylvana looked at the cascading material, collected the sides and did her best to shake off the dirt. She then smoothed out the material and looked up at Klyn. "How do I look?"

Klyn motioned with one hand for her to turn around and Sylvana walked in a slow circle as she held the dress above her ankles.

"Well?" she questioned.

"I can still see specks of dirt and you have a few white hairs on your cleavage."

"Shit." Sylvana exhaled, as she bent further over to take a better look.

"Allow me to give you a fighting chance." Klyn waved his hand, and her hair and dress blew to the side as if caught in a gentle breeze. "I believe you're good now. Even the smell of the *wolf,* as you called it, should no longer be an issue."

Sylvana placed her hands on his forearm and smiled. "Thank you."

"Your gratitude is premature. Thank me after Riordan fails to notice." He opened the door and took her hand in his as she stepped up into the carriage.

"We are going to have to pick up the pace, and it might be a rough ride. The last thing either of us needs is to show up late."

"I'll be fine."

Klyn picked up the reins, gave his lead stallions some slack, snapped the reins and made a clicking noise with his tongue.

The stallions pointed their ears forward, leaned into the harnesses, and the wheels of the carriage creaked as they rolled forward. With another snap of the reins, they broke into a trot, and it was not long before they were galloping down the road.

"I think I'd feel safer on the horse than is this carriage," Sylvana said.

Klyn turned his head and winked. "As would I. Driving a carriage is not what I do."

"What do you do?"

"Normally, I'm one of the Acheron's personal guards. Tonight I'm your escort."

"I appreciate it, but why didn't they send a driver?"

"We take care of our own."

"I don't belong to them."

Klyn laughed aloud. "You sure about that?"

"Yes, I'm sure!"

"We shall see."

"Yes, we will."

"Whoa, whoa," Klyn called out as he pulled on the reins.

The carriage slowed, the stallions fell into a trot and then settled into a walk. Sylvana scanned the fields stretching before them as they headed out of the forest. Her stomach churned as a stampede of nerves coursed through her veins, and she cupped her hands together to stop them from trembling.

As they crossed the fields, she thought about how serene they had become under the bright glow of the full moon. Normally, they would be crowded with serfs whose faces were forlorn and weathered as they worked under the watchful eye of the guards.

The guards stationed at the iron gates pulled them open as they approached and for the first time; none of them stopped, searched, or questioned her. *Well, this is a first,* she thought as they politely acknowledged her with a nod. *They have no idea who I am,* she chuckled to herself.

"We're right on time," Klyn said.

What a relief, she thought.

He passed the market and rather than heading toward the expansive courtyard; he turned a corner and headed down a smooth stone road. "Where are we going?" she questioned.

"They don't live in the main castle. They have a private wing."

Their own private wing? Good to know. Shit, as if I wasn't nervous enough. "Klyn, would you stop for a moment?"

Klyn turned his body, looked at her, and furrowed his brows. "I fell for that once. I won't do it again."

"I'm nervous is all."

"I'm not stopping," he replied as he turned back around.

Sylvana noticed multiple silhouettes stepping into the shadows of doorways and peering from the windows as they passed by and knew they wanted to see who was in the carriage. *Here we go,* she thought with an eye roll.

Chapter 6

Klyn pulled the stallions to a halt, and Sylvana studied the appearance of the four guards who looked nothing like the ones at the main gate. They were impeccably dressed from head to toe, larger in stature, and armed with various weapons. They wore black leather trousers with raised patterns, and matching, knee high, lace-up, black boots. Their deep-blue, pleated tunics stood out from beneath their black leather vests which were adorned with silver studs.

Sylvana was taken-a-back as she stared at the majestic gates, having been forged with thick, black iron, which rose above them and was slightly taller than the courtyard walls. Each of the gate's arches was adorned with pointed tips similar to that of an arrow, and in the center of each gate was a colorful, exotic looking creature, each facing the other, which had also been forged from iron. They had the head of an eagle as white as newly fallen snow and curved, yellow beaks, and two white tuffs of feathers that created their ears. The feathers faded down their necks, and tawny fur took over where a lion's lower body appeared. They stood on their hind legs with outstretched wings which were a deep, umber brown and long, yellow eagle like talons reached forward.

My lord, she thought. *I have never seen something so incredible.*

The clanking of the heavy chains as they fell from the enormous locks broke her fascination with the gates, not realizing Klyn had been watching her until he spoke.

"They're incredible, aren't they?"

"Yes, I have seen nothing like it."

"Watching you admire the gates reminds me of the first time I stood before them."

"How long ago?"

"They were created before the original war as a gift."

"One wouldn't know they were so old by looking at them."

"It took dozens of blacksmiths to create the gates."

"How did they color it?"

"It is said that a powerful Faye Lord conjured the colors and the creatures. They appear only in ancient scrolls."

"What? A Faye?"

"Yes. The Faye legend's say there was a powerful Faye Priestess that could transform herself into the creature known as a Griffin."

"Like a shifter?" she asked.

"Yes," Klyn replied.

Sylvana thought about Amarok and everything he had said to her, which brought about another wave of anxiety. Klyn turned around, snapped the reins, and the horses languidly walked through the gates. The most exquisite courtyard she had ever seen stretched before her, and was protected by a solid stone wall which faded into the distance. *My god, I can't imagine what the inside looks like if this is the outside.* Exotic, flowering plants lined the smooth, marble walkways, while wisteria vines climbed the courtyard walls, and a multitude of aged trees grew thick and wild, while lush bushes were sculpted into various animals, birds, and figures.

Klyn pulled the horses to a halt, hopped off the seat. Once again he opened the door and took her hand in his. "In case you were wondering, I will escort you home whenever you are ready."

"Thank you."

"I'll walk you in, and then we will part ways."

She took a deep breath and smiled nervously at Klyn. She held up her dress with one hand while Klyn held onto the other. With each stride up the smooth, white marble steps, she inhaled deeply, feeling as though she was moving in slow motion. Klyn nodded at two well-dressed gentlemen who were standing on either side of the enormous wood doors.

"Milady, welcome," one of them said as they pulled the doors open.

Sylvana did her best not to laugh, knowing she was not a member of the court.

As they walked in, two young ladies, dressed in gray, were awaiting their arrival. "Good evening, milady. Are you thirsty?"

"Yes. I am," Sylvana replied.

The young lady held out a silver tray; Sylvana reached for a gold goblet and took a generous sip. She swallowed the smooth liquid and the sweetest flavor of ripened cherries, and a hint of spice caressed her tongue. *This tastes amazing!* "Thank you."

Klyn chuckled when Sylvana raised an eyebrow and peered into her goblet. "I think I'll join you. Tis good, yes?"

"Incredible." Sylvana smiled.

"Sylvana, welcome," Kieran said.

Her body flinched when Kieran's voice startled her. "Kieran?" she replied.

"Klyn, good to see you," Kieran said, as he walked over and grasped his forearm.

Klyn returned the gesture and pulled him in for a quick embrace.

Sylvana stared at Kieran, who was only wearing a pair of impeccably tailored, ivory-colored cotton trousers; the only distraction from his muscular chest was a geometrical shaped, garnet pendant hanging from a gold chain with oval links.

"How was the ride?" Kieran asked.

Klyn looked at Sylvana and winked. "Uneventful, other than Sylvana being nervous when a wolf appeared near the road."

In that moment, Sylvana felt like she was going to vomit and leave a burgundy pool at their feet. She placed her hand across her stomach and did her best to smile nonchalantly. "It—I enjoyed the ride."

Klyn laughed as he finished his wine and set the goblet back on the tray. "I'll see myself out. Sylvana, it was a pleasure to make your acquaintance. Enjoy your evening."

"Thank you, and it was a pleasure to meet you as well."

The sound of the large doors closing behind her felt as if they had encased her within a coffin of lies and deceit.

Kieran picked up a goblet, wrapped her arm in his and led her toward a large, ornately carved armchair a few feet from the doorway. "It's good to see you again. Have a seat."

She sat down and smiled at him. "It's nice to see you as well."

The two girls kneeled before her and one of them pulled a water-filled china basin from beneath the chair, while the other lifted her legs one at a time and removed her heels. Sylvana looked at Kieran who had taken a seat in a chair next to her, not understanding what was happening.

"It's customary. Riordan has a certain quirk. No one may wear shoes in our home."

"I don't understand?"

Kieran waved his hand dismissively. "It's just the way he is."

Sylvana looked down as the girls placed her feet in the warm, bubbly water and watched as the lavender pedals floated around her ankles while they scrubbed and massaged them. *That feels amazing, awkward, but amazing,* she thought.

"Tell me about your ride?" Kieran suggested.

"I've been down the road many times, but I have never sat back and enjoyed it from a fresh vantage point."

"From what Nicolai has said, you need to relax more, and in case you are wondering, he will be tied up with Riordan for a bit. I'll show you around."

Sylvana smiled and then noticed how the ladies subtly scowled at each other, as if in disgust when they side-eyed her shoes.

Sylvana leaned forward and placed her elbows on her knees. "Are you displeased with my shoes?" she asked with one raised eyebrow.

"No, milady. I was—I needed to place them elsewhere."

As they lifted her feet from the water and dried them, Kieran stood and held his arm out toward Sylvana. "Get up," he said sternly.

Sylvana jumped from her seat, wrapped her arm in his, and placed her hand on his forearm, afraid she had over stepped her bounds. "I'm sorry—" she began.

"I'm speaking to them," he replied as he motioned his goblet in the girl's direction.

They stood without hesitation and cupped their hands in front of their bodies. "Milord," they stated in unison.

"Was it your intention to make our guest feel unwelcome?"

"No—no, milord, we meant no disrespect."

"I am sure your footwear has been soiled with more piss and shit than Sylvana's. Your services are no longer needed."

They looked at each other, trying to decipher what he meant. "Milord?" one of them said.

"Out the back door," he stated.

Kieran followed behind, all the while keeping Sylvana's arm wrapped in his. She scanned the grandiose surroundings, and then looked down at the long, woven, multicolored rug that was lush and soft underfoot. She glanced at the circular, white, marble stairs and another long rug covering the steps from top to bottom while hand carved, wood rails embellished with intricate carvings, lined the stairs and upper hallway. *Wealth at its finest. I never knew someone could have so much,* Sylvana thought, as she gazed at the statues which were carved in the likeness of warriors, mythical creatures, and animals.

After entering a small room adjacent to a lavish kitchen, the girls bent down to pick up their shoes neatly placed against the wall.

"Leave them," Kieran said.

"I'm sorry, I don't understand?" one of them replied.

"You can walk barefoot back to the Gomorrah you came from."

His callousness shocked Sylvana, and she regretted the decision to confront the girls.

"Milord," they replied with a courtesy. They then glanced at Sylvana with malice filled scowls and quietly shut the door behind them.

Kieran looked down at Sylvana. "Shall we?"

"Yes," she replied, with a forced smile.

"I'd like to show you something."

"What is it?"

"Do you like art?"

Art? I certainly didn't expect to see an art collection. "Yes. And you?"

"Yes. And why is it unexpected?"

"I don't know? And I am going to put a stop to you reading my thoughts," she smiled.

"Do your best," he replied with a wink.

They walked down a long hallway and up another set of winding stairs; on their way up, Kieran moved a large oil painting, so it was slightly askew.

"Why did you do that?" Sylvana asked.

"Just fucking with Riordan. How's your family?"

"They're well. My sister Calista is at home and I'm sure you know of Mira's whereabouts."

"Nicolai told me what happened. Enatta is a malicious imposter. She's always scheming."

"My mother used to tell us stories about her. What will you do if Cadell is titled?"

"Enatta will find herself on the other side of the threshold." He chuckled.

"Good to know," Sylvana said as she chuckled along with him.

He opened a door, and they walked into an extensive library; the walls were lined with tall, dark shelves, and black chandeliers filled with candles hung from the ceiling and lit the room with a warm, ambient light which cast shadows across various, sized, oil paintings hanging on every wall and in-between the shelves.

It smells like old wood and aged paper; she thought as she scanned the titles. *I can only imagine the stories waiting to be read that are written across their pages in black scroll ink.*

She languidly strolled around the room and ran her hand across a green velvet, chaise lounge and looked at Kieran. "I'm impressed." She did her best to focus on her surroundings rather than Kieran's impressive physique.

Kieran walked across the room, opened two stained glass doors and stepped onto the half-round balcony. Sylvana stared at the thick, reddish scar running down his back as she followed behind. She stood next to him, placed her palms on the marble railing, and looked down into the courtyard. "I have never seen anything so beautiful."

"Neither have I," he said, only he was looking at Sylvana, not the courtyard.

She felt the warmth radiate across cheeks from the unexpected compliment; she smiled and turned her face to hide the rosy color of her cheeks.

Kieran lifted her chin with his fingers. "The way you're dressed tonight does you justice. You're stunning."

Her stomach lurched, and her pulsed raced, fearing he was about to do more than compliment her. "Thank you." She stepped back, walked across the balcony, and looked at the rolling, black clouds slowly consuming the glowing moon.

Kieran smirked. "Do not be nervous, Sylvana. It's a compliment, not an invitation." He then held out his hand. "Come, I have something else to show you."

She took his hand in hers, and they walked back into the room. Kieran released his grip and pulled two large shelves opened which revealed a smaller room decorated similar to the library however, the walls were covered with writing, maps and sketches of warriors, animals and demonic looking creatures, as if someone had sketched them with charcoal. At the end of the large room were two tall, gray, stone statues; a male and a female, both of whom were wearing a hooded cloak.

This looks like one hell of a story, she thought as she walked in a slow circle.

Kieran pulled the cork out of a green, glass decanter, poured the amber liquid into two matching cups and handed one to Sylvana; he then draped his arm around her shoulder and pulled her tightly into his body.

She looked up and did her best to smile. "Thank you," she said, sounding quieter than she had intended.

He motioned his glass toward the depictions on the walls. "Do you know what this is?"

Her brows furrowed while looking at the illustration. "I have no idea," she stated.

"It's the story of our ancestors."

"Really?"

"Yes. Would you like to hear it?"

"Of course."

Kieran pointed to the far wall and began. "It was the year 1320, and the Lycan's had invaded and occupied most of Kroyidia, which pushed the mortals to the outskirts of the Country and into hiding. Their ultimate goal was to eradicate them in order to deplete our kind's source of fresh blood."

"My lord," she whispered under her breath.

"Wars between clans broke out and often ended in death when the rising bloodlust ran rampant throughout the region. During the war, the cold indifference between our ancestors and the Lycans created famine, sickness and social decay. The stench of rotting flesh, from the piles of Lycans' partially burnt carcasses, overtook the once fragrant forest, while plums of nauseating smoke filled the air."

"It sounds horrible. I have heard none of this." She looked down and realized at some point she had placed her hand on his forearm. *Shit!*

Kieran took a drink and then pointed to another part of the drawing. "Jarimor Ascelin and Marius Acheron, two of the most powerful Nosferatu Lords, led the resistance against the Lycans and eventually enslaved them before beheading Bastan, and all those who were loyal to his cause prior to their defeat, bringing peace to our war-torn lands."

As Kieran continued, his words faded into the background and became indistinct. Against her better judgement, she was becoming more attracted to him with every passing minute. She breathed in his musky scent and looked down at the muscular forearm draped across her chest, while his hand gently held her bicep. The warmth of his body against her back and how his muscles rippled against her with each subtle movement sent a stampede of chills up her spine. She took another sip and tried to focus on the sound of his voice, doing her best to ignore the unwanted wave of desire she felt rising to the surface.

"In the years that followed, Marius and Jarimor freed the Lycans and banished them to the outskirts of Kroyidia, which became known as The Black Moor—"

"I don't mean to interrupt, but the same Black Moor at the edge of your Kingdom?"

"Yes. Why do you ask?"

"I'm curious, is all. I know of it, but I didn't know its history."

She knows a lot more than she is admitting, Kieran thought. "We believe that Bastan's grandson, Ranan, is leading another uprising as we speak. He is hiding somewhere on the outskirts of the Moor."

Sylvana swallowed hard, and her heart lurched the moment he spoke the name Ranan. She looked up at him and smiled, doing her best to look impassive. "Please, continue."

"Jarimor and Marius outlawed all clans from associating with another race after male Nosferatu took female Lycans in their human form, as sex slaves, which resulted in the birth of a new breed, whom you refer to as Helots. They do not yield the powers of either Nosferatu or Lycan and allowing them to continue to breed would only result in a race that would be vulnerable, pallid, and unable to defend themselves or the Kingdom."

"All this time, and neither my father nor my mother have ever mentioned this."

"Unfortunately, history ends up on worn pages when tongues cease to speak. Never forget your past, Sylvana."

"Is this the reason you keep such an extensive collection of books and scrolls?"

"Yes," Kieran replied.

"Go on," she said.

"Not all agreed with freeing the Lycans and fifty years after they brought the Kingdom back from the brink of destruction, Jarimor Ascelin was assassinated and his clan disappeared. Supposedly, the Acherons, my ancestors, betrayed him."

"Your ancestors killed m—the Ascelins?" she replied, having quickly corrected herself.

"Yes, and by the year 1630, it was said there were a handful of purebred female Ascelins in hiding; had they been discovered, they would have been forced into mating an Acheron as a royal breeder."

Sylvana stopped herself from thinking, knowing Kieran would be listening. She swallowed the last of her drink and flinched when she heard Nicolai's voice.

"I was wondering where the two of you were hiding." He walked over and placed a hand on Kieran's shoulder. "Brother, thanks for taking care of her."

Sylvana stared at Nicolai who was wearing form-fitting, dark gray trousers that laced up the crotch and a crisp, white tunic whose soft, pleated folds fell from his wrists. He was also wearing a pendant identical to Kieran's. *I'm not overdressed after all,* she thought.

Kieran pulled away from Sylvana and placed his hand on Nicolai's shoulder. "I assume you'd like a drink?"

"You know I do." Nicolai looked down at Sylvana and before she could speak, his mouth was on hers and the warmth of their tongues was tangled together. He pulled away ever so slightly and whispered in her ear. "You are simply divine, Sylvana. We couldn't take our eyes off of you."

"We?" She looked behind Nicolai and Riordan was standing in the doorway staring at her.

"Good evening, Sylvana." he said, as he glided across the floor with purpose and authority.

Sylvana studied his appearance momentarily. He was a slightly taller and larger version of his brothers and had the same rugged features and stunning appearance. His deep, russet hair was coiffed to perfection and his amber eyes swirled around his raven black pupils. He was dressed similar to Nicolai and also wore the same pendant and gold chain as his brothers. *There isn't a question in my mind, an original sired them.* "Good evening, milord."

"Call me Riordan."

"Yes, milord."

Nicolai chuckled, and she squinted her eyes at him.

"It might take her a moment to get your name right," he joked.

"My apologies for keeping Nicolai tied up. Have you been enjoying your evening?"

"Yes. Very much so. The library is incredible."

Riordan took a seat in a green, leather chair and placed his glass on a round, black marble table. "One of the evilest things we can inherit is an ignorant mind."

Kieran sat opposite Riordan, and Nicolai took Sylvana's hand and led her to a matching settee and sat down. He laid one arm across the back and stroked her shoulder with his fingers.

Sylvana rubbed her arms, feeling the chill in the air, and looked toward the door when a flash of lightning snaked its way through the library and a crack of thunder rattled the stained-glass panes of the balcony doors.

"Are you cold?" Nicolai asked.

"A little," she replied.

Nicolai waved his hand toward the hearth sitting at the far end of the room and bright, orange flames roared to life and flickered and spit at the curved, blackened ceiling; he then lifted her chin with his fist and stole another heated kiss before pulling away. "It will be warmer momentarily."

"Thank you."

"Did Kieran recount to you the story of our ancestors?" Riordan asked as he motioned toward the walls.

"Yes," she replied.

Riordan placed his palm on a book that sat on the table next to his glass. "Can you read?"

"Yes, my mother taught me," she replied.

"What do you read?" Kieran asked.

"Whatever I can. She used to tell me that knowledge is a powerful weapon."

"That it is," Nicolai agreed.

Riordan slowly spun his glass on the table. "I'm impressed with you."

Sylvana stared at him momentarily. "Why?"

"I expected less."

Sylvana looked at Nicolai and Kieran and then back at Riordan. "What is that supposed to mean?"

"It was a compliment," Kieran replied quickly.

Riordan stood and looked at Sylvana. "Come."

Sylvana walked over and stood next to Riordan, along with Nicolai and Kieran.

"Did my brother mention them?"

"No," she said as she looked up at Riordan.

"The male is our grandfather, Marius Riordan Acheron and the female is Lucinda Sabrione Ascelin—they are alive, Sylvana," Riordan admitted. "It is said the blood of purebred Ascelin can unseal the curse and release them from these tombs."

Holy shit! Ascelin? Is she my ancestor? Sylvana thought, very carefully. "You were named after your grandfather?"

"Yes, I am the eldest," Riordan replied.

"Marius and Lucinda were cursed?"

"Yes, by the original Faye," Nicolai answered.

"Where are your parents?" Sylvana asked.

"Our Father Viktor, and our Mother Lyllith, succumbed to wounds caused by the Faye," Riordan replied before telling her the story. "Six hundred years after the war ended between Nosferatu and Lycans, the Faye rose in power beyond the veil in a Kingdom known as Estraxath. Their Lord, Obernzel, and their council, known as The Mercurial Guardian's, sent demands to Marius and our council, The Guild of Entente, allowing them the right to keep any original Ascelin they located. Neither side could come to an agreement and after a long battle, many deaths, and the original treaty being cast into the fires, our ancestors drove them back into the veil, along with the severed head of Obernzel.

Having suffered far too many losses to continue the fight, The Mercurial Guardians sealed the veil. Roughly one hundred years after Obernzel was beheaded, his offspring yearned to return to the world they once knew. However, the Guild dismissed their pleas and, in order to send a coherent message, they returned the beheaded bodies of those who dared to cross over. Marius took it upon himself to watch over Lucinda and Cathagne after his brother, Anton, met his demise during the war."

"How did Marius and Lucinda end up like this?" Sylvana asked.

Nicolai stroked her hair and took a drink. "It had been five years since the last of the Faye crossed over and all had returned to normal. No one knows what happened for sure? Marius found a note on Lucinda's desk with the royal seal. It read, 'Mother, a Full Wolfbane Moon, the chalice is full. Meet me under the Laxon tree. Cathagne.'"

"Who is Cathagne?" Sylvana asked.

"Lucinda's daughter," Kieran replied.

Sylvana adjusted her stance and wrapped her arm around Nicolai. "I can already see where this is going."

Nicolai smiled down at her. "When neither of them returned, Marius set out to find them. When his guards noticed he was missing, they went looking and found Marius and Lucinda entombed in stone, on the edge of the Black Moor, and they never found her daughter."

"That's awful. Do you think she may still be alive?"

"No one knows for sure, but they assumed they killed her in retaliation. They found nothing more than bloodied strands of her hair, tattered pieces of her clothing and her left hand, which still her mother's royal, emerald ring on her finger laying at the base of the statue."

Sylvana stood motionless as Riordan's canines slid from his gums. He then struck his finger against one of them. She stood with bated breath as her eyes followed the small crimson droplets as they dripped onto the Lucinda's lips, which disappeared as quickly as they fell. Her mind spun, and she felt she had no other choice but to cloak her thoughts permanently regardless if they felt the energy or not. She ran her hand down her face and took a breath before thinking. Her mother's words echoing in her mind. *'You can never speak your sired name. We must remain diligent'. What the fuck have I gotten myself into?*

Nicolai wrapped his arm around her waist. "We believe Lucinda's descendants are alive and well."

Sylvana stood frozen in place, knowing there were three sets of eyes pinned on her. The way the brothers stood around her felt ominous, and the howling of the winds, the streaks of lightning, and the cracks of thunder certainly weren't helping. "I—wow—still alive, are they? And you know this for sure?"

"We know," Kieran replied.

"Where do you think they are?"

"Close, Sylvana," Riordan replied. "We suspect they have been living right under our noses for centuries."

Riordan and Kieran took a seat, while Nicolai walked Sylvana back to the settee.

"Have her thoughts become vacant to the two of you?" Riordan asked telepathically.

"Yes," Nicolai and Kieran answered.

Nicolai took a seat next to Sylvana and held onto her thigh while Kieran refilled everyone's glasses before taking a seat.

She smiled at Kieran as she held up her glass and did her best to remain collected. "Why are the Ascelin females important to you?"

Riordan cocked his head and raised an eyebrow. "The originals sired them. Every Acheron throughout history has sworn their fealty to The Guild of Entente and it's our duty to protect them."

Kieran crossed one leg over his knee. "What my brother is trying to say is an Ascelin female is one of the most coveted of mates."

"Why? There are plenty of other suitable females."

"There are, but they don't possess powers like the Ascelins," Nicolai replied.

Riordan picked up a book which was sitting the table. "That's enough history for the night. Would you do us the honor and read a passage?"

What the hell? Is he testing my reading ability?

Nicolai chuckled at the look that crossed her face. "Hasn't anyone ever read to you while sitting in front of a fire?"

"Yes, my mother used to."

Riordan handed the book to Kieran, who handed it to Sylvana. She slid her hand over the worn cover. "The seer beyond the veil," she read aloud as she glanced at Riordan as if needing approval.

"Go on," Riordan said.

She studied its worn spine and faded back and opened the book. She then placed her thumb on the pages and watched them flutter. "Is there a certain page you would like for me to read from?"

"No. You pick one," Nicolai replied.

Sylvana scanned the pages before settling on a brief paragraph. She slid her hand over the page and was a taken aback when the symbols moved across the page and morphed and twisted into words she understood. She looked at Nicolai nervously and he gave her a reassuring smile.

"Vispera, didst crosseth thy veil and didst ariseth within thy hallow'd temple, beneath thy deepest of moon bright night. Shifter with raven flowing hair, emerald eyes, and ivory linen gown. Thy female, high-lone, stood before thy jeweled altar. She wrapped her hands tightly around thy silver steel and allowed thy crimson gouts to fall into thy time worn chalice. She did turn and walk toward thy entrance and down thy onyx steps. Reaching thy edge of thy moor she stood serenely, staring into thy vespers river. Knowing she wast high alone, unseen, Shifter became thy Faye, and thy Faye became she. On this eve, Vispera traveled high alone in search of a mate to call her own. She paced back and forth, without fear she bowed beneath thy waxing scarlet moon."

It sounds similar to my father's poem? she thought as she closed the book, not wanting to continue; she felt as though her entire world was crumbling down around her. She handed to book to Nicolai, picked up her glass, and took a large drink.

"Your voice is mesmerizing when you read," Kieran said.

"The writing is old," Sylvana replied.

Riordan reached his hand out, and they passed the book to him. "That it is, Sylvana. I think I've taken up enough of your time." Riordan stood, walked to Sylvana, and lifted her hand.

Sylvana smiled but the warmth of his lips against the back of it felt like a viper's tongue tasting its prey.

"It's been a pleasure to meet you," she said, as poised as possible.

Riordan's eyes met hers and he felt the pull his brothers spoke about. *I find myself devastatingly drawn to you.* "Believe me, the pleasure has been all mine."

"Shall we?" Nicolai asked as he stood and held out his elbow.

"We shall." Sylvana smiled.

"Let's lighten the evening up," Kieran said as he held out his elbow.

They walked through the library and heard Riordan's voice echo from the stairway. "Fucking hell!"

"I assume he noticed the picture?" Sylvana asked as she chuckled.

"Yes, he did," Nicolai laughed.

"Do you play games, Sylvana?" Kieran asked.

"My family and I play when the weather has turned."

Nicolai and Kieran escorted her through their quarters and down a long, winding stairway which led into a tunnel beneath the main wing. "Where are we going?" she asked.

"Where the entertainment is," Nicolai replied cryptically.

It was not long before the sounds of music and laughter grew in intensity. Two well-dressed guards opened a set of heavy, ornate doors and when she stepped into the extravagant room arm in arm with Nicolai and Kieran the boisterous sounds became hushed whispers, and the guests eyed the three of them with curious glances. The poet, who was standing amongst the crowd, banged the end of his staff on the stone floor. He then waved it toward Nicolai and Kieran with a slight bow. "May the night continue with riddle and poem for the lord's he hosts."

The crowd turned their attention back to one another and the conversations and laughter continued.

"Where are we?" Sylvana whispered.

"Why are you whispering?" Nicolai teased.

Kieran bent over in a joking manner and waved his free arm in front of the three of them. "'Tis the place where we leave our troubles at the door, milady." He winked.

They were escorted through the crowd and Sylvana watched how Nicolai and Kieran were greeted by everyone they passed, as if vying for their attention. Nicolai motioned for Sylvana to sit on the long, gilded, high-back chair, while he and Kieran sat on either side of her. Fresh goblets of cherry wine were handed to each of them while to guards took their place and stood on either side of the chair.

In the center of the room, the guests were playing a game she had never witnessed before.

She watched in awe as she had never seen lords and ladies running around without regard for their status, titles, or reputations.

"What are they doing?

"Playing a game called Esquivar."

"I have never seen or heard of it."

Kieran leaned against Sylvana's shoulder. "We'll play soon. Watch what they do. You'll get the hang of it."

"You want me to play?"

"But of course." Nicolai chuckled. "There are two teams, each team wears a colored vest. Your team will try to kill the other using the short spears they are throwing at each other."

A roar from the crowd erupted when the last of the blue vested lords was hit. Sylvana took another drink and laughed when a brawl between the two broke out.

"You beskaldi! I caught it!" one of them yelled.

"It was a clear shot to the chest. If it were real, it would have taken your fucking hand!" his opponent replied.

"Allow the Acherons to call the game," another yelled, to the amusement of the crowd, all of whom turned their attention to Nicolai and Kieran.

"Our lady shall decide his fate," Kieran yelled.

Once again, the crowd erupted.

"Kieran! Do not make me decide."

Nicolai leaned in. "Do you think he caught the spear, or do you think it hit his chest?"

"I don't know? I wasn't really paying attention."

"Make a decision. It's not a patient crowd," Kieran teased.

"Great, no pressure," Sylvana replied to Nicolai's and Kieran's amusement.

"If it were real, would he have been able to stop it?" Kieran asked.

"Well, yes, seeing how he is Nosferatu," Sylvana replied.

Nicolai and Kieran laughed aloud. "Good point, but just pick a winner," Nicolai said.

"A thumb up he wins, a thumb down he loses," Kieran explained.

Sylvana reluctantly held up her fist up and momentarily glanced between the players; she then pointed her thumb down. Whoops, hollers, and laugher rang from the winning team, while the males on the losing team gave her a slight bow and the ladies curtsied.

Nicolai smiled and winked at her. "I would have chosen the same."

"I have never seen ladies running around like this," Sylvana said.

"I can't wait to see your skills, Syl," Nicolai replied.

"I don't think you will see them tonight."

"Oh, I believe we are going to see a lot tonight," Kieran said with a coy smile.

Sylvana felt her face flush, and she refused to look at either of them. However, her pulse increased, and she felt a rush of adrenaline pool in her stomach at the mere thought of being with them in such a way.

After about an hour of casual conversation, laughter, and drinking, Nicolai and Kieran stood. "What are you doing?" she asked.

"We are going to play now," Nicolai replied.

"Absolutely not."

Kieran bent over and whispered in her ear. "We can find another game for you to play with us if you like."

Sylvana's eyes widened, and she looked between Nicolai and Kieran, who were obviously not taking no for an answer. *I don't want to know what he meant.* She stood, reluctantly.

"Take out three on blue," Kieran yelled.

The crowd cheered and three of the blue vested players stepped to the sidelines.

Nicolai placed a vest on Sylvana, and Kieran handed her a spear. "Are there rules?" Sylvana asked.

"No. It's more like mayhem. Any strike to the body counts," Nicolai replied.

They lined up, a horn blew, and spears began whizzing past her head and body. Nicolai and Kieran knocked the ones headed in her direction to the floor and then ran along the edges, trying to flank the other team. Players were being stuck and moving off the floor, while others were wrestling for the arrows. The ladies were mostly running around screaming, ducking, and laughing, while the males met each other with more aggression and physical contact.

Sylvana stretched her arm out in front of her body toward her opponent, pulled her other arm back and threw the spear across the floor hitting one male in the head. The crowd erupted with cheers, having witnessed the impeccable throw.

"Fuck yes!" Nicolai yelled from across the floor.

"You have a hell of an arm," Kieran yelled as he tossed her another spear.

Sylvana caught it and immediately ducked, dodging an incoming spear. She spun around and her spear landed in the center of the lady's chest.

"Get 'em, Syl!" Nicolai shouted as he tossed his opponent to the floor and drug his spear across his throat.

The red team was now down by more than half of its players, fewer females than males. The ladies chased each other down as they laughed and yelped while the males grabbed the females in their arms and spun them around, making sexual innuendos and gestures. A few females were lip locked while others were playing hard to get.

Sylvana yelped when she felt someone wrap her in his arms and kiss her neck. She turned her head to the side, and it was Nicolai. "I didn't know this game would become sexual." She laughed.

"Everything is sexual. You have seen nothing yet." He chuckled.

A spear almost hit Sylvana in the back of the head, however Nicolai caught it. "Game's not over," he said as he handed it to her. "Choose your next victim."

Sylvana looked around and threw it toward a male who was running across the floor, and it hit him in the waist.

"Damn, you're one hell of a shot."

"I grew up with a brother, in case you hadn't noticed."

"I noticed." He laughed.

"You're repeating me again," she teased.

"Am I?"

"Nicolai!" Kieran shouted.

Nicolai spun around and saw a group running at them from behind. "Shit! Run Sylvana."

She yelped, and as she ran across the floor, she felt a thud in the middle of her back.

Kieran ran toward her and pinned her against his body. "Never turn your back on your enemy, darling." He cupped her jaw in his hand and his mouth fell to hers before escorting her to the edge of the floor where the fallen players were standing.

Sylvana nervously looked around to see if Nicolai had witnessed the kiss. "Kieran, what was that for?"

"A kiss for the dead." He chuckled.

"You shouldn't have kissed me."

"Don't worry about it, my brothers and I share everything." He winked.

"I'm not a *thing* you can share," she protested.

He raised his hand, snapped his fingers, and she was handed a fresh drink. "I do love a challenge." He then caught another spear headed in their direction and kissed her again before pulling away ever so slightly. "Saved your life," he joked. He held his arms out to his sides and shimmied his chest and shoulders as he backed away. "You know you want this," he teased.

"You're ridiculous." She laughed.

She stood on the edge of the playing area watching Kieran and Nicolai taking out player after player; their movements were fluid, precise, and swift and she could not help but to be impressed as they moved with the grace and agility of a feline stalking its prey.

Kieran and his opponent lunged for one of the few remaining spears; Kieran bent his leg around his opponent's and pulled it out from under him, grabbed the spear off the floor and plunged it into his chest.

Sylvana set her cup on one of the small tables having been set up for the players, clapped and let out a call of approval along with the rest of the crowd. She then noticed one of the few remaining ladies pull an arrow from behind her back and sneak toward Kieran, who was now standing over the fallen player with raised arms. Just as she was about to plunge the spear into his back, he spun around, wrapped her tightly against his body, grabbed the spear, and plunged it into her stomach to the amusement of the crowd.

Sylvana felt a pang of jealousy and rolled her eyes. *Vying for his attention in such an obvious way is pitiful. Ohh, please, as if you are really trying to break free. You're too busy shoving your ass into his crotch.*

"How about a kiss for the kill?" she yelled.

Various words of encouragement and cheers of approval rang out from the crowd. Kieran side-eyed Sylvana and yelled. "As you wish!" He then bent over and kissed the back of her hand and walked to Nicolai, who placed his hands on his shoulders and shook him back and forth.

Kieran looked at Sylvana and winked, and she felt another wave of desire she tried her best to dismiss. She also felt someone burning a hole in her back; when she glanced over her shoulder. the girl who tried to get a kiss from Kieran was standing with a group of ladies, all of whom were staring at her, laughing, and whispering in each other's ears.

"Don't worry about them," Sylvana heard when someone nudged her shoulder.

"What?" Sylvana looked at the young lady who appeared to be about her age, only she clearly belonged with the elite. She was slightly taller, had striking hazel eyes, flawless mocha-colored skin and jet-black hair that was a perfect mix of tight braids and loose strands framing her angular features. Her emerald-green gown was made from the finest silks and perfectly tailored to her svelte figure.

"Ignore them. We refer to them as 'the beasts of court.'" She chuckled.

Sylvana smiled. "They don't bother me. I'm used to it."

"I'm Venthana," she offered.

"I'm Sylvana."

"I see you're with the Acherons. How did you get so lucky?" She winked.

Sylvana smiled. "I don't know how I ended up here, to be honest."

"Why don't you join my friends and I?"

"Thank you, but I don't want to intrude."

Venthana wrapped an arm around one of Sylvana's and walked her to her group of friends. "Ladies, I'd like to introduce you to the Acheron's girl, Sylvana."

"I'm not their girl," Sylvana replied nervously.

"You could have fooled us. They have never brought a girl here," Aurelia said.

"Really?" Sylvana asked.

"*Really*," Venthana replied.

Sylvana glanced at Nicolai and Kieran. "I'm surprised. I'm aware of their reputations."

"They are everything you have heard and more." Stefania chuckled.

Venthana playfully pushed Stefania's shoulder. "Stop messing with her."

"Tis true," she stated.

"Worry about how they treat you, not what others say." Venthana then pulled on Sylvana's vest. "I see you have blue, and we have red."

"That means you're on the beasts' team. They will do whatever they can to embarrass you," Aurelia said.

"Wonderful," Sylvana replied.

"We will have to do something about this. Come girls," Venthana said.

Sylvana watched as they headed toward the girls and, from what she could tell, a minor altercation broke out amongst them. *Apparently, they don't want to give up their colors.* However, it wasn't long before they were headed back wearing blue vests.

"Watch your back. They will come for us," Aurelia laughed.

Another round began and as Sylvana ran across the room with Venthana and Aurelia, someone grabbed her from behind and bent over her and knocked a spear down that almost hit her. "It about took you out, milady," Klyn smiled.

"However can I thank you for saving my life?" she joked.

"I'm sure I can think of a way, eventually," he teased.

Chapter 7

Nicolai was standing on the sidelines with Sylvana wrapped in his arms. "What do you say we go elsewhere and relax?"

"I'd love to. What do you have in mind?"

"Kieran, let's go," Nicolai said telepathically.

Nicolai patted Klyn's shoulder. "We're heading out. Want to join us?

"Absolutely."

Venthana looked at Sylvana. "Are the two of you leaving so soon? Dawn won't be here for hours."

"The three of us are leaving," Kieran replied as he picked his goblet up.

"Klyn, you're coming as well?"

"Yes. If you don't mind?" Klyn replied.

"Not at all." She smiled.

"Sylvana, this Damascus, a friend of ours," Klyn said.

Damascus nodded politely. "Good to make your acquaintance, milady."

"Nice to meet you as well." Sylvana looked at Nicolai. "It appears as if it is a group event? Would it be a problem for Venthana and her friends to join us?"

"If it pleases you, they are welcome to come along," Nicolai replied.

"It does," Sylvana smiled. *The last thing I want is to be alone with four males, one of whom I have never met.*

"Shall we?" Kieran asked.

As the group walked down the hall, a gentle glow of light grew brighter when they rounded the corner. They passed two large columns and standing at the entrance of a bathhouse, which was lit by torches, and filled from wall to wall with exotic plants and statues, while stained glass windows lined the top half of the outer two walls.

"You want to go swimming?" Sylvana questioned.

"Not exactly," Nicolai replied.

"Are you hungry, Syl?" Kieran asked.

"Yes, now that you mention it."

"We are here to feed and relax." Nicolai smiled.

They walked around the main pool, and as the males removed their clothing, Sylvana looked at her girls and smiled meekly, feeing embarrassed not having the desire to get naked in front of everyone.

"It is a normal event, Sylvana," Venthana replied sweetly.

"Normal? Have you done this with Nicolai and Kieran before?" Sylvana asked.

Venthana, Aurelia, and Stefania sat on the stone bench and removed their shoes. "Never with them, and I'm shocked we could come along," Venthana replied.

Aurelia untied the laces on the back of Venthana's dress. "We have never been around them other than what you saw during the games," she whispered to Sylvana.

"You all don't mind getting naked around them?" Sylvana asked as she pulled her shoes off.

The girls laughed and glanced at each other. "I assume you have never been to court?" Stefania asked.

"No, I don't belong to the court."

"The bath houses are just another party," Stefanie explained.

Their dresses fell to the floor, and it was as if modesty was not in their nature as they stared at Sylvana.

"Are you going to sit there all night?" Venthana asked.

Sylvana stood and reached behind her to untie the laces on her corset. "I guess not."

Venthana turned Sylvana around. "Here let me."

Sylvana crossed her arms over her chest when her dress slid off her shoulders.

She turned around, and the girls were chuckling. "We will give you a discrete entry," Stefania offered.

They walked down the steps into the pool in a small group, all the while keeping Sylvana hidden behind their bodies. *Thank god they are here.* Sylvana thought.

Nicolai, Kieran, Klyn, and Damascus were already sitting in the pool, casually leaning against the edge with a drink. Nicolai held out his hand as Sylvana sank into the water up to her shoulders between him and Kieran.

"A shy little kit, are we?" Kieran teased.

"I'm not used to baring all in front of strangers."

"A body is a body, Sylvana. Although I have to give you credit, yours is exquisite from what little I could see," Klyn joked.

Once again Sylvana felt the flush radiate across her cheeks when her girls giggled and Venthana splashed Klyn. "Do not embarrass the girl."

"Then I shall turn my attention to you," Klyn smiled coyly.

"Do as you wish," Venthana stood, held her arms out to her sides, and turned in a seductive circle. "Do you like what you see, warrior?"

"Holy shit," Sylvana whispered.

Klyn raised up from the water, which trickled down every crevice of his muscle laden body as he walked to Venthana and wrapped an arm around her. "Seduction at its finest."

Damascus looked at Sylvana. "Milady, where have you been hiding? I have never seen you in court?"

"I live on the outskirts of the kingdom with my family."

"One wouldn't guess by looking at you. Your skills impressed me tonight." He nodded.

She smiled timidly. "Thank you."

Aurelia tilted her cup toward Sylvana. "We think you would be a fitting addition to court."

"I don't know about that," Sylvana replied.

Nicolai lifted Sylvana's chin with his fingers and winked. "We couldn't agree more."

"It's been a long day for Sylvana. We should go," Nicolai said.

Venthana gently squeezed Sylvana's hand. "It has been a pleasure to get to know you. You should come visit us soon."

"Thank you, I would love to."

Stefania smiled. "When you return, we would be happy to show you around."

"Next time, we'll make sure you're on our team when the games begin. We will show the beasts what's up," Aurelia joked.

Sylvana nodded at Aurelia as she rose from the water, feeling less self-conscious than she had before seeing how the alcohol helped her to feel less inhibited. "Have a good night."

The ladies-in-waiting held up white, cotton robes as they walked up the stairs. Sylvana then walked over, reached for her dress and shoes, but Nicolai gestured dismissively with his hand. "Leave it. The servants will see to your clothing."

Sylvana glanced back at Klyn, hoping he was following her. However, his mouth was planted on Venthana's and her body was wrapped around his. *This isn't good,* she thought before looking at Nicolai. "I can't go home in a cotton robe."

"Who said anything about you going home?" Kieran asked.

"I assumed—" Nicolai took her mouth to his before she could finish her sentence.

He then pulled away and looked down at her. "The roads will be washed out, so you will stay with us for the night."

"With the two of you?"

Kieran smiled and held out his elbow. "Come, Syl."

Sylvana wrapped her arms in theirs and feeling nervous and anxious regarding her sleeping arrangements. *I hope to hell I have my own bed-chamber.*

The sound of Nicolai's voice broke the awkward tension she was feeling. "In case you were wondering, you will share our bed."

"Are you reading my mind again?"

"No, you blocked us in the library, remember?" Nicolai answered.

"Yes, I remember," she replied nervously.

"We can feel your trepidation, is all," Kieran said.

"Will we be sleeping or?"

"Are your nerves getting the better of you?" Nicolai asked.

Sylvana looked up at him. "Yes, I don't make impulsive decisions."

"Then allow me to put your mind at ease. The decision was ours, so technically you are not making an *impulsive decision*." He winked.

"And if I say no?" she asked, as they rounded the corner and headed up an expansive staircase.

"Do you want to say no?" Kieran asked.

"Putting me on the spot is not helping."

Nicolai looked at Kieran. "I didn't hear her say no."

"Neither did I," Kieran replied.

They walked down a long hallway and Nicolai let go of her arm and opened the door for her. She walked into the most opulent bed chamber she had ever seen. The room was dimly lit by a few sconces attached to the walls and they had decorated it from top to bottom with exotic artwork, hand sewn tapestries and various statues. The lavish furniture was overelaborate with decorative gilding while the enormous, hand carved, four post bed was wrapped in a canopy of garnet-colored velvet drapes.

Kieran escorted her into the chamber while Nicolai shut the door behind them.

Nicolai watched the way in which Sylvana scanned the room. "In case you were wondering, this is my bedchamber."

"I don't have the words. Stunning is all that comes to mind."

"You are what is stunning," Kieran offered.

Not wanting to make eye contact, Sylvana looked down at the exquisite rug on which she stood.

"Make yourself comfortable," Nicolai said.

They removed their robes and tossed them onto a chair while Sylvana leaned against a bed post with her arms wrapped around her chest. *Is this really happening?*

They way in which they seductively walked toward her along with their heated gaze was both erotic and foreboding.

"Do not be nervous, Sylvana. We are going to give you a night of pleasure you won't soon forget." The words rolled off Nicolai's tongue like satin, and she could not control her body's reaction. She discreetly squeezed her thighs when her libido screamed from deep within her core.

Nicolai untied the belt, holding her robe closed, and pushed the material open. He then slid his hands around her waist and pulled her close while Kieran moved behind her and slid his hand across her chest and cupped her breast.

As Kieran pressed his body against hers, she wrapped her hands around Nicolai's shoulders.

Nicolai then slid his face up the side of hers whispered. "You're trembling. Have you ever been with another?"

With a barely audible voice, she replied. "I have only been with one other, and it was long ago."

"Relax, and let us take care of you," Kieran whispered as he gently slid the robe off of her shoulders and down her arms. He then brushed the sides of her breasts, which caused slight bumps to rise on her skin as he traced his fingers over her naked body.

Nicolai slid his hand down her stomach, between her legs, and strummed her sex with his fingers; his touch was delicate yet determined as he parted her soft folds.

She ran her hands over his solid chest and muscular shoulders, admiring the intricate tattoos covering most of his upper body.

"The things I want to do to you," Kieran purred from behind.

The sensations of Nicolai's mouth on hers while Kieran massaged her breasts and drug his tongue across her neck, swept her into a heated current, and the desire pooled within her core.

"You're so wet," Nicolai whispered into her mouth as he plunged his fingers into her body.

She let out a gentle moan and slid her hands over his taunt ass while his sizeable erection rested firmly against her stomach and Kieran's was pressed against her lower back.

In this moment, all she wanted was to feel the heat of the orgasm desperate to release.

Nicolai picked her up, and she wrapped her legs around his waist, and felt his member rub against her sex as he walked her to the bed and laid her down. They positioned themselves on either side of her and took turns claiming her tongue, all the while titillating her sex, massaging her breasts, and playing her body like an instrument they were all too familiar with.

"We have been craving you all night," Nicolai growled as he and Kieran 'turned' and the whites of their canines gleamed in the dark. Sylvana felt the pull, and she 'turned' in response.

"I want to taste what drips from between your legs." Kieran whispered. He kissed and licked his way down her body before pushing her thighs apart and sliding his hands under her ass. The anticipation of their words sent a fresh rush of wetness between her legs. He dropped his face between her legs and pulled her nub into the warmth of his mouth and sucked.

"Oh my god." She moaned.

"That's our girl," Nicolai said. He then straddled her and leaned over her face. "Take it, Syl."

She wrapped her hand around his shaft, twisted her fist in circular motions, and licked the tiny droplets spilling from his tip. She then slid as much of his erection as she could manage into her mouth.

"Bloody hell," he muttered.

The harder Kieran sucked her sex and plunged his fingers into her core, the harder she sucked Nicolai's shaft. The feeling hit hard and fast and her sex throbbed with such intensity, she slid Nicolai's shaft from her mouth and pressed her head into the pillow. "Ohh, fuck," she exclaimed.

"We are just getting started," Nicolai said as he and Kieran traded places.

Nicolai slid his fingers into her wet core and rubbed her swollen, sensitive nub with his thumb. She let out a gasp and grabbed the back of Kieran's head and pulled his mouth to hers.

He pulled away, straddled her, and she slid her tongue along the length of his shaft and twirled it around the tip.

The warmth of her hand, the soft flesh rubbing his, brought about a desperate need to come into her mouth. He planted one hand on the headboard and fisted her hair with the other.

Nicolai was relentless between her legs; his fingers sliding in and out and his thumb moving in rough circles over her sex was calling another orgasm to the surface. As soon as the wave of pleasure rose, he slipped them out.

"Not yet. I want you to come around my cock."

Kieran pulled his shaft from her mouth, wrapped his arms around her body, rolled onto his back and pushed her shoulders down. She slid down his body and slid his vein into her mouth while Nicolai lifted her hips to meet his. He rubbed her soft opening with his tip and slowly inserted himself into the slickness of her core.

She pulled Kieran from her mouth and rested her forehead on his stomach. "Wait, your—go slow," she mumbled.

"Fuck, you are so goddamn tight," Nicolai groaned. "Relax your body and take it in. Pain is also pleasure." He then forcefully thrust himself into her core.

Sylvana gasped and bunched up the blanket in her hands. "Shit, that hurts."

Kieran lifted her head and nodded for her to take him. He wrapped a fistful of her hair around his hand and matched the rhythm of her head with his hips. He took a deep breath when the tips of her canines scraped his tender flesh, causing him to flinch. "Shit, be careful, darling," he mumbled.

Nicolai increased the rhythm of his hips and one hard shove, followed by another, and then another, brought about an orgasmic release she had never experienced, forcing her to cry out with high-pitched sounds of pleasure.

"I going to come so hard you will taste my guz in your throat," Nicolai said along with a chesty growl.

"Geza vit," Kieran exclaimed as he released himself into her mouth.

Nicolai and Kieran plopped onto their backs next to Sylvana. Nicolai then pulled her body tightly against his and pulled her leg over his crotch. She rested her head on his shoulder while Kieran placed his hand on her ass.

Nicolai lifted her chin and softly kissed her lips. "We will give you a few minutes to catch your breath."

"A few minutes?" she asked, a bit stunned, not knowing they has such an insatiable appetite for sex.

"You've got five," Kieran joked.

After a short time, Kieran rolled onto his side and pinned one of her legs between his, glided his hand over her inner thigh, and slid his thumb alongside her sex.

Sylvana let out a low moan while Nicolai rose on his elbow, took her mouth to his, and rolled her hard bud between his fingers.

Kieran slid his fingers into her soft opening. "Is this what you want, darling?"

"Yes." She gasped.

He crawled down her body, dropped his head between her legs, pushed her thighs apart, and teased her sex with his mouth and flickering tongue.

She looked at Nicolai, who bent over and plunged his tongue back into her mouth. He then

straddled her, and she slid her tongue along his vein and nipped his tip.

Nicolai flinched in response, placed one hand on the headboard, and grabbed her head with the other. "Goddamn, that turns me on."

Kieran sucked her sex harder, plunged his fingers deeper, and felt her body clench around them.

Oh my god, she said to herself.

"Flip her," Kieran growled.

Nicolai pulled his cock from her mouth, rolled over, pulled her on top of his body, and pushed her down.

Kieran raised her hips and forcefully shoved himself inside her. "Damn, Kieran, be careful."

"Nothing compares to the way your body squeezes my cock." He gently patted her ass. "Relax, it won't hurt as bad," he whispered.

The sharp pains from Kieran's shaft stretching her body soon succumbed to the pleasure.

"Take it deeper," Nicolai rumbled.

Unable to speak with his cock in her mouth she replied telepathically. *"You're going to choke me."*

"So you can speak telepathically?"

"Yes," she replied.

"Good to know." Kieran smirked.

She soon felt Nicolai's cock pulsing; he let out a throaty moan and released himself. After a few breathless minutes, he pulled his shaft from her mouth and fell onto his back next to her.

Kieran crawled up her body, and she wrapped her legs around his waist, her arms around his back, and with a forceful thrust followed by another, and then another, he brought them both the pleasure of another release.

She ran her hands over his ass, up the curve in his lower back and gently glided her fingers over the scar, and his body flinched in response. "Be careful, darling."

"I'm so sorry. Does it still hurt?" she asked.

"Don't apologize, you didn't know. The pain is always there, but it's tolerable. I was struck with a Faye's dagger long ago. Their magic is powerful, and it has never healed properly," he replied.

"Is that the reason you wear loose tunics—or none at all?"

"Yes." He rested his heavy body on hers and stared into her eyes.

"We have yet to find a cure," Nicolai added.

"That's awful. I'm sorry," Sylvana whispered.

"It's fine and we have more important things on our mind," Kieran said.

"Like what?" she asked.

Kieran placed a soft kiss on her lips. "You are ours, say it."

She cocked her head, not sure she had heard him correctly. "I am what?"

"We own you," Nicolai replied.

"I—what do you mean?"

"If we ever find out you have been with another, we will take his head," Nicolai threatened.

Kieran rolled off and lay next to her. "Say it. You belong to us."

She felt the heavy, dragging thuds of her heart against her breast with their sudden and unexpected demands. *What the hell have I done?*

"Speak, Sylvana. This is not a choice we are offering. We need to know you understand what this means."

"I mean, yes. I won't bed another. I have never had loose legs, if that's what you are insinuating?"

"We are not *insinuating* anything. We are making sure you understand who you belong to," Nicolai replied.

Kieran moved his body against her backside, and she tucked his arm under her breasts and laid her head on Nicolai's shoulder.

"There is one more thing," Nicolai stated as he pulled her thigh over his crotch.

Sylvana let out a heavy sigh. "I'm not sure I want to know."

"You will only feed on our blood," Nicolai replied.

"We have feeders and who decided I don't get to choose who I do and do not feed from?"

Kieran gently turned her head toward his face. "We decided."

Sylvana pushed Kieran's arm off and sat up on her knees while they rolled onto their backs. "It's not your decision. I can and I will drink from my feeder whenever I choose to do so."

"This is not up for discussion," Nicolai answered.

"The hell if it isn't."

Nicolai tucked his arm under his head and chuckled. "Sylvana, your feeder can easily disappear."

"This was a mistake." She scooted back and tried to crawl from the bed. However, Kieran wrapped his arms around her waist and plopped her onto her back. He then lay his powerful body on hers and pulled her bottom lip down with his thumb. "Where do you think you are going?"

"Home."

Nicolai laughed aloud and rolled onto his side and sat up on his elbow. "No, no, you aren't."

She planted her palms on Kieran's chest and tried to push him back. "Kieran, get off of me."

"How about I *get off* in you?" Kieran joked.

"This isn't funny."

Nicolai stroked her thigh with his hand. "We are not looking to fight with you, Sylvana. If you were nothing more than our 'bedmate' as you said to me, then we wouldn't give a fuck who you fed from or whom else you bedded."

She glared at Nicolai. "You act as if I am a potential mate."

"Who says you aren't?" Kieran interjected.

"I don't know what games the two of you are playing, but I'm not falling for it."

"This is not a game," Nicolai stated.

"Then what it is?"

Nicolai and Kieran glanced at each other and then looked at Sylvana. "Is it such a terrible thing for us to treat you like royalty?"

"Well, no but—"

Kieran's mouth fell to hers, and after a heated kiss, he pulled away. "How would it have made you feel if we would have had kicked you out of our bed after having our way with you?"

"Like shit, I suppose?"Nicolai turned her face towards his. "Then allow us to treat you as someone who matters to us."

Chapter 8

Calista woke up before the sun had risen and was pacing back and forth in the parlor when she heard the sounds of hooves. She rushed over and looked out the window, hoping to see Sylvana. Between the dark of night and the heavy rains, she could not tell who it was until a flash of lightning lit the area and she realized it was Alaric, heading toward the barn. "Shit!" she said aloud. *Sylvana, where the hell are you?*

She ran up the stairs, closed Sylvana's door and then ran into her room, shutting the door behind her and it was not long before she heard the sounds of Alaric's boots heading up the stairs. She stood against the door listening, hoping he would go to bed. Once she heard his door shut, she breathed a sigh of relief and crawled back into bed. Just as she as was about to fall asleep, she again heard hooves coming down the road. She leapt from her bed, ran down the stairs, and opened the door. Someone wearing a brown, wool cloak was heading in her direction. She grabbed her shawl, covered her head, and ran toward the visitor through the torrential downpour.

Whomever it was, pulled his horse to a halt and removed the hood from his head. "Milady, are you Calista?" the young man asked.

"I am. Who are you?"

"The Acherons sent me to inform you that Sylvana won't be home tonight."

"Is everything okay?"

"Yes, milady."

"Thank you."

The young boy nodded, pulled the reins and headed back down the road.

I better figure out something to tell Alaric, she thought, as she ran back to the manor.

Kadric stood at the edge of the river, feeling uneasy and impatient; he paced back and forth for what felt like an hour before he noticed a silhouette appear from the trees; the figure then leapt across the river and landed on the bank next to him.

"Ranan." He nodded.

Ranan nodded back. "Kadric, sorry to keep you waiting, but I had to be sure no one followed you."

"Is that what the inbred was doing on this side of the river?"

"Yes, we have been sending scouts across for some time now. The uprising of the Faye is no small matter."

"Your treaty with their kind will not serve you well in the end," Kadric warned.

Ranan motioned for Kadric to follow him into the density of the trees. "Let me worry about that. You have bigger issues to contend with."

"What have you discovered?" Kadric asked.

"The Faye have your mate," Ranan blurted out.

Kadric felt the blood drain from his face. "Is she—is she alive?"

"They believe she is a purebred Ascelin and if the truth lies within her veins, I would assume they would keep her alive."

Kadric paced back and forth for a few minutes, feeling terrified for his offspring.

"Is it true?" Ranan asked.

"No," Kadric replied immediately, knowing better than to reveal the truth.

"Then her life would not have been spared."

"What do they want with an Ascelin?" Kadric asked.

Ranan leaned against a tree, concealing himself within its shadow. "They are a means to an end. There is a darkness between the veil and this world and it is slowly consuming the Faye's kingdom."

"Speak fully. I don't have time to decipher what you aren't saying."

"They desire to return to this realm, and should they breed with an Ascelin, they could, in theory, create a race powerful enough to take on the Acherons and all those who are loyal. They could also use their powers against the darkness."

Fuck, Kadric thought, realizing the danger his family was in. "They are going to cause a war which will have unspeakable consequences for the entire country."

"The Acherons have been our enemies for centuries and I desire nothing more than to see them fall upon their knees."

Kadric stepped chest to chest with Ranan, and a low rumble rose from his chest. "You are a part of this?"

Ranan stepped back. "Yes, and now you have a choice to make. The Acherons or your life, which shall you choose?"

Kadric swiftly removed his sword from its sheath and pressed the tip into Ranan's chest. "I will never betray the Acherons."

Ranan fluently moved to the side and pulled his sword. "And I will never betray the Faye."

Kadric bared his canines and stood defensively. "This is where we part and only one of us will walk away."

"Before you decide your fate, you should know I have made a deal with the Mercurial Guardians. Stand with me and I will make sure you have a place in their Kingdom."

"Never," Kadric snarled. He then lunged for Ranan, who evaded the blow and leapt across the river. As Kadric gave chase, he heard the crunching of brush coming from all directions. He stopped mid-stride and cautiously walked in a slow, choreographed circle. The fear and uncertainty gripped him when the shapes drew closer and inbred Lycans appeared from within the shadows and attacked. He leapt into the air above the onslaught of Lycans and a large wind blew past his body, and he landed on the ground with a mind numbing thud. They placed a piece of material over his head and restrained his arms and legs with ethereal binds.

Ranan walked over, kneeled down, and fisted both the sack and a handful of his hair, and wrenched his head back. "I have always considered you an ally, so I will give you a chance to come to your senses."

"I will never betray the Acherons," Kadric snarled.

"Take him," Ranan ordered.

As Kadric was being carried off, Ranan leapt across the river, walked to where Kadric's stallion stood, and raised his blade. It came down with a thud as it cut the leather reins that were tied to a branch; he then slapped his hindquarters. "He will find his way home and it won't be long before the Legion comes looking for him," he said to Dronve, the Faye's High Lord.

"We will be ready," Dronve replied.

Sylvana awoke, looked out the window, and gazed at the dark, turbulent clouds swirling against an ominous, mordent sky.

Nicolai placed his arm behind his head and looked at her. "How are you feeling?"

"Confused," she admitted.

"About what?" Kieran asked.

"Everything that happened last night and everything the two of you said."

"I thought we came to an understanding?" Nicolai asked.

"I know I 'came' to an understanding, multiple times." Kieran offered with a coy smile and a wink.

Sylvana couldn't help but to chuckle with them. "I suppose you did."

"How about we *come*, to another understanding?" Nicolai suggested.

"Unlike the two of you, I don't have anyone to attend to our animals or the fields. I need to go home."

"You can't head home in this storm," Kieran insisted.

Nicolai slid his hand between her legs and over her sex. "We will see you home—at some point. But right now, we have other ideas."

Sylvana grabbed his wrist and squeezed her legs together. "My sister is probably worried sick right now."

"We already took care of it. Now what say we get to it?" Kieran said as he placed his head on the side of hers and slid his tongue across her neck.

"What do you mean?"

"We sent word to your sister last night."

"I appreciate it, but I have to go." Even though she spoke the words, the moment Nicolai slid his fingers into her core, she knew she was not leaving anytime soon.

After the rain had stopped, Cadell saddled the horses in order to see Mira home. He then lifted her up and sat her on a mare. "Thank you," she replied.

Laurent stepped back. "I'll see you soon, Mira."

"Good bye, Laurent. Can I see you tomorrow?"

"Yes." He smiled.

Cadell pulled the reins, and they headed down the road. "Did you enjoy yourself last night?"

She gave Cadell a radiant smile. "Yes, milord."

"Mira, you won't be seeing Laurent for awhile."

"Why?"

"Laurent will be with me. I have clan business to attend to. He is old enough now to come along."

"How long will he be gone?"

"A few weeks."

"Why didn't he tell me?"

"I haven't told him yet."

Mira hung her head and scowled. *I won't see him for weeks, maybe more? What am I going to do? I'll be home alone with my stupid sisters, who will expect me to work all day.* "Milord?"

"Yes, Mira?"

"Would it be okay if I came over to visit Enatta?"

"No, child. She also has business to attend to. I'm sure you can find something to do to pass the time."

"My sisters will force me to work all day."

"Mira, it is not disparaging to work. One day you will be the lady of a manor and you will need to know how to run it."

"I suppose."

"Will you do me a favor?" Cadell asked.

"What is it?"

"Can you see fit to help your sisters while Laurent is gone? I'm sure they could use your help and you seem quite capable."

Mira turned her head to the side and looked up as if something had caught her attention. She then rolled her eyes as far back as they would go before looking back at Cadell. "Yes, milord."

They rode the rest of the way in silence; Cadell was furious with Enatta, and Mira was loathing the thought of being alone with her sisters.

Nicolai, Kieran, and Sylvana crawled out of bed and while Nicolai and Kieran dressed, Sylvana sat on the edge with the cotton blanket wrapped around her body. "I don't see my dress?"

Nicolai walked over and laid a pair of impeccably fashioned black leather trousers and a crisp, white, pleated tunic on the end of the bed while Kieran set a pair of new, black leather boots on the floor next to her feet.

"What's this?" she asked curiously.

"We assumed you would be more comfortable heading home in this rather than a fancy garment."

Sylvana collected the trousers and ran her hand over the silk material. "I can't accept this."

Nicolai looked at her and cocked his head to the side. "Why not?"

"The material in this one outfit is worth more than half my wardrobe." She chuckled.

"What did we tell you last night? Did you think they were hollow words?" Kieran asked.

"Well, no. But what am I to tell my brother if he sees me in this?"

"Tell him we gifted it to you. What else?" Nicolai suggested.

"*Oh boy,*" Sylvana mumbled as she stood and slid her arms into the shirt.

"We would like to see you again tonight," Kieran said as he walked over stood next to her.

"I'm not sure I can. There is a lot for me to do around the manor and the day is half over, if you hadn't noticed."

"We are going to fix that. We don't want you doing a Helots job anymore," Nicolai said.

Sylvana rolled her eyes but said nothing in response.

Nicolai held out his elbow once Sylvana was finished dressing. "Klyn will escort you home, but you will have to ride. The wagon won't be able to cross the road for a day or so."

"I'd rather ride, anyway." She smiled.

They escorted her to the front parlor, where Klyn was already waiting. He nodded to Nicolai and Kieran and then acknowledged Sylvana. "Good afternoon, Sylvana."

"Good afternoon, Klyn."

"Are you ready, milady?"

"I am."

The two guards opened the front doors and Sylvana noticed the magnificent-looking stallion standing tall and strong next to one of Klyn's. She studied the exotic animal whose body, main and tail, were sable-black; its thick, wavy main spilled over its shoulders and rested softly over the side of his face, while its tail cascaded down his hind legs. The leather saddle and reins, having been lined with silver studs, were as black as the stallion. He subtly turned his head and blinked once, slowly, and she was taken-a-back when she stared into its ice-blue eyes. "He is absolutely stunning."

Nicolai strode down the marble steps and patted the stallion's neck. "This is Skadi, he's mine."

"He's yours?"

"Yes."

"You want me to ride him home?"

"Is that a problem?"

"Well, no. I mean, it's not customary for anyone else to ride a lord's personal stallion. I thought—"

"You think too much," Kieran replied before stealing a little tongue. He then lifted her up and placed her in the saddle while Nicolai handed her the reins.

Nicolai kissed the back of her hand. "I expect to see your ass on my stallion when you come tonight."

Sylvana held her hand up. "Hold up. I will not be responsible for your stallion."

Nicolai slid his hand under Skadi's wavy mane. "Klyn, make sure they get back to her manor safely."

"Milord." He nodded.

The guards opened the gilded gates and as they closed behind them, Sylvana felt like she was waking up from a mythical dream. Out of her peripheral vision, she noticed silhouettes moving into the shadows, stopping only when she and Klyn passed by, and their conversations became muted. She looked down at Skadi, not wanting to make eye contact with the judgmental crowd.

"They're curious, is all," Klyn offered kindly.

She looked at him and smiled meekly. "I feel like they are scoffing at me for no other reason than to spread rumors that will defile my reputation."

Klyn laughed aloud. "No one would dare to defile your reputation, Sylvana. You are sitting upon Nicolai's stallion. They would not willingly choose that fate."

"Once my brother hears about this, he will lock me up for good." She chuckled.

"I am quite certain Nicolai and Kieran have the means to free you." Klyn winked.

Sylvana let out a sigh of relief once they crossed the fields and entered the comfort of the forest.

"Feel better?" Klyn asked.

"Yes."

"Did you enjoy yourself last night?"

She felt as if the warmth of her cheeks were telling him more than she wanted. "Yes," she replied quietly.

"Do not be abashed."

"I wasn't expecting anything that took place last night is all.""Now that they have you pinned in their sights, you need to realize your choices, or lack thereof, are no longer yours to make."

Sylvana's head snapped in his direction. "What do you mean?"

"You will figure it out."

They rode the rest of the way in silence as she contemplated what he was and was not saying. Once they made it to the edge of the forest, she pulled the reins, bringing Skadi to a halt, and tossed one leg over his hindquarters.

Klyn furrowed his brows and looked down at her. "What are you doing?"

"Making a choice," she replied as she handed him the reins. "I chose to walk the rest of the way, and I chose to send Skadi back with you."

Klyn leaned on his saddle horn and cocked his head. "Was Nicolai not clear?"

She tossed the reins over Skadi's neck and stepped back. "Thank you for seeing me home. I appreciate it."

"Sylvana, this is not a choice worth making," he stated adamantly. However, she turned her back to him and walked away.

I guess she is looking to find out the hard way what her 'choices' will get her, he thought as he watched her walk across the field.

Riordan walked into Nicolai's bed chamber, waved his hand, and the large curtains covering the widows flapped open.

"What the hell are you doing?" Nicolai asked.

"The two of you have been sleeping all fucking day," Riordan replied.

"Shut the fucking curtains," Kieran snarled.

Riordan ripped the blanket off the bed. "Get the fuck up."

Nicolai placed his arm behind his head. "Don't you have business with the Guild to attend to?"

Riordan took a seat and swept his hand over the table next to his chair and looked at his palm. "Yes, and the two of you will be in attendance."

Nicolai looked at Kieran and rolled his eyes. "It's clean, Riordan."

"How did last night turn out?" Riordan asked.

"She's as innocent as a cub sucking a teat," Nicolai replied.

Riordan adjusted himself and drummed his fingers on the table. "I'm surprised she allowed the two of you to bed her."

"She was as nervous as a thief standing on the gallows." Nicolai chuckled.

"She has lived a sheltered life and I'm certain she has little experience with the world outside of her manor," Kieran added.

"I don't care what you do with your cocks but keep your canines at bay. If she is an Ascelin, we need to bond with her before taking her blood."

Kieran sat up and leaned against the headboard. "We are well aware."

"Milord," Klyn stated from where he stood in the doorway.

"Did you get Sylvana back in one piece?" Riordan asked.

"Yes, milord," he replied as he took a seat.

Nicolai sat up on his elbow and placed his head in his hand. "Is there something else?"

"Yes, she made a choice."

"What the fuck are you talking about?" Nicolai questioned.

"She sent Skadi back with me."

The brothers glanced at each other before looking at Klyn again.

"She did what?" Kieran asked.

"She asked me to stop at the edge of the forest and said she was 'choosing' to walk the reset of the way, and 'choosing' to send Skadi back with me."

Riordan furrowed his brows. "And you 'chose' to go along with it?"

"Milord, there was no stopping her without a fight, but I did not leave until she had entered her manor."

Riordan then looked at Nicolai and Kieran, who were chuckling.

"I said she was innocent. I did not say she was compliant," Nicolai replied.

"It seems as if we are going to have to limit her *choices* from here on out," Riordan stated.

Sylvana snuck through the back door and up the stairs to her chamber. She shut the door and immediately changed into her clothes. She neatly folded the shirt and pants and placed them beneath her clothes in the drawer, and hid the boots in the armoire's corner.

A knock on the door startled her, and she hastily shut the armoire. "Sylvana?" Calista said.

"Come in," she replied with a sigh of relief.

Calista walked in and crossed her arms. "Where the hell have you been?"

"I'm sorry, I would have sent word, but the rain washed the roads out."

"Oh, well, Nicolai sent word on your behalf," Calista snarked.

"So that's what he meant," Sylvana muttered.

"What?" Calista asked.

Sylvana waved her hand dismissively. "Nothing. How did you find out?"

"He sent a young stable boy to let me know you would not be returning. I was worried sick."

"I'm so sorry. I didn't know."

"You are lucky Alaric didn't find out."

"Where is he now?"

"Sleeping."

"Is Mira home yet?" Sylvana asked.

"Yes, and do not change the subject," Calista stated.

"I'm tired and I don't want to discuss this." Sylvana walked past her and headed down the stairs.

Chapter 9

Sylvana wandered through the fields deep in thought, not having the motivation to work nor the desire to take another load to the castle anytime soon. She felt ashamed for having slept with them and afraid she had given them the wrong impression. *As if my reputation hasn't been soiled enough.* She picked a tomato off of a vine and tossed it as far as she could. *I should let it all rot.* She heard the distant drumming of hooves and her pulse quickened, knowing it was Nicolai or Kieran or worse, both. The sounds grew in intensity and Skadi burst through the tree line and leapt over a fallen tree.

Oh fuck me, she thought. Nicolai pulled on the reins, Skadi lowered his butt, and planted his back hooves into the dirt a mere foot from where she stood. She yelped, jumped back, and held up her hands.

"Are you out of your damn mind? You almost ran me over!"

Nicolai failed to reply. He simply stared at her while Skadi pranced in a circle around her.

"What are you doing here?" she demanded.

"Klyn informed us you made a choice?"

"I did," she replied sternly.

"Good to know," he replied calmly. He then locked his eyes on hers.

After an uncomfortable moment of silence, she broke eye contact, feeling as though a hot ember was burning a hole in her mind. "I don't have time for this."

"I'm curious? What put you in such a sour mood?"

"What do you want from me?" she snapped.

"Were we in some way unclear?"

"I will not allow myself to taste a world beyond my means, only to have it taken away when you and Kiran decide to discard me. It's better to not know what you are missing than to miss what you never knew existed."

"That is an eloquent way to defy us."

Sylvana rolled her eyes. "I am not defying you. I am making a choice that is best for me."

"And I am making *a choice* as well."

"And what would that be?"

"You will soon find out."

"Don't be evasive, Nicolai." She walked away, snatched the basket off the ground, and began throwing tomatoes into it.

Nicolai rode beside her on Skadi without responding.

After walking halfway down a long row of plants, Sylvana turned around to face him. "You know what would be great right now?"

"What?"

"If you would stop bothering me, or get your ass down and help?"

Nicolai looked as if she had asked him to scrub a floor. "It's a Helots job."

"I see. So I'm a Helot, and hard work isn't your thing? Got it."

He leaned forward on the saddle horn. "My dear, hard work takes place on the battlefield, not picking shit for mortals and Helots to feed on."

"First off, I don't want their kind on our land and in case you hadn't noticed, we don't live in a castle with endless means. I did not know making money was so beneath you."

He cocked his head and for a moment she thought she saw a hint of a smile as he dismounted Skadi and stood in front of her. "How about I put you *beneath me' in the bed*," he said with a seductively low voice.

"I am not in the mood."

"Well, I am." He wrapped his arm around her waist, pulled her in, and his mouth fell to hers.

She pushed back against his chest and turned her face. "Stop," she whispered.

He turned her face to his again and forced her mouth open.

After another heated kiss, she pulled away. "Nicolai, stop. I won't be another one of yours and Kieran's whores."

"We have not treated you like a whore."

"I have yet to find out, and the rumors about you and your brothers travel far and wide."

"Rumors?"

"Don't play stupid, Nicolai; it doesn't suit you."

"What *suits me* is you."

Once again, he stole a kiss, and she fell prey to his advances. She pulled away and placed her hands on his chest. "Stop, someone will see us."

"And?"

Sylvana furrowed her brows. "It matters to me, Nicolai."

"I don't care who sees, and we are expecting you tonight."

"Don't wait up." She backed up and watched as he mounted Skadi and took off in the opposite direction. *I'm such an idiot! Our family has kept their distance for as long as I can remember, and here I am, spreading my legs for them.*

Sylvana sat on the padded bench in her bedroom, watching the crescent moon rise above the forest's canopy. Even though it was miles away, she could see the faint glow of the castle's windows being illuminated by firelight. It took everything she had not to run to Nicolai and Kieran and she hated herself for desiring them the way she did. She also thought about how kindly they had treated her and felt a pang of regret for having spoken to Nicolai so rudely. *I couldn't be more confused. The Acherons, for all their power and cunning, are driven by the same motivations as their ancestors. Their only desire is to secure their lineage by any means necessary.*

She felt jealous of Venthana, Stefania, and Aurelia, who would surely be in attendance for the nightly games. Her stomach churned at the mere thought of another touching Nicolai and Kieran, knowing the ladies would swoon all over them again. She had never contemplated being a member of the court, yet here she was longing to be a part of a world they had given her a taste of. A tear dripped down her cheek at the mere thought of another being in bed with them.

A soft knock on the door and Calista's voice pulled her from her misery. "Sylvana, you awake?"

She swept the tear from her cheek. "Yes, come in."

Calista quietly shut the door behind her. "I thought you might have a drink with me? I can't sleep."

Sylvana readjusted herself, placed one foot on the floor, and pulled a knee to her chest. "I sure could use one."

Calista handed her a cup and sat next to her. "You can't sleep either?"

"No. Are you thinking about Father?" Sylvana asked.

"Sort of. He's been gone a week now and hasn't sent word."

"It's not the first time he's left on clan business like this. He'll be back," Sylvana offered.

"I know." Calista took a drink and stared out the window in the castle's direction. After a few minutes of silence, she side eyed Sylvana but failed to find the words.

"What?" Sylvana asked. "I can tell you have something else you want to talk about, so out with it."

"When you didn't come home last night, I was really worried," Calista admitted.

"I'm sorry. I didn't have a choice. The storm washed the road out."

"I think there is more to this story."

Sylvana wrapped her hands tightly around the cup and looked at the amber hued liquid.

Calista immediately knew something else had happened. "Whatever it is, you can tell me."

"It's complicated is all."

"'Complicated'? How so?"

"I will tell you everything, but you have to promise me you won't say a word to anyone."

"We have always confided in each other. Tell me, Sylvie."

"Please reveal nothing to Alaric. He will go after Nicolai and Kieran, and if he does, you know what they are capable of."

"You're scaring me," Calista replied.

"It's not you who needs to be afraid," Sylvana said.

"What the hell happened? Did they hurt you?"

"No, not at all. It's just—I slept with them," she whispered.

"You what?"

Sylvana looked out the window, trying to come up with an explanation for her actions. "It just happened. It was an amazing night; we were drinking, playing games and the next thing I knew I was in Nicolai's bedchamber with him and Kieran."

"That is the lamest explanation I have ever heard."

"It is what it is, Calista. I can't take it back now, can I?"

"I can't believe this. Did you really sleep with them? Together?"

"Yes."

"Holy shit. Sylvana, how could you?"

"It was a mistake. Don't make me regret it any more than I already do."

They sat quietly, staring out the window in silent contemplation, awaiting the other to speak.

"I won't tell Alaric or anyone else," Calista said.

Sylvana wrapped her arms around her, and Calista hugged her back and then cupped her face in her hands and stared into her watery eyes. "Do you have feelings for them?"

"Yes," Sylvana whispered.

"How long has this little dalliance been going to on?"

"Remember the night I came home late?"

"I do."

"I was late because Muriel and Lenora asked me to stay and have a drink with them. We ended up at the Viscant Tavern, and Kieran showed up. You know Lenora is mating Tobias, and he showed up with Nicolai shortly thereafter and was not very pleased. He ended up carrying her out."

"Carried?" Calista asked.

Sylvana chuckled. "Yes, as in over his shoulder.

Calista smiled. "If the circumstances were different, I would love to have witnessed it."

"Muriel and I tried to leave, but Nicolai stopped us and asked Muriel to leave without me. He then wanted to know what I was doing in such a place. I stood there looking like a simpleton. I couldn't muster the words. He then escorted me out and walked with me to the stable where Rana was."

"Damn, so he escorted you all the way home?"

"Yes."

"I didn't know you were friends with Lenora?"

"I have to keep most of my life hidden. You know how overbearing Father and Alaric are," Sylvana said.

Calista tipped her cup and winked. "I sure do."

"This following morning I was tending to the horses and Nicolai showed up in the barn."

"Why didn't you tell me? We have never hidden things from each other."

"I didn't know how?"

"I knew something was up when I scared you so. What are you going to do now?"

"I'm not sure?" Sylvana admitted.

"Sylvie, you have to stop this, and now. Neither of them will ever be allowed to take you as a mate, and if they find out who we are—"

Sylvana held up her hand. "I understand, but I like them more than I care to admit. It's not so simple."

"Your heart is going to get broken one way or another. It is better to end it now than to let it drag on."

"I know," Sylvana sighed.

Calista raised an eyebrow. "Just curious. How good are they?"

Sylvana choked on her drink. "Calista!" she whispered.

"Tell me. The only side of the Acherons I know is nothing short of brutal."

"They were amazing. I have to give it them."

"It appears you already *gave it to them*," *Calista joked.*

Sylvana laughed aloud. "It's not funny!"

"It's really not. I see this ending in misery where you are concerned. What are you going to do when they find a mate?"

"I do not know. I don't let myself ponder the thought and you could be a little supportive."

"I'm being realistic. But I have to know, what is their brother Riordan like?"

"He's unreadable. There is something behind the chill in his eyes and his face is vacant of emotion. However, there is more."

"What do you mean?" *Unless,* Calista thought. "Do you think he suspects who you are?"

"I think he has his suspicions."

"Sylvana, this is bad. What gives you that idea?"

"He was there for part of the evening as well. He was very polite, but there was a lot residing beneath his friendly demeanor." Sylvana explained all that occurred in the library, the games, and the bathhouse.

"Father is going to lose his shit," Calista stated.

"He won't find out."

"Do not underestimate him. He is a member of the Legion in case you've forgotten."

"I haven't forgotten."

"You are playing with fire, Sylvie."

"Yes, I am well aware. Nicolai came by today and they want me to go to them tonight."

"Are you?"

"Obviously not or I wouldn't be sitting here."

"How does this work? The turning part?" Muriel asked as she and Lupine walked arm in arm.

"There are only two ways to be turned. You either have to be born into it or you have to be bitten by an original."

"You said you are an original, so there is no way this can go wrong? I won't end up as some sort of mixed breed?"

Lupine chuckled. "No. As you know, my pack came here on the old ships, and I am one of five remaining originals. The Acherons beheaded my great grandfather, Bastan."

"I had no idea."

"You don't know about the original war and all that followed?"

"I only know the basics. I'm not a member of the court, so I suppose no one thought it important."

"I will tell you all you need to know."

"I would appreciate it." She looked up and stared at the moon. "Lupine, how will I change? Other than the obvious."

"You won't have the powers of a pure born. However, it does not mean you will become a feral."

"Promise me. I won't end up like them."

"I promise, my love," he replied, along with a kiss.

They walked into the center of the pack and stood beneath the full moon, surrounded by a cascading landscape of boulders and an endless array of trees swaddled in a layer of vaporous mist.

They completed the ceremony and Cobium, Lupine, and Muriel turned and faced the pack. "It is with great honor I introduce your pack leader, Ranan Lupine, Kashgar's mate, Muriel Kashgar."

As soon as the entire pack lifted their heads and howled, Muriel looked up at Lupine, and smiled. "What now?"

"I will turn you, while our pack celebrates and waits for their newest member to join them." He took her hand in his and escorted her to his small, timber-framed house with a thatched roof.

He unbuttoned her simple, white cotton gown and slid the material off of her shoulders. After a passionate kiss, he picked her up, carried her to the bed, and laid her on her back. He then undressed and crawled over the top of her.

She felt a rush of nervous anticipation as he settled between her legs. "What do I do?" she asked timidly.

"You don't have to do anything. The wolf will come for you."

"I'm scared," she whispered.

"Do not be afraid, my love. It will only take one bite and I will be at your side."

"Will it be painful?"

"Yes. It will be, but you can handle it," he replied bluntly. "Are you ready?"

Her hands trembled, and in this moment, she questioned whether she had made the right decision. She was about to give up all she had known, and the mere thought of the transformation terrified her.

He felt her trepidation and gently stroked her cheek. "I will give you the life you deserve. Do not be afraid."

"I'm ready," she replied.

Sylvana was lying on her back, trying to fall asleep. All the while, she couldn't get Nicolai or Kieran out of her mind, not to mention she told Calista everything. She rolled over for the umpteenth time, bunched up her pillow, and closed her eyes.

She felt the covers tighten around her body and the warmth of someone's breath in her ear. Her pulse raced, and she tried to call out to Alaric. However, a large hand muffled her sounds. "Shh," was all he said.

She gathered her composure and squinted her eyes, only to find Nicolai kneeling over her and Kieran standing next to her bed. "What are the two of you doing here?"

"You were supposed to come to us tonight."

"I told you no."

Nicolai crawled over the top of her and pinned her down. "We won't be leaving, and if you protest too loudly, you will wake everyone." He winked.

She tried to break free, but he had her pinned beneath him. "Get off of me," she whispered sternly.

"I plan on *getting off*, just not in the way you're demanding," Nicolai teased.

Kieran crawled into the bed next to them and ran his hand down her cheek. "Relax, Sylvana, you know you want us," he teased.

"Nicolai, let me up."

He released his grip, sat up, pulled his shirt over his head, and tossed it aside.

Sylvana sat up and pushed his chest. "I'm not sleeping with either of you."

"So serious," Kieran stated coyly.

Nicolai reached down and slid her nightshirt up her thigh. She grabbed his hand, trying to stop him, but Kieran grabbed the hem and pulled it over her head and tossed it to the floor.

"The two of you need to stop," she demanded again, in a hushed whisper.

Nicolai slid his hand over her thigh and between her legs, and she arched her back when he slid his fingers into her core. As much as she wanted to stop them, her body was screaming for more.

"We have waited all day for another taste," Nicolai said.

They removed their trousers and Nicolai settled himself further between her legs while Kieran slipped his tongue into her mouth; she became powerless beneath their touch and couldn't wait to feel them deep inside her. The warmth of Kieran's tongue twirling with hers, and his hands caressing her breasts, sent her body spiraling.

Nicolai placed the tip of his cock against her core and rubbed it over her sex. "Are you sure you want us to stop?"

"We shouldn't be doing this here," she whispered.

"I sealed the room," Kieran admitted. He then lowered his head and pulled her supple bud into the heat of his mouth. "They're perfect," he rumbled.

"Are you hungry?" Nicolai asked.

"I am," she replied.

Nicolai turned his head to the side and the pricks of her canines sent a wave of desire crashing through his body. He reached down again, griped his shaft, and rubbed the tip against her wet core. "Shit, that went right to my dick," he rumbled.

The wave of desire rolling through her body when his blood flowed over her tongue and his tip slid between her folds almost brought about her orgasm.

Nicolai gently pulled his head back. "Enough, darling. Our blood is powerful."

Nicolai and Kieran glanced at each other, knowing they were struggling with the unrelenting desire to feed from her.

"*We need to remain in control now more than ever,*" Kieran said telepathically.

"*Fuck me. Her blood is summoning my name,*" Nicolai admitted.

"*Mine too,*" Kieran replied.

She reached for Kieran's thick shaft, gripped it in her hand, and massaged it.

Nicolai laid on his back, pulled her on top of him and placed his tip against her core. "Take it."

As she slowly lowered herself onto his shaft, Kieran kneeled behind Nicolai's head and fisted her hair. She slid his vein into her mouth while Nicolai thrust his hips, matching the rhythm of her body. "Damn, you are so wet," Nicolai murmured.

Her nub rubbing against his crotch and the sharp pains radiating between her legs ignited her orgasm.

"Take it deeper," Kieran said.

Sylvana did her best to oblige and took it as deep as she could.

"We'll come together," Nicolai said.

As soon as her orgasm peaked, she tasted the salty liquid spilling from Kieran's shaft as it glided down her throat; at the same time, she felt Nicolai's shaft pulsating as he released himself into her core.

Once they finished, Kieran pulled his shaft from her mouth and she lay on top of Nicolai's body; after a few minutes, they readjusted themselves and wrapped her body within theirs.

"Sex with you is intoxicating," Nicolai said. He then slid his tongue over the vein in her neck and she felt his canines scrape her skin.

"Please don't," she whispered.

"We won't be feeding from you tonight, darling," Nicolai said as he nipped her neck, which sent an electric jolt through her body.

Kieran draped his arm over her body. "Why didn't you come to us tonight?"

"No reason." She sighed.

"You have your reasons," Nicolai replied.

After she failed to speak, Nicolai sat up on one elbow and stared into her beautiful emerald eyes. "I assume it has to do with mating?"

"Why would you think that?"

"You keep saying you don't want to be another bedmate. The only alternative is mating," Nicolai replied.

"We can never be mated, so why do you continue bringing it up?"

Kieran stroked her hair. "We can take any mate we chose."

"The Guild says otherwise," Sylvana replied.

"We don't take orders from the Guild." Kieran chuckled.

"I don't need the two of you making false promises. Neither of you have any intention of taking me as a mate. I am not a purebred Ascelin."

"She brought it up. Now is as good a time as any to beg the question," Nicolai said to Kieran telepathically.

"There are rumors a purebred Ascelin is near," Kieran said.

Her stomach fluttered, and her mind spun into an abysmal coil of paranoia. "What?"

"We know the Lycans have been sniffing around," Nicolai admitted.

Shit. "I've never heard a more ridiculous rumor."

Kieran also sat up on his elbow and looked down at her. "Rumor, huh?"

"Yes, my father would have warned us if it were true."

"You may as well fess up. We are going to find out," Nicolai said.

"I have nothing to fess up to."

"Well, we do," Nicolai said.

"Great. What?" Sylvana asked, not sure she truly wanted to know.

"We came here to punish you for making the wrong choice today," Kieran said.

"Punish me?"

They sat up, pinned her arms above her head and spread her legs apart. Sylvana wanted to speak, but the words became lodged somewhere in her throat.

"I am going to punish your tits," Nicolai said as he nipped her bud with his canines, making her flinch.

Kieran cupped his hand over her sex and shoved a finger in. "I am going to punish your pudenda."

They released her arms, flipped her onto her stomach, and Nicolai slapped her ass. "Dammit, Nicolai!" she stated.

"There's more," he replied, along with another playful slap.

Kieran crawled over her body, grabbed his shaft and slid the tip between her butt cheeks and drug it up from her core and stopped before penetrating her ass.

"Kieran, please don't. I've never—" she began.

He cut her off and whispered in her ear. "If you ever defy us again, we will punish your virginal ass."

They flipped her back over and Nicolai took her mouth to his while Kieran suckled her erect bud.

Chapter 10

Sylvana awoke the next morning and was startled to find herself wrapped in Nicolai's and Kieran's arms.

"What are you still doing her?"

"Sleeping, what else?" Nicolai replied softly.

"Nicolai, it's not funny. The two of you have to leave before someone sees you."

Kieran placed one arm behind his head and squeezed her thigh with the other. "We don't have to do anything."

"Please. You need to leave."

"No," Nicolai replied.

No? she thought. "I'm not asking. I'm telling the two of you to go."

"We can also defy an order." Kieran smirked.

"Get out!" she demanded, again.

"We will go on one condition," Nicolai said.

"What is your *condition*?"

Nicolai parted her mouth and after a heated kiss he whispered, "Let's finish what we started last night, then we'll go."

After another passionate round, they lay quietly wrapped in each other's arms and Sylvana dozed off; the sounds of the goats bleating outside woke her. "Shit! I have to get up. If I'm not downstairs soon, Calista will come for me." She shoved Nicolai and Kieran. "Go."

"You are persistent, I'll give you that," Nicolai said as he slapped her ass before rolling out of bed.

"Owe! Why do you keep doing that?" Sylvana snapped.

"I like the way it sounds," Nicolai replied.

Kieran rolled on top of her, squishing her into the mattress, and his mouth fell to hers.

She turned her head to the side and laughed. "Kieran, get off. I can't breathe."

After getting dressed, Sylvana walked to the window and awaited them to leave. However, instead of leaving cloaked, they walked toward her bedroom door, and she ran in front of them and stood with her back against it.

"Are you out of your damn minds? You haven't even cloaked yourselves," she whispered assertively.

"There's no need. You think we see you as nothing but a bedmate, so we're letting you know you're wrong. Now you can either move and walk with us willingly or I will throw your ass over my shoulder and carry you down in front of your entire family," Nicolai threatened.

"You most certainly will not!"

"So be it." Nicolai swept her into his arms and tossed her over his shoulder.

"Put me down right now," she demanded.

"I will if you agree to walk on you own."

"I'm begging you, please don't do this."

Kieran reached for the doorknob. "Walk or be carried. You decide."

"I'll walk. Now put me down!"

He gently set her down, and as Kieran opened the door, she felt her panic rising, and each step was more terrifying than the last.

"It's about time you got up." Calista said. She turned around and dropped her cup of fresh cruor the moment she laid eyes on Nicolai and Kieran; she dared not speak or move, not having a clue why they were there.

"Good morning. I'm Nicolai Acheron," he offered.

"I'm Kieran Acheron. I assume you're Calista?"

"Good morning—yes, milords, I'm Calista," she stammered. She then looked at Sylvana. "Is everything okay?"

"It's fine, he—they stayed the night," Sylvana admitted.

"Um, do—are you staying?" Calista asked.

"Not for long," Kieran replied.

Nicolai looked down at the mess on the floor, waved his hand; it disappeared, and the cup was back on the counter. "We wanted to introduce ourselves to Sylvana's family."

Calista and Sylvana stared at each other awkwardly, not knowing what else to say before it dawned on Calista. *Alaric is outside. Fuck!*

"We would like to make his acquaintance as well," Nicolai replied.

"Umm, I think—it's not a good idea," Calista stated as she fumbled for words, realizing he had read her mind as easily as Sylvana said they could.

Sylvana wrapped her hand around Nicolai's bicep. "Please, can we do this another time?"

Nicolai placed his hand over hers and looked down at her. "No."

"Shall we?" Kieran said as he headed for the door.

Florin stood next to Alaric while he tossed the saddle on his stallion. "Are you escorting Muriel to the ceremony?"

"Yes," Alaric replied, as he tugged on the cinch. "How is Brienne?"

"Last night she was fantastic," Florin joked.

"Has her father granted you permission to take her as your mate?" Alaric tugged on the straps one last time; when Florin failed to answer he looked up, and Florin was staring in the manor's direction with a look of shock. Alaric turned, only to see Nicolai and Kieran standing with Sylvana and Calista.

"What the fuck?" Alaric stated.

Florin slowly walked between the stallions and stood next to Alaric, who was glaring at Sylvana and Calista.

"Alaric," Nicolai said with a slight nod of his head.

Alaric lowered his head and placed his fist against his chest as he addressed Nicolai and Kieran. "Milords, what are you doing here?"

"We came to pay your sister a visit."

The look Alaric shot Sylvana's way tore through her body like a knife to linen.

"What do you want with my sister?" He asked as respectfully as he could manage.

"We have been spending time with her and see no need to keep it a secret."

It felt as if someone had punched her in the gut and she could not look at her brother. Instead, she stared at the ground, wishing it would open up and swallow her.

"Seeing my sister? You mean treating her as a whore?" he seethed.

"We have never treated her like a whore." Kieran walked around the stallions and patted their hindquarters. "They are beautiful. There is nothing more stunning than a purebred," he offered.

As soon as the word 'purebred' left Kieran's mouth, Alaric glared at Sylvana, who again failed to make eye contact.

"What is it you want, milords?" Alaric asked.

"I heard a rumor Lycan's have been here. Do you know anything?" Nicolai asked.

"No, milord."

"Interesting. I would assume you would have gotten word of it from the Legion—no?"

"No, milord."

Kieran walked over and stood face to face with Alaric. "I think you might know a little something, seeing how they are looking for a pure-bred Ascelin," he stated accusingly.

Alaric's thoughts became disordered and frenzied, and he feared they would sense his panicked state of mind. *Control yourself, they won't know what you don't show them,* he thought. "I told you I know nothing about it, and I would appreciate it if you left."

"That's rude," Nicolai said.

"Rude is intruding in on someone else's manor without invitation. Now leave."

"Alaric!" Sylvana snapped.

Nicolai held his hand up in her direction and looked at Kieran. "Do we take orders from anyone?"

"Not that I can recall?" Kieran answered.

"Milord, Alaric has answered your question. I have not received word of this either," Florin stated, in defense of his friend.

Nicolai and Kieran glanced between Alaric and Florin. *"They know,"* Nicolai said to Kieran telepathically.

"Of course they do," Kieran replied before addressing Alaric and Florin. "I don't suppose you would mind if we looked around?"

Alaric stepped to the side and in an over exaggerated manner, he placed one arm behind his back, and motioned with the other for them to have free rein of the property. "No, milords. We have nothing to hide."

Nicolai glanced around and walked back to Sylvana. "I see no reason to suspect your family is hiding anything." He then looked at Alaric again. "Just so you know, we will escort your sister to tonight's ceremony."

"The hell, if you will," Alaric stated.

Florin placed his hand on Alaric's shoulder before he did or said anything that would make the situation worse than it already was. "Alaric, pull it back—" he began.

Nicolai took one step toward Alaric. "Say again?"

Alaric stood his ground. However, he softened the tone of his voice. "My apologies. It is up to our father, not me."

"Where is your father? We will inform him."

"He's not here."

"Why don't you send word and ask him to return?"

Alaric and Florin side eyed each other, feeling like Alaric had backed himself into a corner.

"I'm waiting and my patience is thin," Nicolai said.

"He won't be back for some time," Alaric admitted.

"How long has he been gone?" Nicolai questioned.

"A few days."

"A few days or one week?" Kieran interjected.

Sylvana approached Nicolai and gently squeezed his forearm. "Nicolai, please."

"Klyn will come for you this evening." He then looked at Alaric. "I assume you will also be in attendance?"

"Yes, milord."

Nicolai and Kieran walked to Sylvana, and they each placed a kiss on her forehead. "We look forward to seeing you tonight." Nicolai winked.

Once Nicolai and Kieran were out of sight, Alaric rushed toward Sylvana. "You stupid, stupid girl! Do you know what you have done? Riordan wears a crown without mercy, and you have put us all at the tip of his blade!" he bellowed.

"I'm sorry—"

"You're sorry? Fuck, this is beyond sorry."

Florin grabbed Sylvana's arm and spun her around to face him. "Sylvie, what the fuck were you thinking, sleeping with them?"

"Florin, do not raise your voice at me and it is none of your goddamn business. It just happened!"

Alaric was furious. "You *just happen* to fall into the bed of Riordan's brothers?"

"I never said I slept with them," Sylvana snapped.

"Sylvana, your actions are like an impetuous child," Alaric scolded.

"And you are acting like an *impetuous* ass."

"I have known you my entire life. I never expected you would pull something like this." Even though Florin was speaking out of anger, he was genuinely concerned for her. After all, he and Sylvana had been each other's first love and first sexual encounter when they were younger.

Alaric pushed his hair back and interlaced his fingers on the top of his head. He was truly at a loss. "When father finds out what you have done, he will drain the Ascelin blood from your fucking body."

Calista grabbed Alaric's forearm. "Stop it! You have said enough."

"Alaric, we should take this matter to the Cynfadels. They may be able to get word to your father before this shit takes a turn for the worse."

"*This shit* has already taken a turn for the worse. Did you hear how he enunciated purebred when talking about the stallions?"

"Loud and clear. We should go, like now," Florin replied.

Alaric and Florin mounted their stallions, and as he rode past Sylvana, he stopped momentarily. "We will discuss this when I return."

"I'm sorry Alaric. I never meant for any of this to happen."

"Unfortunately, your utter lack of judgement has brought the Acherons to our doorstep."

Cadell picked up on the distant sound of hooves heading in his manor's direction. He walked to the entrance of the stable and narrowed his eyes, sharpening his acute sense of sight, and realized it was Alaric and Florin who appeared to be riding as if they were eluding or chasing an adversary.

Once they met Cadell, they pulled their stallions to a halt and he could see the concern on their faces. "Alaric, is everything all right?"

"I came to ask for your help," Alaric replied.

"Anything. What do you need?"

Alaric and Florin side eyed each other as their stallions pranced in place.

"Whatever it is, say it," Cadell demanded.

"It's Sylvana—it's bad, Cadell."

"Is she ill?"

"Only in her head," Florin replied.

Cadell cocked his head. "I don't understand?"

"I don't know how to tell you?" Alaric replied.

"Alaric, spit it out," Cadell demanded.

"Nicolai and Kieran are bedding Sylvana," he said, feeling as if he was going to choke on the words as they left his mouth.

Cadell stared at Alaric with wide eyes and adjusted his stance. *It cannot be, she cannot be?*

"There is more," Alaric admitted.

"What more could there possibly be?"

"They are looking for a purebred Ascelin and I am positive they suspect it is Sylvana."

"How do you know this?" Cadell asked.

Florin looked at Alaric, who appeared to be at a loss for words. "They didn't come right out and say it, but it was clear," Florin replied.

"If you know where Father is, you need to send word," Alaric said.

"Alaric, I can't."

"Why the hell not? They slept in Sylvana's fucking bed chamber last night, and I hadn't a clue they were there!"

Cadell could clearly see his desperation and he felt terrible. "We will take this matter to Lord Cynfadel, but I need you to speak the truth. The rumors? Are they true?"

Fuck, If I speak the truth there is no hiding it. If I don't, the consequences could be worse. He looked at Florin, desperately trying to figure out what to do.

Florin shrugged his shoulders, not having an answer.

"Alaric, your father is my friend and I will not betray him, nor will I betray his family. I can't help if I don't know the truth."

Alaric straightened his back. "It's true."

"Are you, Calista, and Mira Ascelins as well?" After a brief pause, the blank expression on Alaric's face told him what he needed to know. "There is something I need to tell you," Cadell admitted.

"Sounds ominous," Florin mumbled.

"Enatta knows about Mira," Cadell said.

"What do you mean?" Alaric asked.

"Mira showed Enatta her ability to create life."

"Oh, fuck me. I'm going to kill her."

"I've spoked to Enatta, and I've demanded she remain silent. It is the very reason I am keeping Mira and Laurent apart. I told Mira when I brought her home this morning Laurent would be leaving with me for a few weeks."

"First Sylvana and now Mira? What the hell am I supposed to do?"

"I assume you will be in attendance for the ceremony tonight?"

"Yes," Alaric muttered.

"Then we have little time. Go back to your manor and do nothing. I will go to Lord Cynfadel."

"Will you be at the ceremony?" Alaric asked.

"No, I will remain as guard for the villages, along with several other members of the Legion, as required."

Enatta was sitting in the shade of an aged wisteria vine watching Laurent, who stepped forward and drew his sword, cutting upwards toward Ilial, his tutor. The sword glanced off Ilial's shield with a loud clang. Ilial spun around and brought his blade down on Laurent and reversed the attack. Laurent drew back, his shoulder a mere inch from Ilial's blade. He then brought his sword around in a tight circle and stepped forward, repeating the cut. With a resounding clank, Laurent's sword hit the ground and slid across the dirt.

"Shit," Laurent said, slightly breathless.

"Well done," Enatta shouted.

Laurent collected his sword. "Well done? I dropped my damn sword."

"Yes, you did," Ilial replied as he patted Laurent's shoulder. He then spun his sword in a small circle. "Let's go again."

"Laurent, enough for now. Would you walk with me?" Enatta asked.

"I'm training. Can it wait?"

"No. I need to speak to you."

Laurent twirled his sword and looked at Ilial, who nodded and placed his sword back in its sheath. "Go with your mother. We will continue when you return."

"What is more important than my training?"

Enatta wrapped his arm in hers and gently nudged him. "I need to speak to you about Mira."

"Is she okay?"

"Yes, of course. Your father wants you to keep your distance from her for a few weeks." Laurent stopped mid-stride and pulled his arm away. "Why would I do that?"

"Your father is not asking, Laurent. I don't agree either. However, I cannot defy him, and neither will you."

Laurent crossed his arms. "Explain. Mira and I have done nothing wrong."

"We never said the two of you did anything wrong. It is complicated."

"*Complicated*? I'm old enough to choose whom I spend my time with."

"This is not permanent, Laurent. It will only be for a few weeks."

"What are the reasons for this? Yesterday, you were all about her being with us."

"You are aware of her powers, yes?"

"Yes. Why does it matter?"

"There is not a simple answer, but for now, being around her may put you at risk."

Laurent uncrossed his arms and paced back and forth. "Father is being paranoid. How is it putting us at risk when no one else knows?"

Enatta reached for his arm but he pulled away. "I will not allow you and father to keep us

from seeing each other."

"Laurent, you will do as your father says."

"The hell I will—"

"Laurent! Do not speak to me in such a manner."

"Does Mira know of this?"

"Yes, your father planned on to telling her this morning."

"Great. Thanks for interfering in my life—again!"

Enatta ran her hands down her corset, struggling with the situation. *I will find a way around Cadell.*

"Since you have nothing more to say, I'm going to find Mira."

"Laurent, you will do no such thing. I don't agree with this either and I will speak to your

father, but for now, you will do as you are told."

"We will see," Laurent mumbled under his breath as he stormed off.

Calista sat with Sylvana in her room, trying to comfort her.

"I don't think I can go tonight after what happened this morning," Sylvana stated.

Calista rubbed her arm. "They came for you last night. Do you think tonight would be any different?"

"No. I suppose not?"

"Look, we can't do anything about this right now. I assume they are only suspicious. If they knew more, I'm sure things would have ended differently. Now let's get you dressed. I want you to enjoy yourself tonight."

They heard the door slam shut and the heavy thumping of boots on the stairs. "Ah shit. Alaric is back," Sylvana said.

They waited with bated breath, thinking Sylvana's door was going to slam open. Instead, they heard Alaric's slam shut.

Calista's face lit with amusement. "One of these days, you are going to push him over the edge."

"I think the vein in his forehead was throbbing," Sylvana replied.

Through their laughter, they heard hooves coming down the road; they leapt off the bed and rushed to the window.

"It's Klyn," Sylvana said.

"What is he doing here so soon?" Calista asked.

"I don't know? But I suggest we greet him before Alaric does," Sylvana stated.

They ran down the stairs and out of the front door just as Klyn rode up with Skadi in tow. "Sylvana, good to see you again. Good afternoon, Calista."

"Hello Klyn," Calista replied.

"Why are you here so early?" Sylvana asked.

"The ceremony is tonight, or have you forgotten?"

"I didn't expect to see you so soon. I'm not dressed."

"It's fine. They want to see you now, and I suggest you wear the outfit they gave you."

Calista looked at Sylvana. "What outfit?"

Sylvana motioned dismissively toward Calista and then looked at Klyn again. "Why do I need to wear the outfit?"

"It would be a polite *choice*." He winked.

"Whatever. I'll be back."

"I'll be waiting."

Sylvana and Calista headed back into her chamber and Sylvana pulled out the clothing and dressed.

"Damn." Calista walked over and ran her hands over the fine material. "I would steal this from you if I had anywhere to wear it," she joked.

Muriel awoke feeling as though she had been beaten from head to toe. She glanced around her new home and studied the modest surroundings. The bodies of two rabbits hung from the hearth above the glowing embers, while various pelts hung from the walls and the room smelled of aged wood and smoke; the only furniture other than the bed was an old wood table, two chairs and an armoire.

Lupine walked over and sat next to her. "How do you feel?"

"Tired. My entire body hurts, and I remember nothing." She ran her hands down her face, sat up, draped her legs over the edge of the bed, and noticed her soiled feet; it was as if she had been running barefoot through the forest. "What happened last night?"

"After you turned, we ran with our pack until dawn."

"It's over then?"

"Yes. Your new life begins today."

"What's next?"

"We will figure it out, but for now, you need to return home and allow Alaric to escort you to the ceremony, as if nothing has changed."

"It wouldn't feel right." Muriel sighed.

"You don't have a choice. If anyone discovers we have mated, the Guild will force us to stand trial. Their archaic way of thinking has withstood time and reason, and they will tighten the noose around or necks."

"Maybe Sylvana would speak to the Acherons? She has been spending time with them."

He laughed aloud. "Tell me you aren't naïve enough to believe she is more to them than their next conquest?"

"I don't know what to think? But I know she would never be someone's whore."

"She will be whatever they want her to be."

"I am supposed to be helping her find information regarding her mother."

"Muriel, you are a predator now and you need to leave your family and friends behind. Whatever you were conditioned to believe in as Nosferatu, no longer applies."

"What do you mean?"

"Did I stump you?" he chuckled.

"It's not funny, Lupine. How do I simply stop being Nosferatu and become the wolf?"

"You stopped being Nosferatu the moment you changed. You can't be both. It's not possible."

"I'm confused, is all. It's as if the life I have lived is already fading from my mind."

"It's normal and soon the wolf will take over your mind as she did your body."

"I don't know if I am fully prepared to walk away from everyone and everything I've ever known?"

"Do you want to live the rest of your life in servitude, or do you want to discover a whole new world? A world where you no longer live beneath the boots of the Acherons."

"I want a new life with you, but I feel I owe Sylvana. She is—was my friend."

He leaned in and, after a heated kiss, he pushed her onto her back and rested his heavy body on hers. "As a gift to my new mate, I will help you, but you will need to bring her to me. They cannot see me near the castle and after which, you will sever all ties."

"You would really do that for me—for us?"

"Yes, but right now I am going to fuck my new mate ."

Chapter 11

Klyn dismounted his stallion and escorted Sylvana into the parlor; two young servants greeted them and once again, they pulled the wash basin from beneath the chair and motioned for her to take a seat.

Sylvana looked at Klyn, who was watching her as if amused; she smiled at him and subtly rolled her eyes, and he chuckled aloud. "I assume you're not used to this kind of personal attention?"

"No. And it's awkward," she replied quietly.

"You better get used to it," he said.

"Sylvana, I'm glad you could make it," Riordan said as he entered the parlor.

"Milord," she replied, along with a subtle curtsey as she stood.

"No need to great me so formally, Sylvana." He then looked at Klyn. "I'll take it from here."

"Milord." He nodded and turned to Sylvana. "I will see you tonight."

Riordan walked over and held out his elbow. "Nicolai and Kieran will be here soon."

She wrapped her arm in his and did her best to quell her beating heart, feeling as though she was a rabbit scurrying into the den of a wolf.

"I heard what happened earlier," he said.

"My apologies if Alaric offended Nicolai and Kieran."

"Do not apologize on his behalf. It is his duty to look after you and your sisters. Your brother is protective. I would expect nothing less."

"I can look after myself."

Riordan looked down at her and winked. "I am well aware."

He escorted her to Nicolai's chamber, and three ladies who were waiting in the hallway greeted them.

"Milord," one of them said as she opened the door and stepped aside.

"Milady, we are here to help you dress," another offered.

Sylvana walked in and they had spread an elegant gown out on the bed.

Riordan took a seat and crossed one leg over his knee while one of them handed him a drink. "I hope it is to your liking, milord."

Riordan nodded. "I believe Sylvana would like a drink as well."

"Yes, milord." She filled another goblet and handed it to Sylvana.

"Thank you," Sylvana replied.

Riordan tilted his head, curious why Sylvana was staring at him, as if waiting for something. "Is everything okay?"

"Yes. Are you staying?" Sylvana asked.

"Yes. Is that a problem?"

"Well, no. I mean—I have to change."

"I'll divert my eyes."

She noticed a hint of a smile as he looked at the table and set his goblet down.

"Milady, are you are ready?" She picked up the dress and Sylvana followed them into a bathing area, where they spent a great deal of time getting her ready.

"There. Look," one of them said.

Sylvana stood from the bench and looked at her reflection in a large mirror hanging over the bureau. *Damn, I have never seen myself like this. My face—the colors are beautiful. I wish Calista could see me.*

She subtly turned from side to side, admiring how the silk material cascaded down her body and pooled on the floor around her feet. The midnight-blue color faded down her body and seamlessly melted into lighter bluish tones, while a black, leather, studded strap wound its way around her waist and then crisscrossed beneath her breasts, accentuating her cleavage.

"Riordan is waiting, milady."

Riordan was leaning against the window and the moment he saw Sylvana, he was taken aback. *Ahh fuck, she is a vision to behold.* Her auburn hair was loosely pulled back from her forehead and braided over the top of her head, while luxurious, wavy locks flowed over her bare shoulders. He walked in a slow circle around her, admiring her appearance.

"Do I look okay?" Sylvana asked nervously.

"Impeccable. However, something is missing?"

She ran her hands over her hips and looked at the girls and then into a tall, ornate mirror standing in the room's corner across from her. Riordan opened a drawer in the bureau and pulled out a silver box. He then removed a pendant and draped it over his hand.

She immediately realized it was a replica of the pendants he and his brothers wore. "Riordan, it's stunning."

"As are you," he said as he placed his hand on her shoulder. "Turn around."

Sylvana turned her back to him and he placed it around her neck and gently pulled her hair from beneath the gold chain and looked at her reflection in the mirror.

"It is known as the Sanguis Murielrum and it is only one of six. As you know, my brother's and I each have one. Everyone in attendance will know you belong to us."

Sylvana placed her hand over the amulet and looked back at his reflection. *I don't know if I should cherish this or run like hell?* She turned to face him. "Riordan, I don't know what to say?"

He leaned over, lifted her chin with his fingers, and slid his tongue into her mouth. After a heated kiss, he pulled away and whispered into her ear. "Cherish it, Sângele Nostru. A rabbit cannot outrun the wolf."

Not having expected the kiss, she was too overwhelmed to move or speak; ominous thoughts squirmed in the back of her mind, realizing he had read her mind even though she had cloaked her thoughts before arriving. *Don't think,* she told herself.

"*Think* whatever you want." He winked and held out his elbow. "I look forward to seeing you in a few hours. In the meantime, *I thought,*" he enunciated, "you would like some company while you wait for Nicolai and Kieran."

He walked her down the hallway and into what appeared to be a formal parlor on the upper floor.

"Milord," Venthana said.

Riordan nodded and left.

Venthana rushed over and grabbed her hands. "Sylvana, you look incredible!"

"Thank you, and you are stunning. What are you doing here?"

"Rayna brought me here and said I was to keep you company."

"I am so happy you are here," Sylvana said, as they took a seat on the chaise lounge.

"Miladies, would you care for a drink?" Rana asked.

"Yes. Thank you," Sylvana replied.

Venthana looked at the amulet resting against Sylvana's chest. "May I?"

Sylvana lifted the pendant and placed it on her palm. "Of course."

"Where did you get this? It's the same one the brothers wear."

"Riordan gave it to me."

"Sylvie, does this mean—are you mating them?"

Sylvana laughed aloud. "No."

Venthana gently placed it against Sylvana's chest. "Why didn't you come to the games last night?"

"I was at my manor with Nicolai and Kieran."

"They stayed at your place?"

"Yes, and they ended up introducing themselves to my family this morning."

"Damn, how did they take it?"

"Not well."

"You are the talk of court."

"Great. What are they saying?"

"A lot." Venthana chuckled. "The envy runs deep."

"Just what I need," Sylvana said. "I'm nervous enough as it is."

"Don't worry about it. Stefania and Aurelia will also be in attendance, and they are excited to see you.

Florin pulled up to the manor and hopped out of the carriage. "I'll be back momentarily."

Brienne smiled and nodded. "Take your time, my love."

He walked into the parlor and Alaric was pacing back and forth with a drink.

"I hope the rest of the day was uneventful," Florin said as he filled a cup with ale.

Alaric leaned against the table and crossed his legs. "I am afraid of how tonight is going to play out."

"Alaric, it will be fine. Most of the Cynfadel clan, and other members of the Legion, will be there. Not to mention Cadell has your back."

Alaric tipped his cup to him. "Not one of them carries enough power or influence to go toe to toe with the Acherons."

"I don't disagree, but I also think nothing is going to happen."

Alaric reached behind him for the pitcher and filled his cup up again. "I want nothing more than to get through this night, and then I am going to kill Sylvana."

Florin took Alaric's cup from him and set it down. "Go easy tonight. The last thing I want is to see you say or do something you will regret."

"Another one of my many concerns is Muriel has been hanging out with Sylvana. The last thing I need is to find out she has been involved in or has any knowledge of this."

Florin laughed aloud. "The women in your life are going to be the death of you."

"In the literal sense." Alaric chuckled half-heartedly.

Laurent was standing behind the barn, waiting for Alaric to leave. Once the carriage was out of sight, he snuck through the back door, peered around the corner, and heard someone coming down the stairs. As Calista walked through the parlor, he stood with his back against the wall and held his breath. Once he heard the door close, he ran up the stairs, down the hallway, and knocked softly on Mira's door.

"Go away!" she yelled.

"Mira, it's me."

The door flew opened, she grabbed his arm, and pulled him into her chamber. "What are you doing here?"

"I came for you."

"I thought you were with your father?"

"He lied to you. Mother told me he does not want us to see each other for awhile."

"Why? Did I do something wrong?"

"No, it's complicated. If I asked, would you leave with me?"

"Leave? And go where?"

"We can stay in our cottage for now. It's only a few hours from here."

"And how will we live?"

"I will take care of you. We need to let them know they cannot keep us from each other. Father will come to his senses."

Mira looked around her room and then back at Laurent. "Okay, I am sick of my sister's anyway." She pulled a small bag from her armoire and stuffed what she could into it.

Venthana stood without haste when she heard footsteps on the other side of the door and Sylvana looked up at her and gently squeezed her hand. "Why are you so nervous?"

"Because I am not the one in your position," she replied.

Kieran walked in and stopped mid-stride the moment he laid eyes on Sylvana.

Nicolai wasn't expecting Kieran to stop so abruptly, and he bumped into his back. "What the hell, Kieran?" He then looked at Sylvana and placed a firm hand on Kieran's shoulder. *"My heart just skipped a beat,"* he said telepathically.

"My dick is hard," Kieran replied.

Sylvana and Venthana were awestruck with Nicolai's and Kieran's appearance. They were wearing midnight-blue, leather trousers, a studded leather strap that crisscrossed just below their chests, similar to Sylvana's, and silk tunics that were awash in the same colors as her dress.

Holy shit, Venthana said to herself. *I think I am the one who is envious.*

Nicolai walked over and stole a heated kiss. He then raised her arm and gently spun her around. "You look sensational."

"Thank you, as do the two of you."

Kieran also stole a kiss and then nodded to Venthana. "Will you see yourself out?"

"Yes, milord," she said along with a polite curtesy.

"Who decided on the matching outfits?" Sylvana asked.

"It's customary," Nicolai replied.

"I thought it was only customary for mates and clans?"

Kieran picked up the amulet and gently cupped it in his fist. "We decide what's customary."

"Brothers," Riordan said as he strolled into the room.

"You weren't exaggerating earlier," Nicolai replied.

Damn. He can dominate a room without having to say a word, she thought.

The only difference between him and his brother's outfits was that Riordan was wearing a silver crown and had an intricately designed silver brooch attached to the leather strap in the center of his chest. Although the crown wasn't as opulent as one would expect, it was impeccably detailed none the less. However, standing there looking at him, it was merely a symbolic formality. The power and authority clearly resided within Riordan, not the crown.

Riordan placed his hands on Nicolai's and Kieran's shoulders and addressed Sylvana. "It's time for us to formally introduce you to the court."

Although she was feeling anxious and self-conscious, she also appreciated their generosity. "I would like to thank you for the dress and the hospitality you have shown me."

"We are just getting started." Riordan winked.

"Shall we?" Nicolai said as he and Kieran held out their elbows.

Sylvana took a deep breath. "I suppose."

Kieran looked at her with a half-cocked grin. "Do not be nervous. We will be with you for the duration of the evening."

Nicolai, Sylvana, and Kieran walked arm in arm as they followed Riordan into the main castle. Once they reached the top of the expansive staircase, the exuberant crowd turned their attention to them.

Sylvana scanned the grand hall and was stunned by how impeccably decorated it was. Bouquets of every size and shape filled large containers while floral garland made of fresh flowers were wrapped around the marble pillars, draped on the walls, and hung from the stone railings lining the upper hallways. On the walls hung long intricate tapestries, each telling a story of their own. From the enormous, black iron chandlers, having been filled with hundreds of candles, came a radiant arc of golden light being cast across the entire hall. The guests' clothing was fashioned from exotic fabrics with brilliant colors, while bracelets, pendants, and rings complimented their outfits. All the while, musicians, poets, and jesters were entertaining the guests. Armed guards who were wearing intricately designed, leather vests with their specific clan's emblem over their hearts flanked the entire hall.

Sylvana glanced at Nicolai and Kieran, and they looked down at her and smiled. Kieran placed his hand over hers and gave it a gentle squeeze. "Relax."

Riordan stepped forward and held out his arms. "Lords and ladies," he hollered. "Tonight we are here to celebrate the bond between Tobias Severn Acheron and Lenora Isadora Phelan!"

The crowd erupted into cheers and chants, and Riordan looked to his right and bent his left arm behind his back and nodded. Tobias and Lenora made their way over and stood next to him.

He placed his hand on Tobias's shoulder and whispered in his ear; Tobias dropped his head and laughed, and Riordan patted his shoulder and turned his attention back to the spirited crowd.

"If there is one amongst you feeling queasy or apprehensive at the thought of what lies ahead, I assume it is Tobias, who has now formed a lifetime bond with a lady of court!"

The crowd burst into a round of wholesome laughter, after which Riordan held up his hand.

"Tobias should know how fortunate he is. He has acquired a beautiful mate, a kind heart, and someone who will keep his bed warm, and his desires fulfilled. As for Lenora, she has acquired a beautiful gown!"

Tobias grasped Riordan's shoulder and let out a belly laugh while Lenora placed her hand across her stomach and her mouth parted with laughter.

After a few minutes Riordan held up his hand once again.. "The Guild of Entente has accepted the blood bond. And on behalf of myself, Nicolai Theron, and Kieran Malachi Acheron, it is our honor to welcome Lenora Isadora Acheron as the newest member of our clan."

"Aru—Aru—Aru!" the males shouted in agreement.

Vispera leaned against the wall next to one of the numerous windows in her bedchamber and ran her hands over her arms, feeling a chill in the air when a shadow cast over. She looked toward the door, having heard the sounds of footsteps. "Salve, darling," she said as Dronve walked in.

He strode over and wrapped his arms around her. "Greetings, my love."

"You appear solemn. What are you thinking?" he asked.

"About our choices," she replied.

"Limited, they are," he acknowledged.

"I fear this may be thy end of Estraxath. The shadows within thy veil grow stronger with each passing moon and thy Acherons beyond thy veil have proven undefeatable."

He kissed her cheek and held her tighter. "Thy Ascelins are thy key to our survival."

"Can Ranan be trusted?" Vispera asked.

Dronve looked at himself in the clear panes and reflected on his own doubt for Ranan. "He's always had ulterior motives, and I'm afraid if we allow him into Estraxath, we will only encourage his tendency to demand more."

Vispera took a sip of her briar wine. "Your words are not hollow. He knows much and shares only what is in his best interest."

"He approached me earlier and has taken a mate whom he believes has a connection to thy Ascelin."

Vispera was taken-a-back. "Who is she?"

"She is—was Nosferatu."

Vispera slipped from his embrace and paced back and forth.

"Thoughts, my love?" he asked.

"Why would one who holds thy powers of Nosferatu give it all up to become a creature who is untamed and savage? They have no morality, no sanctity, and are duplicitous by nature."

"I too have thy same questions."

"Follow him. Make sure he brings thy Ascelin to us. Should he refuse, kill him and his mate," Vispera said.

"Consider it done, my love."

"What would he have to offer her?" she questioned aloud.

"We don't know what her life was like. Maybe it was her chance to start anew with a powerful mate?"

After a few moments of silent contemplation, Vispera tipped her chalice toward him. "He has offered her a place by his side in Estraxath."

Dronve nodded in agreement. "Tis logical. Most would leave all if offered a life of abundance. Regardless of what it costs them."

"She is thy first of many. Soon, he will offer homage to his entire pack, and it won't be long before Lycan overrun our kingdom," Vispera stated.

"'Tis a reasonable thought. He is taking advantage of thy treaty."

"Have you spoken to thy Mercurial Guardians?" she asked.

He walked over and took the chalice from her hand and set it down. "Yes, my love." He then lifted her chin with his fingers and kissed her passionately.

"Take me to bed, my love," she whispered.

Sylvana glanced through the crowd and glimpsed Alaric, who was look-ing in her direction. She gave him a forced smile, and he tipped his cup to her. "Nicolai, I would like to say hello to Alaric."

He placed his hand on her lower back and nodded in Alaric's direc-tion. The crowd parted before them and closed in behind them as they walked across the great hall.

Once Alaric, Nicolai, and Kieran had greeted each other, Alaric stared at Sylvana.

"Alaric, it's good to see you." Sylvana smiled.

Alaric leaned in, kissed her cheek, and squeezed her hand. "You look incredible tonight."

"Thank you. As do you."

"Milords, I would like a moment with my sister, if you don't mind?"

Kieran patted her butt. "Go."

Alaric offered her his arm to her; they walked outside, and stood on the wide veranda overlooking the courtyard.

"I am truly sorry for what took place this morning," Sylvana said.

"I know you are." He let go of her arm and turned to face her. "You look as if you belong here."

Sylvana looked down at her dress. "I may look like it, but I certainly don't feel like I do."

"Are the ladies giving you trouble?"

"Not so far. I met a few of them the other night and they have been wonderful."

"The other night?"

"Yes."

"I don't want to know, do I?"

"No. You really don't."

He stared at the pendant and lifted it up. "The Acheron's pendant? What are you doing with it?"

"Riordan lent it to me."

"Riordan? They don't just *lend* you something like this. What the fuck have you gotten yourself into?"

"It is not what you think, Alaric."

Alaric rolled his eyes and took a sip of his ale. "We shall see." He then glanced over her again. "I can't get over the way you look."

"Neither can I. But off the subject, what pulled you out of your sour mood?"

"Muriel." He winked.

"Where is she?"

He subtly nodded toward the courtyard. "Over there with Brienne and Florin. I wanted to find you to make sure you were okay."

"I'm *okay*. Are we *okay*?"

"Yes, but there is much to discuss," Alaric replied.

"I agree," Sylvana said.

"Would you like to say hello to Muriel?" Alaric asked.

"Yes."

Mira wrapped her arms tightly around Laurent's waist as Rhone galloped down the road. "Laurent, you need to hurry. We shouldn't be out here this time of night."

"We are almost there, Mira. Hold tight."

Off in the distance, the trees thinned, and a field of grass spanned out before the cottage. He pulled the reins and Rhone slowed his pace. "There it is," Laurent said.

She loosened her arms and looked at the cottage. "It doesn't look like anyone is there?"

"Let's wait a few minutes to see if any of the caretakers are around."

They heard a twig snap and their heads spun in the noise's direction. "What is it—"

Laurent held up his hand and turned Rhone around. "Shh!"

"Go, we need to go—go now, Laurent," she whispered firmly.

Laurent kicked Rhone's hindquarters, and as he darted across the field, they then heard the thundering of hooves approaching from behind. "Laurent, someone is following us!" Mira yelled.

"Hang on!" He squeezed his thighs and leaned forward.

They had only made it halfway across the field before six warriors surrounded them; two of whom rode up on either side of Rhone, reached down and grabbed the reins hanging beneath his neck.

"Whoa, whoa!" one of them yelled.

Rhone tossed his head up and planted his back hooves into the dirt.

Laurent and Mira looked at the warriors whose silver helmets partially obscured their faces, while wing like flaps covered their ears and extended down their necks.

"What do you want?" Laurent demanded.

No one spoke as they reached over and pulled them off of Rhone. Laurent did his best to fight back while Mira kicked and screamed at the one who had grabbed her.

Another warrior rode up and grabbed a fistful of Laurent's hair and waved his free hand over his face. Laurent fell still and the warrior who had pulled him off Rhone draped his body across his thighs.

"Laurent! What did you do to him?" Mira screamed.

The same warrior rode up to Mira and ran his hand over her face and she too fell still.

Chapter 12

Sylvana stood with her friends and a few other members of the court they had introduced her to. They were enjoying each other's company and watching a large group of ladies playing games in the center of the courtyard. Sylvana glanced over and smiled to herself when he saw Alaric laughing along with Florin and other members of the Legion. *He is actually having a good time.*

"Ladies," Nicolai said as he approached Sylvana from behind.

"Milord," they replied, along with a gentle curtsey.

Kieran slid his hand across Sylvana's lower back. "You seem to be enjoying yourself."

"Very much so." Sylvana smiled.

"Can we get you anything?" Nicolai asked.

"I'm fine, thank you."

Nicolai took the goblet from her hand and looked into it. "It's empty?"

"Yes. The servants haven't been around for a while."

"Ladies, are all of your cups empty?" Nicolai asked.

"Yes, milord," Venthana replied.

Kieran side eyed Nicolai and looked around and then morphed out of sight.

Sylvana looked up at Nicolai. "What is he doing?"

"Fetching you a drink." He winked before bending over and stealing a little tongue.

"Shit," Muriel whispered.

Sylvana pulled away from Nicolai and looked over, only to see Kieran briskly walking in their direction and had a grip on one servant's shoulders. He nudged him forward once he approached the group. "You will see to their every need for the rest of the evening."

"Yes, milord. I—I was told they—the ladies were not drinking."

"What the fuck are you waiting for?" Nicolai asked.

"Miladies." He nodded politely and then darted across the lawn, leapt onto the veranda, shouted at two servants, and pointed in Sylvana's direction. They grabbed a pitcher in each hand and rushed back over and filled all of their goblets.

Nicolai bent down kissed Sylvana's forehead. "We will be right over there. If you need anything, let us know."

"I'm fine. Thank you."

"Holy shit!" Stefania exclaimed.

Brienne placed her hand on Sylvana's forearm and winked. "I think it's safe to say they have feelings for you. We have never seen them treat anyone else this way."

"We will see how long it lasts," Sylvana joked.

"Oh shit. Here come the beasts," Venthana interjected.

"What do we have here?" Elsa asked.

"Shouldn't the four of you be on your backs in servitude somewhere?" Aurelia snarked.

"It appears as if Sylvana has already been on her back whoring for the Acherons," Elsa snarked.

Sylvana leaned over and ran her face up the side of hers. "You smell like a fucking Helot's cocotte."

Sylvana's friends laughed aloud and moved closer to her. "The greenish hue on your repulsive faces is unbecoming," Stefania snarked.

Nicolai looked over when he tuned into the conversation between Sylvana, her friends, another group of ladies. "Brothers."

Kieran looked over and just as he and Nicolai took one step, Riordan placed his hands on their shoulders. "I'm curious? I want to see how she handles herself."

They stood shoulder to shoulder watching and listening as the altercation unfolded.

"What makes you think we are jealous of a field hand? Sylvana is nothing more than a blackbird hiding behind the feathers of a peacock." Nora laughed.

Sylvana stepped forward. "I would tread lightly. I am not bound by the rules of the court."

"You are not *bound* because you don't belong here. The Acherons will discard you as easily as they do the rest of their whores," Latavia replied.

Elsa acted as if she tripped and poured her entire goblet of cherry wine down the front of Sylvana's dress. Her friends looked on in horror when Sylvana gasped and stepped back; they watched as the fine linen absorbed the burgundy liquid.

"Oops, I tripped." Elsa laughed and covered her mouth with her hand while her ladies laughed under their breath and mocked her.

Riordan, Nicolai, and Kieran's canines slid from their gums the moment they saw the liquid splash against the front of Sylvana's body.

Sylvana looked at Elsa and bared her canines; the blood splattered across Elsa's face when her fist landed squarely on her nose.

"Oops, I tripped," Sylvana snarled.

Riordan, Nicolai, and Kieran let out a belly laugh while the ladies winced, and/or shrieked.

"We should handle this before it gets further out of control," Riordan stated.

They sauntered over, and when Riordan turned Sylvana to face him, he felt her trembling.

"I—I am so sorry, milord. I didn't—I just reacted."

Riordan watched as her eyes glossed over with moisture. He lifted her hand and wiped the blood from her knuckles with his thumb. "Are you hurt?"

"No. I'm humiliated."

"Then I shall have to fix that."

Nicolai pulled her between himself and Kieran while Riordan stepped in Elsa's direction. "You have made a grave mistake," he growled.

Sylvana was terrified by the look upon the brother's faces, and how the color of their eyes shifted from their normal tones to a glassy, coal black.

"Milord, I am very sorry. I—I tripped. I will help her clean up." She reached over as if she was going to grab Sylvana's hand.

A low rumble rose from Nicolai's chest, and he stepped forward, gripped Elsa's shoulder, and pulled her back. "I would spill your fucking blood for what you have done. However, I don't want to get it in my mouth," he said as he side-eyed Sylvana.

The corner of Sylvana's mouth turnt up with a modest smile, knowing what he was alluding to. "There are other ways to kill," she said.

The tears streamed down Elsa's face. "Milords, it was an accident—"

"It was a grievous error in judgement," Kieran interjected.

Riordan wrapped his fists around her wrists and yanked her toward him. "Let's make sure you never spill another."

"Yes, milord. It will never happen again."

Riordan looked at the guard standing behind her. "Take her fucking hands," he stated calmly.

"What? Noo! I beg of you!"

"Yes, milord." He grabbed the back of Elsa's neck and drug her out.

Riordan then turned his attention to her friends. "Sylvana will take your places at court, and you will spend the rest of your days tending to my fucking fields with the Helots." He flicked his hand and the guards drug them away. Riordan then turned to Sylvana. "Sângele Nostru, I believe you have soiled your dress."

"It appears so." She chuckled and ran her hands down the material, and then subtly shook them.

Riordan stepped back, waved his hand over her body, and everything dissipated as if nothing had happened.

Tobias and Lenora walked over and she pulled Sylvana into a tight embrace. "I am so sorry. Are you okay?"

"I'm fine, really. Just embarrassed," Sylvana replied.

A look of amusement crossed Tobias's face, and he cocked his head. "I have never witnessed a lady of court land such an impeccable blow."

"I'm not a lady of court," Sylvana replied.

"No, no, you aren't, but based on the amulet around your neck, the court will soon *belong* to you," he replied, along with a wink.

"Holy shit, Sylvie." Lenora said. "That was one hell of a punch. Did you see the blood splatter?"

"I believe you broke the skýla's nose," Klyn laughed.

Lenora wrapped her arm in Sylvana's. "Let us put this behind you and go inside. My mate has promised me a dance."

Sylvana smiled as she watched the guests moved seamlessly around the floor, each step in sync with the harmony of the music.

"Shall we?" Nicolai asked as he and Kieran bent over, placed one arm behind their backs, and held their hands out.

"We shall, milords." Sylvana curtsied, and they spun her around between them, and melted into the crowd and easily fell into step with one another. A smile spread across Sylvana's face as they glided together, drifting serenely across the floor in unison with the rest of the crowd.

"The way you handled yourself with Elsa was impressive," Kieran said as he twirled her body around his.

"It was embarrassing. I shouldn't have lost my temper during such an important event."

"You stood up for yourself. There is nothing to be embarrassed about," Nicolai replied.

"I can't recall the last time I heard Riordan laugh so hard." Kieran smiled.

When the music faded, Nicolai dipped Sylvana in his arms, and admired how her mouth parted in laughter and the way her emerald-green eyes sparkled. He raised her up, slid his hand over her thigh, held it against his hip, and took her mouth to his.

Riordan placed his hand on Nicolai's shoulder. "Not to interrupt, but I believe the next dance is mine."

"Don't keep her all night," Nicolai joked.

Riordan placed his hand on her lower back. "I make no promises."

The tempo of the waltz changed, the guests slowed their steps, and drew each other into a tight embrace. Riordan held her tightly against his body and glided across the floor. The simple gestures of their hands, the way they looked into each other's eyes, and the unexpected eroticism of their bodies swaying together, made her deaf to envious whispers and unwanted glances. Riordan swept her off her feet, and she wrapped one leg around his waist and nestled her face into the crook of his neck and gently cupped the back of his head in her palm.

"You have been a surprise—one we never saw coming," he whispered.

"As have you and your brothers."

The seductive movements of his body, the rich, velvety tone of his voice and his intoxicating, earthly scent evoked a desire and longing that both frightened and aroused her.

He pulled her head back and stared into her eyes before parting her lips. After a long, passion filled kiss, she felt the warmth of his breath in her ear.

"She sleeps beneath the covers, her body soft and still, while he watches from afar. He stands silently in the shadows, breathing in her scent and pondering his intent. Controlled by desires, stirring deep within, is it her blood or his sins calling to him from within?"

In that moment, she knew her secret was clawing its way to the surface.

"Milord, we have them," Riordan heard telepathically. He then set her down and spun around and around, which forced her to let out an amused squeal.

"Where are they now?" Riordan asked.

"They are in the veiled, turrent chamber."

"We will be there momentarily." Riordan then called to Klyn telepathically. *"Klyn, take Sylvana to the floor."*

Klyn materialized behind them and placed his hand on Riordan's shoulder. "Milady, would you do me the honor?"

She looked up at Riordan and he ran his hands down her arms. "My brothers and I need to attend to a small matter. Klyn will keep you company."

"Is everything okay?"

"Yes. You are not the only one who knows how to throw a punch," he replied, along with a wink.

Klyn placed his hand on her lower back and moved across the floor. "What did he mean?" Sylvana asked.

"The altercations when a large group of warriors have been tipping the cup all night are not unexpected."

"I suppose not. I'm glad I'm not involved this time."

"As am I." Klyn chuckled.

Laurent woke up and scanned the dark room, and realized they were in a cell. He slowly sat up and shook Mira, who was still asleep. "Mira, wake up," he whispered.

He shook her harder and moved her hair off her face. She let out a gentle moan and her eyes fluttered.

"Mira, wake up!"

Her eyes gradually opened, and it took her a minute to gather her senses. "Laurent, what happened?"

"We were taken. Now wake up." He placed his arm behind her shoulders and helped her to sit up.

Once Mira regained her senses, she wrapped her arms around Laurent, and he held her tightly against his body. "Where are we?" she whispered.

"I don't know."

Four small torches provided only a somber amount of light, and the wafting shadows that seemed to beckon to her, felt as ominous as they looked. She closed her eyes, tucked her head against his chest, and wept.

Laurent tightened his arms around her body and rested his chin on her head. "Don't cry, Mira. I will protect you."

"Who has taken us? Are we prisoners?"

Laurent gently stroked her back, doing his best to re-assure her. "I don't know, but my father will come for us."

Their bodies lurched when they hear the loud clanks of the locks being pulled from the door.

Riordan, Nicolai, and Kieran walked in and while Kieran and Nicolai approached Mira and Laurent, Riordan leaned against the wall and crossed his arms and legs.

They jumped to their feet, and Laurent straightened his back and, with a slight bow, he addressed them formally. "Milords."

"Milords," Mira said with a courtesy and a sigh of relief. *It's Nicolai, he's come for us.*

"Milords, why are we here?" Laurent asked.

"Why were the two of you traveling through the forest so late at night?" Kieran asked.

Laurent and Mira side-eyed each other but failed to speak.

"It would be best for you to answer my questions voluntarily," Kieran warned.

"I—we were leaving," Laurent replied.

"Why?" Nicolai asked.

"My father, he said we couldn't see each other. I was taking Mira away."

Kieran chuckled and looked back at Riordan and Nicolai. "It seems we have caught a couple of young lovers on the run." He then turned back to Laurent and Mira. "Go on."

"He didn't say why."

"There is a reason—yes?" Nicolai asked.

Mira looked at Laurent with pleading eyes, begging him to keep her secret. "Father said mother wants me to mate another," he lied.

"*Mate another*?" Nicolai repeated.

"Yes. Someone who belongs to the court."

Kieran stepped to the side. "Ohh, I see."

Riordan cocked his head and pushed himself from the wall. "Did you know when you are lost in slumber, the wild one slips through your window to steal the secrets you keep?"

Mira felt the tears pooling in her eyes, realizing Nicolai was not there to save them and she looked at Laurent for reassurance.

Riordan kneeled before her and gently grasped her jaw in his hand. "Do not look at your lover to answer for you. I believe the secret you keep runs deep within your veins."

"Milord," Laurent began as his voice trembled. "She is not keeping a secret."

Riordan let go of Mira's face and stood. "Then maybe it is you who has a secret?"

"No, milord."

Riordan pulled his sword from the sheath that hung on his hip and lifted his chin with the tip. "Are you willing to die to keep her secret safe?"

Mira's breathing accelerated and her body trembled uncontrollably. "Please, milord—please don't hurt him."

"I suggest you speak truthfully. My brother is not very patient," Kieran warned.

As Laurent and Mira stood silently, she heard the faint whisper of her father's words in her head. *On a cold winter's night, the Wolf's Bane moon will rise high into the dark night sky and part the clouds with blood blossomed blooms. Do not listen to the tales like a trembling fool, be still like the wolf or the wolf will come calling for you.* She cupped her trembling hands together when she remembered what the moon looked like when night fell. *It's a full Wolf's Bane moon tonight,* she said to herself. A veil of terror consumed her when Riordan's blade cut through the air as if in slow motion.

"No! Laurent!" She flung her arms out to her sides and a plume of black smoke billowed from her palms before morphing into a trove of bat-like creatures. Their high pitched screeches radiated through the air and echoed off the stone walls as they surrounded Riordan, Nicolai, and Kieran. Laurent dropped to his knees, covered his head, and cowered from the demonic creatures.

Mira stood in place and watched as the winged creatures were easily and swiftly struck down by the Acheron's swords. They dropped from the air and landed on the stone floor all around her; after their twitching bodies became listless, they floated into the air like blackened embers.

Riordan looked at Mira. "Well, hell, that was unexpected."

"The power of life," Nicolai replied.

"Pretty fucking impressive," Kieran added.

Riordan grabbed Laurent's tunic and pulled him to his feet. "Stand, bairn." He then looked at Mira. "Is this the extent of it?"

"Yes, milord," she answered.

"Is Mira an Ascelin?" Kieran questioned telepathically.

Riordan nodded and then looked at Laurent. "I was curious how far Mira would go to save your life. I assume you knew about this?"

Laurent straightened his back and stood firm. "Yes, milord," Laurent stated, not wanting to show any weakness.

Riordan lifted Mira's chin with his fingers. "I will only ask once. Your family, are they purebred Ascelins?"

Mira looked at Riordan and his face blurred, as if he had stepped behind a thin veil of water, knowing she was about to betray her family in the worst possible way. "No, milord," she whispered in a barely audible voice.

He raised an eyebrow and glanced at Nicolai and Kieran before looking at Mira again. "No?"

"No. Not my family, milord."

"Explain, bairn. I will not hesitate to take Laurent's head if need be," Riordan threatened.

She glanced at Nicolai, who raised his sword, tapped it against his shoulder, and nodded toward Laurent.

"I can create life, but Sylvana is the only one whose blood is Ascelin," she admitted.

"Is she a purebred?"

"Yes, milord."

"How do you know this, for sure?"

"Sylvana's mother is a direct descendant."

"What do you mean, *Sylvana's mother*?"

"Mine, Calista's, and Alaric's father took her mother as his mate a few years after ours passed. Sylvana is not his sired offspring."

"Who is Sylvana's father?"

"I don't know?"

"You are awfully young to know of such things. How do we know you are not being deceitful?" Riordan asked.

"It is the truth. Mother told me."

"Does Calista know?"

"Yes, milord."

"Does Sylvana know?" Nicolai asked.

"Yes, milord."

Riordan removed his hand, turned to Nicolai and Kieran, and placed his hand on one of the guard's shoulders. "Move them into the tower chamber. I don't want anyone to so much as hear their whispers."

"Yes, milord."

As they left, Mira spoke up from behind. "Are we your prisoners?"

They turned ever so slightly and looked at her. "Consider yourselves our guests," Nicolai replied.

"You will regret this when Sylvana finds out what you have done."

"Mira!" Laurent snapped.

They glanced at each other, and a look of amusement crossed their faces. "Is that so?" Riordan asked.

She crossed her arms and lifted her chin. "Yes, milord."

Laurent nudged her with his shoulder. "Stop it!" he whispered.

"Sylvana will find out soon enough," Nicolai stated.

Mira glanced at Laurent and then back at the brothers. "Are you going to tell her?" she asked.

"Yes," Kiran replied.

The heavy door shut, and Laurent spun Mira around to face him. "Never speak to them in such a manner again! Do you want to get us killed?"

She plopped down on the tattered mattress, pulled her knees tightly against her chest, and sobbed. "Sylvana is going to hate me!"

Laurent walked over and stroked her head. "She will understand, Mira."

"She will never forgive me, and neither will my family!"

After siting with her for a few minutes, Laurent wandered around the cell and then placed his ear against the door and listened; all he heard were a few ghostly moans and intermittent cries of pain echoing from somewhere off in the distance. He jumped back when the lock clanked and hurried over to Mira.

"Come with us," the guard stated.

The guards escorted them up numerous sets of stairs and down various hallways before coming to the end of another corridor. The guard opened the door, ushered them in, and then shut and locked it. They looked around and it was an elaborate chamber rather than another cell.

"Are we really their guests?" Mira asked, feeling confused.

"I don't know what is going on. First, we were in a cell and now we're here?"

They walked over to the large windows at the opposite end and realized they were at the top of the Castle. Laurent turned the lock and tried to open a window, but it was sealed shut. "We are still locked up." He sighed.

Mira looked through the beveled glass and stared at the moon. "What have I done?" she stated softly.

"You didn't have a choice. They will understand."

"I like the bairn. She has Sylvana's courage." Nicolai chuckled.

"Yes, she does," Riordan replied.

"How the fuck did Kadric take a purebred Ascelin as his mate and go undetected?" Nicolai asked.

"There is only who knows what took place. We need to find Kadric," Riordan replied.

"There is a lot more to this story," Kieran stated.

"There sure is," Nicolai replied.

Riordan placed his hand on their shoulders as they walked. "I'm not sure I buy it?"

"Neither do I. Something is amiss. It doesn't add up," Nicolai agreed.

"The Wolf's Bane Moon will be at its peak tonight," Riordan said.

"We no longer have any doubt who Sylvana is," Nicolai replied.

"Have you brought this up to the Guild?" Kieran asked.

Riordan squeezed his shoulder. "No."

"I am not sure Sylvana will agree?" Nicolai chuckled.

"She will choose wisely," Riordan replied.

"Have you had anymore shifter encounters?" Klyn asked with a coy smile.

"No." Sylvana smiled.

"Other than your little altercation, have you enjoyed the evening?"

"Very much so."

Klyn nodded in the opposite direction. "It appears Alaric has put the blade down." He spun her around and she looked at Alaric, who had Muriel wrapped in his arms as they glided across the floor.

"For now anyway," she replied.

The music slowed and Klyn looked down at her. "Would you like a drink?"

"I would."

He placed his hand on her lower back and he escorted her to her ladies.

"Where are your three overlords?" Venthana joked when she and Klyn walked over.

"I think another fight broke out," Sylvana replied.

"I would expect nothing less from this crowd." Venthana chuckled.

Riordan appeared behind Klyn, placed a couple of hard pats on his shoulder and looked at Sylvana. "Is he still dancing with feet made of clay?"

"No." She chuckled.

Riordan then spoke to Klyn telepathically. *"Keep a sharp eye on Alaric."*

"Yes, milord."

Riordan turned his attention back to Sylvana. "There is someone you need to see."

She glanced at the brothers. "Who?"

"A special guest of ours," Riordan replied.

"Shall we?" Nicolai asked as he and Kieran held out their elbows.

Chapter 13

Kadric awoke to the sounds of the lock rattling and slowly sat up, feeling groggy and out of sorts. A young gal walked in carrying a tray with a single silver goblet. She had a sculpted figure with a tapered waist and a burnished complexion. A pair of arched eyebrows framed her sweeping lashes, and her constellation blue eyes stood out against her raven-black hair. Kadric noticed a shadow move serenely behind her as she shut the door. *She is not alone,* he told himself. He stood defensively, not knowing what was in store for him.

Her hair fell over her shoulder when she set the tray down on the stone slab and as she swept it back over her shoulder, she subtly dragged her finger across her throat. Kadric picked up the cup and looked at the burgundy liquid and swirled it around. "What's this?" he asked.

"Fresh cruor," she replied quietly.

He set it back down. "I'll pass. They have drugged me once already."

"'Tis clean. You may drink freely," she replied.

She looks familiar, he thought. "What is your name?"

Without moving her head, she glanced behind her. "I will leave it. Should you change your mind?"

As she collected the tray, he noticed a deep scar across her opposite wrist.

"Do not drink," she stated telepathically.

"Who are you?"

"I have only ill begotten memories. But I know I do not belong here. Your scent is familiar. Are you Nosferatu?"

"I am. And you are as well?" Kadric asked.

"Yes," she replied.

"Do you know why, or how long you have been here?"

"I know not why, and I have been here as long as I can remember. I serve thy Faye Priestess."

"Maybe we can help each other?" he replied.

"'Tis impossible. Word of warning. I learned long ago to cloak my thoughts. Do not think what you do not want them to know. They are listening."

"Can you tell me anything?"

"You are now at their mercy." She suddenly straightened her back, tucked the tray under her arm and left.

Mira and Laurent jumped to their feet when they heard the lock on the door clink. Sylvana was in shock when she saw Mira and Laurent. "What the hell?"

Mira ran to her and wrapped her arms around her waist, and Laurent stood quietly by the window. "I'm so sorry Sylvana, I didn't—they made—I didn't have a choice." She sobbed.

Sylvana pulled her arms from around her waist and kneeled down and held her hands. "Mira, calm down and take a breath."

Mira let out a few breathless sobs, pulled her hands away, and wrapped them around Sylvana's neck.

Sylvana held her tightly, looked at Laurent, and held her hand out to him. "Come here, Laurent."

He walked over and she wrapped her arm around him and then walked them to the settee. She then looked at the brothers. "One of you had better explain to me what the hell they are doing here?"

Riordan took a seat and crossed one leg over his knee and set his goblet down on the table. "Mira and Laurent ran away tonight. I'll let the bairns explain."

She kneeled down before them. "Mira, what is going on?"

"I'm sorry Sylvie," was all she managed to say in-between her heavy breaths.

"Laurent, tell me what's happened," Sylvana said.

He nervously eyed the brothers, and Riordan nodded. "It is true. Father said Mira and I were not to see each other for a-while so Mira and I left. We were only planning on being gone for a few days."

Sylvana knew immediately based on Mira's emotional state of mind and how Laurent failed to make eye contact with her, there was more to the story. *This is bad on so many levels,* she thought.

Mira placed her hand on Sylvana's, discretely turned her palm up, and opened and closed her fist. Sylvana looked into Mira's eyes, feeling as though someone had just shoved her off a cliff. She took a deep breath and closed her eyes. *They know everything,* she said to herself. After a moment of gathering her composure, she stood protectively in front of Mira and Laurent, turned toward the brothers, and crossed her arms. "So now what?"

"*So now* we have a real conversation, but I think it's best if Mira and Laurent weren't present," Riordan replied.

"What are you going to do with them?"

"They will not be harmed. They will be down the hall," Nicolai replied.

Riordan called to the guard telepathically. *"Take Laurent and Mira to the chamber two doors down."*

He walked in and nodded. "Milords." He then motioned for Mira and Laurent to follow.

Mira wrapped her arms around Sylvana. "I never meant to tell them. Please forgive me," she pleaded.

Sylvana hugged her tightly. "It will be okay, Mira." She then lifted her chin and smiled. "I won't let anything happen to you or Laurent, and Alaric is also here."

"Do you hate me?" Mira asked.

Sylvana cupped her face in her hands and smiled. "I could never hate you, Mira."

Nicolai walked over and reached for Sylvana's hand, but she pulled it away. "Do not touch me."

"Have a seat, Sylvana," Riordan stated.

She sat on the edge of the settee while Nicolai and Kieran took a seat opposite her.

"How did you find them if they ran away? And why did you bring them here?"

"As you are aware, we have been monitoring the acreage around your manor. Our warriors found them deep in the forest and brought them here for their own safety," Riordan stated.

"For their own safety? Bullshit, you could have taken them home," she stated.

Riordan spun the glass in his hand and took a sip. "We could have. However, your lives are in jeopardy and the sooner we uncovered the truth, the sooner we could make arrangements for you and your family."

"What arrangements? And why are our lives in jeopardy?"

"The Lycans are aware of your existence, and we fear the Faye is as well," Riordan replied.

"And what about my father?"

"We have yet to locate him, and I assume he has gotten himself into a precarious situation," Riordan answered.

"What about Calista and Alaric?"

"Alaric is here, we have eyes on him, and a few of our warriors will stay back to watch over Calista when they take Laurent home."

"I want to be the one to explain things to them."

"As you wish." Riordan nodded. "There is one thing you need to know. We have blocked you from speaking to Calista and Alaric telepathically outside of these walls."

"Why?"

"We don't want someone hearing a conversation that would relay pertinent information they could use against you and/or your family."

"I don't appreciate the way you all are making these decisions without my knowledge, much less my opinion. Calista and I can cloak our own damn conversations."

"As well as you did with Riordan?" Nicolai questioned.

Her head snapped in Nicolai's direction, and Riordan held up his hands as a gesture of peace. "There are others, Sylvana, who can listen as easily as I," Riordan said.

Sylvana cupped her hands together, rested her arms on her knees, and looked down, fearing the worst. "Will you find my father?"

"We are doing our best. I have ordered a legion of Barouqe Warriors to locate him."

"What are you going to do with him?" she asked nervously.

"It will depend upon the circumstances. We will not tolerate dissonance, nor will we tolerate betrayal against the Guild. If your father is simply seeking answers, as we all are, then we will release him. He has been a loyal member of the Legion and a high-ranking warrior for the Cynfadel's. We will give him the benefit of the doubt—for the time being," Riordan answered frankly.

Sylvana cocked her head and furrowed her brow. "Are you willing to kill my father?"

"It is not our intention. To hurt your father would be to hurt you. However, if he has gotten himself involved with Ranan, he may have already sealed his own fate."

"Do you think he's dead?" she asked.

"It's too early to make such an assumption," Riordan replied.

"Fuck me," Sylvana stood, paced back and forth, and then walked to the window, leaned against the pane, and stared at the swirling, magenta moon.

Nicolai meandered over and wrapped his arms around her shoulders and chest. "I know this much to take in, but we need you to trust us."

"How am I to trust this entire situation?" she asked.

Kieran walked over and turned her face toward him. "Darling, have we not made it clear all along how we feel about you?"

"I think it has more to do with me being a purebred. Would either of you ever laid sight on me if you had not been suspicious?"

"It is true we sought you out, thinking you may be a purebred. However, Nicolai and I felt an undeniable pull toward you the first night we met, and Riordan felt it the night we were in the library."

She looked over at Riordan. "Speaking of which, when you asked me to read from the book, was it some kind of test?"

"Yes," Riordan answered as he stood. "It was written in an ancient Faye dialect, and you read it flawlessly."

"So all this time you have known who I am and yet not one of you had the decency to tell me?"

"It was of no consequence. We found you and it's all that matters. It wouldn't have changed anything for us. However, had we told you under different circumstances, I think it's safe to assume you or your family would have made a rash decision, one which would have left you vulnerable to both the Lycans and the Faye," Riordan replied.

"This is too much to comprehend. I don't know what to think?" Sylvana shrugged.

"My brothers had already made up their minds so regardless of whether you were or were not a purebred, they were not giving you up," Riordan stated.

Sylvana stared at Riordan momentarily. "And what about you?"

"I have feelings for you I am unprepared to describe in words, but I will honor you in every way. It's as if a fountain of life has emerged from a barren past."

"And had other purebreds presented themselves, would you still have chosen me?"

"Yes," the three of them answered in unison.

"And what if a female with majestic looks, or a female with title and status, or a female who didn't have dirt under her nails, stood at my side? Would you have looked at me then?"

"Without a doubt," Nicolai stated.

"It's not what your reputations suggest," Sylvana replied. "I fear you are only choosing me because I am your only choice?"

Nicolai leaned against the window next to her and glanced at the moon before looking down at her. "For centuries we have been living in a self-imposed cage, never to be free with thought, nor desire, nor love. Call it wanderlust, if you will, but we have always known our hearts, our blood belong to only one. There has been nothing, no one, who has affected us the way you have."

"Nicolai speaks the truth. You are our perfect match in every way, Sylvana," Kieran added.

Riordan placed his fingers beneath her chin and gazed into her eyes. "There are others, Sylvana, and we choose you."

"*Others?*" she questioned.

"Yes. They are being sought as we speak, and we have entrusted their care to the Guild. We have no desire for another," Riordan replied.

"I don't know what to say or what to do?" Sylvana stated.

"You need to make a choice before we leave here," Riordan stated.

"What choice would that be?"

"We plan on taking you as our mate tonight," Riordan admitted.

Sylvana cocked her head to the side. "You expect me to mate the three of you—tonight?"

"What Riordan is trying to say is we would like for you to agree to become our mate," Nicolai interjected.

Sylvana looked at Riordan. "And if I don't agree?"

"You have said all along you don't want to be our bedmate, and we have never been deceitful with you regarding our feelings where you are concerned," Kieran answered.

"You can't kidnap Mira and Laurent. Tell me about my father and then spring this *choice* on me."

"We took them in order to uncover the truth for many reasons. Had the Lycans found about Mira first, I can assure you the consequences would have been dire," Riordan explained.

"Why didn't you just ask me?""Would you have told us the truth?" Nicolai asked.

"Well, no—I mean maybe. Hell, I don't know?"

Riordan ran his hands down her arms. "Sylvana, you are a purebred Ascelin. You deserve to be respected, protected, and loved. We will hold you in the highest of regard and you should not have to live your life hiding in the shadows. Have we given you any reason to think that we would cause you or your family harm?"

"No, you haven't."

He cupped her amulet in his hand. "Sângele Nostru, agree to become our mate."

"What does Sângele Nostru mean?"

Riordan kissed her cheek. "It means our blood."

"Your blood?"

"Yes. You belong to us," Riordan replied.

"I don't belong to anyone, and what about my family, and Laurent? Not to mention Calista must be worried sick."

"We will make it known your family is under our protection. I will send Laurent back to his manor tonight unscathed, and Mira will remain here."

Sylvana backed away, walked over to the table, and picked up Riordan's glass. "I can't think right now. And I am certainly not worthy of what you are offering me."

"Look at me and tell me you do not desire us as much as we desire you," Riordan said.

"I won't even try to deny it," she replied. "Who has wronged you so badly you think yourself unworthy?" Nicolai asked.

Sylvana looked out the window, not wanting to make eye contact. "You have witnessed for yourselves the way I am treated. Enatta, the ladies of court, as well as the Helots in the fields. I am deemed no better than a serf by anyone with status—shall I go on?" She finished the drink and set the glass back down, trying to do anything other than look at them.

The brothers glanced at each other and felt terrible seeing her looking so forlorn. *"If we have played any role in this—"* Nicolai said telepathically.

"We will have an eternity to make it up to her," Riordan replied.

Kieran placed his hand on her shoulder and gently squeezed it. "I'm sorry, Sylvana."

"Sylvana, look at us. We need a decision," Riordan urged.

"If I agree, how will this work?"

"All you have to do is agree. We will worry about the details," Riordan replied.

Kieran walked over and wrapped her in his arms. "We have waited a lifetime for you, and you need to know there is nothing we would deny you."

"You need to decide, Sylvana," Riordan stated again. "The Wolf's Bane Moon won't rise for another two seasons. I know this situation is difficult. It is not easy for any of us to be here with the choices that are being thrust upon us, but you are the better part of us. Allow us our destiny and we will show you a life you never dreamt of."

Nicolai lifted her chin and stole a heated kiss. "Is this not what you want?" he whispered.

"I do," she replied in a hushed tone.

Riordan picked her up and held her firmly against his body. "You won't regret this."

"I sure hope not."

"Laurent?" Enatta called out. Not getting a response, she headed up the stairs to his bedchamber, opened the door, and noticed his window was open; she rushed over and looked down. "Cadell! Cadell!"

He appeared in the doorway. "Enatta, what the hell is wrong?"

"I can't find Laurent anywhere."

He walked over to the window, leapt out, and headed for the barn. As he pulled the door open, Rhone was also missing. "Dammit that bairn!"

Enatta appeared behind him. "If anything happens to Laurent, I will never forgive myself!"

"I assume he's run away with Mira. This is not the first time they have disappeared. I will go to the Orfaedo's manor. Maybe Calista has seen them?"

"Cadell, I have a terrible feeling something is wrong. A mother knows."

He wrapped his arms around her. "My love, I will find him. I will send word to the Legion, and they will help in the search. Stay here and call to me if he returns."

"Aren't they all at the ceremony?" she asked.

"You know we have never left the villages vulnerable to attack. There are enough warriors around, and they will help me search for them."

He mounted his stallion and headed for the Orfaedo's. "Calista?" he called out as he knocked on her door. "Calista, it's Cadell."

Calista opened the door and covered herself with her shawl. "Cadell, what's wrong?"

"Laurent is missing, and I believe he may be with Mira," he replied calmly.

"Shit!" She turned, ran through the parlor and up the stairs while Cadell followed. "Mira?" she said, as she opened her chamber door and glanced around.

"She's not here. Damn that girl!"

They walked around the room and then opened the armoire doors only to notice her bag was missing. Meantime Cadell had walked over to the bureau; one drawer was partially askew and the clothes were disheveled. "At least we know they are together."

"We have to go find them, and I need to let Alaric and Sylvana know they are missing," Calista stated.

"You can't speak to them," Cadell replied.

"Why not?"

"There is an energetic veil blocking all communication from being relayed. If you're outside the walls, you can't communicate to anyone on the inside. If you within the castle walls, you can't communicate with anyone on the outside."

"How is it possible?"

"Only the Acherons and the Guild know its secret. It has been this way since the end of the war. For security reasons, they grant the only outside communication to those who serve the crown, such as the Barouqe Warriors."

"I had no idea," Calista replied. "It explains why I couldn't get a hold of Sylvana the night she didn't come home."

"Stay here and let me know if Mira returns. I have called upon the Legion, and they are headed here as we speak. We will go in search of them," Cadell said.

"I'm coming with you. We both know she's not coming back tonight."

"I think it would be best for you to remain here."

"Absolutely not. I need two minutes to change and if you don't take me with, I will go on my own."

Cadell stared at her and how she tilted her head to let him know she would not waiver.

"I'll be waiting outside. I assume your mare is in the barn?"

"Yes."

As they headed outside the Legion's stallions were galloping down the road. She mounted her mare and they met the warriors halfway.

Cadell placed his fist to his heart and nodded. "As you know, Laurent and Mira are missing. I can only think of one place they would feel safe for the night. I would assume they have headed for our country estate."

"Then we have no time to waste," Leodion replied.

Their stallions thundered down the winding dirt road; once the trees thinned, they slowed and then came to a stop at the edge of tree line.

"It's awfully dark in there," Cadell stated.

"I assume they wouldn't light the lanterns if they were trying to be discrete," Markus replied.

Cadell kicked his stallions' hindquarters, and they trotted across the field. He looked down and noticed multiple sets of fresh imprints. "Leodion, someone else has been here."

Most of the members of the legion spread out in a defensive position while the rest dismounted and walked around the area.

"It looks like they headed away from the manor," another stated as he studied the tracks.

"Shit!" Cadell mounted his stallion, who broke into a gallop toward the cottage. "Laurent?"

"Mira?" Calista yelled.

"We will surround the manor," Markus said as he motioned for a half of the warriors to head in opposite directions. Meanwhile, Leodion had dismounted his stallion along with a few others, all of whom followed Cadell.

Cadell slowly opened the door, cautiously walked in and they spanned out. "It doesn't appear as if anyone has been here."

"I can't sense anyone," Leodion stated.

"Laurent?" Cadell called out.

"Mira, if you are here, come out right now!" Calista demanded.

"They have not been here," another stated as he appeared from around the corner.

"The tracks in the field. I fear someone has taken them," Cadell stated.

"It appears so," Leodion agreed. "We followed one set of tracks here and there are multiple tracks heading in the opposite direction."

"Cadell, please tell me they are going to be okay," Calista stated.

Cadell turned to her and placed his hand on her shoulder. "We will locate them, but I think it would be best to have you escorted back to your manor. I don't know what or who we will be facing."

"I cannot go back and sit all night worrying. I need to go to the castle and inform Alaric and Sylvana."

"Lass, they will have it heavily guarded it tonight. You will not make it past the front gate," Leodion replied.

"Cadell, we have company," Markus said telepathically.

They rushed outside and noticed a large group of warriors in the tree line. "What the hell?" Cadell stated.

They mounted their stallions and drew their swords. "Calista, go inside, lock the door and do not come out," Cadell demanded.

Calista stood momentarily as she stared at the warriors.

"Go, now!" Cadell stated firmly.

She ran inside, shut the door, and peered out the window.

"Defensive line!" Markus ordered.

They squinted their eyes, sharpened their eyesight, and noticed their elaborate helmets.

Cadell, Markus, and Leodion glanced at each other. "They are the Acherons Baroque Warriors," Cadell stated.

"What the hell are they doing here?" Leodion asked.

They placed their swords back into their sheaths and waited as the Baroque warriors headed in their direction.

Each of them placed a fist over their hearts and nodded respectfully when they met them in the middle of the field.

"I am looking for Cadell Marque," one of them stated.

"I am Cadell Marque," he replied.

"The Acherons sent us."

"On what business?" Cadell asked.

He looked behind him, waved his hand, and as the warriors parted Laurent appeared on Rhone.

"Laurent?" Cadell said.

"Father!"

They dismounted, and Cadell caught him in his arms when he leapt toward him. "Why do you have my son?"

"The Acherons asked us to bring him back. We know nothing more."

Calista ran up from behind. "Where is Mira?"

"Under the protection of the Acherons."

"Why? Has something happened to Sylvana?"

"No. Two of my warriors will escort you to your manor and will remain as guard for the time being," he replied.

"Tell me! What the hell is going on?"

Cadell's head snapped in her direction. "Mind your tongue, Calista," he stated firmly.

"Milord, I appreciate you escorting my bairn home and let the Acherons know I owe them a debt of gratitude," Cadell stated.

The warrior pulled his stallion's reins, and they left.

Calista looked at Cadell and whispered. "Why are they placing us under guard?"

"I don't know?" He then looked at Markus and Leodion and spoke telepathically. *"This can't be good."*

"No," Markus replied.

"Markus and I will stay at your manor tonight and I will have the others remain close by until we figure out what is happening," Leodion said.

Cadell nodded and turned his attention back to Laurent. "Let's get you home. Your mother is worried sick."

"Father, I am so sorry." Laurent tried to be stoic, but his body's innate reactions failed him; he could not stop trembling and tears dripped from his eyes.

Cadell wrapped Laurent in a tight embrace, and he rested his head on his father's shoulder and faced Calista. "Calista, I'm sorry. I did not mean to get Mira in trouble."

"It's okay, Laurent."

"Calista, I would like for you to stay at my manor tonight," Cadell offered.

"I appreciate the offer, but I will feel more comfortable at home."

"Considering the recent situation, I insist."

"Not to be rude, but I am not comfortable being around Enatta. You know how she feels about us."

"I understand, and I will speak to her before arriving. I will give you a formal order if needed. Your brother will most likely be gone all night, and after what has just taken place, I will not leave Kadric's daughter to fend for herself."

"Cadell, please."

"Let's go," he replied.

Laurent rode up next to Calista. "I won't let my mother bother you."

"That's very sweet of you, Laurent." She smiled. *I'd rather be in a fucking cell for the night than stay with that wretched lady.*

Chapter 14

Sylvana looked at Riordan when they passed Nicolai's door. "Where are we going?"

"To my chamber," he replied.

Sylvana's face paled, and each step felt as if it was in unison with the slow, dragging beat of her heart. "All of us?" she asked meekly.

"No. It will be you and I, for now."

He opened the door and held it open with his palm. Nicolai kissed the back of her hand while Kieran kissed her forehead.

"We will return," Nicolai stated.

It was as if she had walked through an energetic veil when she stepped across the threshold; his bedchamber was as opulent and regal as Nicolai's.

"Do not be nervous. I will only bite once," he said with a half-cocked grin.

She glanced up at him and smiled nervously. "Only once?"

He filled two glasses and handed her one. "I want you to feel comfortable." He took a seat on the settee and motioned for her to sit next to him.

Feeling too nervous to strike up a casual conversation, she looked down at their feet and then at Riordan. "I believe we forgot to take our shoes off."

"I think we'll live." He winked.

"Can I be honest with you?" she asked.

"I expect nothing less," he replied.

"I'm afraid I'm making a rash decision," she admitted.

"What can I do to put your mind at ease?"

"I'm not sure?" she replied.

"You have brought up our reputations frequently and I can assure you there will never be another and we would do nothing to dishonor you." He waited momentarily and when she didn't reply, he pulled her thoughts. "You are worried about those we have bedded?"

She looked up at him and furrowed her brow. "I will stop you from listening."

"Never." He smiled.

"How many?" she asked.

"What does it matter?"

"It matters to me, Riordan. How many of the ladies of court will I have to contend with, knowing they have been with you and your brothers intimately? I should at least have a heads up after what happened earlier."

"If it would make you feel at ease, I have no problem dismissing them from court."

"How many, Riordan?"

"We would lose half the court," he joked.

Sylvana's eyes widened, her face froze, and she didn't know how to reply.

He chuckled and squeezed her thigh. "I'm joking, Sylvana. We have never bedded the ladies of our own court, for many reasons. The altercation that took place earlier is a prime example of why we don't."

Sylvana let out a sigh of relief. "Good to know. I'd hate to run into a bunch of scorned lovers."

Riordan chuckled, placed his hand on her neck, and stroked it with his fingers. "May I ask you a question?"

"Yes."

"Nicolai and Kieran said you have only been with one other. Is it true?"

Instead of reciprocating his gaze, she looked down at her glass. "Yes. Why do you ask?"

"Who was it?"

She looked up at him, not expecting his bluntness. Although, if she were being honest with herself, she was not the least bit surprised. "What does it matter?" She asked, doing her best to not let his name cross her mind.

"It matters to us," he replied as he pulled his boots off.

"I—I mean, I don't want to betray him."

He picked up one of her legs at a time and removed her shoes. "Sylvana, we are about to be mated. There has to be trust amongst us."

"What are you going to do if I reveal his name?"

"Nothing, unless he gives us a reason."

"And what reason would he give you?" "As long as he respects the fact you belong to us, he will not cross our minds."

"You promise you will do nothing?"

"I give you my word, Sylvana."

"It was Alaric's friend, Florin. It was a lifetime ago. We were only about seventeen years old, and it only lasted one season."

"Does Alaric know?" Riordan asked.

"I don't think so? I can only assume Florin wouldn't have dishonored me by telling him."

"All this time, why have you not been with another?"

"I don't know? I guess I never wanted to let anyone get close to me. In the back of my mind, I was afraid I would reveal my true bloodline to him."

Riordan lifted her chin and his mouth fell to hers; after a passionate kiss, he pulled away ever so slightly. "Those days are over."

He stood, pulled her to her feet, cupped the back of her head in his hand, and took her mouth to his again.

She slid her hands up his solid chest, over his shoulders, and melted in his arms. He led her across the chamber and stopped at the edge of the bed.

"What I feel for you, I will never understand," he admitted.

She placed her hands on his chest. "I'm scared."

He lifted her chin and gazed into her eyes. "You will have nothing to fear again, least of all myself or my brothers." He then removed her leather strap and slowly unlaced the back of her dress.

Her hands trembled as she slid them up his chest and undid the straps over his shoulders securing his vest. He pulled it off, tossed it to the side, and then seductively kissed the crook of her neck as he slid her dress down her arms. "Your skin is as soft as silk," he whispered, as he pulled his tunic over his head.

She glided her hands up his chest, and over his muscular shoulders as he pushed her dress the rest of the way down her body. He then slid his tongue down her neck, and a soft rumble rose from his chest. "Your blood is calling to me."

Once her dress fell to the floor, he cupped her breast in one hand, and slid the other over her ass. He then removed his trousers, picked her up, and laid her on her back.

"I can hear your blood coursing through your veins." He glided his hand across her stomach, up her body, and then cupped her breast in his hand and suckled her erect nipples.

He pushed her legs further apart with his and dragged his canines down the vein on her neck, which forced her heart to skip a beat. He then slid his hand up her thigh and massaged it, all the while slowly rocking his hips back and forth, rubbing his hardened erection against her nub.

Damn, I want him, she thought, as she slid her hands across his back, feeling his muscles flex and relax each time he moved. "You feel amazing," she whispered.

"You pull my desire like no other," he stated.

He glided his hand up her waist and across her ribs; he then ran his thumb over her hard, pink bud and a soft moan escaped her mouth, yearning for more.

His lips brushed hers just long enough to inhale her breath. The way she tasted, and the nervous beat of her heart ramped up his need to possess her in every way. With each gentle touch of his, her moans grew with a nervous anticipation.

He pulled away and peered into his soon to be mate's eyes. "You are making the right decision, and we will do nothing to make you regret it," he whispered.

"I believe you," she replied.

He kissed her neck, slid his tongue across her throat and over her hammering pulse. He then trailed gentle kisses down her neck, slid his hand between her legs, and slipped his fingers into her wet core.

She gasped and arched her back, needing, wanting more. He rubbed her sex with his thumb, all the while sliding his fingers in and out of her core. He licked and kissed his way down her stomach, and her body quivered beneath his touch.

He moved further down, placed his face between her legs, pushed her knees to the side, and swirled his tongue around her sex.

Her moans grew in intensity, and the sensation overtook her as he suckled her nub. She grabbed the back of his head with one hand and bunched the blanket in the other.

"Riordan," she whispered. "I want you inside me."

He sucked harder, shoved his fingers deeper, and her sex pulsed beneath his lips.

"Riordan," she moaned with a raspy whisper. "I want you now," she said as her climax rose, and her body convulsed with its release. He continued to tease her body until the heated orgasm consumed her.

Once she had finished, he crawled up her body and shoved his tongue back into her mouth. With a gentle thrust, he inserted his cock into the heat of her throbbing core and gently turned her head, exposing her neck. "Say the words, agree to become my mate."

"Riordan, wait," she whispered.

"All you have to do is say yes, Sângele Nostru."

"Ye—yes," she stammered. She felt the bite in her very core when his lips sealed tightly around her neck. A painful sensation danced across her nerve endings when his canines sunk deep into her tender flesh. "Oh, shit," she said quietly.

Her blood flowed over his tongue, and every swallow brought about his need to cum inside her, to consume her, to possess her. He was also shocked at the intensity with which her blood hit him. *Ahh fuck, it's ancient, cold even. I have tasted nothing like it.*

After taking what he needed, he released his grip and offered his vein to her. "Take my blood, darling, and it will bond us for an eternity."

Her canines pierced deep into his musky flesh, and she savored every drop. However, the unexpected intensity of his blood coursing through her body hit her immediately; it was as if he was consuming her from the inside out.

"Not too much, darling. Your body will need to adjust to the power of my blood." He pulled away ever so slightly and rocked his hips with greater intensity and she reveled in the painful, erotic pleasure of his large, solid shaft.

He pumped harder, lifted her leg further over his hip. She arched her back and grabbed a fist-full of his hair.

"Riordan—what's happening? It feels like our worlds are colliding," she said as she moaned.

"Shh, don't fight it."

The pulsing of her core around his shaft, along with the knowledge she was his blood

bonded mate pulled his orgasm to the surface; he dropped his head to the side of hers and let out a deep chested growl as he released himself into her core.

"Oh, damn," Sylvana cried out when her body was swept into another heated release.

He fell on top of her and laid there quietly, as their chests rose and fell together. After a moment, he raised up, removed his amulet, and placed it around her neck. "You are mine, say it.

"I am yours," she whispered.

He rolled over and wrapped her in his arms and they lay quietly for a time, each contemplating the power and intensity of the bond. "What are you thinking, darling?" he asked.

"How amazing it feels to be in your arms," she replied.

"From here forward, everyone will know you as Sylvana Phaidra Ascelin-Acheron."

"You are letting me keep my sired name, Ascelin?"

"Yes. I told you once, never to forget your past. The name Ascelin deserves to stand next to ours."

"Phaidra was my mother's name."

"We know," Riordan admitted as he gently stroked her neck and shoulder.

"Why does it not surprise me?" She drifted her hand up his stomach and over his chest. "Riordan?"

"Yes, darling?"

"Tell me I did the right thing. I feel as though I let my desire overtake my reasoning, but I can't imagine my life without you in it."

He rose onto his elbow and moved her hair off her forehead. "On my honor as an Acheron, my life is yours. There is nothing I wouldn't give to you and nothing I wouldn't do for you."

"I never expected to feel such a powerful bond," she said.

He rolled on top of her and stole another heated kiss. Her lips were warm and soft as they parted slightly, allowing his tongue to slip inside. "I should take you again. However, I believe my brothers are anxiously awaiting their turn to bond with you."

"I'm anxious as well," she admitted.

"I should make them wait until the moon is about to disappear into the horizon."

"What would they think?"

"They would wear a path in the rug." He chuckled. "On a serious note, are you ready?"

"I am."

Enatta heard the sounds of stallion's hooves clacking against the stone road leading to the front of her manor. She ran outside and Cadell, along with a dozen warriors, were headed in her direction. She ran down the steps and called out. "Cadell, do you have Laurent?"

He pulled his stallion to a halt, and she reached up and placed her hand on his thigh. "Yes. He is safe, my love."

The warrior's parted, and Laurent rode up, and Calista was riding next to him. She glared at Cadell with furrowed brows.

"I expect you to be courteous and make her feel welcomed. Understand me?" "I will be as pleasant as she is."

Cadell placed his hand on hers and squeezed. *"You will do better, or you will find yourself sleeping in the barn,"* he threatened telepathically.

She pulled her hand away and rushed to Laurent. "Laurent, you scared me to death."

He dismounted, and they wrapped their arms around each other. "I am sorry, Mother. I never meant for any of this to happen."

She pulled back and cupped his face in her hands. "Laurent, what happened? And where is Mira?"

Cadell placed his hand on her shoulder. "Let's go inside and I'll explain." He then walked to Calista and held her mare's reins. "It will be fine."

She dismounted and reluctantly followed him and as they walked past Enatta, Calista gave her a forced smile and although Enatta smiled back, her eyes remained cold and judgmental.

She is a smug and disingenuous shrew. I can't, for the life of me, figure out what Cadell sees in her? Calista thought.

Riordan called to Nicolai and Kieran telepathically. *"It's time."*

They materialized at the edge of the bed, removed their clothes, and crawled over Sylvana's body while Riordan got out of bed, filled a glass, and took a seat on the chair.

"Our turn," Nicolai whispered as he slid his hand between her legs and massaged her sex. Kieran twirled his tongue over her soft buds and suckled them while Nicolai parted her

mouth with his. After a moment, Nicolai pulled away. "Are you ready, love?"

"I am."

"All you have to do is say yes." He then bent down and whispered in her ear. "First, I need you to know I truly love you."

"I love you too, Nicolai, and yes." She turned her head to the side, and his canines pierced her flesh. After taking what he needed, he turned his head to the side. "Take my vein, darling."

Nicolai's blood flowed over her tongue, and with each swallow, the same sensation took over; he too, was attaching himself to her from the inside out. She pulled her canines from his flesh and he took her mouth to his, reveling in the taste of his own blood on her tongue. He then pulled away and removed his amulet and placed it around her neck. "You are mine. Say it."

"I am yours."

Kieran cupped her face in his palm and gazed into her emerald-green eyes. "Say yes." "Yes."

Having completed the bond, he placed his amulet around her neck. "You are mine. Say it."

"I am yours."

Kieran grabbed her, playfully rolled over, and pinned her arms above her head. "My cock is already throbbing." He scooted up and slid his tip across her lips while Nicolai spread her legs and shoved his cock into her core. She let out a small gasp and Riordan, who was already on the bed, rose on to his knees and nodded to Kieran, who moved to the other side of her.

Sylvana wrapped a fist around Riordan's and Kieran's shafts and took them into her mouth, alternating between them. She suddenly stopped and looked at them with a devious smile.

They cocked their heads, looked at each other, and then down at Sylvana. "What are you up to?" Riordan asked, curiously.

"I want to drink from your vein," she replied.

"As you wish," Riordan replied. He began to pull back, and she wrapped her fist tighter around his shaft. "I want to drink from this vein." She then slid her canines along the length of his shaft.

Nicolai pushed himself deep into her core and held himself steady as he, Kieran, and Riordan glanced at each other.

"Is that a problem, milord?" she asked playfully. She then nipped his tip, and he flinched.

"Riordan, you're not afraid, are you?" Kieran joked.

"No. I've just never had someone ask if they could bite my cock."

"If you're not afraid, why do you hesitate?" Nicolai teased.

"I believe your cock belongs to me," Sylvana said seductively.

Nicolai and Kieran laughed aloud. "She's not wrong, Rio," Nicolai said.

Riordan let out a low rumble, nodded at her, and then playfully slapped her lips with his dick. "Don't damage the goods." He winked.

The brother's watch in anticipation as she licked, kissed, and sucked Riordan's shaft. She then bared her canines, and he placed one hand on Kieran's shoulder and fisted her hair with the other. "Fuck me, this is an unexpected turn on," Nicolai mumbled. He rocked his hips, unable to remain still any longer.

"You're telling the truth," Kieran replied, as he cupped his shaft in his fist and massaged it.

Riordan took a deep breath and a jolt of pain radiated from his cock and spread throughout his body.

Sylvana watched Riordan as she pulled his blood into her mouth, and other than his eyes widening, his expression remained stoic. "Oh fuck, I'm going to cum," he groaned.

She retracted her canines, and he slid his shaft as far into her mouth as he could, and the liquid spilled from his tip.

She then looked at Kieran. "You're next."

Riordan tilted his head and chuckled at the look on Kieran's face. "You're not afraid, are you?"

Sylvana looked down and Nicolai and winked. "Move up here. I'm drinking from yours as well."

Nicolai held himself steady and looked at Riordan and Kieran, not expecting her to want to drink from his cock as well.

"Do as your mate says," Riordan joked as he crawled down the bed and jokingly pushed Nicolai to the side. "It's my turn to watch." He laid his body on hers, slipped his tongue into her mouth, and his cock into her core.

She then felt the warmth of his breath in her ear. "I have never felt something so painfully erotic."

"Did I damage the goods?" she asked lightheartedly.

"Apparently not, because I'm ready to fuck the breath out of you."
He sat up, and readjusted himself as well as Sylvana.

She took turns teasing and pleasuring Kieran's and Nicolai's cocks
while they waited in anticipation of the pain that was sure to come.

Kieran's body also flinched when he felt the scraping of her canines
on his skin. He cupped the back of her head with one hand and grasped
Nicolai's shoulder with the other when she pierced his shaft. It was not
long before the liquid spat from his tip; she quickly took him into her
mouth and finished him. "Just when I think I can't come any harder,"
he growled.

"Fucking hell," Kieran rumbled.

Nicolai didn't know what hit him. Without warning, Sylvana's canines pierced his flesh. "Ahh, shit!" he yelled to Riordan's and Kieran's
amusement.

After satiating her thirst, she slid his shaft into her mouth and swallowed the salty liquid. Once Nicolai finished, Riordan fell on top of
her body and thrust himself so hard she cried out. "Dammit, Rio," she
muttered, as she placed her hands on his hips to hold him back.

He grabbed her wrists and pinned them down. "Allow the pain to
guide your orgasm as it did ours."

She arched her back when a powerful rush of pleasure crashed to the
surface. "You feel amazing," she mumbled.

Riordan lay on top of her body and slowly pulled himself out. He then
rolled over and Nicolai lay next to her while Kieran lay between her legs
and rested his head on her stomach.

"I don't think I've ever gotten off so intensely," Nicolai said.

"The combined pain and pleasure were like nothing I've felt before,"
Kieran agreed.

Riordan gently stroked his shaft.

"Everything okay down there?" Sylvana chuckled.

"Yes. It's still in one piece." He readjusted his body, lifted her leg with his and slid one finger between her butt cheeks and pressed down. "I let you bite my cock. You need to let me take your ass." He winked.

She grabbed his wrist and pulled it back. "Absolutely not!"

The brothers laughed aloud. "She denied us the pleasure as well," Nicolai said.

"It was quite a turn down," Kieran added.

"We can be quite convincing when we want to," Riordan said.

"Convincing my ass," she joked, to their amusement.

They flipped her onto her stomach and pinned her down. "No, wait—I don't agree," she said.

Riordan pushed her legs apart and placed his tip against her core. "Do you agree with this?"

She moaned softly as she spoke "Yes."

Riordan raised her hips, and Nicolai and Kieran kneeled in front of her and wrapped her hair around their fists. She stroked and massaged their shafts with her hands and moved her mouth from one to the other.

Chapter 15

Riordan walked into his bedchamber and Sylvana, Nicolai, and Kieran were still wrapped around each other and sound asleep. He knelt over Kieran and kissed Sylvana's forehead. "Wake up, darling."

"When did you leave?" she asked.

"Not long ago."

"Don't let him fool you. He's been gone for hours," Kieran mumbled.

"And the two of you should have been up hours ago as well."

"We are nocturnal by nature, or have you forgotten?" Nicolai replied as he placed his arm behind his head.

"How long have we been sleeping?" she asked, feeling sore and exhausted.

"You have slept for two days, darling," Nicolai replied.

"What? How? Calista and Alaric must be worried sick."

"They know where you are, Sylvana," Riordan replied. "As for the two of you, you need to get your asses out of bed."

They sat up and leaned against the headboard and Sylvana wrapped a blanket around her body and sat on her knees. "Why did you all let me sleep for so long?"

"Our blood is untainted, and your body needed time to adjust," Riordan explained. He then set the box on the end of the bed; Sylvana crawled over and ran her hand across the top. "What is this?"

"A gift, for my mate," Riordan replied.

"Your mate," she repeated. "Yes, *our mate*." He winked.

She looked at him with bright eyes and a radiant smile. "Thank you." She opened the box and two grayish-blue hands were laying on a plush, velvet pad. "What the hell?" She slammed the lid shut and jumped back.

"Are you displeased?" Riordan asked.

"Well, no—I mean, I appreciate the gesture, but my god Riordan, what am I to do with them?"

"Whatever you like." He cocked his head and stared at her.

"Are those—Elsa's hands?"

"Yes."

Nicolai and Kieran let out a belly laugh. "I don't think she has the stomach for your *gifts*, brother." Nicolai then wrapped his arms around her and pulled her between himself and Kieran.

"I didn't realize you were serious last night?"

"Did I stutter?" Riordan asked.

"No, you didn't, but don't you think it was a little extreme?"

"No," he replied unemotionally.

"Sylvana, when Riordan speaks, they listen for a reason," Nicolai interjected.

"I appreciate the sentiment I really do, but if you wanted to give me a gift, a puppy would have sufficed." She held up her hand. "Let me clarify. I mean one who is still breathing. I would have also been happy with a flower."

Riordan pulled her face to his and slipped his tongue into her mouth. He then shook his head and scoffed under his breath and mumbled to himself. *A puppy or a flower, that's absurd.*

Nicolai grabbed Sylvana and tossed her onto her back. "I have a gift of the flesh you will actually appreciate," he teased.

She placed her palms on his chest and playfully, pushed back. "Nicolai, stop." She chuckled.

"Sylvana, you may go back to bed, but Nicolai and Kieran are coming with me."

Nicolai dropped his head onto her chest and twirled his tongue over her soft bud. "Apparently, we are going to have to finish this later."

Kieran rolled over and a strange sensation hit him. He subtly rolled from side to side and there was no pain. "What the fuck?"

The three of them looked at Kieran and glanced at each other. "Brother, what's wrong?" Riordan asked.

He jumped fron the bed, walked across the chamber, and looked at his back in the mirror. "The scar, it's changed and it doesn't hurt at all."

"What?" Nicolai asked as he walked to him.

"There is no pain at all," Kieran reiterated.

The brothers looked at Sylvana and stared at her.

"What?" she asked.

"Your blood. It must have healed my wound?" Kieran questioned.

"How is that possible?" Sylvana asked.

The brothers studied his back and the red, swollen skin now appeared to be nothing more than a faded scar.

"Your blood—it has the ability to cure Faye wounds?" Riordan questioned.

"Holy shit," Nicolai stated.

She draped her legs over the edge of the bed. "Why are you all looking at me like that? I had no idea."

Kieran rushed to her and swept her into his arms. She wrapped her arms and legs around his body and he spun around. "This is the first time in over four hundred years I have felt no pain or discomfort."

She kissed the crook of his neck. "I am so happy for you."

He placed his forehead on hers and then pulled her head back, and there was a glint in his eyes she had never seen before. "I know I haven't said it yet, but I love you."

"I love you too." She smiled.

He wound his fingers through her hair, and the passion in his kiss conveyed more than his words.

Once they finished, Riordan placed his hand on his shoulder and rubbed Sylvana's back. "Not to interrupt, but we need to keep this to ourselves."

"I won't say anything, but should I be worried?" Sylvana asked.

"No. This is incredible." Riordan smiled. "You have no idea what this could mean for our kind, so we need to handle this discretely. However, I struggle to find the words to express our gratitude."

"There is no need to thank me."

Kieran set her down, and the unexpected emotions wrapped within Riordan's kiss took her breath away. He wrapped her tightly in his arms and patted her butt. "Go back to bed, darling. We have business to contend with. But I believe a celebration is in order when we return."

"I don't want to go back to bed. By the way, are the clothes I wore yesterday still in Nicolai's chamber?"

Riordan motioned toward the window, and there was a pair of leather trousers and tunic neatly folded on the chair. "I brought another outfit over this morning."

She walked over and pulled the cream colored trousers on and laced them up, and then pulled the dark gray tunic over her head and turned to Riordan and smiled. "Thank you. I need to go home."

The brothers glanced at each other and then stared at Sylvana.

"What?" she asked.

"You need to stay here," Riordan replied.

"I *need* to be going home."

"I insist," Riordan stated firmly.

Sylvana crossed her arms and cocked her head. "And I *insist* on heading home."

Riordan stepped closer. "This is your home now."

"I understand, but I need to see Calista."

"We will take you to see them later. Until then, you are free to do whatever you want as long as you do it in our wing."

"Let's get one thing straight. We may be mated, but you will not control what I do or where I go."

"We can and we will," Riordan stated firmly.

"Is that so?"

"It is," Riordan replied.

She walked to the door; all the while, she heard the increased whooshing sounds of her heartbeat in her ears, not knowing how they would react when she walked out. She opened the door, headed down the long hallway and then down the stairs. She subtly looked behind her and they were leaning on the marble railing with their forearms, watching her as if amused. *Funny, is it?* she thought.

She walked across the parlor and noticed her boots had been placed by the chairs. She quickly pulled them on and stepped toward the door, however the two guards placed an arm behind their backs, shifted their stance, and blocked the door.

"Please move," she requested.

"Milady, we are following orders," one of them replied.

"I am not asking. I am telling you to move." She took one more step, and neither of them so much as flinched.

She spun around and looked up. "I thought I was your mate, not your prisoner?"

"You are our mate, hence the reason you will not be leaving," Riordan replied.

"Riordan, tell them to move!"

They leisurely strolled down the stairs, and she glanced to her left remembering the door Nicolai had sent the ladies out of the first night she was there. She turned and darted down the long hallway. However, she did not make it halfway before Riordan swept off her feet and tossed her over his shoulder.

"Riordan, put me down!"

He plopped her down onto her back on a large lounge and kneeled over her. "We said you are not leaving." She placed her palms against his chest. "Get off me!"

"Your defiance does nothing more than to get me hard." Riordan stood up, and when he swirled his hand, a book appeared, which he placed on the settee next to her. "You can entertain yourself with a book until we return."

He walked away, and she stood up and snatched the book off the lounge. "How about you read a book!"

He spun around, caught the book, and tossed it to Nicolai. "I don't think she liked what I chose."

"*Thy tale of four mo'rs,*" Nicolai read aloud as he handed it Kieran.

"It is an interesting read," Kieran replied.

"This is not funny, and the three of you are not the least bit amusing," she snapped.

"Maybe not, darling, but you certainly are." Nicolai chuckled.

Kieran set the book on a table as they walked away.

"What am I supposed to do all day?"

"Whatever you like, as long as you do it here," Riordan reiterated.

"The three of you are unbelievable!" she yelled. *There are plenty of doors and windows. I just need to look around.*

After wandering about and finding guards at every entrance, she went into the formal sitting room and closed the door behind her. She walked over to the window and tried to open it however, it would not budge. *What the hell?* She stepped back, closed her eyes, held her hands in front of her and an icy-blue mist hit the window and dissipated like fog. *You have to be kidding me? So I need to up my game as well.* She closed her eyes, drew a deep breath, waved her hands and heard the crackling glass. *That's how it is done,* she chuckled to herself. Once she twisted the lock and pushed, all of its pieces splintered, fell off, and the window creaked open. She slipped out and ran, keeping her body low to the ground and close to the wall so the guards inside would not see her through the windows. Once she rounded the corner, she raised up and bolted toward a gate nestled at the far edge of numerous rows of tall hedges. Riordan, Nicolai, and Kieran suddenly stepped out of one row and blocked the gate. Stopping mid-stride, along with a yelp, she slipped and landed on her ass.

"Going somewhere?" Riordan asked

"Yes. I am going home."

Nicolai looked down at her and made some clicking sounds with his tongue. "We told you not to leave."

"And I told you I won't be controlled."

Kieran held out his hand and winked, and she took it in hers and he pulled her to her feet and wiped the dirt off her butt. "Are you okay?" He chuckled.

"Other than my pride, yes."

"Your powers are impressive," Riordan said.

She placed her hands on her hips. "Was this another test?"

"Yes. We were curious how far you would go. Now we know." Riordan then took one step forward.

"So you want to play games?" she asked, as she took one step back.

"This is not a game, Sylvana," Riordan replied.

She spun in a circle and consumed them in a thick, icy mist obscuring everything from view, and ran toward the gate.

She tried to leap over the gate and screamed when one of them wrapped their arms around her waist and pulled her back. "You will need to do better," Nicolai laughed as he gracefully landed on the ground with her dangling over his shoulder.

"This is not funny! I want to go home."

He set her down and Riordan and Kieran stepped into view appearing to be amused rather than angry, to her relief. "We can do this all day," Kieran said with a half-cocked grin.

"Would you like to walk inside, or would you like to be carried?" Riordan asked.

"Neither," she protested.

"We should punish her for her disobedience," Nicolai said.

"I have a few ideas," Kieran added.

"Stop it," Sylvana demanded.

Riordan spun his hand in a circle and red, silk rope appeared. "Ties and binds would be fun." He then draped it around the back of his neck and held the ends. "We will even give you a head start if you want to run."

They took one step toward her, and she held her hands up and stepped back. Even though she was angry, she could not help herself, and she started chuckling. "I'm not playing your stupid games."

Kieran jokingly lunged, acting as if he was going to grab her; she yelped and jumped back and they laughed aloud.

Riordan slid the rope from around his neck and wrapped the ends around his hands; before she knew what happened, she was face to chest with him and the rope was around her lower back, holding her firmly against his body. "I must admit I'm turned on." He slid his hand down her pants and strummed her sex with his fingers. "Wet already?" He winked.

She placed her forehead on his chest and her hands on his waist.

"I say we take her right her," Kieran added. He stood behind her and slid his hand under her tunic and massaged her breast while Nicolai fisted her hair, pulled her head back and seductively, slid his tongue across her full lips. Her mouth parted with desire, and she placed her palm on the back of his head and pulled his mouth to hers.

She moaned softly when Riordan pushed two fingers into her core.

"Is this what you want, Sângele Nostru?"

"Yes," she whispered.

He removed his hand and cupped her face in his palms. "This will have to wait. We have business with the Guild."

"Wait—what?"

"Riordan, you cannot be serious," Nicolai stated.

"You want us to show up with hard-ons?" Kieran joked.

"It's called self-control, brothers." Riordan then draped the rope around her neck and tied it in a loose knot between her breasts. "Keep this safe for us. We plan on using it later."

Riordan took her hand in his and led her back into their home. "Just a heads up. I will have this place as secure as an iron tomb." He then kissed the back of her hand as they left. Nicolai and Kieran looked back and rolled their eyes before shutting the door to the formal sitting room.

She plopped onto her back on the settee and sighed. *I will not sit here by myself all day,* she thought while slipping the silk rope between her fingers. *"Ven, can you hear me?"*

"Sylvie?"

"Yes. Will you come over?"

"Of course. Where are you?"

"Locked in the brothers' wing." Sylvana heard her laugh aloud. *"It's not funny, Ven."*

"I'm sorry. I'll be there as quickly as I can. Are they going to let me in?"

"Honestly, I am not sure."

Florin's carriage pulled up to the Marques manor, and they noticed two stallions wandering around in the small pasture next to the barn. "Those belong to Marius and Leodion," Florin said.

"Cadell said he was going to the Legion."

Just as they stepped out of the carriage, Cadell, Markus, and Leodion walked out of the manor and headed in their direction. "Milords," Alaric and Florin said as they greeted them with a subtle nod and a forearm grasp.

Cadell placed his hand on Alaric's shoulder. "Come, there is much to discuss."

"You look troubled," Alaric said.

Cadell led them into a private room off the main parlor and shut the door. He then revealed all that had occurred. "Alaric, take a seat. We will figure this out. You are going to wear a path in the rug pacing back and forth," Cadell said.

"I need to find my father."

"I'll go with you," Florin offered.

"I'm afraid no one is going anywhere. The Barouqe Warriors have their orders," Markus stated.

"They cannot stop me from searching for my father," Alaric replied.

"They can and they will. This is not a fight you want to bring to the table," Leodion replied.

Alaric sat down and placed his elbows on his knees. "We can't sit here and do nothing while Sylvana is at the mercy of the Acherons."

"She was wearing their amulet, Alaric. There isn't anything we can do for her," Florin stated.

Cadell, Markus, and Leodion glanced at each other and then stared at Alaric. "Ahh, fuck," Cadell mumbled.

"Sylvana said it wasn't what I thought when I asked her about it last night," Alaric replied.

"What did she think it was?" Cadell asked.

"I have no fucking idea," Alaric replied.

"I think it is best if you accept the fact she will not be returning," Markus replied.

Alaric interlaced his fingers behind his head and leaned back. "What do we do now?"

"We wait," Cadell answered.

"Where is Calista?" Alaric asked.

"She was escorted back to your manor this morning," Cadell replied.

Venthana pulled the reins on her mare when she made it to the gilded gates. "Sylvana Orfaedo sent for me."

"Your name, milady?" one of them asked.

"Venthana Lynexia Mehira."

He nodded, and they opened the gates; a stable boy took her mare's reins and walked her to the front entrance. "I will care for her, milady."

"Thank you." She walked up the steps, and when the doors opened Sylvana was standing in the middle of the parlor with her arms crossed, looking as mad as a spring hare.

"Milady," a young lady-in-waiting said as she motioned toward the chair near the door.

Venthana took a seat and looked at Sylvana with a questioning expression.

"It's a thing Riordan has," Sylvana replied.

Once they were done, Venthana walked over and took Sylvana's hands in hers. "Someone's a little heated." She winked. "What happened?"

"Not here," Sylvana stated as she furrowed her brow at the guards.

Another one of the young ladies approached and curtsied. "Milady, may we fetch you and your guest anything?"

"Yes, a decanter of cherry wine. And is there a private sitting room?" Sylvana asked.

"Yes, milady. Follow me."

They followed her down the opposite hall and she opened two elaborate doors and stood aside. "Damn," Venthana said as she looked around. "I have never seen such opulence and I'm a member of the court."

"Neither have I," Sylvana replied as they took a seat.

"Miladies," one of the young maids stated as she set down a silver tray holding a glass decanter and two matching goblets. After filling the goblets, she handed them over and curtsied. She then pulled a small gold bell from the pocket of her skirt. "We will be right outside the doors. If you need anything ring."

"What are your names?" Sylvana asked.

"I am Lysa and she is Delia. We are a few of your personal chamber maids, milady."

Once they shut the doors the Sylvana and Calista looked at each and giggled. "Ring a bell?" Sylvana questioned.

"I don't even have a bell." Venthana picked it up in a joking manner and shook it and there was a soft knock on the door and Lysa and Delia walked in and curtsied. Venthana hastily cupped it in her hand. "I'm sorry. I didn't mean to ring it."

"Tis all good, milady," Lysa replied.

Once she left, they fell into a heap of laughter.

Venthana jokingly tugged on the silk rope. "A new fashion statement?"

"No. They threatened to tie me up with it when I tried to sneak out and go home. Seduction at its finest," she joked.

Venthana laughed aloud. "I had no idea being friends with you would be so entertaining."

"I'm glad you're amused." She chuckled.

"Don't keep me in suspense. What happened last night?"

"I don't know where to begin, so I'll just say it. "I mated Riordan, Nicolai, and Kieran last night."

Venthana's jaw dropped, and her eyes widened.

"Say something, anything," Sylvana urged.

"I—umm. I'm sorry, I don't know what to say. I am truly at a loss for words."

"Is it that bad?" Sylvana asked.

"Bad? Hell no. It's fabulous! I just—I'm shocked is all. There was no announcement?"

"It's a long story, but before I get into it, there is something else you should know."

"What the hell more can there be?" Venthana chuckled.

"I don't know how to tell you. I have told no one."

"You can confide in me. I will never betray your trust."

Sylvana took a large drink, looked out the doors, and stared off into the distance.

Venthana placed her hand on her thigh. "Tell me, Sylvie. Whatever it is, I am here for you."

Sylvana looked at her and took a deep breath. "I am a purebred Ascelin," she blurted out.

Venthana was stunned, and once again struggled to find the right words. She raised the goblet to her mouth and took a much needed drink, unable to comprehend that she was sitting next to someone she had only heard of in legends. She set the goblet on the tray, readjusted herself on the settee, and faced Sylvana. "I am shocked, to be honest. I never really believed rumors to be true." She then squeezed Sylvana's hand. "Forgive me, I am being impolite."

Sylvana smiled. "Please, don't apologize. I was hoping this would be the extent of your reaction and honestly I feel like my next words should be 'please don't tell anyone,'" she joked.

Venthana chuckled. "I'm sorry, but I can't believe Elsa purposely spilled her drink on a purebred Ascelin. And here I thought I needed to protect you."

Their chuckling grew in intensity, and they soon found themselves rolling in laughter. "Ohh, that's a whole other story," Sylvana managed to say in-between her laughter.

Venthana wiped her eyes. "Sylvie, I don't think I can take much more."

Sylvana squeezed her forearm. "Riordan, he—he gifted me her hands in a gilded box this morning."

Venthana slid off the settee onto her knees and placed her hand over her stomach. "I can't breathe—I'm done—no more," she said as she held up her other hand.

Chapter 16

When Riordan, Nicolai, and Kieran entered the Chamber of the Guild the members took a knee, bowed their heads, and placed their fists over their hearts. "Milords," they stated in unison.

The brothers placed their fists over their hearts and nodded. "Milords," they replied.

"It was quite the ceremony last night," Astaroth stated, as he grasped Tobias's forearm.

"Yes, it was," Tobias replied.

"The ladies of the court are rather quiet this morning." Mordeci chuckled.

"As it should be," Riordan replied.

"How is Sylvana faring after the altercation?" Rhazien asked.

A slight smile crept across Riordan's face. "Your sister is with her now."

"Did I see a hint of a smile and a glint in your eyes?" Astaroth questioned.

Riordan placed his arms around Nicolai's and Kieran's necks in a joking manner. "I'm sure you did," he admitted.

The members of the Guild glanced at each other. It was a rarity to witness Riordan acting in such a lighthearted manner. "I assume you have good news regarding Sylvana?" Astaroth asked.

"Everyone take a seat. We have much to discuss," Riordan said.

"What news do you have?" Norix asked.

Riordan glanced at Nicolai and Kieran and then turned his attention back to the Guild. "We have taken Sylvana Ascelin as our mate."

It became so quiet one could hear a leaf fall on the forest floor. They stared at the brothers with frozen expressions; the only hint of emotion was the shock in their eyes.

After a few minutes, Astaroth spoke. "Sylvana is indeed an Ascelin?"

"She is as pure as they come," Nicolai replied.

Astaroth leaned back and taped his palm on the table. "Did her sister reveal the truth last night?" "The words spilled from her mouth like an upturned cup," Nicolai chuckled.

"Holy hell," Mordeci stated.

"And you are mated?" Norix asked, making sure he heard correctly.

"Yes. We plan on making the announcement tomorrow," Riordan said.

"Well, hell, this shall be a celebration to remember." Astaroth stood, held up his cup, and everyone followed suit.

"Aru—Aru—Aru!" they shouted.

"In honor of Riordan Demidicus, Nicolai Theron, and Kieran Malachi Acheron, who have fulfilled their one true desire, followed their destinies and have been bestowed their coveted mate. As the highest ranking member of the Guild, we accept your blood bond with reverence and fortitude. From this day forward Sylvana Acheron will live under the protection of the Guild of Entente."

"Aru—Aru—Aru!"

Riordan, Nicolai, and Kieran placed one arm behind their backs and acknowledged them with a slight bow.

"We are honored," Riordan replied. "Sylvana has lived a sheltered life and has little experience with the outside world. In our absence, we ask that you be her eyes and her ears, her sword, and her shield."

"It goes without saying," Astaroth agreed.

Kadric lay on his back on the stone slab, trying to regain his senses the powerful sorcery had assaulted, and it felt as though every thought coming to the surface was being dragged through the mud. The door opened and harsh, ethereal light flooded the small cell; Kadric squinted his eyes and sluggishly sat up. He draped his legs over the edge, and rested his feet on the cold, stone floor. Two amorphous silhouettes lingered in the brightly lit threshold and then Ranan stepped into the cell and the door closed behind him. He took a seat in a chair next to a decrepit table in the corner, set a copper pitcher and two cups on the table, and filled them. Kadric pushed himself off the slab and pulled a chair out.

"I assume I am on the other side of the veil?" Kadric asked.

"Yes. You are in Estraxath," Ranan replied.

"Where is my mate?" Kadric asked.

"She took her own life," Ranan replied unemotionally.

Kadric placed his forehead on his clenched fists, doing his best to hold back his rage. His heat was heavy, and he could not come to terms with the fact he had failed to protect her.

"Kadric, I did not want you to find out like this, but you left me with little choice," Ranan said.

Kadric looked up, filled his cup, and dropped the pitcher onto the table with a heavy thud. "What now?"

"Have you made a decision?" Ranan asked.

"I will not betray the Acherons," he stated firmly.

"Kadric, do not think of this as *betraying the Acherons,* think of it as a promotion of sorts."

"*A promotion*? Is that what you tell yourself to ease your mind? Your dissonance against the Acherons, not to mention the Guild, with be met with deadly force."

"Why do you choose to side with the enemy, when you and your family could live a life of grandeur?" Ranan asked.

"Did my mate live a fucking *life a grandeur*?" he snarled.

"Had she not made such an impulsive decision, she would have."

Kadric leaned back and rapped his fingers on the table. "Why would I betray one lord only to be at the mercy of another? The Faye has a long axe to grind with us. What reasons do I have to believe I will not eventually become expendable?"

"The Faye want peace and prosperity in the world they once thrived. They will reward, not punish, all those who are loyal."

"History has an ironic way of repeating itself and I fear going to war with my kind will put yours as well as the Faye's lives to rest permanently."

Ranan poured more of the effervescent liquid into Kadric's cup. "You may change your mind when you find out the Acherons have taken an interest in your daughter."

Kadric desperately racked his mind for something, anything, he could say to explain their interest in Sylvana but came up blank. "What makes you think such a thing? Mira is far too young and Calista and Sylvana spend their days in the fields."

"You know damn well I am speaking about Sylvana."

"What are you alluding to?"

"I am *alluding* to the fact I believe you have done a splendid job hiding her true identity."

Kadric leaned back and laughed aloud. "True identity? I believe I know who my bairn is."

"As do we, and *your bairn* is a purebred Ascelin."

Kadric took another drink and tilted his cup at Ranan. "Whatever gave you such an absurd idea?"

"We know, Kadric, and it would be in yours as well as Sylvana's best interest to accept the Faye's offering."

"I will not waiver. Sylvana is my blood, and you will leave her be," he snarled.

"She is the blood of Phaidra Myrine Ascelin."

Kadric placed his forearms on the table and leaned forward. "You can call a serpent a dragon all you want, but at the end of the day, it does not become a dragon."

Ranan stood up and slammed his palms on the table. "I am fucking offering you a way out of a war that is inevitable!"

Kadric jumped to his feet and the loud clanging of the copper pitcher and cups hitting the floor along with the bang of the table having been upheaved reverberated off the walls. Kadric grabbed a fistful of Ranan's tunic and yanked him forward. "Nothing is fucking inevitable! You can stop this!"

The motion was so quick Kadric, in his befuddled state of mind, having been bound by Faye magic, didn't have time to comprehend what was about to happen; one moment he was staring down Ranan and the next his body was bouncing off the stone wall.

"Let's see what you have to fucking say when Sylvana is standing before you!" Ranan bellowed.

Kadric stumbled to his feet and Ranan slammed the door behind him. He sat on the stone slab, placed his elbows on his thighs, and rested his forehead on his fists. *On all that is merciful, I pray Sylvana is with the Acherons. They will protect her regardless of what motives they may have. If Ranan, and or the Faye, get a hold of her—they will destroy her to use her.* He then thought about his mate and the tears dripped from his eyes. *My beautiful Myrine, you took your own life to protect Sylvana's identity. You should have awaited me, and now I fear it is too late to protect Sylvana.*

"I can't fathom all of that took place last night," Venthana stated.

"My mind is still reeling, and now I'm locked up and I can no longer penetrate the energy surrounding us," Sylvana replied.

"They are powerful, Sylvana. I am not surprised in the least. We all know that no one goes in and no one goes out without their permission."

"Do you know where it comes from? If I have an idea, maybe I can work around it."

"All I know, based on the stories passed down, is the brothers faced the Faye four hundred years ago when they crossed the veil. The Barouqe Warriors had captured a member of the Mercurial Guardians who led the attack."

"I have never heard of this," Sylvana replied.

"Then I will tell you the story. The night of the attack, the starless sky was coal black and even the clouds seemed morose; the only light came from the half-crescent Blood Moon. They crossed the river and into the Black Moor all the while the cold, north wind howled and caterwauled through both the forest and the bodies of the Warriors. They gripped their cold steel and raised their shields, which glinted cruelly under the ominous rays of the moon. The Lycans and Faye swarmed before them with a legion numbering in the hundreds. Riordan, Nicolai, and Kieran stood before their warriors, raised their swords and ordered them forward. The sounds of the enemy's feet hitting the frozen ground echoed throughout the forest like rumbling thunder. They met the brothers and their army head on with a tempest of barbed arrows arching their way across the sky as they advanced. Steel met steel with a thunderous crash and bodies were being tossed onto the ground, while roars of pain and rage rose from the chaos. Unarmored bodies spilled their blood and organs, saturating the ground beneath their feet.

"My god, it sounds awful," Sylvana said.

"I can't imagine being there," Venthana agreed before continuing. "Riordan was attacked by a Lycan who tried to cleave his head. However, he leapt to the side, evaded the deadly blow, and brought his sword across its chest. He was then attacked by another and knocked to the ground. He grabbed it by the throat and plunged his blade into its chest, all the while its enormous jaws were snapping mere inches from his face. Kieran came from behind, grabbed a handful of its fur, pulled its head back and decapitated it. He then fell to his knees next to Riordan and let out a guttural roar. He hadn't seen the Faye who dropped from the tree above him, but the Faye's lifeless body fell to the ground next to him. When he looked up, Nicolai was standing there, the blood dripping from his blade. Riordan and Nicolai pulled him to his feet, but his wound was not healing."

"The scar on his back, was it the Faye's blade?" Sylvana asked.

"Yes. It was tainted with a caustic substance."

"Go on. I'll tell you about his scar when you're done," Sylvana replied.

Venthana took another drink and continued. "They say the battle lasted until dawn, and just as the sun rose, the Lycans and Faye retreated. A dozen of their Barouqe Warriors appeared, having captured the Mercurial Guardians Lord Ulfganger, who had led the attack. Having been captured, they say he begged for his life. Riordan and his brothers had no intention of releasing him, and Riordan made an offhanded remark about sparing his life. In exchange, Ulfganger would bestow upon him and his brothers the powers of the Faye. The story fades from there and only Riordan, his brothers, Tobias, Klyn and the members of the Guild know exactly what occurred. Once again, they saved an empire that has stood for a thousand years and Riordan, Nicolai, and Kieran now have the powers of both Nosferatu and Faye."

"Holy shit," Sylvana replied. "How have I never head of this?"

"It was so long ago no one really speaks of it anymore," Venthana replied.

Sylvana filled her cup and took another sip. "When were you told the story?"

"As a child. My clan has a long lineage of nobility, and we are required to be educated in such matters prior to becoming a member of the court. My brother Rhazien is also a member of the Guild."

"Really? I had no idea." Sylvana looked down, feeling as though she were an uneducated Helot.

Venthana lifted her chin and smiled. "Never feel you are beneath anyone, Sylvie. You are a purebred Ascelin and from what Klyn told me, you are well educated in your own right and a flawless reader."

"That's another story." Sylvana chuckled.

"I can't take another one of your stories," Venthana joked.

"On a serious note, thank you, Ven. What you said truly means a great deal to me coming from someone of your status."

"My status?" She gently held her amulet up. "I believe you outrank us all, Sylvana Acheron."

Sylvana scoffed and rolled her eyes. "By name only."

"Well, the name carries more weight than any. Now, what were you going to tell me?"

"Riordan and his brothers told me to keep this private. You swear an oath to me you won't speak a word of it."

"On my honor as a Stelion, I do swear an oath. I will never betray you."

"The morning after we mated, Kieran was lying in bed and suddenly jumped up and when he looked at his back in the mirror, the scar had healed."

"Are you serious?"

"Yes. They say it was my blood."

Once Venthana came to terms with what she had been told, she squeezed Sylvana's hand. "Never speak of this to anyone else, sweetie, and you should let your mates know you told me. Secrets here have dire consequences and I have no desire to be on the receiving end of their wrath."

"I will. I assume the reason my mates allowed you into their wing is because your brother is a member of the Guild? They also know you and I speak freely and have said nothing about it."

"Yes. My brother told me they were going to ask me to look after you. And on that note, I have something to tell you," Venthana admitted.

"What is it?"

"It's about Muriel. You should be cautious around her."

"Muriel? Why?"

"There are rumors."

Sylvana's eyes widened, and her pulse quickened, knowing they had shared quite a bit of information with each other, not to mention she was with Alaric at the ceremony. "I don't understand?"

"I don't know much, but apparently after you and the Acherons left last night, she was seen in the market talking to one of the Helots."

"I don't know what to think. I mean, she has been a friend of mine and Lenora's for some time now. Maybe she was selling food on the side?"

"They are just rumors, but I thought you should know. She does not belong to the court and you are well aware how the ladies treat an outsider. However, Lenora told me this morning Tobias doesn't want her associating with her."

"Great. I wonder why my mates haven't said anything?" Sylvana replied.

"Well, she wasn't in the fields handing out food to the workers this morning."

They looked at each other and took a drink, both having the same thought regarding her sudden disappearance. "Riordan?" Sylvana questioned.

Venthana simply shrugged her shoulders.

"Has the plan been set in motion?" Riordan asked.

"Yes. Our warriors have captured a Faye who were scouting the area just beyond the veil. Our scouts saw Dronve with Ranan two weeks ago," Rhazien replied.

"Well, hell, it couldn't have worked out better. They will tie him to Ranan," Riordan said.

"We also believe the Lycan's and/or the Faye have Kadric Orfaedo. They found his stallion grazing in the fields outside his manor last night and there was the subtle scent of a Lycan on him," Mordeci added.

"Where is the Faye now?" Nicolai asked.

"Sequestered and guarded on the south side of the Black Moor," Astorath replied.

"Then we head out today, and we need to look for any sign of Kadric," Kieran stated.

"My brothers and I will go with you. We want to make sure this goes according to plan," Riordan said.

"Has Tobias made the preparations for the inbreds?" Nicolai asked.

Mordeci pointed to an area on the map. "Yes. This is where he has laid the bait."

Riordan tilted his cup toward Astaroth. "Before we leave, there is something you need to know regarding Sylvana."

"We are listening," Astaroth replied with a slight nod.

"Kieran," Riordan said.

Kieran stood, removed his tunic, tossed it on the table, and turned his back to the Guild. Various words were mumbled under their breath and the members looked at each other, not believing what they were seeing.

"May I?" Astaroth asked.

Riordan nodded and Astaroth walked over and studied what appeared to be nothing more than a large scar. "It's healed? How—how is this possible? Did—you said Sylvana?"

Kieran turned around and smiled. "After taking her blood last night, the wound had healed by the time I awoke."

Astaroth handed Kieran his shirt. "This—this is incredible. I find myself at a loss for words."

"Wounds of the Faye are no longer a threat to us?" Norix questioned.

"Apparently," Kieran replied.

"It is imperative this information does not leave this room," Riordan demanded.

"You have our word as your brothers. This will remain within these walls."

"Rhazien, we have granted your sister with access to our mate. Do we have your word she will reveal nothing Sylvana tells her, or do I need to make it clear?" Riordan asked.

"Venthana is trustworthy. I will speak to her before we leave to make sure she fully understands her position and what is expected."

The door opened, and Venthana stood. "Milords," she said, along with a slight curtsey.

"Venthana," Riordan replied.

"Good afternoon, milord."

"You look a little more relaxed," Riordan playfully grabbed the rope and pulled Sylvana into his body.

She poked him in the chest. "I'm still mad, you know."

He grabbed her finger and stole a heated kiss before answering. "If this is you being mad, I'll take it."

"Venthana, your brother would like a word with you," Nicolai said.

"Milord," she replied. She then looked at Sylvana and smiled.

"You may speak freely," Riordan said.

"Thank you, milord. Sylvana, if it's okay with your mates, would you like to have a drink later? Lenora, Stefania, and Aurelia will be in the gardens for tonight's games, and they asked if you would be there."

"I would love to." She then glanced at Riordan, Nicolai, and Kieran.

Riordan nodded. "You don't need our permission to see your friends, my love."

"I will see you later, Sylvana."

"I look forward to it."

Kieran held out his elbow. "Shall we?"

"Where are we going?" she asked.

"Would you like to go for a walk in the gardens?" Nicolai asked.

"Of course. Is everything okay?"

"Things couldn't be better." Riordan smiled. "We have a few things to discuss, is all."

"Like what?" she asked as they leisurely strolled down the hallway.

"We met with the Guild today and they have accepted our bonds," Kieran replied.

"We also informed them your blood has the ability to heal Faye wounds," Nicolai added.

"Why would you tell them?"

"They had to know, darling. They have also sworn their allegiance to you," Riordan said.

"What do you mean?"

Riordan casually picked a flower off of a shrub and handed it to her. "It *means* from this day forward; you are under the protection of the Guild."

Sylvana took the flower, smelled it, and looked up at him with adoration. "Thank you."

He winked and pointed to a large, curved bench beneath a shade tree. She sat on the satin cushion between Riordan and Nicolai while Kieran pulled a chair closer and placed her legs over his.

"We have to leave soon," Riordan said.

"Why?"

"Matters of the Guild," he replied.

"Are you going to be gone all night?"

Kieran shrugged his shoulders. "It depends on how things go."

"In that case, I would like to see my family."

Riordan picked up a goblet the servant had set down and took a sip. "They will be here shortly. We have made arrangements for them to say in three of the chambers in the main castle."

"They agreed—more specifically, Alaric, agreed to this?" Sylvana asked

"Yes, with a little prompting," Kieran replied.

"Where are they now?"

Nicolai rubbed the back of her hand with his thumb. "At the manor with one of our advisors who is explaining the situation. They too, are under our protection now."

"I know the three of you are keeping more from me."

"We are," Nicolai replied causally.

"Why? I deserved to know what is going on."

"The only thing we are keeping from you are matters of the Guild," Riordan replied.

"Have you heard anything about my father?"

"No. But we are doing everything we can to locate him," Nicolai answered.

"You should have let me speak to my family."

"Sylvana, it is not safe right now. You need to come to terms with it," Riordan stated firmly.

She scanned their faces and it dawned on her. "The Lycans know who I am, don't they?"

"We believe so, but as long as you and your family are behind these walls, you are safe," Riordan replied.

"I have something to tell you all as well," Sylvana admitted.

"Go on," Nicolai smiled.

She looked at Kieran. "I told Venthana about my blood healing your wound."

"We expected as much," Kieran replied.

"You're not mad?"

"On the contrary. It pleases us you have someone to confide in," Kieran replied.

"Is that why her brother wanted to see her?"

"Yes. Now let's talk about something we think will please you," Nicolai said.

"What would that be?" she smiled.

"Our mating ceremony," Riordan replied.

Sylvana smiled and looked down at her cup. "That sounds—" she began as her voice trailed off.

Riordan lifted her chin and cocked his head. "What's wrong? We thought you would be excited?"

"Don't get me wrong, I am. It's just—will everyone be told I'm an Ascelin?"

"Yes, and we understand your trepidation," Riordan replied.

"I have hidden my identity for so long, I feel as though I am betraying my mother."

Nicolai leaned over and kissed her forehead. "You are not betraying her. You are claiming your identity."

"We know you told Venthana we are mated, but please do not reveal this to anyone else until we make the formal announcement," Nicolai added.

"Can I tell my family?"

"Of course," Riordan replied. He then nodded toward the flower she was spinning between her fingers. "What color flowers would you like for the ceremony?"

Sylvana was in the sitting room with a book in her hand, waiting for Venthana to arrive. "Milady, your guest has arrived," Cassius, her personal guard, stated.

She set the book down and headed for the parlor with him in tow. "Are you ready?"

Venthana asked.

"Yes." She wrapped her arm in Venthana's and they headed down the long hallways toward the main wing. "I heard your brother wanted to speak with you regarding me."

"Yes. He reiterated what I already knew. What is said between us stays between us."

"I'm sorry. Being friends with me shouldn't come with a warning," Sylvana joked.

Venthana laughed. "Being a member of court comes with many warnings, Sylvie. You are an Acheron and with that comes a higher level of responsibility and discretion. Lenora is now in the same position."

"I appreciate you understanding," Sylvana replied.

"Listen, I felt an innate connection to you the night we first met at the games. I truly enjoy your company whether you are an Acheron or not. To be honest, you have been a breath of fresh air. The ladies of court are tantamount to a spider web; their intricately spun beauty is just a distraction from the huntress's true intensions. I also feel somewhat isolated, seeing how my brother is a member of the Guild."

"An eloquent way to put it." Sylvana laughed. "I am happy I met you."

Venthana jokingly bumped her shoulder. "As am I."

"Milady, I hate to interrupt but your family has arrived," Cassius interjected.

"Your family is here?" Venthana asked.

"Apparently. Will you excuse me? I need to go see them."

"Of course. Come down later and bring them along."

Chapter 17

Sylvana stood outside Calista's chamber door and took a deep breath. *Relax,* she told herself as she slowly opened the door.

"I will be right outside, milady," Cassius said before pulling the door closed.

"Sylvana!" Mira ran over and leapt into her arms. "Are you mad at me?" she whispered.

"No sweetie, not at all." She set her down and looked at Calista, whose cold expression and body language let her know she was not happy.

"I thought I heard your voice," Alaric said, as he walked through the adjoining door.

"Mira, go to your room. We need to speak to Sylvie," Calista said.

"Why do I have to leave?"

"Go, Mira," Alaric stated firmly.

"Fine!" she snarked.

Calista closed the door and turned to Sylvana. "You have a lot of explaining to do."

"What the fuck took place last night?" Alaric snapped.

"I don't know where to start?" she replied.

"At the beginning," Calista stated.

"They know who I am," Sylvana admitted.

"No shit," Alaric replied, as he sat in a chair and crossed one leg over his knee.

"What your 'bedmates' put Mira and Laurent through last night is unacceptable," Calista snapped.

"I agree," Sylvana replied.

"I told you all along this was going to be a fucking disaster," Alaric said.

"It's not as bad as you think—"

Calista cut her off mid-sentence. "Not as bad as we think? Are you kidding me? They kidnapped Mira and Laurent, an advisor and a half dozen Guards showed up at our manor first thing this morning and told us we were to move in here. Father has no idea what is going on, and I had to stay with the bitch Enatta last night!"

"Calista, I am so sorry. I didn't mean for any of this to happen."

"I fucking told you to stay away from them," Alaric scolded.

Calista walked over to the bureau, filled two cups with ale, and took a large drink as she handed one to Alaric. "Why are you here still? More importantly, why are we here?" Calista asked.

"What the fuck have you done, Sylvana?" Alaric interjected as he took the cup from Calista.

"I—I'm not sure how to tell you—"

"Sylvana, spit it out," Calista demanded.

"I agreed to let Riordan, Nicolai, and Kieran take me as their mate last night," she blurted out.

The dead silence and the expressions crossing their faces made her feel as though she had betrayed them in the worst possible way. "Say something," Sylvana mumbled.

Alaric stood, paced back and forth, and ran his hand down his face while Calista simply stared at her as if in shock.

"Why the fuck would you mate them?" Alaric bellowed after a few heart pounding moments of silence.

"I'm in love with them," she admitted.

Alaric laughed aloud. "'In love with them'? You are not in love with them. You have been masterfully manipulated by three of the most cunning and lethal lords in the kingdom!"

"Alaric, they have done nothing but show me kindness and they brought the three of you here to protect you!" Sylvana barked.

"Protect us? My god, Sylvana, I have never taken you for a fool, but this—this is—I don't even fucking know what this is?" Alaric stammered.

Calista looked at Sylvana's eyes as they glossed over and knew she was truly in love with them. "Alaric, calm down and let her explain."

"There is nothing to explain. What has been done can never be undone. And now we are all at their mercy, not to mention their fucking beck and call!"

Calista walked over and wrapped her arms around her. "I get it, Sylvana. I knew this was going to happen."

"How the fuck did you know this was going to happen?" Alaric demanded.

Sylvana and Calista glanced at each other and then looked at Alaric without speaking.

"Have you have been covering for her all this time?"

"In a way," Calista replied nonchalantly.

"Father is going to lose his shit when he finds out you mated the fucking Acherons under my watch. I promised him I would look after the three of you and I have failed miserably. And on another note, Mira doesn't know the truth, so did you reveal mine and Calista's identities as well?"

"Alaric, please, let me explain. They are looking for father, they fear he is in trouble with the Lycans and no, I did not."

"Why do they think that?" Alaric asked.

"Alaric, if you would calm the hell down and let her explain without losing your temper, you would find out," Calista stated.

Their stallions thundered through the stillness of the forest, and they reached the Black Moor just after the sun had dipped beyond the horizon and were met by Klyn and a legion of their Barouqe Warriors.

Riordan and his brothers dismounted and followed Klyn. "Have you located an inbred?" Riordan asked.

"Yes, we have eyes on him. We were waiting until you arrived. How do you want to do this?" Klyn asked.

"Discretely," Riordan replied.

"Have you secured the surrounding areas?" Nicolai asked.

"Yes. The South side of the river is silent. We haven't seen so much as a rodent."

"Good," Riordan replied as he stepped over a rotten log.

Klyn motioned to where they had the Faye chained and gagged, and Riordan walked over, pushed his body with his foot, rolled the Faye onto his back and kneeled down. "You will be the beginning of the end of your treaty."

The Faye looked at him through his matted, golden locks partially obscuring his face, with a malice filled glare. He rubbed his battered face on the ground to remove the gag.

Riordan pulled the gag from his mouth. "Speak your peace, for they will be your last words."

"Holding me prisoner shall do nothing for you," he snarled.

Riordan grabbed a fistful of his hair and pulled his head back. "We have no intention of taking you prisoner. We are going to leave you to the inbred."

His eyes widened, and he blinked once. "Doth as you wish. Thy treaty shall never be broken."

"Based on the look in your eyes, I believe you know it will be the tear in your fragile little treaty."

"I am prepared to die for my own. I assume you did prepare to die for yours?" he snarled.

"We have extinguished your flames of war for centuries. This time, it will be at the cost of your entire fucking race."

"Your confidence shall be your death," he replied.

"Your name is Dronve, is it not?" Riordan asked.

"My name matters not."

"I believe it does. We know you and Ranan have been leading the excursions outside of the veil. What will they think when Ranan's ally turns up dead at the hands of his own kind?"

His pointed ears twitched, and he bared his jagged teeth. "We have a surprise awaiting. Killing me shall not stop thy war," he threatened.

"And we have a surprise for you." Riordan looked up at Klyn and held his hand out. "Give me his dagger."

Klyn removed it from its sheath and handed it over. Riordan flipped his cloak to the side and pulled his sleeve up. He then placed the blade against his wrist and pulled. The blood spilled from the gash, and Riordan noticed how Dronve's body stiffened, and his face became ashen as he watched the wound heal. He pulled the gag up and shoved it back into his mouth. "Apparently you have been rendered speechless." Riordan winked.

Dronve curled his body up, shoved his legs, pulled against the chains binding his wrists, and yelled. However, his words beneath the gag were unintelligible and muffled. "Take him across the river," Riordan ordered.

"Milord," Rhazien replied.

"A bold move, milord," Mordeci stated. "How did you know for sure the wound would heal?"

"I didn't, but I have enough of my mate's blood in me. I thought it would be a good time to test our theory," Riordan replied.

"We know now," Mordeci replied.

After an hour or so of explaining what had occurred and all she knew, Alaric had finally calmed down. "I really am sorry it happened this way," Sylvana said sincerely.

Calista gave her a warm hug. "Sylvie, I understand, and I am truly happy for you."

To her shock, Alaric stood up, walked over, and pulled her in for a tight embrace. "When this shit falls apart, I will not abandon you," he whispered.

"It will not fall apart, and it means the world to me," Sylvana replied, and she hugged him back.

"I'm going to the tavern. Cadell and Florin are waiting for me, and I can't wait to fill them in on all this bullshit."

Sylvana rolled her eyes. "I am going to take Calista and Mira to the courtyard to meet my friends," Sylvana replied.

"Be ready, Sylvana. I feel there is a storm on the horizon," Alaric replied, as he pulled away.

"Alaric," Sylvana said.

"There better not be more," he replied from the doorway.

"You will have a personal guard, and you can't tell anyone they have taken me as their mate," Sylvana said.

"Fucking fabulous. And I won't."

Once the door shut, Sylvana plopped onto the bed on her back. "Holy shit, that was exhausting."

"I still can't believe you mated the Acherons," Calista said, as she sat down next to her.

"Honestly, neither can I, but I really am happy."

"And I'm happy for you, but you are going to be the death of Alaric," she laughed.

"I hope it is not in the literal sense," Sylvana replied, as stood and pulled Calista to her feet in a joking manner. "I don't know about you, but I need to get the hell out of here."

"I'm right there with you. What do you have in mind?"

"A few of my friends are in the gardens for the games taking place. Would you like to go?"

"I would love to."

"Let's get Mira. She can tag along," Sylvana suggested.

Sylvana and Calista walked into Alaric's chamber, and Mira jumped up and ran over to them. "Look, I have my own lady-in-waiting. Her name is Pelana."

Pelana, stopped pulling the bed covers down and politely cupped hands together. "Miladies," she said, along with a subtle curtsey.

"Nice to meet," Sylvana and Calista replied.

They then looked at a young lady, who appeared to be about Mira's age, and she curtsied and smiled as well. "Miladies."

"And who would this be?" Sylvana asked.

"This is Lexie.She's my new friend." She then walked over and sat down on the rug in front of the hearth, and Lexie sat next to her.

Sylvana kneeled beside her."Would you like to meet a few of my friends?"

Mira gave her a radiant smile. "No. it's okay."

"Are you sure?" Calista asked.

"Yes. I'm sure."

"Okay, we will check on you in a bit."

Mira smiled and turned her attention back to Lexi."

"If Mira needs anything, we will be in the gardens," Sylvana said.

"Yes, milady," Pelana replied.

After Nicolai, Kieran, and Klyn staked Dronve to the ground, Riordan kneeled over his body and ripped his shirt open. Dronve let out muffled screams of agony when his skin parted beneath the tainted steel. "The smell of fresh blood will draw the inbred to you," Riordan said. "It's also rewarding to know you will feel your own poison."

When Klyn walked over, Riordan stepped back. "I'll remove our scent," he stated as he waved his hands over Dronve's body. They then leapt into the canopy, cloaked themselves, and waited while another group covertly pushed the inbred into the immediate area.

After what felt like hours, they heard the snapping of branches and heavy panting as the creature drew closer. The brush parted and its enormous head appeared and swayed from side to side. It then lifted its nose into the air, drew a few deep breaths, and retracted its blackened lips, and snarled. The thick saliva dripped onto the ground and its yellowish eyes glowed in the dark when it pinned its sights on Dronve.

Dronve twisted his body, kicked his legs, and fisted the chains, doing his best to yank the stakes from the ground all the while the sounds of his muffled screams of terror rose into the canopy.

The creature cautiously stepped closer, cocked its head, and twitched its ears. It let out a thunderous roar, leapt towards its prey, slammed a heavy paw onto Dronve's chest, and bared its enormous canines; with an explosive series of strikes and bites, it tore chunks of flesh from his body.

"Now!" Riordan called out telepathically.

They dropped from the trees and while Nicolai, Kieran, and Klyn held it back, the rest of the warriors stood in a half-crouched position, ready to intervene.

Riordan shoved Dronve's dagger into its abdomen in rapid succession; the creature let out a ground shaking roar and flung its heavy body to the side, which forced them to stumble to the side and partially release their grip. It then lunged at Riordan, who leapt out of the way, spun around, and shoved the dagger into its flank multiple times.

"Release him!" Riordan ordered.

They leapt out of the way, cloaked themselves, and watched as it stumbled through the brush and disappeared.

Riordan tossed the dagger onto the blood saturated ground next to Dronve's remains. "That should do it."

"Is everyone accounted for?" Nicolai asked telepathically.

"Yes, milord." Rhazien replied.

Nicolai walked over and stood next to Riordan. "Let's hope this works."

"Nicolai, I need you and Kieran to stay behind and make sure the area is cleared of any sign of our presence."

"Will do," Nicolai replied.

"Rhazien, you and your warriors need to sweep the South side of the river one more time before heading back. Klyn, you and yours will come with me so we can make another sweep on the North side."

Riordan and his warriors traveled through one of the village's market which on a usual day would have been raucous and hectic, however because of the heavy downpour it was as quiet as a grave. A faint sound caught his attention; he pulled the reins and cocked his head in its direction.

"Milord?" Klyn said, as he stopped next to him.

Riordan held up his hand and listened intently before dismounting Skadi. All those riding with him fanned out to secure the immediate area.

Riordan kneeled down and moved a bit of debris to the side, and found a small puppy shivering in a corner. He picked it up by the scruff of its neck, held up and stared at it.

"Milord, what are you doing?" Klyn asked.

"I have no fucking idea," he mumbled. After a moment of silent contemplation, he tucked the puppy beneath his cloak and stood.

Klyn laughed aloud and patted his shoulder. "A gift?"

"At least it's breathing," he replied.

"I assume this has everything to do with Sylvana?"

"I think it has to do with me losing my fucking mind," Riordan replied.

Klyn smiled and laughed under his breath as he mounted his stallion and the other warriors looked at him with a questioning expression.

"Is Riordan okay?" Tobias chuckled.

"He has not lost his mind if it's what you are thinking, only his heart."

"The shit we will do for our mates," Tobias replied as he kicked his stallion's hindquarters.

Riordan, Tobias, and Klyn walked into the bathhouse and kicked their boots off. Once Riordan removed the saturated cloak, the ladies-in-waiting looked at each other, as if confused, when they noticed the small puppy tucked under his arm.

"Milord?" one of them said curiously.

"Would you like us to take care of it?" the other asked.

"No." He sat the puppy on the ledge and the three of them hopped into the pool and washed the stench off their bodies.

Tobias sank into the water, leaned against the edge, and one of the ladies handed him a drink. "You're not going to take the filthy thing to your chamber, are you?"

"Yes, after I clean it up." He lifted the puppy above his head and then washed him off in the warm water.

"This is a sight I never thought I would witness." Klyn laughed.

Tobias slid over and held out his hand, and Riordan handed him the puppy. "Based on the size of those paws, he is going to be rather large."

"Let me see the scraggly little thing," Klyn said.

Tobias handed it to him and he, too, held it up. "I hope you realize this is not an ordinary puppy."

"How the hell am I supposed to know what an ordinary puppy is?"

Tobias and Klyn laughed aloud. "I believe this is a Dire Wolf," Klyn said.

Riordan took the puppy back and stared at it. "What the hell would it be doing in the market?"

Klyn shrugged his shoulders. "Who knows? It may have gotten separated from its pack, and was scavenging for food?"

Riordan rose from the water and one of the ladies held his robe open when he walked up the steps. "Whatever it is, I'm committed now."

"Leaving so soon?" Tobias asked.

"Yes. My mate is in bed and hopefully she's naked," he joked.

He ran his hand down Sylvana's shoulder. "Wake up, darling."

She rolled onto her back and held her hand out. "Did you just get back?" she mumbled.

"I did, and I have a gift for you."

"*Oh boy,*" she chuckled to herself. "I can't wait to see what it is."

She sat up and he cupped the back of her head with his hand and pulled her in for a kiss. She heard what sounded like a whine and pulled away.

"Your gift," he said as he handed her the puppy from behind his back.

She looked up at him with a radiant smile. "You got me a puppy?"

"Yes. And it was filthy," he replied.

She held it up and then tucked it against her chest and caressed its head. "Where did you get her?"

"Him, and I found it in a market."

"He's shivering, the poor thing." She sat on the edge of the bed and stroked its back.

"I have a feeling I am going to regret this," Riordan said.

"Well, I will never regret it."

She scooted back and set him down and it shook its ragged body, wagged its tail, and whimpered.

"He's so skinny, we need to feed him."

Riordan raised an eyebrow. "And what are we to feed the mongrel?"

"Is there goat's milk anywhere we can warm up and maybe some bits of meat? He might be old enough to eat solid food."

"The servants can come up with something."

Sylvana handed Riordan the puppy while she slipped her silk robe on. "I'll go to the servants' kitchen."

"No need. I will have them bring it." He handed the pup back to Sylvana and reached out telepathically.

It wasn't long before there was a soft knock on the door; he walked over and motioned for the young lady to enter. "Milord, you wanted warm milk in a bowl and some meat?" she asked, sounding confused.

Sylvana smiled. "It's for my puppy, not Rio."

She placed the bowls down and Sylvana put the pup in front of them and he drank and ate as if he had not fed in days. "The poor baby is starving."

Riordan sat on the edge of the bed, watching Sylvana, who seemed to be enthralled with him. After he finished eating, Riordan looked at the servant. "Take him to our stable. He can sleep there."

"Absolutely not," Sylvana protested. "He's sleeping with us."

"Say again?"

"Rio, he's tired, he's scared, and he needs a warm body."

"And where, exactly, do you plan on him sleeping?"

"With us, he's clean after all," she teased.

"I will not be sharing my bed with that thing."

"Rio, please."

He rolled his eyes and picked up a blanket, folded it neatly and set in on the floor next to the bed. "I will allow it in our chamber, but not in our bed."

Sylvana held the pup up and walked toward him. "Rio, come on. Look at his face."

"I will not waiver."

"Fine, he can sleep on the floor." She kneeled down and tucked the pup into the blanket and Riordan knelt behind her, slid his arms around her waist, and kissed the crook of her neck. "Since you're awake, I have other things on my mind." He walked over to the chair, picked up the silk rope, and snapped it in her direction; she screamed and leapt across the bed.

"You didn't think I forgot, did you?"

"No, but I did." She chuckled.

He subtly leapt in one direction and as she leapt in the opposite direction, he jumped onto the bed and she jumped off and ran across the room; he leapt after her, wrapped an arm around her waist, swept her off her feet, tossed her onto the bed and pinned her down. He then tied her wrists together above her head and clenched the rope in one hand. She held her breath, feeling strangely excited and nervous at the same time.

"It's a dangerous thought, the things I can do to you in this position." He trailed his fingers up her inner thigh and over her sex, continuing up her stomach. Small bumps raised on her skin with his delicate touch. He cupped her breast in his hand and suckled her petite, hard nipples. He then kissed his way down her stomach, lowered her arms, grasped the knot between her wrists, and braced her hands firmly on her stomach.

Her body was on fire, and her mind was spinning with the thoughts of being so helpless. She watched as his head dipped between her legs.

She pushed her head into the pillow when she felt his warm breath blow across her sex and the tip of his tongue caress it. She raised her hips, desperate for more when he slid his tongue between her folds and then pulled her sex into his mouth.

"You like that?" he asked.

"Yes." She moaned softly as she tried to pull her hands free.

He looked up at her and made sharp, clicking noises with his tongue. "Don't move unless I tell you to."

She spread her knees further apart when his fingers penetrated her core. As he pushed them deeper and shoved harder, she felt her orgasm clawing its way to the surface. "Rio, don't stop. I—I'm going to."

He abruptly stopped and pulled them out. "Not yet. I want to hear you beg." He then alternated between licking and sucking her sex, which drove her into a desperate need to come.

She could not move her hands, but she had her legs locked around his neck. Once he felt her nub swell, he pulled away again. "On the verge again?" he asked.

"Rio, please," she murmured.

"Please what?"

She should have gotten off multiple times, however, he kept slowing down or stopping to prolong it. "I want—I need you inside me."

He crawled up her body and pinned her arms over her head again, gripped his shaft, and slid the tip across her lips. "Take it, darling."

She slid her tongue up the length of his shaft, twirled it around the tip, and then cupped her lips around it, and glided it into her mouth.

Just as the feeling rose, he pulled it out and rolled onto his back, taking her with. She straddled him and slid herself down on his shaft, placed her hands on his chest, and rocked back and forth with firm and steady movements. He reached up, cupped the back of her head in his hand, pulled her mouth to his, and bucked his hips in unison with hers. The feeling of her sex rubbing against his crotch nearly undid her.

"Not yet." He grabbed her hips and stopped her from moving.

"Rio, I can't take much more."

He pulled her onto his chest, rolled over, and forcefully shoved his hips forward. "Shit," she mumbled.

"Fuck me, you feel good," he said, as he rocked back and forth. "I'm hungry."

"Then I shall feed you." She turned her head, and he dragged his canines along the vein on her neck and felt her shiver as the cool tips caressed her skin before he sank them into her flesh.

He lifted his head and gazed into her eyes. "There is an ambrosial flavor within your blood that sways my immortal mind," he whispered, as he turned his head.

The sharp stab of her canines radiated into his shaft, and he let out a deep chested rumble.

She released her grip, shoved her head into the pillow, and cried out when the waves of pleasure finally consumed her.

"Music to my ears," he whispered.

The wetness pooled around his shaft, and as he released himself, he let out a long, deep growl, and fell on top of her body. After their breathing returned to normal, he rolled over, untied her wrists, and draped his body over hers.

"That was amazing," she said.

"Yes, it was," he agreed, as he stroked her back with his fingers.

"Rio?"

"Syl?"

"I love you."

He rose onto his elbow, tucked her hair behind her ear, and gazed into her eyes with a heartfelt smile. "And I love you more than you will ever know." After a passion filled kiss, he pulled away and cupped her face in his palm. "If there is ever a time where I seem harsh or unemotional, never doubt my feelings for you."

"I won't."

Chapter 18

Riordan was trying to sleep. However, the puppy's incessant whining was as aggravating as a cricket under a floorboard. He rolled over, picked it up by the scruff of its neck, and held it above his face. "I should have left you in the fucking market." He then laid him down on the other side of Sylvana. "You better not shit on our bed."

Sylvana laughed aloud. "If he does, I'm sure you are capable of cleaning the mess."

"Is that so?" He scooted the pup to the side, rolled over, and pinned her beneath him. "I will not be responsible for him."

"Rio, I can't breathe. Get off." She laughed.

"You've held your breath longer when my dick was down your throat." He winked.

"Rio!"

He laughed aloud and rolled over.

"Haven't you had enough for one night?"

"No."

"Well, I'm tired."

He kissed the crook of her neck and wrapped her in his arms. "If he wakes me again, your body is mine."

"Fine." She chuckled.

Nicolai and Kieran quietly tossed their robes onto a chair and crawled into the bed and Nicolai jumped up when a high-pitched yelp startled him. "What the fuck?"

"What the hell is that thing doing in our bed?" Kieran asked.

Sylvana woke up and grabbed the puppy. "Shit. You're okay, little one," she said as she cuddled it in her arms. She then looked up at Nicolai and Kieran. "Didn't Riordan tell you?"

"No," Nicolai stated.

"Fuck me, I have finally fallen asleep and the three of you are as loud as lords in a fucking tavern."

"Can one of you explain why there is a mangy pup in our bed?" Nicolai asked.

"He's not mangy, and Riordan gave him to me," Sylvana replied.

"Say what?" Nicolai asked.

"Riordan—gave you a puppy?" Kieran questioned.

"Yes," Sylvana said.

Nicolai looked at Riordan. "Why is it in our bed?"

Riordan draped his arm over his face. "Will everybody go to fucking sleep?"

Sylvana began laughing under her breath, and it wasn't long before Nicolai and Kieran joined in on her amusement.

"At least it's the whole pup and not its paws," Nicolai joked.

Kieran let out a belly laugh, and Sylvana slapped his chest. "Nicolai, that is not funny!"

Nicolai placed his hand on Kieran's shoulder. "Can you imagine what the legions are going to say when they find out that Riordan Demidicus Acheron gifted his mate a scraggly little pup?"

"I'm sure word has spread already," Riordan grumbled. He then tossed the covers off, walked over to the liquor cabinet, and filled a cup. "If the three of you cannot quell your amusement, Kieran and Nicolai, I will kick your asses out."

"We should name him after Riordan, Rio for short," Kieran joked as he held the puppy up in one hand.

Sylvana placed a pillow over her face to muffle her laughter while Nicolai and Kieran continued to taunt their brother.

After gathering her composure, she tossed the pillow to the side, sauntered over to Riordan, and slid her hands over his chest. "Come back to bed, my love."

Kadric was lying on his back with his arm draped over his face when he felt a presence. He looked over, and a silhouette materialized into a svelte looking woman with waist-length, golden hair streaked with silver strands. Her iridescent-green eyes shone bright against her sienna colored skin dappled with golden flecks.

She calmly walked over, collected the upturned chair and sat; she then smoothed out the satiny, amaranth-colored material of her dress, crossed one leg over the other and the material slid to the side bearing her toned thigh.

Kadric sat on the edge of the stone slab and stared at her, and with one smooth motion of her hand, the table was upright, along with the other chair. "Take a seat," she said in a melodious tone.

"I'll pass," he stated firmly.

"As you wish," she replied.

"You're not speaking in Faye tongue?" he asked.

"We adapted long ago. Communication is best when all understand thy dialect."

"Why are you here? I will never betray the Acherons."

"Help us and we shall reward you generously."

"You're wasting your breath."

The Faye's expression hardened, her melodic voice adopting a noticeable edge. "Ranan has asked twice. Please, don't make me repeat myself. Rewards will be plentiful, and refusal will be painful."

"The same way in which you rewarded my mate with a *plentiful* bounty?" he snarled.

"It was unfortunate. We made her an offer, and she chose to close thine eyes. We assume it was in order to protect herself as well as her offspring's identity."

"As I told Ranan, you are chasing a dragon that doesn't exist," he stated.

"Dragons exist. You must know where to look," she replied.

"What is your name?" he asked.

"Vispera," she replied.

"The mythical Faye Shifter," he stated.

"One and the same, Vampyre."

"Well, let me make myself clear, Faye. I will never be fucking indebted to you." he said, as he stole a glance at another Faye, who was towering over him.

"Free will is only an illusion, Kadric Orfaedo."

"*Free will* is all I have, Vispera."

"Such a shame. I was hoping you would see reason. I would hate to have to use Sylvana as motivation. And in return, I shall use you as motivation for Sylvana."

"I can assure you I am motivated, Vispera."

As she stared at him, there was a burning intensity pooling around his black irises, and it sent a chill of warning up her spine.

Vispera's pointed ears subtly flicked in his direction. "Kadric, refuse for now, but I believe you will act later."

He jumped to his feet, but before he made it two steps, the male Faye slammed him face down onto the stone slab.

"You have no power here. Take heed of the only warning I am going to give. You have two days, Kadric Orfaedo," Vispera warned.

Riordan slipped out of the bed and after dressing, he quietly opened the door and heard a thump. When he turned around, the puppy was standing behind him eagerly, wagging his tail. *Ahh, fuck. We are not starting this,* he said to himself. He then picked the pup up and laid it on Sylvana's pillow and, as he turned to leave, he heard another thump. *You have got to be fucking kidding me?*

He left, and the puppy followed behind. As he walked down the stairs, it whined incessantly. Riordan rolled his eyes and when he turned around, he was standing on the top landing trying to get down the step however, he only moved forward and back. He put a paw down, picked it up, and wagged and whined.

"You wanted to come, so jump," Riordan said.

The pup awkwardly made the leap and tumbled head over heels. Riordan reached out, picked him up by the nape of his neck, and held it in front of his face. "Keep this shit up and I might be inclined to take you back to where I found you." He then carried it the rest of the way and set him down at the bottom.

He playfully ran around Riordan's bare feet and let out a few playful high-pitched barks and Riordan looked down and furrowed his brow. "I assume you want me to feed you?" He walked to the kitchen and a young servant curtsied.

"Milord, may I help you?"

"I need meat and goat's milk," he replied.

She looked at him and tilted her head. "Milord, you—want to eat?"

"It's not for me. It's for the fucking puppy."

"My apologies, we don't have anything here, but I will run to the servants' kitchen and be back momentarily."

"Make it quick. I don't have time for this shit."

Once she was out of sight she ran down the long hallway and burst through the door. "Quick! I need meat and goat's milk, and now."

"Liza, what is the rush?" one of them asked.

"Riordan, and he wants it now," she replied, as she grabbed a pitcher of milk.

"What the hell does he want with this?" she asked.

"He has a puppy." The young gal laughed aloud. "Riordan has a puppy? I have to see this!" She quickly cut up small chunks of meat.

"Apparently," Liza chuckled.

She followed Liza, who returned without haste. Riordan nodded toward the puppy, and they set the bowls down while he leaned against the table, crossed his arms, and watched him devour his food. "Keep this kitchen stocked. I won't wait again."

"Yes, milord," Liza replied with a curtsey.

Riordan pushed himself off the table, opened the door, and waited patiently while the puppy took care of its business.

Riordan walked into the Guild's chancery and shut the door behind him.

"Riordan," Astaroth said as he greeted him with a forearm grasp. He heard a high-pitched yelp and jumped back. "What the hell?"

All the members walked over and studied the puppy and then stared at Riordan with a look of curiosity.

Riordan gave them a dismissive wave. "It belongs to Sylvana."

"Why is it with you?" Tobias asked.

"I don't fucking know? Ask it," Riordan snarked.

They turned their backs and took a seat, doing their best to quell their amusement.

Riordan sat down, leaned back, and looked at Astaroth. "Have the Faye located the remains yet?"

"As of an hour ago, no. However, the inbred is face down in the dirt."

"Has Rhazien reported back with information on who else Dronve and Ranan have ties to?" Riordan asked.

Astaroth crossed one leg over his knee. "Other than their ties to each other, we don't know any more than we did."

Riordan leaned forward, spun the map around and pointed to various areas. "We need to secure the outlining areas of the kingdom. I want a legion of Barouqe Warriors scouting these areas, and another line here, here, and here."

"They will be sent out tonight," Astaroth replied.

They looked up when the door opened and Nicolai and Kieran walked in. "It's about time the two of you showed up," Riordan stated.

The puppy jumped up from where he was laying at Riordan's feet, ran to them and Nicolai picked it up and held it out. "I see you have all met Rio," he joked.

"Rio?" Tobias laughed.

"Yes. We named it after his father," Kieran replied.

They all looked at Riordan, whose eyes were pinned on Nicolai's and Kieran's, and laughed aloud.

Vestal nodded to Riordan. "Congratulations on your new bairn," he joked.

Riordan's eyes snapped in his direction. "It belongs to Sylvana. Now, if you all are done fucking around can we get back to the matters at hand?"

Nicolai set him down, and they took as seat. It ran back to Riordan, jumped on his leg and barked; he casually pushed it down trying not to draw more attention to himself and the puppy.

Astaroth's face became serious. "We know the Faye have taken Kadric Orfaedo. Lucias and his warriors picked up on his scent and it disappeared where the mists meets the veil."

"Ahh, shit," Nicolai said, as he glanced at his brothers.

"I have spoken with Cadell and he believes he went in search of his mate, Myrine," Phaone added.

"Why go alone?" Vestal asked.

"At this point, I can only assume he didn't want to get anyone involved with his personal matters," Phaone replied.

They tried to remain on topic, but the way in which the puppy was growling, and Riordan was subtly moving his leg under the table made it all the more difficult.

"We should lock the main gates as well—" Astaroth began, before he was suddenly interrupted.

"Owe! Dammit," Riordan yelled, as his body lurched, and his chair slid back.

"What the fuck is wrong with you?" Nicolai asked.

"Fucking thing bit my goddamn leg," Riordan snapped.

Their laughter was as rich as the woodland thunder.

"Sylvana!" Riordan called out telepathically.

"Darling, what's wrong?"

"Come get your goddamn puppy."

"Where are you?"

"I'm in the chancery with the Guild."

"I'll be down shortly."

"Sylvana—"

"Okay. I'm coming right now." She chuckled.

Riordan picked up the puppy, carried it over to Nicolai, and set it in his lap. "Since you are so amused, you can hold him until Sylvana gets here."

Riordan waved his hand at Astaroth. "What were you trying to fucking say?"

"I'm—I'm not sure," he stuttered through his laughter.

"Darling, I'm outside the door," Sylvana said.

"Come in, love."

"I'm not going in there. Bring him to me," Sylvana protested.

"I should have stayed in fucking bed," Riordan rumbled. He opened the door, placed one arm behind his back, gave Sylvana a slight bow, and waved his opposite hand toward the chancery.

"Rio, I'm not going in there," she whispered.

Nicolai and Kieran moved behind her and walked forward, forcing her to enter the

room. *You two, stop,* she demanded telepathically.

They chuckled and kept ushering her forward.

"Milords," she stated nervously, along with a curtsey.

They immediately stood, placed one arm behind their back, their fists over their hearts, and nodded politely. "Milady," they replied.

"I would like to introduce you to our mate, Sylvana Phaidra Ascelin-Acheron," Riordan said.

"It is good to meet you, milady," Astaroth said, as he walked over and kissed the back of her hand.

"It's my pleasure to meet you as well, milord," she replied, in a shaky voice.

"If there is ever anything you need, we are at your service, milady," he offered.

"Thank you." She looked down when she felt the flush in her cheeks.

Nicolai then handed her the puppy. "Rio is driving Riordan crazy." He winked.

I should go now, she replied telepathically.

"Are you ready for us to make the announcement?" Riordan asked aloud.

"As best as I can be."

"We won't be much longer, love," Nicolai stated.

Riordan patted her butt. "Get dressed and we will be up soon."

He closed the door behind him, and they took a seat. "Now, can we get back to business?" Riordan asked.

"She is stunning," Rhazien said.

"Yes, she is," Kieran agreed.

"Her trust in others is going to be an issue," Nicolai replied.

"She is still as shy as she was the night we met her in the tavern," Tobias added.

"Don't let her shyness fool you. She is more than capable of going toe to toe with anyone of you." Nicolai chuckled.

"Yes, she is. I witnessed the punch," Tobias joked.

"She threw a book at Riordan's head the other day," Kieran chuckled.

"She sure did," Riordan agreed.

"Now that is a scene I would have loved to have witnessed." Astaroth laughed.

"Shit, his dick was so hard he could hardly walk," Kieran joked.

Another ripple of laughter filled the room.

"My dick? You had to unbutton your fucking pants, and your brother leaned against the wall for five minutes," Riordan said in jest.

"We should adjourn, since we are obviously getting nowhere," Astaroth suggested.

"We will re-convene after the announcement," Riordan said.

"I will call the court to order, and we will see you soon," Tobias said.

"I'm so nervous," Sylvana said as Calista pulled the ties on her amber corset.

"It will be fine. We will all be there," she replied.

"You have no idea how happy I am you are living here," Sylvana offered sincerely.

"I'm not sure about the living here part, but I wouldn't have missed this for anything."

She turned Sylvana around and they gave each other a warm embrace, and Sylvana pulled away and looked Calista up and down. "You are gorgeous."

"I never thought I would be wearing the finest of silks." Calista smiled.

The door opened, they turned around and her mates walked in wearing identical, form-fitting, gray cotton trousers that laced up the crotch. Their pant legs were slightly bunched in soft folds above the top of their black leather boots, and their pleated, amber tunics matched her dress perfectly.

"Calista, it's good to see you again," Nicolai said.

"Milords," Calista replied, along with a curtsey. *Damn, they are stunning*, she thought.

"You belong to our clan now, Calista. There is no need to address us formally," Riordan offered.

"Yes, milord," she replied, as she glanced at the crown on his head.

"This sounds familiar," Nicolai joked.

Calista looked at Sylvana, who waved dismissively. "I'll tell you later."

"Where are your ladies in waiting?" Riordan asked.

"I dismissed them," Sylvana replied.

"Why? Have they have done something to upset you?"

"No, my love. My sister and I have always dressed each other."

"Makes no sense, but they can dress you both," he replied.

She slid her hand over his chest. "It's fine, Rio. We are used to taking care of ourselves."

Riordan took her mouth to his and then stepped back, and his eyes dropped to her cleavage. "You are perfection, my love." He smiled. "As for taking care of yourself, those days are over."

"You're a decadent sight, Syl," Kieran replied.

A young lady stood in the doorway, and Nicolai looked at Calista. "She will escort you to you place with Alaric and Mira."

She gave Sylvana another hug. "I'll see you momentarily, and breathe. It will be fine."

Riordan held out his elbow. "Shall we?"

"Yes." Sylvana smiled.

Nicolai and Kieran walked behind them and as they stood before the large, ornate doors veranda doors. Riordan looked down at Sylvana, having felt her hand trembling. "Relax, love. This is just the announcement. It won't take long."

She smiled up at him and then looked behind her at Nicolai and Kieran for reassurance. Nicolai bent over and kissed her forehead. "We are right here with you."

"I know," she said, along with a radiant smile.

Riordan nodded to the doormen, and they swung the large doors open. They stepped onto the veranda and stood on the landing above the steps.

Astaroth walked over and placed his hand on Riordan's shoulder. "Are you ready?"

"I've been ready for this my entire life."

Nicolai stood next to her, held out he elbow and smiled down while Kieran stood behind her and placed his hands on her shoulders and gave them a gentle squeeze.

She scanned the enormous crowd and Alaric, Calista, and Mira were standing front and center. Calista winked at her, Mira smiled from ear to ear, and Alaric nodded. She scanned the crowd again and noticed Cadell and Enatta. Cadell nodded politely, and she smiled back. Enatta, however, side eyed Cadell and then looked at Sylvana and scowled.

Nicolai leaned over. "If you think she is scowling now, just wait," he joked.

Sylvana chuckled under her breath and smiled up at him. "Doesn't she always look like that?" she replied in jest.

He gently patted her ass. "I think she was born with a scowl."

She looked down at the ground, doing her best to not laugh.

Astaroth walked down two steps and held up his hand and the crowd became as still as the calm before a storm. "We have called you all here today to make an announcement."

"It is my pleasure to announce the Acherons have taken a mate!"

Hushed gasps, whispered chatter, and transfixed stares greeted Sylvana. It only took a moment for it to sink in before the shocked crowd erupted with bellows of cheers, chants, and claps.

"The Guild of Entente has accepted their bond and in three days-time there will be a mating ceremony you will not soon forget!"

Another round of cheers erupted, and the crowd seemed to be genuinely happy and excited, to Sylvana's relief.

"I would like to introduce you to Sylvana Phaidra Ascelin-Acheron!"

The crowd stilled momentarily when they heard the name Ascelin. Sylvana watched how they fell silent, glanced at each other, whispered in each other's ears, and looked at her as if in disbelief.

"I know this comes as a surprise to all and yes, Sylvana Acheron is a purebred Ascelin."

Kieran leaned over and she felt the warmth of his breath in her ear. "They will need a moment to come to terms with who you are. This was to be expected."

She looked up at him and smiled.

"Aru—Aru—Aru," rang out from the warriors as well as the members of the Guild, breaking the awkward silence.

"The Acherons have found their Ascelin!" someone shouted from within the crowd.

"This is wondrous news!" another shouted.

Rhazien, who was standing behind Alaric, Calista, and Mira, raised his sword and the crowd turned their attention to him.

"Alaric, Calista, and Mira Ascelin now belong to the Acheron's clan are under the protection of the Guild," Astaroth announced.

Mira turned around and smiled at Laurent; he nodded and smiled back and Enatta winked at her.

Calista felt a hand on her lower back so she turned around to see who it was. "I am Venthana's brother, Rhazien. I would be honored if you would join me for a drink later?"

"Did she or Sylvana put you up to this?" Calista asked.

"Venthana may have mentioned something about Sylvana having a stunning sister who could use someone to show her around."

"How can I turn down such an eloquent offer?" she chuckled.

"Very well," he said as he kissed the back of her hand. "Meet me on the veranda in an hour."

"I will be there with baited-breath," she joked.

"And I will count down the minutes." He winked.

Once he was out of earshot, Alaric turned to Calista. "Don't you start this shit."

"Relax, Alaric. I met Venthana last night and she and Sylvana are very close."

"Based on the flirtatiousness in your voice, I assume this was not unexpected?"

"She may have mentioned his name, and I was not flirting."

"If you say so."

"Alaric, it's fine."

"He is a member of the Guild, Calista. Do not get involved with him. I already have to explain to father Sylvana mated the Acherons. I'd rather take the next shanty boat out of port than tell him you mated a member of the Guild."

She laughed aloud, wrapped her arm around his, and playfully nudged his shoulder. "I think you are the one who could use a drink."

"Alaric, can I go see Laurent?" Mira asked.

"Yes. But do not leave the grounds with him or I will give you a well-deserved spanking," he threatened lightheartedly.

Mira rolled her eyes. "You wouldn't dare." She then laughed and ran off.

"We need to watch Enatta around her," Calista said.

"Cadell won't let her step out of line where she is concerned."

"I hope you're right."

The door closed behind them, and Sylvana sighed. "I'm happy it's over."

"It wasn't so bad, was it?" Riordan winked.

"For the three of you, maybe. I thought I was going to vomit." She chuckled.

Her mates laughed aloud and Nicolai swept her into his arms, spun around and she let out a squeal of delight and tucked her face into the crook of his neck. He set her down and Riordan held her hands and walked backward down the hall. "We wanted to make the announcement prior to the ceremony so you would enjoy yourself."

"I appreciate it. I'm relieved I won't have to look at the shock on their faces again."

"They will move onto more salacious gossip in a couple of days," Nicolai joked.

Riordan opened the door to his chamber and held it with his palm.

"I have salacious gossip for you," she said nervously.

"What salacious gossip could you possibly have?" Kieran chuckled as he took a seat.

Sylvana sat on the edge of the bed and twisted her hands together and looked down.

"Sylvana?" Riordan said.

She looked at them with a forced smile. "Promise me you won't be mad."

"I suppose it will depend on what you have to say," Riordan replied.

She took a deep breath and glanced at them. "Go on Sylvana, we won't be mad," Nicolai urged.

"Alaric, Calista, and Mira are purebred Ascelins as well," she blurted out.

The brothers stared at her momentarily and then glanced at each other. "Why have you not revealed this earlier?" Riordan asked.

"Alaric asked me not to."

"The story Mira told us about her, Alaric, and Calista having a different mother was not true?" Nicolai asked.

"No. They weaved a story for Mira. She is so young they were afraid she might slip and reveal the truth to the wrong person. Not to mention she can be very impetuous."

"Why does she know about you?" Nicolai asked.

"She overheard mother and father talking. Honestly, I'm surprised she has kept it to herself all this time."

"We will inform the Guild, but until things settle down, let's keep this between us," Riordan said.

"Soo—none of you are mad?"

Riordan walked over and pulled her into his body. "No, darling. We've had our suspicions, and Mira's story was a little far strung."

"We need to meet with the Guild. What are your plans for the rest of the day?" Riordan asked.

"I'm taking Calista to the gardens to meet up with the girls and watch the games." She turned around and tugged on the laces behind her back. "Will you untie me? I'd like to change into something more appropriate."

"I'd love nothing more than to get you naked," Riordan replied.

She turned back around and slid her hand over his ass. "We should all get naked."

Nicolai and Kieran removed their tunics and sauntered over to her. "We need to make this quick," Kieran said as his tongue met hers. He slid her dress down and cupped her breast in his hand while Nicolai moved in behind her and kissed the crook of her neck.

Riordan pulled her dress the rest of the way down and twirled his tongue over one of her erect nipples while Nicolai slid his hand between her legs and rubbed her sex.

Riordan then slid his face up the side of hers and whispered, "We don't have time now, but we are going to punish you later for keeping secrets."

"Sounds intriguing," she replied.

He picked her up in his arms, laid her on her back, moved down, and pushed her knees to the side. He nipped her sex, teased it with his tongue and slowly, he slid his fingers into her core.

Nicolai's mouth fell to hers, and Kieran cupped her breast, and pulled her supple bud into the heat of his mouth.

"Sit with your back to me." Riordan patted her ass and sat against the headboard.

Nicolai and Kieran kneeled on the bed in front of her and she wrapped Nicolai's shaft in her hand and massaged it with firm, twisting motions while she sunk her mouth down on Kieran's.

Riordan reached around and titillated her nub with his fingers as she rode him, all the while she was pleasuring both Nicolai and Kieran.

Kieran let out a guttural moan, grabbed the back of her head, and moved it up and down as she took as much of him as she could. "Ohh, damn." He moaned.

Riordan felt the wetness of her core pool around his shaft, bringing forth his own release.

Nicolai's shaft swelled, and he released himself into her mouth; once he was done, she moved to Kieran's, bringing forth his orgasm.

They plopped onto their backs, and Sylvana chuckled. "I never knew there were so many ways to have sex with multiple partners."

"We have a lot more to show you." Kieran smirked.

"I can't imagine how much more there can be?"

"We will take you as far as you are willing to go," Nicolai said.

"Have you ever heard of bondage, Syl?" Riordan asked.

"No," she replied.

Riordan kissed the back of her hand. "The rope last night was a simple example."

"Wait—you used the rope without us?" Nicolai asked in a joking manner.

"Sure did," Riordan stated.

"Are the two of you mad?" Sylvana asked.

"Absolutely not," Kieran answered.

"Syl, there will be many times when you are alone with either one or two of us. Never be nervous about doing anything with us individually. There will never be jealousy or anger," Nicolai said.

"Promise me. I could not stand it if one of you was ever mad at me over something I did—I mean sexually."

"You have our word, Sylvana," Kieran replied.

Riordan pulled her on top of his body and caressed her back. "Listen darling, if there is ever a time where you feel like being with only one of us, all you have to do is say so. Your needs come first and foremost. There is nothing you could do sexually that would ever make us angry."

Nicolai rolled over and gazed into her eyes. "Riordan speaks the truth. The last thing we ever want is to make you feel inhibited or ashamed for having sex with us."

"I understand. This is so new to me, I'm afraid I'll do something wrong."

"You can do no wrong in our eyes, Syl," Nicolai reassured her.

Riordan slapped her ass, and she yelped aloud. "Owe! What the hell?"

"This has been sweet and all, but we have to go," Riordan stated.

Chapter 19

Sylvana, along with Calista and her friends, were sitting in the garden, having a few drinks while the minstrels' soft melodies filled the air and a group of ladies played multiple games comprising balls and thick sticks, each competing against the other.

"Are you all coming to the games tonight?" Lenora asked.

"Yes," Sylvana replied.

"Calista, will you be joining us?" Venthana asked.

"Yes. I can't wait to see what Sylvie has been talking about."

Sylvana felt a pair of eyes on her; she turned around and noticed Muriel looking at her from where she was hiding behind the gates. She motioned with her head and disappeared. Sylvana looked at Venthana and thought about her words of warning. *Shit. I don't know what to do. I should at least give her a chance to explain what's going on. I mean, she is here and if she has done something terrible, I am sure my mates would have told me.*

Sylvana handed Rio to Calista. "Will you hold him for a minute?"

"Where are you going?" Calista asked.

She placed her hand over her stomach. "I'm not feeling well. I just need a minute."

"I'll go with you," Calista offered.

"No, really, my stomach is upset. I can handle this alone," Sylvana replied.

Once she was out of earshot, the ladies glanced at each other. "Are you thinking what I am?" Venthana asked.

"Do you think she's carrying their bairn?" Stefania asked.

"I wouldn't be surprised. It's all Tobias talks about," Lenora replied.

"That would be amazing," Aurelia added.

Sylvana headed into the parlor and looked at Cassius. "I need to lie down for a few minutes."

"I'll be right outside the door, milady," he stated, as he pulled it shut.

She quietly opened one of the balcony doors, slipped out, hopped over the railing, and snuck around the back of the main wing, remaining as close to the wall as she could, ducking under multiple windows along the way. She came to the end of the courtyard and pulled on the lock securing the iron gate. *Shit.* She closed her eyes, held out one hand, and the lock popped beneath the icy freeze. She then ran down the long row of shrubs and found Muriel waiting in their usual spot behind the main castle.

"Where have you been?" Sylvana asked.

"I know the ladies of court are spreading vicious gossip about me. You have to know whatever they are saying is not true."

"Why were you with the Helot the night of the ceremony?" Sylvana asked.

Muriel looked down, reached for the amulet, and gently picked it up. "I heard you are mated to them. I am truly happy for you."

Sylvana slipped the amulet beneath her tunic and smiled. "Thank you but answer my question."

"He wasn't a Helot. He's a friend of mine and he said he heard a few of the guards talking. He knows where your father is, and he is in trouble."

"What? Who is this friend and how the hell would he know when my mates don't?"

"They know Sylvana. A few of their Baroque Warriors found your father's stallion the other night. They say he was looking for your mother."

Sylvana was taken-a-back and too stunned to speak. "I—I don't know what to think. It's not possible. At least I never really believed it was." She placed her hands on her hips and paced back and forth. "What's your friend's name?"

"Pascal."

"I am going to ask my mates right now." She turned around, but Muriel grabbed her forearm.

"Sylvie, we don't have time. Do you know a shifter named Amarok?"

"How the hell do you know Amarok?"

"Pascal introduced us the other morning, it's the reason I wasn't working. Amarok said he would be back today, and he's waiting for you in the forest."

"I can't go there alone. It's too dangerous right now. Go and tell him to come here. I would try to call to him, but I know my mates might be listening if I speak telepathically."

"Sylvie, you know the guards would sniff him out before he made it through the gates, and I certainly can't sneak him through the tunnel. If someone saw, it would be the end of us both. I am not in your position, least you forget." She smiled.

Sylvana took a moment to contemplate the situation. "Shit, I can't."

"Do you think your mates are going to tell you the truth? They haven't even told you they found your father's stallion. You have been looking for information on your mother for so long I thought you would be excited, but if you don't want to go, I'll tell him to leave." She then removed a small flask from the pocket of her shawl and took a sip. "Would you like a drink?"

Sylvana's mind was spinning, and her heart was beating against her breast. "Yes."

"Sylvie, he's not far beyond the tree line, just out of sight of the guards. I will be with you the entire time. We are friends. You can trust me."

Amarok would never betray me, and he will certainly protect me, she thought. "Fuck it, let's go."

"We need to hurry. It won't take them long to find out you are missing and I would like to keep my head attached to my shoulders." Muriel chuckled.

After another drink, Sylvana reluctantly followed Muriel. They made it to the forest without being seen, and Sylvana leaned against a tree, and did her best to quell her beating heart. "Where is Amarok?"

"Wait here so you don't have to venture too far. I'll go get him."

Sylvana's body flinched when she heard a branch snap off in the distance. "Muriel?" she whispered.

When she did not get an answer, she took a few steps forward, scanned the immediate area, and listened intently. It was ominously silent, and she knew she was being watched; she froze when she heard the crunching of brush getting louder. "Muriel? Amarok?" she whispered again.

"Hello, Sylvana," Amarok said, as he and Muriel appeared.

She placed her hand over her chest and let out a sigh of relief. "Shit! You all scared me half to death."

"He walked up to her, rubbed his large head against her legs, and looked up at her. "Let's walk."

"I don't have much time. What have you found out?" Sylvana asked.

"The Faye have your father and mother," he said.

Sylvana stopped mid-stride and stared at him with a blank expression. Muriel ran her hand over her shoulder, handed her the flask, and Sylvana took another large drink.

"Amarok, how do you know this?" Sylvana questioned.

"I heard a few of the Lycans speaking to the one named Ranan."

She looked at Muriel and then back at Amarok. "Ranan?"

"Yes. Ranan saw them fighting with your father and heard them speaking of his mate. I can only assume it was your mother they were referring to."

"Is she alive?"

"I wouldn't think so?"

"I can take you to where he was last seen, but we need to go now," Amarok offered.

A stampede of chills marched up her spine. *There is something strange in his voice?* she thought. "Amarok, thank you for telling me, but I'm not comfortable getting involved alone."

"Sylvana, I will go with you if you like?" Muriel offered.

Venthana's warning. I need to leave now. "No, thank you. I really need to go."

She turned and as she darted between the trees, there was a rush of wind, and her legs flew out from beneath her body when something crossed her throat. The air exploded from her lungs when she landed on her back. Having 'turned', she did all she could to fight back against her attacker, but it was as if she had no connection to her powers. She felt herself being lifted off the ground and she let out another large belt of air when her body hit the hard soil face down.

"Amarok? Muriel?" she screamed.

"I'm so sorry, Sylvana," she heard.

Unintelligible words were being spoken from numerous males, but she could not see through the strange material draped over her head and secured around her neck. More than one large male pinned her down, while another bound her wrists and ankles. "Why are you doing this?" she bellowed. "Muriel what have you fucking done? Amarok!"

The heavy weight of their bodies disappeared, and she lay there doing her best to hear anything that would indicate who had taken her, or why they had taken her.

She was picked up and thrown over someone's shoulder and after what felt hours, they placed her face down and although she was freed from the binds around her wrists and ankles, she could not move; there was an ethereal energy pinning her down. Someone pulled the material off her head and as she looked up, Amarok morphed into a large male Lycan who was crouched over her. "Who the fuck are you?" she snarled.

He kneeled down and grabbed a fist-full of her hair. "My name is Ranan." He then nodded toward Muriel, who was standing a few feet away with tears streaming down her cheeks. "I would like to introduce you to my mate, Muriel."

"You fucking bitch! How could you betray me?"

"I am so sorry, but Ranan offered me a life I could never achieve under the Acherons' rule."

"There will be no mercy for your betrayal!" She swirled her hands but nothing happened, she tried again to no avail. "What have you done?"

Ranan held the flask up. "A little Faye alchemy to hold you still." He then drug her a few feet away and shoved her to the ground over a naked male who had been savagely beaten to death. He rolled the body over with his foot and she realized it was Amarok in his human form.

"Oh! God! Amarok, I am so sorry," she cried, as she cupped his battered face in her trembling hands. She looked up at Ranan and bared her canines. "You have made a grave mistake."

The crack from the back of his hand stung her cheek and her head snapped to the side. He then grabbed her jaw in his hand; it was clear he was beyond reason and he looked cruel and unpredictable. "Speak another word and I will fucking cleave your tongue from your mouth."

She flung her head to the side, grabbed his forearm and sunk her canines deep into his wrist, doing her best to sever his artery. She ripped a large chunk of flesh off and spit it in his face.

Ranan let out a guttural roar; the pain radiated across her rib cage and forearm when her body slammed into a tree. He picked her up and held in out in front of him, having grabbed a fist full of her tunic. She wrapped her hands around his forearms and tried to break free.

"A message for Riordan." He pulled back his arm and it felt as if her cheek had exploded.

"A message for Nicolai." Another blow caused her vision to blur, and her knees buckled beneath her. He then ripped her tunic off and slammed her face down. "This is a message for Kieran."

All she felt was a burning sensation from the steel as it slid down her back, and the warmth of the liquid running down her body; the last thing she heard was Muriel's voice.

"Ranan Stop!" Muriel screamed.

The Lycan who had mated them stepped over and grabbed Muriel's jaw in his hand and snarled in her face. "You are Lycan now, and you will stand with our pack!"

The fear rose from Muriel's stomach and into her chest. *What have I done?*

"Yes, alpha. Say the words," he demanded.

"Yes, alpha," she replied, with a shaky voice.

"An Acheron whore is what the bitch is," Ranan roared, as he kicked Sylvana in the stomach.

"Should we inform Vispera we have acquired the Ascelin?" another Lycan asked.

"No. We can't trust the bitch. We will keep her until I have more assurances."

"You are defying the Faye?" he asked.

"They do not fucking control us, and this whore is the key to getting our lands back once and for all."

"As you wish," he replied.

"I'm so sorry, Sylvana," Muriel whispered under her breath as the tears streamed down her face.

Ranan walked over and lifted her chin. "She is not worth your tears and given the chance, she would have you thrown into the gutter should she tire of your friendship."

Her body trembled and she fell to her knees, placed her face in her hands and wept. "I just betrayed my best friend," she cried.

"You honored your mate," Ranan stated, as he kneeled before her. "There are always casualties of war. However, we have no intention of taking her life."

"It's not the point, Ranan. I betrayed the only friend I had as well as her family!"

"You will have a chance to convince *your friend* to do as she is told."

"She will never forgive me," Muriel said coldly. She then looked over at Sylvana's limp body, and immediately regretted what she had done. "Not only have I betrayed Sylvana, I have betrayed her family!" she snapped.

"Are you speaking of Alaric?" Ranan snarled.

"Yes. He treated me as if I am no different than anyone else, and he never looked down on me, and neither did Sylvana."

"I am your fucking mate now and should another thought of him ever cross your mind, I won't be as kind." He pulled her to her feet. "Forget your past, Muriel. Your home is with me now."

"If there is nothing more, we should adjourn for the rest of the evening," Astaroth suggested.

"Agreed," Riordan replied.

"Your mating ceremony is a welcomed distraction from everything taking place," Rhazien said.

"Just like my cousins to steal my thunder," Tobias joked.

"It's not difficult when your thunder is more like a distant rumble," Kieran replied in jest.

"What the fuck?" Riordan exclaimed as he shoved his chair back, and looked at Nicolai and Kieran, who had also jumped to their feet. They picked up their amulets and a gentle, red glow was radiating from the center.

"Sylvana," Nicolai snarled.

"What's wrong?" Astaroth asked as he stood.

"Something's wrong with Sylvana," Nicolai replied.

Everybody followed the brothers as they ran from the chancery. *"Cassius, where the fuck is Sylvana?"* Riordan asked telepathically.

"Milord, she is resting. I am outside the door of the formal sitting room."

"Get your ass in there!" Riordan demanded.

Cassius burst through the door and frantically looked around. *Fuck me!* He thought, as he hurried over and ripped the veranda doors open.

"Sylvana, answer me," Nicolai said.

"Sylvana, can you hear us?" Kieran asked.

"Milord, she—she is gone," Cassius stated nervously.

They all materialized in the sitting room, and Cassius was standing on the veranda looking down. They rushed out the doors, leapt over the railing; Riordan kneeled down and ran his hand over the small impressions left behind. He lifted his nose to the air and followed her scent to the gate.

"She fucking snuck out," Riordan snarled. He then turned to Cassius. "You had one job! One. Fucking. Job," he snarled, enunciating every word.

"Milord—" Cassius hadn't seen Riordan's hands move until they were on either side of his face. He then heard a large pop before completing his sentence and found himself staring at the iron gate that had been to his back. Nicolai and Kieran plunged their daggers into his chest and the gate slowly faded away as his body slumped to the ground.

"Blow the fucking horns," Riordan demanded telepathically.

"Yes, milord," another warrior replied.

"Klyn, secure the grounds. I want every warrior prepared for battle."

"What's happened?" Klyn asked.

"Sylvana is in trouble," Riordan replied.

Vispera was sitting on her throne sipping from a chalice and listening to The Mercurial Guardians discussing their plan of attack.

"Once Ranan brings us thy Ascelin, thine only purpose Kadric will serve will be as bait for his offspring," Ninbae said.

"Any word on Ranan?" Diaspor asked.

"He left hours ago and as long as his mate does her job he should have an easy time sequestering her," Stronbo replied.

"Dronve will ensure he does not have other plans," another stated.

"Has anyone received word from Dronve?" Vispera questioned.

"No, Priestess," Diaspor replied.

She took a sip, set the chalice down on her gilded table, and spun the jeweled bands around her wrist.

Two of the Guardian's suddenly opened the golden doors in the center and four Faye warriors walked in, one of whom was carrying what appeared to be a body draped in a white linen, saturated with blood.

All those in attendance took a knee and lowered their heads. "Priestess," they said.

Vispera stood, placed her hands across her stomach and gasped. "Dronve?" she whispered. Mascuriel placed the body on the floor and stepped back as she ran down the steps.

She hastily pulled the linen away and fell onto her ass. "Noo!" she wailed. She pushed herself onto her knees and looked at his face, which was unrecognizable. She fell over his body and cradled him in her arms. "Who did this? Who killed my mate?" she wailed.

She looked up and glanced amongst Guardians who were standing around in a circle around her. Diaspor kneeled down behind her and placed his hands on her shoulders. "Priestess, we will punish whoever did this."

"Where is Ranan?" she screamed.

"We do not know. It appears as though a feral Lycan killed Dronve," Eoin replied. He then pulled Dronve's dagger from his waistband and handed it to Vispera.

"The feral are Ranan's scouts," Diaspor said.

She lifted it to her face, and her nostrils flared as she slid her tongue along the flat of the blade. Her eyes widened, and her face contorted with rage. "Ranan is a fucking traitor!" Vispera roared. She stood up, flipped a table, and then turned to the Guardians. "Find him! Kill them all!" She then fell to her knees again, rocked back and forth over his body and wailed.

After a few minutes, Diaspor gently placed his arms around her and lifted her to her feet. "We shall place him on thy altar, Priestess." He nodded to the Guardians, and they picked up his body.

Sylvana regained consciousness and was lying on her stomach where she smelled the heady scent of aged wood. Out of her peripheral vision, another large piece of wood slightly askew was obscuring the attackers. The energy holding her down slowly dissipated, and as she painfully rolled over, a shadow grew overhead, and she realized she was being sealed in a wooden box.

She pounded her fists on the smooth planks, which did nothing more than to cause trickles of dirt to cascade down on her face, causing her to choke on the dust and debris. She could barely see out of one eye which was swollen shut, and her other was watering, having been coated in a thin layer of dirt. It wasn't long before she the sounds of the dirt thumping against the top of the coffin became muffled and the last trickle of light shining between the planks from the lanterns swaying above disappeared.

Her labored breathing, due to her injuries, became all the more dif-ficult when the claustrophobic confines of the small structure consumed her, and she became panic-stricken. "Why are you doing this?" she screamed.

She did all she could to try and find a weakness in the coffin, which did nothing more than cause excruciating pain and more debris to fall on her face, which stung her eye like the venom from tiny vipers. She closed her eyes and held her breath to slow her accelerated breathing.

After a moment, she slowly opened her good eye and used her keen sense of sight. She slid her fingers over the planks, took a deep breath, and waved her hands across the lid. A yellowish-orange glow grew in intensity and seemed to dissolve the icy-blue mist flowing from her palms. Symbols, and writing in a language she only seen in books and scrolls of morphed and twisted above her body.

"Powers of the Faye," she said aloud. The tears spilled from her eyes. "No one is coming. No one even knows I left. I'm suck a fucking idiot," she cried. *"Riordan, can you hear me? Nicolai—Kieran? Fucking listen to me!"* she screamed telepathically.

She pulled the amulet from beneath her tunic, cupped it in her hands, and held it to her forehead. "Please, please hear me." She rolled onto her side to alleviate the pressure on the gaping wound on her back and continued calling to her mates.

The sounds of the deep horns blowing interrupted the conversations and laughter, and a wave of silence fell over the gardens.

"Why are they blowing the horns?" Calista asked.

"Shit!" Venthana stood up and grabbed Calista's hand. "They are the horns of war."

"Where is Sylvana?" Calista asked, feeling frantic.

"We need to go find her," Lenora replied, doing her best to not let Calista see how frightened she was.

"Let's go," Venthana said as calmly as she could manage. Once her back was to Calista she placed her hand over her stomach and took deep breath.

Guards were running in all directions, and the entire scene erupted into chaos. Calista tucked Rio under her arm and they ran toward the castle, calling out Sylvana's name. They frantically searched the grand parlor but did not see sight or sound of her.

Calista ran out onto the veranda when the thunderous sounds of hooves echoed into the parlor. She stood and watched the enormous parade of stallions in a full gallop, headed out of the main gates carrying fully armed warriors. Others were running along the parapets and lining the battlements and defensive towers.

"Sylvana, where are you?" Calista asked telepathically. *"Sylvana?"* She turned to the girls. "She's not responding." She then reached out to her brother. *"Alaric, I can't find Sylvana. What is happening?"*

"I don't know. I'm meeting with the Legion now. Find Sylvana dammit. She couldn't have gone far, and get Mira."

"Mira?" Calista called out telepathically.

"Why are the horns blowing?" Mira asked sounding frightened.

"Where are you?" Calista replied.

"Senna made me and Lexi go to our chamber and there is a guard outside the door. Calista, I'm afraid."

"There is nothing to be afraid of. Stay there."

"Calista, what's happening?" Mira questioned again.

"I'll be up momentarily and I'll explain when I see you. Everything is okay."

"Lenora, where are you?" Tobias called telepathically.

"I'm on the veranda and we can't find Sylvana."

"I need you to lock yourself in our chamber and don't leave for any reason," Tobias replied.

"What's going on?"

"Sylvana is missing," he admitted.

Lenora placed her hand over her stomach. "Oh, my god," she said aloud.

"We will find her, my love."

"Lenora, what's wrong?" Venthana asked.

Lenora looked at Calista, doing her best to appear calm and gently squeezed her hand. "Sylvana is missing."

"What? How?" Calista stammered.

"Sweetie, they are going after her," Lenora replied.

"Milady," a guard said, interrupting Lenora. "I am here to escort you to your chamber."

Calista looked around, feeling uncomfortable and out of place. *At least if I were back at my fucking manor, I would know what the fuck to do and where to go.*

The chaos of the gardens spilled into the main parlor. Warriors were moving about, ladies were being escorted away, all the entrances were secured, and all those still trying to enter were being stopped and questioned; only those with personal guards were allowed through the large crowd. Calista glanced at the four guards surrounding her and the girls and assumed they belonged to Lenora by the way in which they had her protectively surrounded.

One warrior walked between the others and nodded at Calista. "I am here to escort you to your chamber, milady."

"Calista?" Lenora said. When she didn't respond, she squeezed her hand. "Calista, you can stay with me and the girls in mine and Tobias's chamber. You shouldn't be alone."

Venthana placed her hand on Calista's lower back and wiped the tears off her cheek with her thumb. "It will be okay, darling." *I simply can't lose Sylvana. She has to be okay,* Venthana thought.

Lenora looked at Victor. "Please fetch Mira. She is in the west tower."

"Yes, milady. I will have another bring her to you, but I must insist we move."

Flames rose from the Mercurial symbol sitting a-top of the tower and it was not long before a wave of warriors spilled over the hills and into the valley below, while the Mercurial Guardians lined up along the large parapet beneath Vispera's tower. She stepped forward, her right hand gripping the jeweled hilt of her sword as if she were prepared to remove it from its leather scabbard attached to her left hip. Her right shoulder was protected by silver, three-layered, rounded rerebraces tucked tightly under her shoulder plate, while smaller layers ran down her arm, stopping just shy of her wrist. Two shadow-black wings, shimmering in shades of iridescent green, woven into the braids just above her ears, fluttered with the gentle breeze.

She held up her hand and the sounds of the warriors pounding their swords against their shields fell still. "Ranan has slain your High Lord Dronve, whose corpse now rests on thy sacred altar! Ranan is a traitor, and we shall show nay mercy! Arise with courage and meet our enemy visage to visage, sword to flesh and staff to bone. Arise and put your armor on and let them hear our cries of triumph. Arise and paint thy forest with thy blood of thy soulless wolf!"

Chapter 20

Kadric paced back and forth after having searched every corner of the cell looking for any sign of weakness when he felt a presence behind him, he spun around and noticed a spectral form that appeared to be walking through the stone wall and a cold chill swept over his body. *Vispera?* he wondered.

"No, my love," a seraphic voice said.

"Myrine?" he questioned.

"Yes, darling," she replied, as her evanescent form took shape.

I see with my own eyes, but I don't believe it. It has to be the Faye tonic. Unless Vispera is fucking with my mind, he thought, as he closed his eyes and pinched the bridge of his nose. He then felt a coolness on his cheek; his eyes snapped opened and Myrine was standing before him, having cupped his cheek in her hand.

"Darling, I am here," she said.

"How—this can't be—you can't be?"

"In this world, our presence dwells in the eternal light. We hear all, we know all, we see all."

"I don't understand?" Kadric replied.

Kadric felt Myrine wrap her arms around his neck, and he held her in a tight embrace. "How is this possible? I can feel you. I can smell you," he whispered.

"I have missed you my love. Nothing else matters."

"Why did you do it? Why did you take your own life?"

"My blood is all they needed to solidify their powers."

Kadric pulled back, ever so slightly and looked into her eyes. "I will avenge you, my love, for all they have stolen from us and our bairns."

"Tell me about them," she requested.

"Alaric is strong and ambitious and Sylvana is as spirited and stubborn as her mother." He winked. "Calista is stoic and reasonable, and Mira is a spitting image of you, and as impetuous as ever."

"I would die a thousand more deaths if it meant I could hold our bairns one more time," she replied.

Kadric placed his forehead on hers. "I would choose to die here and now if it meant I could be with you, but our bairns are being hunted by both Faye and Lycan."

"Yes, and it is time for you to go to them," she replied.

He pulled back and tilted his head. "How?"

"Come, my love. I will guide you, but you need to feed from me first."

"Feed from you? Is that possible?"

"Yes."

She tilted her head to the side and images of the life they had lived flashed through his mind with each swallow of her decadent blood.

She gently pulled away and walked toward the cell door that speckled like a starlit night. She waved her hand and disappeared.

Kadric heard a clank and as he pushed on the door, to his surprise, it opened. He followed Myrine through a labyrinth of hallways and winding stairs. Myrine walked through another door and as he pushed it open, an indiscernible aroma washed over him. The forest was awash in a palate of colors glowing beneath the rays of the two silvery moons surrounded by a halo of colorful light. Myrine disappeared before him and he ran, following nothing more than her scent.

He didn't know how far he had run or how long he had been running, but he came to a sliding stop when a tidal wave of blackness appeared before him like an impenetrable iron wall.

Kadric stared into the soundless void; even the silvery rays of the moons seemed to have been swallowed by the darkness.

"This is where we part ways, my love." He heard.

"Do not leave me. We can figure something out?"

"You are standing before the veil. Step through," Myrine replied as she slowly dissipated from view.

"Myrine, where are you? I can no longer see you." His stomach churned and his heart sank. *I cannot lose her all over again.* "Myrine!" he stated again.

"I have to go, my love."

"I beg of you to come with me," he replied.

"I cannot. I belong here now. I will never escape the shadows. I love you Kadric Armond Orfaedo."

"What shadows?" Myrine? Myrine?" he whispered harshly. "Do not fucking leave me," he demanded.

He paced back and forth and reached his hand out, when he noticed a shimmer in the blackness, and it hit some sort of invisible barrier. *Shit! What am I to do now?* he wondered as he paced back and forth dragging his hand through his hair.

"There is a tear in the fabric. When the snow-crested owl appears overhead, follow her, I will hold it open," He heard.

Follow a fucking owl? Okay, I'm either dreaming or I have lost my fucking mind.

Riordan pulled his stallion to a halt. "We are close enough to head the rest of the way on foot. As they dismounted, Riordan held up his hand and cocked his head; Nicolai and Kieran walked over, stood next to him and tilted their heads; they heard a veritable cacophony of sounds, so continuous they blended into a single withering echo which seemed to be miles away.

"The Faye have gone to war with the Lycans," Riordan stated.

"All we have to do is stand back and let them destroy each other, and then we can finish whoever is left," Mordeci replied.

"Sylvana is somewhere in the mix of the war," Nicolai said.

"How are we going to search for her without either the Faye or the Lycans sensing our presence?" Kieran asked.

"We don't know if she is with the Lycans or beyond the veil," Tobias said.

"I assume the Lycans have her. It was their scent we picked up on," Riordan answered.

"So they have either gone to war having found Dronve or there is the possibility the Lycans have Sylvana and the Faye found out?" Astaroth questioned.

Riordan paced back and forth, contemplating both scenarios. "We will use this to our advantage. While they are distracted, I want half of our warriors to search the edge of the veil and remain cloaked within the mists. The rest of us will search the surrounding areas on the outskirts of the battle."

"How do we know she hasn't been caught in the middle of the shit?" Nicolai asked.

"We don't," Riordan replied. "Mordeci, Rhazien, and Norix, take your warriors and search the edge of the veil. Tobias and Astaroth, you will accompany us."

Sylvana awoke in the pitch black, and when she slowly rolled over, she realized her wounds had failed to heal when a searing jolt of pain radiated through her body the moment her back touched the wood. She opened her palms and a soft blue light chased away the darkness, but it could not relieve the desperation and fear gnawing at her. Her mind was spinning in turmoil. She wanted to cry out, to call to her mates, but knew it was of no use. She kicked at the wood and pounded the side with her fist, if for no other reason than to do something, anything rather than lay there and accept her fate. However, it wasn't long before she was out of breath and exhausted. She slid her parched tongue over the gash on her lip, and spit the dirt and blood from her mouth; she could no longer decipher her tears from the sweat dripping down her face.

She did not know how long she had fallen asleep again when she woke to the sounds of scraping and trickling dirt. She listened intently and whatever it was, panted and dug in the same rapid manner as a dog; the scraping of claws crossing the top of the box scared her all the more. *Shit! Whatever it is, it has picked up on the scent of my blood.*

"Hold on, Sylvana, I'm coming," she heard from a voice in the distance.

"I'm here! I'm here!" she called out. However, she felt as though she was merely whispering, her voice was so hoarse.

The lid slowly scraped to the side and then someone lifted it open. "I'm so sorry, Sylvana. I had no idea they were going to do this."Sylvana looked up and beneath the gentle glow of the lantern, Muriel was staring down at her.

"You fucking bitch! How could you do this to me?" Sylvana cried.

"Sylvie, I didn't know—I would never have helped them," she whispered.

Sylvana slapped her hand away when she reached down for her. "Don't fucking touch me!"

Muriel stepped into the box and kneeled over her body. "You have to let me help you. I know you fucking hate me, and you have every right. But we have to go—now." Muriel placed Sylvana's arm around her neck and helped her to sit up.

Sylvana listened to the ominous sounds drifting through the forest from somewhere off in the distance. "What is happening?"

"The Faye and Lycans have gone to war. Now get up—I need you to move."

With Muriel's help, she crawled out of the shallow grave and took a deep breath; the cool air felt as if it were a breath of life. She dug her fingers into the soft dirt and pulled herself the rest of the way up and fell onto her stomach.

"Sylvana, get up," Muriel demanded. "We have to go—we have to go now."

She pushed herself off the ground and Muriel helped her to her feet and ran as quickly as she could manage having to drag Sylvana along in her weakened state.

"Why are you barefoot and in nothing but an oversized cloak?" Sylvana mumbled.

"It doesn't matter," Muriel replied.

Sylvana's mind was clouded and disoriented, and the pain from Muriel's arm wrapped around her back was almost too much to bear. Sylvana's muscles cramped with spasms, and she tripped over a branch causing both of them to fall to the ground.

"Come on, you can do this," Muriel coaxed, as she helped her to her feet again.

Sylvana's entire body was knotted with pain and as they ran and stumbled through the rough terrain, the sounds of the battle faded further into the distance.

"Where are you taking me?" Sylvana asked.

"There is a cave I can hide you in. You will be safe, and I will do everything I can to get to your mates and tell them where you are."

"After everything you did, why are you helping me now?"

"It wasn't supposed to happen this way. Ranan said he would take care of you. He gave me his word, as my mate, you would not be harmed. Wouldn't you do the same for your mates?" Muriel questioned."

"I would do a lot of things for them, but I would never betray a friend the way you did."

"You say that but until you are in the situation you don't know what you would do. He promised me he wouldn't hurt you. Would you have reason to believe your mates would deceive you?"

"I suppose there is some truth behind your bullshit, but I can feel it. I'm going to fucking die because of you," Sylvana rumbled sarcastically.

Muriel let out a forced laugh. "You are not going to die, Sylvana. I won't let you."

Sylvana fell onto her knees again and placed her forehead on the ground. "I can't—I can't go on." She looked to the side when her stomach churned, and liquid spewed from her mouth.

"It's the toxin, Sylvana. Can you call to your mates?"

"Don't you think I've been fucking trying? What did he do to me?" Sylvana bellowed.

Muriel cupped her hand over her mouth. "Shh, be quiet!" she demanded, as she helped her to her feet again. After what felt like an hour, they were crawling over boulders and fallen logs. "Sit here for a minute."

Muriel gently set her down and then pulled a few large logs out of the way. She picked Sylvana back up, led her into the cave and laid her down. She then pulled the logs back over the entrance and pushed the pine branches between them. She removed a satchel from her back, hastily opened it, pulled out a thin, wool blanket, laid it over Sylvana, and held out her wrist. "Drink, you need your strength."

Sylvana slapped her arm to the side. "I would rather die than drink from you right now." She cupped the amulet in her hands and placed it against her forehead. *Nicolai, can you hear me?* When she didn't get an answer, she curled her body into a fetal position and wept; all the while she continued calling to her mates.

Muriel opened a small leather pouch and pulled out a few leaves. "Sylvana, suck on these. They will help with the pain."

When Sylvana didn't respond, Muriel gently moved her hair from her forehead, and cupped her swollen, bruised cheek in her hand. "Sylvana, please, it will help. Ranan got the tonic from a Faye and it's stopping you from healing. I assume it is also what is preventing you from using your powers. Please trust

me—"

Sylvana's good eye snapped opened and she looked at the blurry image of Muriel's face. "Trust you? *You want me to fucking trust you?* After what you did? How do I know you are not drugging me in servitude of that piece of shit Ranan?"

"I fucked up, Sylvana! And I know you have no reason to trust me now, and there are no words that can be spoken to make you believe me." The tears streamed down her face, and she sobbed. "I can't apologize enough, but I want to make this right. I will do everything I can to get word to your mates."

Sylvana stared at her and based on the look in her eyes and on her face, she reluctantly reached for the herbs and placed them in her mouth.

"I need to look at your back." Muriel pulled the blanket to the side, held the lantern over the wound and gasped under her breath.

"I assume it's bad?" Sylvana mumbled.

"No, I just—it—it looks a little infected is all, but it's not bad," she replied, as she placed the blanket back over her.

Mordeci and his legion covertly walked along the edge of what seemed to be a never ending black void, having cloaked themselves within the swirling, ghost-gray mists. They listened intently as the sounds of the battle being waged off in the distance seemed to grow closer the further they traveled.

"Pay attention and try to pick up on any scent, no matter how minute that would indicate Sylvana was in the area," Mordeci relayed telepathically.

Although the air was cool and crisp, there was a dead flavor to it, as if hundreds of bodies had been left to perish on the battlefields of the past. "The dead are all around us in this godforsaken place," Rhazien said to no one in particular.

"The void feels more like a wall than an energetic field," Mordeci added.

What sounded like a whirlwind of disorder and violence growing closer stopped them mid-stride. They readied their swords, stood with their backs to the void, and listened intently; the anger they heard was ingrained in a Faye's muffled words. They then heard a loud thud, which sounded as if a body had been slammed onto the ground.

"Keep moving," Mordeci said.

They walked a bit further and a body exploded from the mists, nearly slamming into two of the cloaked warriors. The Lycan rose to his feet and spun around, having picked up on their scent, and as they slowly backed away, a blur of color and vicious movement appeared and lunged for the Lycan.

"Take them out," Mordeci ordered.

Two of them lunged for the Faye, covered his mouth, and held him back while another plunged his dagger into his heart. Mordeci and Norix, along with a few others, surrounded the Lycan and diverted his attention toward them while Rhazien snuck up from behind and swung; the Lycan's head rolled from his shoulders and his body slumped to the ground.

Mordeci waved his hand over the bodies, leaving only their ashes behind. "The mists will take care of the rest. Keep moving."

One of their warriors in the center of the line called out. "Anyone else feeling a ripple in the air?"

"Yes," another replied.

"Split your line, and ready yourselves on either side," Rhazien demanded.

Rhazien, Mordeci, and Norix ran down the line and met in the middle where the ripple was being felt.

"It feels like water parting," Rhazien said.

"Is it opening?" Norix asked.

"I am not sure but be ready. We have no idea what is about to enter or leave the veil if it is opening," Mordeci said.

As the ripple grew, the warriors stepped back and noticed a small whiff of smoke swirling from within the void carrying with it an unfamiliar scent."

"Stand fast and be prepared. Whatever, whomever, it is we need to end this as discretely as possible," Mordeci said.

The ripple grew in intensity and a colorful glow radiated from what looked like a rip in a piece of fabric. It expanded and contracted multiple times and without warning, the loud screech of an owl cut through the silence when it appeared from the tear and disappeared into the mists.

"A fucking owl?" one warrior questioned.

"If it can get out, we can get in," Mordeci replied.

"Should we go in?" another asked.

Mordeci reached his hand out, and it disappeared within the tear. "It's definitely a way in—"

Before he finished his sentence, the ripple let out a rumble, and it appeared as if someone had been tossed out based on how he rolled across the ground.

They surrounded whomever it was and Mordeci lunged, wrapped his arm around his neck, covered his mouth with his hand, and pinned him face down on the ground. "Anything more than a whisper, and I will slit your fucking throat. Who the fuck are you?" he demanded.

Whomever it was, held out his hands as soon as he realized who had a hold of him and relaxed his body in order to let him know he was not fighting back. Mordeci slowly removed his hand. "Mordeci, it's me Kadric Orfaedo."

"Kadric? What the fuck is going on?" Mordeci replied, as he released his grip and stood.

Kadric rose, kneeled before him, and continued to hold his arms out. "You need to send word to the Acherons. The Faye are planning an invasion and they are looking for my bairn, Sylvana Orfaedo."

"Get up," Mordeci replied. "Milord, we have Kadric Orfaedo. He just appeared from the other side of the veil."

"What? How?" Riordan asked.

"We haven't gotten that far, milord, although he said to warn you. The Faye are planning an invasion."

"No shit," Riordan replied.

"I'll leave him to you. I have no intention of stopping the search for Sylvana. Have a few of the Baroque Warriors escort him back to the castle and lock his ass up."

Kadric stood and glanced amongst the familiar faces. "What are you all doing here?"

"What are you doing here?" Rhazien asked.

"I don't have time to explain, but I can assure you I never once intended to betray the Acherons. Ranan said he knew the whereabouts of my mate, Myrine. However, it was a deception."

"Why would he want to deceive you?" Mordeci asked.

"Ranan said they offered me a life of opulence if I would join their fight against the Acherons. I refused and attacked Ranan. However, it had been a trap all along. They took me, and a Faye, named Vispera, offered me one of two choices. Join them or they would use me to get Sylvana to do their bidding."

"If you refused, how did you manage to escape through the veil?" Norix asked.

"I don't have time to explain. We need to warn the rest, and I need to get to Sylvana before they do."

"You have time now. Explain," Mordeci demanded.

"Myrine, she showed me the way out," he stated with a heavy heart.

"She is alive, then?" Mordeci asked. "Why didn't she come with you?"

"She took her own life, but somehow—she—her spirit is alive," Kadric tried to explain.

Riordan, Nicolai, and Kieran had been listening in on the entire conversation. *"Kadric Orfaedo, this is quite the story,"* Riordan said.

"Milord, I know it sounds like bullshit, but I can assure you it is the truth. Vispera is also alive and well, and she has ordered the invasion."

"And what part of this does Ranan play?" Riordan asked.

"He has sworn his allegiance to them and has signed a treaty. The Lycans have sided with them." Kadric could no longer ignore the unrelenting noise raging in the distance. *"Have they invaded already?"*

"Sylvana is missing, and we are looking for her. You said Ranan, do you know if he took her?" Riordan asked.

"Fucking hell! Tell me they don't have her?" he rumbled.

"Someone took her this evening," Riordan replied.

Mordeci saw the look crossing Kadric's face. "If you want us to find your bairn, do not yell out."

Kadric dropped onto one knee and the dirt spewed from beneath his fist. "Ranan is a fucking traitor. I know for sure now he took her. If Vispera had her, they would have made it known to me without question."

"Then we know she's not beyond the veil, which means she is out here somewhere," Riordan replied. *"Mordeci, forget about searching the veil, move forward and converge with us on the North side of the battle and have Kadric escorted back to the castle and secured."*

"Yes, milord." He motioned to a few of the Mordeci and they grabbed a hold of Kadric.

"Milord, I beg of you to let me accompany you in your search. She is my bairn."

"I will show you a snippet of mercy for Sylvana's sake. I will give you one opportunity to explain your involvement when you stand before the Guild at which time they will render a judgement," Riordan replied

"Yes, milord," Kadric replied, having no other option.

Chapter 21

Ranan walked amongst the bodies of the fallen, his chest expanding and contracting with each heavy, panting breath. His yellowish eyes stood out against his thick, dark fur which was matted with blood and debris. He stepped on a body with one foot, dug his curved claws into the flesh, and swayed his head from side to side, scanning the battlefield. *It seems as if no one is winning this battle, but I will be damned if I fall. I have that Nosferatu scant and they need her, which means they need me.*

The hackles along his back rose and as he spun around, the Lycan's feet landed squarely in the center of his chest and his back hit the ground with a solid thud. He rolled over, curled his blackened lips, bared his enormous canines, and let out a guttural roar. "Have you gone mad?"

The Lycan landed in a half crouched position and as it stood, it shook its large body and morphed into another form. "I now face thy enemy I look most forward to killing," Vispera seethed.

"You lit the fucking flame of war," Ranan snarled.

"You murdered Dronve! You are a traitor to all Faye, and I shall walk across your corpse when it lies with thy rest of your dead!"

"Dronve? I had nothing to do with his death!"

"My warriors brought his body to me. He was murdered by one of your ferals!"

"It was a fucking setup," he replied as he cautiously took one step after the other, following Vispera's movements.

"The one who is about to perish would say anything to save his life." She made a whistling sound, and a dozen of her warriors surrounded Ranan.

"It seems we are at an impasse. You should know I have the Ascelin. Kill me and she will fucking die."

"All thy more proof I need. Dronve has been watching you for some time, and now he is dead, and you have thy Ascelin female. Quite thy coincidence, don't you think?"

"It is quite *thy coincidence*, isn't it?"

Riordan, Nicolai, and Kieran pulled their amulets from beneath their tunics after feeling the heat against their chests, and when they held them together, the crimson light of each amulet pulsed. They kneeled down and placed their palms on the moist ground and felt a subtle vibration.

"She's close," Riordan said.

Nicolai closed his eyes and took a deep breath through his nostrils. "The scent of her blood," he snarled.

"She's hurt," Kieran replied.

Riordan stepped between them and walked forward. And it was not long before they were following her scent.

"Scan the entire fucking area for the slightest of nuances," Riordan said.

Nicolai stepped between Riordan and Kieran. "She should be right fucking here."

Riordan walked through an entanglement of shrubs and noticed the fresh pile of dirt, a wood lid someone had tossed to the side, and a partially buried box. "Oh, fuck!"

Nicolai and Kieran kneeled down and Riordan stepped down into the box, swept his fingers across the wood planks and smelled them. "She was here and recently. Her blood is still fresh, but there is something else."

Nicolai and Kieran followed suit and Kieran looked at them and furrowed his brows. "It's the same scent the wound on my back had when I was struck by the Faye's blade. Someone has fucking stabbed her," Kieran snarled.

"There is also the scent of a Lycan?" Nicolai said as he tossed a handful of dirt into the box.

Riordan sifted through the dirt and picked out a small tuff of fur and held it to his nose. "Why is the scent so familiar?"

Nicolai and Kieran also smelt it and then looked at each other with the same expression. "Are you thinking what I am?" Nicolai asked.

"Yes. It smells like Muriel," Kieran replied.

"If she had anything to do with this, she will feel pain she never knew existed," Riordan snarled as he threw the tuff of fur down.

"Milord—Lycan," Rhazien said.

They stalked toward the sound of its breathing and as they surrounded it, the skin on the Lycan's muzzle rippled back when it lifted its head, smelled the air, and twitched its ears as it slowly retreaded.

"A female," Riordan said, as he, Nicolai, and Kieran glanced at each other.

"Is it Muriel?" Nicolai questioned.

"Based on her scent, yes," Kieran replied.

They lunged and Riordan flipped her body over his head, slammed her onto her back, and pinned her down. "Wait!" she yelled.

They stared down at her as she transformed back into her human form. "Milord?" she said with wide eyes.

"Where the fuck is our mate?" He growled.

"I—I saved her. I have her hidden. I came to find you."

Riordan grabbed a fist-full of her hair and pulled her to her feet. "Take us to her."

"Yes, milord," she replied nervously.

"Muriel?" Sylvana said in only a raspy whisper. "Muriel?" Each movement was torturous as she rolled over feeing delusional and weak. She crawled onto her knees and her body trembled from the cold, the pain, and the unrelenting fear. *She left me here? Maybe she went to find my mates, or maybe she went to for Ranan? Don't be a fucking fool. You cannot trust anything she says or does after what she did.* "Get the fuck up," she coaxed herself aloud. "No one is coming. I have to save myself."

She pulled the blanket over her bare shoulders and after a few minutes and multiple failed attempts, she stood up and stumbled toward the entrance using the wall as a crutch. With each sluggish step, she edged closer to the entrance. She pushed on the logs and once they gave way, she fell through the entrance, and tumbled onto the branches and boulders. She cupped her mouth with her hands to mute the sounds of her cries of pain.

I am an Ascelin. Get up and move before she returns, or worse, returns with Ranan. She listened momentarily to the sounds of the sky rumbling off in the distance and a gentle breeze crossed her body, which was more invasive on her skin than the cool night air. *If I lay here and do nothing, I will freeze to death when the rains come. You can do this,* she coaxed herself.

She crawled over the logs and boulders and looked down when she reached the edge. *It's not far, just slide down.* She slid her legs over the edge and lowered herself down until she felt the damp earth beneath her toes. She released her grip to move further down and slipped; her body tumbled down the hill, and she came to a stop when she hit the trunk of a tree. It hurt to cry, it hurt to move, and it hurt to breathe. She looked up through the trees towering above her and stared at the endless array of stars dotting the sky and watched as the turbulent black clouds slowly consumed them. Her body shivered, and she looked over and tried to reach for the blanket laying a few feet away to shield herself from the small droplets of rain but could not reach it; she just looked up again and watched the stars slowly melting into the darkness.

"Sylvana, you're safe now," she heard. She moaned and felt the warmth of someone's hands cupping her cheeks, and she slapped them away. "Don't fucking touch me," she snarled.

"Sângele Nostru, it's us. It's Riordan, Nicolai, and Kieran. We're right here."

"Riordan?" she mumbled.

"Yes darling. I've got you."

"It's just a dream, get up," she said aloud.

"It's not a dream, my love," Nicolai replied as he and Kieran gently rolled her over.

The moment they looked at her back, their eyes met and an unfamiliar feeling descended over Riordan; there was a pressure wrapped around his heart, and if only for a moment he diverted his eyes, unable to bear the sight before him. His knees sunk into the earth, he cupped her cheeks in his hands, and whispered. "I've found my weakness, and I really need you to pull through. I can't fathom my life without you." He then looked at Nicolai and Kieran. "We should have been there. We should have fucking known."

"What have they fucking done to her?" Kieran snarled.

Nicolai removed his cloak and draped it over her half naked body and Muriel discretely backed away. However, a firm hand landed on her shoulder.

"Going somewhere?" Astaroth asked as a low rumble rose from his chest.

"I have to get back. If they find out, I took her, they will kill me," she lied.

"Muriel," Sylvana moaned. "It was—she took me—"

"She saved you?" Kieran asked.

"Yes—but—she helped them."

Riordan's, Nicolai's, and Kieran's eyes snapped in Muriel's direction and there was a fury intricately woven behind their onyx-black irises, letting her know the end was near, a very painful end. Muriel hadn't seen Riordan move, but she was now face to face with him, her feet were no longer touching the ground, and he had a vice like grip around her throat.

She grabbed onto his forearms and, other than his narrowed eyes, his face was absent of emotion. Although a low rumble rose from his chest, he spoke with an ominously calm and monotonal voice. "There will be no mercy. No one will come for you, no one will save you, and no one will take away the pain my brothers and I are going to inflict upon you. Now look upon me with one eye, as my mate does now."

She felt an intense spike of pain when his elongated finger nail slid across her pupil. She tried to cry out, but the grip he had on her throat muffled any and all sounds.

Riordan then tossed her into one of his warriors. "Take her."

"You need to feed, take my blood," Kieran offered. He slit his wrist and let the tiny droplets fall into Sylvana's mouth.

She cupped her lips around the slit and took a few meager swallows. "I'm not healing," she moaned as she released her grip.

"Shh, darling, it's okay," Riordan said, as he picked her up in his arms.

She tucked her face into the nape of his neck and sobbed. "Rio, I'm dying."

He carefully adjusted her body and gazed into her eyes. "Look at my face. Is there one expression leading you to believe my mate is going to die in my arms?"

"You always look like that. Where's Nicolai and Kieran?"

"We're right here, baby," Nicolai replied as he stroked the back of her head. "Riordan is correct. You are not dying."

"Everything hurts," she cried.

Kieran kissed the top of her head. "I know it does, my love. We are taking you home now."

"Open the gates!" one of the guards yelled when he noticed the royal stallions heading in their direction from where he stood on the parapet.

They pulled the gates open, stood to the side, and the stallions thundered through the main entrance. "What are they doing?" another asked when the warriors spanned out in all directions.

"I am not sure," another replied.

When Klyn heard the thundering sounds, of hooves he kicked his stallion's hindquarters and headed to meet Riordan and his brothers. *"Riordan, do you have Sylvana?"* he asked telepathically.

"Yes. We are headed back now."

"What do you mean 'you are headed back now'? You just entered the main gate."

Riordan, Nicolai, and Kieran looked at each other, confused. *"What the hell are you talking about? We are nowhere near the castle,"* Riordan replied.

One warrior who was with Kadric interrupted Riordan's and Klyn's conversation. *"Milord, the stallions are gone and their tracks are leading back home."*

"It's a fucking ruse," Nicolai stated.

"Fuck!" Riordan yelled. He then turned his attention back to Klyn. *"Klyn, it's a fucking breach!"*

"Shit!" Klyn called out to the warriors. "Attack at will! It's not the Acherons!"

The warriors leapt from the stallions and an army of Lycans and Fayes shifted back into their forms and attacked whomever was in the immediate area. Vispera and her warriors surrounded the area in a subtle mist and a reddish halo settled over the cloaked warriors who were on foot, revealing their whereabouts.

"Two lines and push back!" Klyn ordered.

Their stallions leapt over the hedges, appeared from between the trees in the gardens and in two separate waves, moving in opposite directions, they rode between the enemy and the castle; they then attacked head on to drive them back.

They weaved their way through the fray, dogging with their stallions while the warriors slashed both Faye and Lycan with their swords; the rains, aided by the burst of lightning and heavy winds, caused the blood to run down their bodies like paint on a canvas.

Klyn was knocked off his stallion when a Faye leapt at him from the side; he hit the ground and rolled to his feet. He then grabbed the Faye by the arm, spun him around, and twisted his arm in a direction it was never meant to go, breaking the elbow, and separating the shoulder. The Faye bellowed, did a back flip and his knee met Klyn's chin, which forced him to release his grip. The Faye landed in a half crouched position, gripping the hilt of his sword while his broken arm hung at his side. As he lunged, Klyn sidestepped and with a vertical slash, the Faye's head split open.

The girls rushed to the windows when they heard the sounds of splintering shields, ringing sword, the roars of Lycan's and the shouting of orders. The trails of rain running down the glass made it virtually impossible to see what was occurring, so Lenora quietly opened the window just enough so they could look down and were horrified when they stared down at the nightmare below.

"Oh my god," Lenora gasped. "How did this happen?"

"I don't know," Venthana replied.

"We have to do something," Calista stated.

"Like what?" Venthana asked.

"I don't know, but I can't stand here and do nothing." Calista then turned to Mira, kneeled down and cupped her hands in hers. "Mira, I need you to pay close attention. Your gift. How big can you make the things you control?"

"I don't know, Calista," she replied with a trembling voice.

"It's okay. I will help you. We are going to need to stand on the balcony, and I need you to do exactly as I say."

Mira pulled away and back up. "Go out there? No, I can't,"

"Calista, what are you talking about? You and Mira cannot go out there," Venthana stated firmly.

"You are going to find out eventually, so you may as well know. We are purebred Ascelins and we have certain abilities which I don't have time to explain."

The girls were shocked at her sudden admission, and they glanced at each other, but in this moment they did not know what to say or how to respond.

Calista looked at their blank expressions and she reached for Lenora's hand. "I think it would be best for you all to leave in case either Faye or Lycan come for Mira and I."

"We are not leaving you," Lenora stated. She rushed across the chamber, pushed a large painting to the side, pulled out two swords, and handed one to both Venthana and Lenora, and then took another for herself. "We know how to fight, and we will stand with you."

"Milady, what are you doing?" Victor asked as he materialized before them.

"Calista and Mira are Ascelins and they are going to help," Lenora replied

"I don't care who they are. You are not leaving," he stated.

Lenora gripped the hilt of her sword tighter. "We are not leaving. Now you can either stand with us or you can leave."

"Milady, I have my orders and I am telling you to stand down."

Lenora turned to Calista and nodded. "We are ready. Whatever you are up to, do it now."

"Mira, I will stand right behind you, okay?" Calista said.

Mira looked at the girls and then at Victor, who was staring at her and Calista as if he was waiting for them to make a move so he could intervene.

"We will also be right here, Mira," Venthana said.

Calista took Mira's hand and tried to open the balcony doors. However, Victor was suddenly standing beside her and had placed his palm on the center of the doors. "I cannot allow you to open the doors."

"Victor, I know you don't know me, but I am begging you to trust me." She then turned to Mira. "Darling, show him what you can do, but keep it small."

Mira closed her eyes, cupped her palms together, and when she opened them, a small creature flapped its coal-black wings and rose from her palm to the shock of everyone in the room. "I can make them bigger."

Victor stared in disbelief, and then glanced at Calista and Mira. "Make them bigger?"

"Yes, sir," Mira replied.

"How much bigger?" he asked.

"Between the two of us, they will be large enough and aggressive enough to distract the Lycans and the Faye. If even for a moment, it will give our warriors an opportunity to strike," Calista answered. "Is there any way you can let them know?"

"I can, milady." His palm slid from the door, and he held it up in a gesture for them to wait a moment. *"Klyn?"*

"Speak," Klyn replied telepathically, sounding breathless.

"Let the others know something is coming their way from above. Do not let them distract you," Victor replied.

"What the fuck are you talking about?" Klyn asked.

"It's Calista and Mira. I am not sure what they are up to, but from what I just witnessed, there will be some sort of flying creatures raining down on the Faye and the Lycan."

"What you are saying makes no fucking sense," Klyn stated.

"I agree, but as their commander, they will trust your word."

"I don't understand what the fuck is going on up there, but I trust you and I will get the word out."

They materialized where the stallions had been, and Riordan handed Sylvana over to Kadric. "I have ordered you to be placed under guard, but in light of the situation I will put it aside. Take our mate, and hide her until either myself, Nicolai, or Kieran call to you."

"What's happening?" Kadric asked.

"The Faye and the Lycans have breached the main gates. I will leave twelve of my warriors behind to ensure your safety."

"She is still my daughter, and I will protect her with my life, milord." Kadric took her in his arms and called to Cadell telepathically. *"Cadell?"*

"Kadric? Where the hell have you been?"

"I don't have time to explain, and I need your help. There has been a breach at the castle. I have Sylvana and she's in bad shape."

"We are well aware of the breach." Cadell replied. *"We are on the outskirts of the castle fighting the Faye and Lycan. Where are you?"*

"I'm on the North side of the Black Moor and I'm heading to my manor now. I need you to secure Alaric, Calista, and Mira."

"You don't know?" Cadell questioned.

"Know what?" Kadric asked.

"The Acherons have taken them and secured them in the castle," Cadell replied.

"You have to be fucking kidding me?"

"There is much to discuss. We will talk when we meet," Cadell said as he helped Leodion with the Lycan. After which, he turned to Markus and Leodion. "I have to go. Kadric has Sylvana and he needs my help."

"I will go with in case you run into trouble," Markus replied.

"As will I," Leodion offered as he ducked under another swipe of a Lycan's clawed hand.

Cadell, Leodion, and Markus ran through the fray, leapt over the fallen, and headed for Kadric.

Kadric adjusted Sylvana in his arms and reached out to his son telepathically. *"Alaric, it's your father. Where are you and your sisters?"*

"Father? Where the hell have you been? It's fucking mayhem here!"

"Where are you?"

"Inside the castle walls. It wasn't the Acherons who returned, the Faye and the Lycans shifted, and we are under attack."

"Get your sisters!"

Alaric grunted and Kadric heard the clang of sword meeting sword.

Alaric?" When he did not get a response he focused on getting Sylvana out of harm's way for the time being. *If something happens to my son, I will never forgive myself for not being there with him.*

After warning the warriors about what was happening, Klyn propelled himself forward and attacked another Lycan who fluently leapt over his head; he spun around, brought his sword down, and it crossed the Lycan's bicep; it let out a deadly roar and lunged. Klyn hit the ground, somersaulted once, and brought his blade up the front of the Lycan's leg as he jumped to his feet. He felt a spray of moisture cross his face when the Lycan's neck tore open; except for the sounds of its gurgling breaths, it was silent as it dropped to its knees and fell forward, revealing another warrior who had yielded the deadly blow from behind.

"Where are those things you spoke of?" the warrior asked, as he spun around to face another oncoming Lycan.

Its long arm swiped in Klyn's direction, and he ducked and stepped to the side and swung. "I have no fucking idea."

Another warrior looked down when he felt a subtle vibration beneath his boots. He cautiously stepped back and noticed a bubble rise to the surface from beneath a large puddle of water and could not tell if it was caused by the heavy drops of rain or something else. He took a few more steps back; a form emerged, and the water and mud ran down the opaque figure and a set of iridescent green eyes were pinned on his. A burning sensation radiated across his midsection, and he stumbled back. Vispera stepped forward and swung; his sword met hers with a resounding clang, which knocked him to the side. His eyes widened, his head rolled from his shoulders, and his body slumped to the side.

"One of many whom will die this night," she said aloud. She then ducked and swung at a large, rabid looking creature with leathery wings and fervid, scarlet eyes when it dove for her and slit her cheek with a long curved claw. She looked up and an explosion of the creatures appeared from within the heavy rains.

"Kadric, we are close," Cadell said telepathically.

"I am headed toward my manor."

"I think it would be best to take her to mine. It has been secured."

"Father?" Sylvana mumbled when she woke.

"Yes, darling. I've got you," he replied.

"Where have you been?"

"I'm here now. Nothing else matters," he replied.

She wept and her body writhed from the pain having been carried in her father's arms. "Put me down. I can't take it anymore."

"I'm sorry, darling, but we can't stop."

"Father, please, I—I need a minute."

Cadell and his warriors appeared, and they scanned her battered body. "She's not healing?"

"No. She was struck with a caustic Faye blade," Kadric replied.

"Father," Sylvana winced.

He looked at Cadell, who nodded. "Give her a moment of relief," Cadell suggested.

Kadric gently laid her on her side and moved her hair from her face. "When was the last time you fed?"

"I don't know? Where are my mates?"

"Your mates?" Kadric asked, as he looked at Cadell.

Cadell placed his hand on his shoulder and looked down at him. "The Acherons have taken her as their mate."

"When the fuck did that happen?" Kadric snapped.

"I am not sure? It was announced this morning before all of this took place."

Kadric rested his forearm on his knee and clenched his fists. "This is my fault. It's all my fault," he mumbled.

Cadell squeezed his shoulder. "They are taking care of her as any mate would. It's not what any of us thought it would be."

Feed her, Kadric heard. "Feed her?" he questioned.

Cadell cocked his head, not understanding. "Feed her? You want me to feed her?"

Kadric waved his hand dismissively. "No, just hold her up for me."

Cadell kneeled down and cautiously lifted her shoulders and head while Kadric slit his wrist.

Riordan, his brothers, and their warriors leapt over the walls and landed in the center of the mayhem. "Klyn, we're here. What the fuck is happening?" he asked when they saw the Faye and Lycans being attacked by malevolent winged creatures.

"Calista and Mira, they are doing this," he replied.

"They were supposed to be secured? Where the fuck are they?" Riordan asked as he rushed toward a Faye, doing his best to both fend off the creatures and remain focused on the surrounding chaos.

Riordan ran forward, barreled his body into the Faye, which sent him spiraling to the ground; he then brought his blade down on his neck, severing his head.

Klyn ducked and met the Faye's blade with his. "Lenora's chamber, or I should say on the balcony with Victor."

Riordan and his brothers looked up, and Calista, Mira, and Victor were looking down at them from the balcony. Riordan nodded and he, his brothers, and their warriors continued to carve their way through both Faye and Lycan.

Calista looked back at Victor. "They've returned."

"Yes, milady. And whatever the two of you are doing, it appears to be working. Keep it up and the Acherons and their warriors will see to the rest."

"Calista, I'm getting tired," Mira said.

"Keep going, Mira. Stay with me and I will take over as much as I can. I can't create those things. I can only make them bigger."

"I have to stop. My palms burn and I don't feel well."

"Mira, you have let nothing get in your way before don't start now. If they don't stop this, Laurent will be in danger."

"Okay, I—" Mira screamed and dropped to her knees when a body popped over the railing and raised his blade; the girls standing near the door yelped and raised theirs in response. Victor shoved Calista to the side and his sword crossed the Faye's midsection and he landed a solid front kick to his chest, which sent the Faye backward over the railing. He then called to the warriors outside the main door to the chamber. *"Send in two warriors and pull another two from down the hall to stand guard at the door."*

"Guard this door," one of them yelled, before materializing behind Victor.

Calista grabbed Mira's arm and pulled her to her feet. "Keep going."

Chapter 22

Sylvana stood in the darkness gazing into the forest; she gasped when she felt a hand on her shoulder from behind, but it held her gently. She turned around and her mother was standing there.

"Mother?"

"Yes, Sylvie." Myrine cupped her face in her hands and looked at her with a radiant smile.

Sylvana wrapped her arms around her neck and clung to her. "What happened to you?"

"I now stand with all those who have passed before us."

It's just a dream, Sylvana told herself.

Myrine pulled away and lifted her chin with her fingers. "It is not a dream, my love. I am here with you."

Sylvana looked over her shoulder and her father was kneeling at her side along with Cadell, while numerous warriors were standing nearby, some of whom were sheltering her from the rain with their shields. "Am I dying?" she asked, realizing neither she nor her mother were getting wet.

"No, my love. Your body is healing."

The tears ran down Sylvana's cheeks. "What happened to you?"

"There is no time for tears my, darling girl. It is time for you to rise up."

Sylvana tilted her head and looked at her, not understanding. "*Rise up*?" She looked over her shoulder when a strange, haunting sound drifted with the wind from off in the distance. "What it is?" she asked as she looked back at her mother.

"The war is upon us."

"What war?"

"The Lycan's and Faye have attacked. You need to wake up and release the grasp of the circumstances having pinned you down."

"I don't understand?"

"You have been laid bare, but you have not yet been defeated. Face your enemies without doubt and without fear."

"You want me—to fight the Lycans and the Faye?"

"Yes. Look for the one named Vispera. You will know her when you see her."

"Vispera? I read about her."

"She is the Faye's High Priestess."

"She did this to you, didn't she?" Sylvana asked.

"She ordered my capture and your father's, and she is seeking you out." Myrine cupped Sylvana's amulet in her hand. "You now have the powers of the Faye in your veins."

"The blood of my mates," Sylvana replied, as she looked at her mother's cupped fist.

"Yes. Vispera cannot defeat you." She then kissed her cheek and stepped back. "I must go now."

"Mother, wait. Do not leave me," she pleaded.

"Rise up, Sylvana, and become the master of your fate."

"We need to go," Cadell said as he rose to his feet.

"Sylvana, open your eyes," Kadric urged, as he stroked the back of her head.

She let out a gentle moan, and her eyelids fluttered. "Father?"

"Yes, darling. We have to go now."

After gathering her senses, she sat up, with her father's assistance, and as she looked over her body, she lowered the tattered blanket and rested her head on her knees. "Is it healed?"

Kadric was stunned. He gently ran his hand over what appeared to be nothing more than an old scar. "The wound of the Faye has completely healed. How do you feel?"

"I feel strong." She held out her arm and Kadric took it in his and stood.

"Can you walk on your own?" he asked.

"I can do more than that." She rolled her head in a circle, closed her eyes, and took a deep breath. She then looked at her father. "I need a tunic."

He pulled the blanket higher over her shoulders. "You can clean up and dress when we get you back to Cadell's manor."

"We are not going to Cadell's."

"What are you talking about?"

"We are going home."

Kadric glanced at Cadell. "Home? Our manor is not safe."

"I'm talking about the Castle. It is my home now."

Kadric gently grabbed her arm. "The hell if you are. You are not going anywhere near there," he stated adamantly.

"You can either go with me or I will go alone," she replied defiantly.

"Sylvana, we cannot allow it," Cadell interjected as he stepped forward.

She looked at her father. "Have you seen and spoken to mother?"

"I have. Why do you ask?"

"Did she tell you what to do?"

"She did," he acknowledged.

"Did you do it?"

"I did and I assume you have also seen and spoken to her?"

"I have."

"Did she tell you what to do?"

"She did."

"And you are going to do it, aren't you?" Kadric asked.

"I am." She then cocked her head and raised her eyebrow. "Are you going to give me your tunic or am I doing this half naked?"

"Sylvana—" Kadric began.

"Father—" Sylvana interjected.

"Shit. You are as stubborn as she is. I don't assume there is anything I can say to change your mind?" He removed his tunic and held it up while everyone else diverted their eyes when she dropped the blanket.

"No." She slid her arms into the large tunic, buttoned it up, tied it in a knot at her waist, and rolled up the sleeves. "I need a moment," she requested.

"Alaric, Calista, can you hear me?" she asked.

"Sylvana! Oh my god, are you okay?" Calista asked.

"Sylvana, I hear you," Alaric replied.

"I need to you to do something, and it needs to be done now."

"Anything," Calista replied.

"I don't have time for this," Alaric replied, sounding breathless.

"Alaric, go somewhere safe. I need you to listen to me without distractions."

He looked around and ran across the garden and stood between one wall and a tall shrub. "This had better be fucking good," he replied.

"I need the two of you to get to the library. There is another room behind the far wall."

"What?" Calista and Alaric asked in unison.

"I'm with father and Cadell and we are coming. Now do exactly what I say."

Sylvana turned back to her father. "How close are we to the castle?"

"About halfway. Do you have the energy to go the distance cloaked?"

"I do."

Kundar, one of the Barouqe warriors, stepped before her. "Milady, I cannot allow you to go to the castle."

"I am going," she replied.

"I have my orders, milady. I will stop you."

"I am the Acheron's mate, and I am telling you to step aside."

Kadric, Cadell, Markus, and Leodion protectively stepped closer to her. "You need to trust her," Kadric said.

"We are not under your command. It is our duty to protect her at all costs and we will go through you if needed," Kundar threatened.

The four of them pulled their swords, and the Barouqe warriors followed suit.

Sylvana took a few steps back, turned around, rolled her shoulders and held out her hand. A small, flickering, iridescent, blue light danced above her palm. She then closed her fist and threw it at a tree.

They watched in disbelief when the tree was consumed by what appeared to be a thin layer of ice wrapping itself around the trunk like the icy fingers of winter's fist. The bark crackled and splintered and the sounds of shattering of glass cut through the heavy drops of rain drumming against the forest's canopy.

After a moment of silence, Kundar stepped forward and nodded. "Milady, we will stand by your side, but you understand, it may cost us our lives for disobeying a direct order."

She wrapped her hand around his forearm. "They will understand."

He simply cocked his head and stared at her.

"I will make them understand."

"I don't believe anyone has that kind of power over them, not even you, milady."

She glanced at her father and Cadell, who had the same look upon their faces. *They do not believe I can intervene, either.* She knew there was nothing she could say to convince them otherwise. She looked up at Kundar. "I can do this alone."

"We will not leave your side, milady. We will either die at the hands of our enemies, or we will die at the hands of the Acherons, but we will not die as cowards." He held out his hand and gave a slight nod. "Shall we dance amongst their frozen corpses, milady?"

She took his hand and nodded back. "We shall."

Nicolai and Kieran were fighting side by side with Riordan as they carved their way through the barrier of slashing Faye blades; all the while, the battle outside was spilling over the walls when the Faye and Lycans managed to make it across the fields avoiding the warriors who followed closely behind. All around them was a whirlwind of chaos and violence; the smell of death contaminated the pure smell of the gardens, the sounds of war replaced the melodic sounds of the birds, and the earth beneath their boots was now discolored and slick from the blood, organs and bodies scattered throughout the kingdom.

Riordan looked over and noticed one Lycan in particular who was discretely walking between the tall stone wall and a row of bushes. *Ranan,* he said to himself. *"Nicolai, Kieran—I've found Ranan,"* he called out telepathically.

They rushed through the fray and surrounded him; Ranan rose on his hind legs, curled back his leathery lips, and roared with such ferocity the ground rumbled beneath their boots.

Riordan spun his sword in a circle and then gripped the hilt with both hands and pointed it toward him. "We have finally come face to face, Ranan."

Ranan looked at the resolute expressions on the brothers' faces who had him pinned between them and the wall, and he knew facing them would be a losing battle. He spun around and tried to leap over the wall. However, the brothers lunged just as quickly, and the dank puddle of water splashed in all directions and the air exploded from his lungs when his back hit the ground.

Ranan snarled and growled, and his large jaws snapped at anything and nothing at all out of sheer panic.

They let him up, re-sheathed their swords, and surrounded him. "I never thought you would try to run like a fucking coward," Riordan snarled.

Nicolai got into a defensive stance. "We are going to dismember you one piece at a time for what you have done to our mate, but first things first."

The blood sprayed from Ranan's snout when Nicolai's fist made contact; Kieran and Riordan then lunged, and Ranan frantically spun around and lashed out, returning the brother's fury. One blow crossed Nicolai's face which caused him to stumble back. He then took a swipe toward Kieran, who jumped back. However, his claws crossed his chest, creating three sizeable lacerations.

Ranan absorbed the pain and did his best to fight back and defend himself. However, the brothers pummeled him mercilessly and ceased only when he fell to the ground and began to lose consciousness. The brothers stepped back and watched as Ranan slowly returned to his mortal form. His face was unrecognizable, his breathing was labored, and his broken body failed to heal with the transformation.

Ranan let out a pain-filled roar when Nicolai's blade separated one arm from his body.

"You will never win the war," he bellowed.

Kieran bent down and grasped a hold of his contorted jaw. "You will never know." He then stood, swung his blade, and separated his other arm.

Riordan spun his sword at his side and then brought it down and across his thighs and Ranan's legs rolled to the side, and the brothers watched as his eyes glossed over.

"The Faye—the High Priestess, they will—defeat," he stuttered, as his head languidly turned to the side when he took his last breath.

"Vispera is next," Riordan said, as he pulled Kieran's tunic up to access his wounds.

"I'm good, brother. You should check the gash on your bicep, not my chest," Kieran stated.

"It's fine," Riordan answered

"Have you seen her?" Nicolai asked.

"No, but she is here somewhere," Riordan replied.

Kieran held up his hand and looked at the wall. "Do you hear that?"

There was a disquieting crackling sound echoing from the other side and a bluish-colored light flickered and flashed and lit the darkness in quick successions. The brothers remained still, in anticipating of another wave of Faye warriors. However, a fraudulent calm followed the flashes and then the disquieting sounds of shattering glass broke the eerie silence.

"What the fuck is going on?" Nicolai asked.

"Another wave of Faye?" Riordan questioned.

They leapt onto the top of the wall and crouched down; frozen bodies, both standing and lying on the ground, were scattered across the out lining forest, and instead of their warriors fighting Faye and Lycan, they were cutting the heads off what appeared to be statues carved in ice. A group of warriors then appeared from the forest and stood at the edge of the field.

"Holy shit! It's Sylvana," Nicolai stated.

"Are you thinking what I am?" Kieran asked.

"Yes. Sylvana, putting the fire out at the barn," Riordan replied.

They leapt off the wall, ran across the field, ducking and dodging both Faye and Lycan, and came face to face with Sylvana. Kadric, Cadell, and the rest of the warriors who had her surrounded in a protective half circle.

"Sylvana," Riordan called out. She ran toward them, leapt into Riordan's arms and clung to him. "What are you fucking doing here?" he asked.

"My mother sent me. She told me to take control of my destiny."

He set her down and Nicolai and Kieran each pulled her in for a tight embrace. "Baby, you shouldn't be here," Nicolai said.

"Darling, you've healed?" Kieran questioned.

"My mother's blood healed me, and I came to help." She looked at their torn and blood-soaked tunics. "Holy shit, are you all okay?"

"We're fine, darling," Kieran replied.

She pulled his tunic up and slid her hand over his wounds. "They're mostly healed."

"No pain at all." He winked.

Riordan stepped face to face with Kundar. "Who the fuck told you to bring her here?"

Sylvana cupped his forearm in her hands. "Rio, please. I insisted,"

"*You insisted*?" He replied as he looked down at her. He then looked back at Kundar. "So she insists, and you decide to disobey a direct order?"

Kundar nodded respectfully and placed his fist to his heart. "Yes, milord. I will not try to defend my actions."

"Rio, look around. I showed him the powers I possess. He has been by my side the entire time," Sylvana explained.

Riordan, Nicolai, and Kieran glanced around. "So this is you? Not the Faye?" Riordan smiled.

"Yes, and that's not all—"

Kundar's voice interrupted her when he called out. "Swords!" Except for Sylvana and the brothers who circled her, they spanned out and met a dozen Faye blade for blade.

Sylvana spun around and the brothers watched as a wave of iridescent-blue mist radiated from her palms like a wave of water, stopping the Faye mid-stride. Their feet froze to the ground and a thin layer of ice crawled up their bodies, like creeping vines, freezing them inch by inch. They flailed their arms and one of them brought his sword across his legs and they shattered beneath him; his body hit the ground, and he frantically clawed at the dirt, and pulled himself across the ground. Sylvana stepped forward and with another wave of her hand, a thin layer of ice consumed the remainder of his body.

"Holy shit," Nicolai said as he looked at Sylvana. "We had no idea you had ice in your veins." He winked.

Sylvana looked at Riordan with pleading eyes. "Kundar had a good reason for his actions."

After a moment of contemplation, Riordan placed his hand on Kundar's shoulder. "My mate speaks the truth, and your actions were admirable. However, I expect this won't happen again without our permission?"

Although Kundar's face remained stoic and expressionless, a wave a relief swept over his body, and he felt as if he could breathe for the first time since deciding to return with Sylvana. "Without question, milord."

Sylvana placed her hand on Kundar's forearm and winked, and she noticed the subtlest hint of a smile when he looked down at her.

"Enough small talk. We need to finish this," Nicolai said.

Riordan bent down and whispered in her ear. "Darling, we will be right behind you, but if you ever pull something like this again without our permission, you will be punished in *so* many ways, some of which you will enjoy and some of which you won't."

Sylvana pulled back. However, before she could speak, Kieran bent over and his mouth fell to hers. She cupped the back of his head in her hand and, after a heated kiss, he placed his forehead on hers. "Let's do this."

"Klyn, open the gates," Riordan said telepathically.

"Open the gates? Why?"

"Look over the wall," Riordan replied.

Klyn leapt over onto the parapet above the main gate and looked across the field. *Holy shit.* "Open the gates!" he called out.

The field was a graveyard of frozen statues in various positions and facial expressions, as if time had suddenly ceased to exist; warrior after warrior fell in line behind Sylvana and her mates while Faye and Lycan retreated into the forest. The sound of shattering glass replaced the sounds of the battle, and the iridescent-blue light flickered and flashed like lightning against the blackness, revealing the fertile fields where slaughtered Faye, Lycan, and Nosferatu bodies littered the ground.

The doors leading onto the marble veranda swung wide open and Marius Acheron and Lucinda Ascelin stepped onto the veranda and lunged, attacking whoever was within reach. They sunk their canines deep into the flesh of the Faye warriors' necks and fed with a pent up blood thirst rivaling any swing of a sword; after which they tossed their drained bodies to the ground and grabbed another and then another. It was not long before both Faye and Lycan retreated over the walls in a disorganized and chaotic frenzy.

Marius spread his arms out to his sides, lifted his chin, and let out a thunderous roar which diverted everyone's attention away from the battle, essentially bringing the fighting to a temporary halt.

Vispera heard a roar reverberate through the air, embodying a promise of death; she spun around and her warriors, along with the Lycan's, were being tossed aside as if they were nothing more than flies being batted away. She took a step back and stared at the most formidable looking opponent. His yellowish eyes were fiery, aglow with rage and determination as he attacked his next victim; with each fresh kill, the blood flowed through his veins and his thin, skeletal body transformed little by little. His gray hair became thick locks of shoulder length chestnut, the concave features on his face filled in, the muscles on his body strained against his skin, and verged into defined, well-built curves.

Diaspor and Mascuriel ran to her side and Diaspor grabbed her arm. "We must leave."

"No! We have come too far and are much too close," Vispera protested.

"It is far too dangerous! It will be impossible to accomplish this now," Mascuriel stated.

"We have one chance. Do you still carry thy ethereal binds?"

Diaspor lifted the rope attached to his hip. "Yes, Priestess."

"Follow me." She backed up toward the main gate and turned around to run. However, she stopped mid-stride when noticed Sylvana and a legion of warriors walking toward her.

"I've been told you are looking for me?" Sylvana questioned.

A ripple of defeat crept through Vispera's body with the realization she had lost all control; she had not anticipated Sylvana would become a dangerous and unpredictable threat, nor had she accounted for Marius and Lucinda, who were emerging from the fray behind her with deadly intent. Although her entire world had just shifted off its axis, she remained calm and unemotional, and Diaspor and Mascuriel remained at her side.

There was a brief interval of silence when everyone laid eyes on Marius and Lucinda. The brothers glanced at each other and then looked at Sylvana. *"How can this be?"* Nicolai asked telepathically.

"I have no idea? It's not possible for Sylvana to have freed them?" Riordan replied.

"It appears I no longer have to chase the dragon," Vispera replied, interrupting the queer silence of all those standing there.

Sylvana glanced at her mates and then back at Vispera and her two warriors. "Your executions will be wrought in iron," she threatened.

Vispera held her arms out and walked in a slow circle. "All my enemies in one place, makes thy dreadful work of tracking you down one by one a less tedious task. Just like thy seasons, your world can change with a gentle breeze. Now let's make a deal, shall we?"

Riordan let out a nefarious laugh. "What could you possibly offer us?"

"Cathagne," Vispera replied nonchalantly.

With long strides, Lucinda advanced and stood face to face with Vispera, looking as poised and regal as she did the night she disappeared. "You dare to speak my daughter's name?"

Everything in Vispera's body told her to flee. However, she stood confidently, with her feet grounded in the mud. "Yay, and I will return her unharmed. In exchange, I choose thy Ascelin."

Nicolai and Kieran stepped on either side of Sylvana, and Vispera felt the cool steel of their blades on either side of her neck. Diaspor and Mascuriel dropped their swords when they too felt the tips of the blades settle on their throats.

"Our mate is not on the bargaining table, but your heads are," Riordan threatened as he stood directly behind Sylvana.

"Should you fail to negotiate, I will sit on my throne and smirk as thy cries of terror, indistinguishable between Nosferatu and beast, fill my ears when you bathe in thy poison of darkened souls. Demons fraught with a brutal desperation to arise, will claw their way across your lands when I open thy dark side of thy veil and unleash them."

"Should you fail to return my daughter—unharmed, I will see that every one of your kind lay bloodless, and bare-boned, on the ground of your own kingdom," Lucinda stated sharply.

Vispera, Diaspor, and Mascuriel dropped to their knees and a violent, rotating column of Snow Crested Owls rose and consumed them all.

They struck them with their blades, and it was not long before the column rose into the dark of night, revealing three doppelgängers identical to Sylvana standing there, each of whom looked at either Riordan, Nicolai, or Kieran.

Having dropped to his knee, Kieran rose, grabbed one of the girls and pulled her tightly into his body. "This is not Sylvana," he said, as he shoved her back.

"What happened?" another asked.

"Where did Vispera go?" the third asked.

"They are shifters!" another yelled as she pointed toward the other two and backed up.

Riordan, Nicolai, and Kieran placed a hand on the lady's shoulders and pushed them into the center of the crowd; all the while, everyone standing nearby was at a loss. They had no idea which one was the real Sylvana. The brothers looked at each other and then back at the lady's.

"Smell that?" Riordan asked. He then cocked his head and stared inquisitively at Kieran.

"Yes. Her scent is strange," Kieran replied as he smelt his tunic.

"Not one of them is our mate," Nicolai snarled.

Kadric shouted aloud and held his hand out when the Acheron's blades cut through the air as if in slow motion. "Wait!"

Nothing but swirling, gray smoke followed the motion of their swords as they slashed through the lady's bodies.

"To the veil. Vispera has Sylvana!" Riordan ordered.

Just as they morphed out of sight, branched lightning lit the acheronian morning sky, whose light was concealed behind the rolling, black storm clouds, and the undulating mass looked fit to fall upon them.

"What the hell is happening?" Klyn questioned.

"It has to be Sylvana," Riordan replied, as he leapt into the air. Except Lucinda, the others followed. When they passed through the mass, it felt as though they had transcended through the cold breath of winter, and their bodies were covered in a thin layer of crystalline flakes.

"Fucking hell," Nicolai snapped, as landed on the ground.

"Give her a moment," Marius replied calmly. "We cannot fight the unseen."

A splintering sound fractured the air all around them and bolts of iridescent-blue radiated outward, along with an ear-piercing screech. They all leapt back when a crystalline-blue dragon appeared overhead. A layer of hoarfrost covered its skin, and her pointed wings were as jagged as the ice that lay along a frozen shoreline. With each beat of her wings, a cold breeze blew, and a gentle snow swirled around their bodies as they stood in disbelief.

"Never in my life did I expect to see such a sight," Rhazien stated.

"Where the fuck is Sylvana?" Nicolai asked.

"Is she the dragon?" Kieran questioned.

"I have no answers," Riordan replied. He then turned to Klyn. "Get a legion of warriors to the veil and be ready for anything."

"Milord, I would like to accompany Klyn in case Sylvana shows," Kadric requested.

Riordan nodded. "Go."

The dragon drew back its glacier-blue lips, revealing a triple row of jagged, iridescent skeens that gleamed like ice cycles hanging from an eave in the early morning sun. It looked down into the forest, opened its mouth, and exhaled a wave of ice, not flame.

Another creature suddenly burst from the tree line. It had the head of an eagle as white as newly fallen snow and a curved, yellow beak. Two white tuffs of feathers created its ears, while the feathers faded down its neck until its tawny fur took over where its lion like lower body appeared. Its hind legs and outstretched wings were a deep, umber brown. It let out a death defying screech, stretched its yellow, eagle like talons forward and attacked the dragon.

"Have we all gone mad?" Kundar asked.

"Holy shit," Tobias stated.

"It's not possible? Maybe it's another Faye ruse being used as a distraction?" Astaroth suggested.

"It's Vispera, and the Griffin is real," Lucinda replied.

They stood briefly, feeling powerless as the creatures clashed above the forest canopy in an explosion of fury and aggression.

Riordan turned to Lucinda. "In our absence, it would only be fitting for you to step in."

She wrapped her arms tightly around Riordan. "I will do what is needed. Just bring my daughter back."

"If she is there, I give you my word." He pulled away and looked at Astaroth. "Remain here, and protect Lucinda. See that the gates are closed and the grounds and outlining areas are manned. Tobias, take you men and get to veil." Riordan then placed his hand on Marius's shoulder. "Grandfather, are you up for another battle?" Marius returned the gesture. "Riordan, I have dreamt of this day for what feels like eons."

Riordan then addressed the legion of warriors who had gathered around. "Attack!"

Except for Lucinda and Astaroth, Riordan, his brothers, and their warriors headed for the Griffin. Just as they surrounded it, its claws slid along the dragon's chest and stomach, and shards of icy scales rained down. The dragon dipped, and then dove straight up, and as it hovered above the Griffin, it let out an explosive wave of ice. The warriors made an evasive move, the Griffin rolled to side, and the dragon's breath caught the tip of one of it's wings, freezing the feathers. The Griffin then expanded its wings, tucked them against her body and, with an explosive burst of power, flew toward the veil, and the dragon gave chase.

"Follow them!" Riordan called out.

Chapter 23

Tobias and his warriors avoided the mayhem between the Faye and Lycans in the surrounding areas near the veil. *"It sounds as if they have turned on each other?"* Rhazien stated telepathically.

"They are accusing each other of the loss," Tobias replied.

"Excellent," Mordeci stated.

"This is it," Tobias said.

After walking along the veil for a short period, Mordeci held up his hand. "Kadric, this is the spot where you appeared."

"Why don't you explain to us all that took place? Maybe there is something we missed that would be of help?" Tobias suggested.

Kadric explained what had occurred, and although it did not provide them with any solid information that would help them cross the veil, it revealed something else of importance.

"The girl you met whose wrist looked like it had been severed. Could it have been Cathagne?" Tobias questioned.

Kadric looked at him when the realization struck. "I knew I had seen her before. Is she the girl in the painting in the grand hall?"

"Yes," Tobias replied.

Cadell walked over and placed his hand on Kadric's shoulder. "You are lucky to have made it out."

"If it wasn't for Myrine, I would still be there. On another note, I do not have the words to express my gratitude, but I want to thank you for all you have done for my bairns in my absence."

"There is none needed. I know you would do the same for Laurent."

"Without question," Kadric agreed.

"In that case, I may need you to save him from his mother," Cadell joked.

A loud screech echoed from off in the distance, capturing their attention. "Ready your swords, and should the veil open, be prepared to follow. If Sylvana is there, secure her first and then, if at all possible, search for Cathagne," Tobias ordered.

Thunderous roars and high-pitched screeching rang out overhead. Tobias and his warriors could not see through the thick, gray mists, so they levitated themselves for a better view. They looked down when they heard the stampede of warriors rushing toward the veil where they had been waiting only moments before.

"Be prepared, if we make it in, as will they," Mordeci warned.

The dragon dove in front of the Griffin as if blocking its path to the veil, and the Griffin slammed its body into the dragon, who locked its jaws around the Griffin's neck. The Griffin drug its gigantic talons down the side of the dragon, tearing it open, and sounded as if the wind had carried an errant object through an enormous, glass pane. As the dragon released its grip, layer after layer of opaque scales formed over the lacerations.

Riordan appeared, along with a legion of warriors, and the Griffin's wings spanned out and then slammed into its body as it dove through a small expansion in the veil as it began opening.

"Go. Now!" Riordan demanded.

Lucinda and Astaroth walked the grounds, surveying the damage, and making sure there were not any Faye or Lycans in hiding or breathing. All the while, Astaroth was calling out orders and making sure the warriors were manning the parapets, walls, and towers.

Shards of glass crunched beneath their feet when Alaric and Victor walked onto the veranda, with the girls following behind. The heady smell of smoke and the scent of burning flesh met them, and based on the bright glow, it looked like a dozen campfires had been lit on the other side of the wall. The once exotic gardens were unrecognizable; the ponds were now filled with debris and discolored, and the tiered fountains and stone statues had been knocked over and were laying in pieces; shrubs were broken, bare and trampled, and the lush lawns were saturated, muddy and filled with the bodies and entrails of the dead. Stable hands were rounding up the stallions who were wandering about, and the warriors and Helots were tossing bodies over the wall where they were being burned in the fields.

"My god," Lenora stated.

"It's unrecognizable," Venthana added.

Alaric turned to Calista and squeezed her hand. "With so many having left with the Acherons, we are all being called to arms. Are you and Mira going to be okay?"

Calista wrapped her arms around him. "Go. We will be fine."

Mira wrapped her hand around his forearm. "Alaric, don't leave."

He pulled her to him and hugged her tightly. "I'm not leaving, but duty calls. Stay here with the girls. I will check on you later."

"Okay," she whispered.

He pulled away and cupped her face in his hands. "You were incredible tonight, by the way." He winked.

"Really?" She beamed.

"Yes. Really. Father is going to be so proud of you." He then stood and looked at Victor, who nodded and stepped forward.

"There are rumors you and Calista might have had something to do with freeing Marius and Lucinda. Is it true?" Victor questioned.

"I know nothing about it," he replied nonchalantly.

Victor placed his hand on Alaric's shoulder. "No one will forget what you and your sisters have done tonight."

Alaric nodded. "Will you watch over Calista and Mira?"

"It goes without saying."

"Alaric!" Florin stated as he bounded up the steps.

They grabbed each other's forearms and patted each other on the shoulder. "We survived to fight another night," Florin stated.

"We sure did," Alaric agreed, as they headed down the steps.

"Calista?" Mira said, as she stood with her back to her.

"Yes?"

"Is Sylvie going to be okay?""She's going to be fine. Her mates will let nothing happen to her." Calista then looked solemnly at the girls.

Lenora placed her hand on Calista's back and smiled. "They will bring her back," she mouthed.

Mira turned ever so slightly and looked up at Calista. "Is Sylvie really a dragon?"

"No, darling. She creates them the way you created the winged creatures."

The girls looked at each other and then tilted their heads, listened intently, and heard the faint sounds of the dragon's roars and the Griffin's shrieks coming from miles away. They felt terrible when they saw the look of sadness and concern cross Calista's face.

"There is nothing we can do out here. Let's go back to my chamber," Lenora suggested.

"Calista, let's go. You and Mira must be exhausted?" Venthana added.

"Calista, can I sleep with Sylvana's puppy tonight?" Mira asked.

"Yes, darling. Sylvana would appreciate you looking after Rio."

Ninbae and Eoin stood on the balcony of Vispera's watchtower holding the veil open and the moment they lay sight of the Griffin being chased by a dragon as well a legion of Nosferatu warriors, a rush of adrenaline seared through their bodies. Not only had Nosferatu breached the veil, so had a wave of Lycans, who were mixed in with their Faye warriors as they scrambled through the opening in a chaotic frenzy.

"Close thy veil!" Eoin yelled. He then looked at the Faye warriors who were standing on the parapets. "Attack!"

"We cannot close thy veil. Half of our warriors are on thy other side!" Ninbae protested.

"Do you not see thy number of Lycans and Nosferatu below? How many should we allow in before thy entire kingdom is overrun? Now close thy fucking veil!" He then turned to Stronbo. "We must find Vispera!" As they ran down the winding staircase toward the back entrance, the walls suddenly shook, and the windowpanes rattled as if the castle had been struck by a bolt lightning.

The dragon exploded from the force of the impact when it careened to the ground. Large shards of ice radiated outwards, and the warriors ducked and held up their shields to protect themselves from the sharp projectiles. Sylvana's body, which had been launched yards away from the center of the impact, came to a rolling stop.

They rushed to her, and Riordan carefully rolled her listless body over, and pulled her tunic up to access the wounds. He traced his fingers over the large lacerations that were in the later stages of healing. Riordan shook his head and scoffed under his breath. "Fuck."

"Come on, darling," Kieran urged as he cupped her face in his hands. However, her body recoiled when he touched her; he let go and backed away. "She must be in a great deal of pain?"

Nicolai and Riordan looked at him curiously. "Why are you backing away?" Riordan asked.

"I don't want to hurt her."

Kadric kneeled at her side and moved her hair off of her forehead, and even though she was unresponsive, to their relief, she was breathing. "She will be okay. Her body needs rest," Kadric offered.

"Has she done this before?" Nicolai asked.

"Not to this extent. Her mother warned me, but I did not know she possessed so much power," Kadric answered honestly.

"We need to get her out of here," Riordan stated.

"Kadric Orfaedo." He looked around and noticed a silhouette standing in the trees. "Milord, it's Cathagne."

"What? Cathagne? How do you know?" Riordan asked, as they all looked in the same direction as Kadric.

"She is calling to me."

Marius placed his hand on Riordan's shoulder. "It is her, as sure as I am standing here."

"Rhazien, remain here with our warriors. We will be back momentarily. If Faye or Lycan come into view, attack at will," Riordan ordered. He gathered Sylvana off the ground and into his arms.

"Yes, milord," Rhazien replied.

"Cathagne, do you remember me?" Marius asked as he stepped toward her. *I can't believe my eyes.*

She cautiously stepped back. "I do not."

Marius held up hands. "Do not be afraid. I mean you no harm."

Kadric stepped forward and held up a hand. "It's okay, Cathagne. They have come in search of you. Marius is your uncle."

Cathagne briefly stared at Marius, trying to remember. "My uncle?"

"Yes. Your mother was mated to my brother, Anton. I took care of the two of you after the Faye killed your father. I couldn't have loved you more if you were my own bairn," Marius explained.

Nicolai placed his hand on Marius's shoulder having felt his sorrow. "It will just take time."

Marius nodded, but did not take his eyes off Cathagne.

Feeling confused and overwhelmed, she looked at the only familiar face in the group. "Is this all true, Kadric Orfaedo?"

"Yes, Cathagne. They mean you no harm and only wish to return you to your mother."

"Why did you return, Kadric Orfaedo?"

"I followed my daughter, Sylvana."

She looked at Sylvana and cocked her head. "Sylvana, thy one Vispera has been seeking?"

"Yes," Kadric replied.

"You should not have come back. Vispera will never allow you to leave," Cathagne answered.

"I gave your mother my word I would bring you back to her, and I have every intention of honoring it," Riordan said.

"*My mother*? 'Tis not possible. The Lycans killed my mother, or so I was told."

"She is alive and well," Marius replied.

"Kadric said you remember nothing prior to being here?" Tobias stated.

"'Tis true. As I explained to Kadric, I have nothing more than ill begotten memories. But I have always known I don't belong here."

"We don't have time to explain. Is there somewhere safe for you to go?" Riordan asked.

"Yes. There is a place where thy molten moon flows over thy falls."

Riordan looked down at Sylvana. "Will you take Sylvana there? I will have a few of my warriors ensure your safety."

Kundar stepped forward. "Milord, my men and I will look after them, if you can spare us?"

Riordan nodded in agreement and handed Sylvana to Kadric. "Cadell, go with them. We will come to you as soon as we are able. Notify us the minute she wakes."

Eion and Stronbo, along with a host of Faye warriors, followed the sounds of the branches snapping and popping and trees toppling over under the heavy weight of the Griffin's body as it plummeted into the forest, causing an explosive plume of debris. As they rushed toward the body, large feathers and leaves languidly floated to the ground all around them. They frantically searched for Vispera's body and once they located her, they gathered her off the ground and headed for her veiled wing.

They laid her down on a large, ornate altar and placed a folded piece of material over the laceration in her throat. "She is not healing?" Stronbo questioned.

"Thy wound is strange. I have seen nothing like it," Eoin replied.

"Thy bite of the dragon. Her skin appears to be freezing around thy wound," Lakomi stated, as he ran his fingers over it. A stinging sensation radiated through the tips of his fingers. "What thy hell is this?" he questioned as he held his hand out. "My fingers, what is happening?"

Except for Eoin, the others stepped away, and without hesitation he removed the dagger from his hip, slammed Lakomi's hand, palm down, on the stone altar, and brought the blade across his fingers.

Lakomi cried out, fell to his knees, and stared at the blood as it spilled from where his fingers had been severed. His body trembled as he grasped his wrist, and a strange numb feeling took over, as if his adrenaline were a sedative.

"Get the Sirona!" As Eoin wound a piece of cloth over the wound, he felt someone's hand slide across his shoulder and looked in Vispera's direction. He grabbed Lakomi's other hand and carefully cupped it over the saturated material. "Hold it tight. This may or may not have worked."

Putting their fear aside, the others rushed to Lakomi, helped him to his feet, walked to the other side of the room, and sat him in a chair.

Turning his attention back to Vispera, Eoin cupped her hand in his. "Goddess, are you able to speak?"

She shook her head no.

"Then you shall speak without your voice. *Are you in pain?*" he asked.

"*Yes,*" she replied telepathically. "*Where are thy others?*"

"Priestess, I am here," the Sirona said, as she leaned over her.

Vispera held up her hand and remained focused on Eoin. "*Go on.*"

"See to Lakomi." He said to the Sirona. He then looked back at Vispera. "*Thy situation is not good, but we are handling it.*"

"*I don't have time for evasive answers.*"

"*Then I shall be blunt.* He went on and explained all that was occurring and had occurred.

"*Well, this is a conundrum,*" Vispera replied, as if unaffected by the news.

"*We have suffered a great loss, and I fear it won't be long before thy Acherons seize our kingdom.*"

She grasped his forearm. "*Thy battle is not lost until we lay down our blades. Now help me up.*"

"*Priestess, you should rest.*"

He knew, based on her hardened expression, resting was not an option. He wrapped his arm around her lower back and helped her sit up. She reached her hand up to feel the wound on her throat, and he pulled it back and nodded toward Lakomi. "*Do not touch it. I had to remove his fingers after he did.*"

The ancient trees stretched toward the burnt-orange sky, and their twisted branches reached out like time-worn fingers. Gnarled roots dipped in and out of the ground, and varicolored mosses partially covered their trunks, rough with age. Winding vines spiraled their way around the trees, while their thick tendrils hung independently from the canopy. The leaves were varying shades of green, some of which were still budding while the grown fan-like leaves, brushed in colors of jade, reached outward to catch the meager amount of sunlight. A strange cacophony of sounds and melodies drifted through the air from the abundance of exotic birds and insects, while the faint rustling of brush could be heard from the creatures scampering through the overgrowth.

Cadell looked down at the florescent rays of colorful light penetrating the thick canopy, casting an unearthly orangish-red luminescence over the ground. "It's as if we are in another world," he said, as he looked at the unfamiliar surroundings.

"That we are," Kundar replied.

"Do not let its beauty deceive you. If you think thy Faye and Lycan are a threat, you have yet to discover thy creatures that slip through thy dark side of thy veil," Cathagne warned.

"The dark side?" Kundar questioned.

"Yes." She held up her hand and closed her eyes. "If you listen carefully, you can hear their moans."

"I think she has been here far too long," Kundar said to his men telepathically.

"We need to keep an eye on her," another replied.

Her eyes snapped open and she hastily walked ahead of them. *They think I am not of sound mind,* she said to herself, feeling as though she was being disparaged once again, having listened to their conversation.

After a long trek, the sounds of rushing water grew in intensity. "This is the place," Cathagne stated.

The trees parted before them, and they stopped at the edge of a large river whose water sparkled and glinted beneath the rays of the sun as if someone had poured stardust into its depths. They were taken-a-back when they looked up at the enormous silver orb, looking as though it was sitting a-top the waterfall. Its molten-silver colors swirled as if being pushed by the rushing swells. A wave of liquid silver poured over the rocks and into the hollow of a pool which spilled down the side of the mountain, feeding a smaller waterfall which plunged into the aquamarine river mere feet from where they stood.

Cathagne leapt across the river and led them up a thin, winding path, which led them around the opposite side of the waterfall. She pulled a large branch, pushed it aside, and a makeshift door opened, revealing a rather large cave.

Cathagne walked in and stood next to a makeshift bed and looked at Kadric. "She can rest here."

Kundar looked at his warriors. "Check the outlining areas." He then followed Kadric and Cathagne into the cave. As he walked around, it was clear she had turned it into a makeshift shelter. Not only did she have a small bed made of timber, there was a table and two chairs, a cracked mirror hanging from a root traveling along the cave's wall, a few of her belongings, and a dozen paintings leaning against the walls, and placed on makeshift shelves.

Kadric pulled a small blanket over Sylvana and looked around. "What is this place?"

She turned, faced Kadric and crossed her arms over her chest. "I stay here whenever I can. It 'tis my only escape from thy cruelty of thy Faye."

Kadric placed a hand on her shoulder and gently stroked it. "I am sorry you have suffered so, but you are safe now."

For the first time since meeting him, she smiled. "You are very kind, Kadric Orfaedo. Sylvana is lucky to have you."

Chapter 24

Riordan and his warriors had rushed into the fray, attacked the wounded and exploited the weakness of those who were battle worn and in a weakened physical state first. Arrows were hissing through the air, the sounds of metal meeting metal and the roars and screams from the fallen and wounded surrounded them in an illusion of chaos and violence. Nosferatu, Lycan, and Faye fought with controlled movements, thoughts, and ages of experience on the battlefields. However, having turned on each other, small groups of Faye and Lycan were being surrounded and slaughtered by the Nosferatu warriors.

One of the Faye warriors was grappling on the ground with a wounded Lycan; their bodies clenched around one another, fighting for dominance. The Faye warrior hooked his leg around the Lycan's neck and rolled his body on top of the Lycans and just as he raised his dagger, Marius leapt on top of the Faye and drove his body into the Lycans with his foot. He then plunged his sword through them both; immediately he pulled his blade from their bodies and brought it across their necks, severing their heads.

He stretched his arms out, lifted his chin, and a guttural roar overshadowed the sounds of battle. Seeking another victim, he noticed Riordan, Nicolai, and Kieran fighting close to one another across the field. *They have become a force to be reckoned with. I have missed their early years. I will not miss their latter*, he thought.

Another Faye attacked from the side, and he swiftly ducked, grabbed the Faye by the throat, and drove his blade through his chest. The Faye's eyes widened, and he wrapped his hands around the sword. Marius slowly pushed the blade further through his body and watched his pupils dilate.

"I take your life in the name of vengeance." Marius recoiled his blade, tossed the Faye to the ground, and turned his attention back to his grandsons. He then scanned the immediate area for any threat headed in their direction.

Riordan pounced on a Lycan's back, and before it had time to react, Riordan drove his sword through his flank. The Lycan roared, whipped his right arm around and it crossed Riordan's temple, knocking him back. Riordan landed in a half-crouched position and as he stood, he felt two large hands seize his neck, the elongated claws burrowing into his flesh. He reached behind him, wrapped an arm around the Lycan's neck, flipped it over his body, slammed him to the ground, and drove his blade through his heart.

As Riordan backed up, he heard Marius's voice yell his name from across the battlefield as if warning him. He spun around and found himself face to face with Kieran, who placed one hand on his shoulder and drove his blade through his chest.

Riordan grabbed a fist full of Kieran's vest and looked at him with a thousand-yard stare, and Kieran's eyes were cruel and pitiless.

It took a moment for Nicolai's horror-filled thoughts to register Marius screaming his name, and the sight of Kieran attacking Riordan slammed all those witnessing the attack into silence.

Nicolai leapt to Riordan's side, and with a swift front kick, sent Kieran spiraling backwards.

"What the fuck have you done? Are you out of your goddamn mind, brother?" he roared.

Riordan grabbed the hilt of the sword with both hands and stared at it.

"Rio let go," Nicolai said, before pulling the blade from his chest. He then tore Riordan's tattered vest and tunic open, and the blood ran down Riordan's chest and stomach.

Riordan grasped Nicolai's shoulder with one hand, and covered the gaping wound with the other. He then pulled it back and looked at the blood as it dripped from his palm and ran down his wrist. He looked at Nicolai, whose face was ashen.

"You're going to be okay, brother." Nicolai said with a trembling voice. Tobias and Rhazien appeared next to them. "What the fuck did Kieran do?" Tobias raged.

Riordan dropped to his knees; Nicolai dropped with him, and Tobias and Rhazien kneeled on either side of them. Marius, however, materialized over Kieran and grabbed a fist full of his vest and snarled in his face. "What the fuck have you done?" With a swift punch Marius knocked him unconscious.

The rest of their warriors allowed the remaining Faye to retreat as they formed a large, protective wall around Riordan, Kieran, Nicolai, and Marius, not sure what to think or what else to do in this moment. However, leaving them unprotected was not an option.

They laid Riordan on his back and impatiently awaited the wound to heal, and although the bleeding slowed, it did not heal. Nicolai placed his hand firmly over the wound. "Rio, why aren't you healing?" he questioned, feeling frantic. "Tobias, place your hand over mine and press down when I pull it out."

Tobias did as asked. "I got it."

Nicolai bit down on his wrist and placed it against Riordan's mouth. "Feed, brother."

Riordan took what he could and then pushed his hand away. "It's not working." His breathing was labored, and he was feeling weaker by the minute.

"Marius!" Nicolai shouted.

Marius shouted at a few of the warriors standing next to him. "Secure him!" He then rushed over, kneeled at Riordan's side, and slit his wrist. "Take my blood, Grandson."

Again, Riordan drank what he could, and the skin fluctuated around the wound but failed to heal.

"We need to get him out of here," Marius stated.

Riordan grasped Nicolai's forearm. "Nicolai, I need you to give me your word. You will get our brother back. Kieran did not do this of his own volition. He is not to be harmed. When they took Sylvana, somehow, they got to him."

"Rio, no one will lay a hand on him. We will figure it out together."

"Nicolai, listen to me. If I don't make it, tell Sylvana she was my last thought, my last desire, and my one and only true love."

"Stop, Rio. You can tell her yourself. Her blood healed my wounds. It will heal yours as well."

"I don't think I'll make it," Riordan said in a raspy voice.

Tobias ripped off his tunic, folded it and placed it over the wound, and wrapped one of his straps around his body to secure the material. Rio gasped when he pulled the ends of the straps as tightly as he could and tied it into a knot.

"Fuck me," Riordan mumbled.

"We need to get him to Sylvana," Nicolai said frantically.

Sylvana gasped for a breath and sat up. "Where are my mates?"

Cathagne jumped when Sylvanas sudden outburst startled her. Kadric, however, rushed over and kneeled before her. "They are fine, Sylvie. They are all together, finishing the last of the Faye and Lycan."

She tossed the blanket to the side and cupped her amulet in her fist. "They are not fine! "Riordan?" He is not answering me—something terrible has happened!" She then called to Nicolai and Kieran and did not get a response.

"Kundar looked at Kadric and called out to Riordan telepathically. *"Milord, Sylvana is awake. Is everything okay?"* When he did not get a response, he reached out to Nicolai and Kieran. When they failed to respond, he called to Tobias.

"Kundar, it's bad. We need to get Riordan to Sylvana. Where are you?" Tobias asked.

"We are not too far. I will come for you."

"Make it quick," Tobias stated.

Sylvana grabbed Kadric's forearm and stood. "We have to go to them—now. They are not listening."

"Sylvana, you can barely walk," Kadric replied.

She stumbled out of the cave, stretched her arms out to her sides, and tried to transform. However, the pain took her breath away, and she crumpled to the ground.

Kadric kneeled beside her and stroked her back. "Sylvana, I will go to them. You cannot transform the energy again so quickly."

She placed her forehead on his knee and sobbed. "Father. Rio is dying and I can no longer feel Kieran's energy."

"Kadric, I need to go. Tobias said they need to get Riordan to Sylvana." Kundar then looked at his warriors. "I need twelve men."

"I'm coming with you," Sylvana said.

"No, milady. You will only slow us down," Kundar replied, as he and his men dissipated.

Cathagne placed her hand on Kadric's shoulder and nodded. She then kneeled down and draped her arm over Sylvana's back. "It's going to be okay, Sylvana."

"Nicolai? Dammit, answer me!" Sylvana demanded.

"Syl, are you okay?" he replied.

"Holy shit! Why have you all not replied to me?"

"I will explain when I see you. We are on our way."

"Where are Rio and Kieran?"

"We will be there soon."

"Answer me! What has happened to Rio and Kieran?"

"Rio has been hurt, and Kieran is out of his fucking mind."

"I'm coming," she replied.

"Sylvana, stay put! Don't you dare come this way."

Feeling panicked, she jumped up and ran down the path.

"Sylvana!" Cathagne yelled as she chased after her.

Cadell, Kadric, and the other warriors appeared on the path before her, and Kadric held out his hands. "Sylvana, you are not leaving."

"Father, get out of my way," she snarled.

She looked to her right, and then to her left, trying to find a way around. However, they had her surrounded. She waved her hand in their direction and a small whiff of icy mist dissipated as quickly as it had appeared. The meager amount of energy it took caused her to stumble.

However, Cathagne grabbed a hold of her, and kept her upright. "Fuck me," she bellowed. "Father, I beg of you. My mates need me."

"Sylvana, they are on their way as we speak. The best thing you can do to help is to gather your strength. What good will you be to them if you incapacitate yourself?" He walked over and wrapped his arms around her, and she clung to him.

Cathagne moved Sylvana's hair off of her face. "Come, sit over here with me. We shall wait together."

They sat on a ledge overlooking the river and Sylvana pulled her knees to her chest and waited impatiently for any sign of them.

Kadric sat beside her. "Sylvie, you should feed. You will need all of your strength should one of them need your blood."

She looked up at him. "You know Rio and Kieran are in trouble, don't you?"

"I am only thinking ahead. But based on your feelings and Kundar leaving, you need to be prepared for the worse-case scenario, darling. The stronger you are, the better," he said, as he held out his wrist.

"Have you received word from Diaspor?" Vispera asked.

"Everything is going according to plan," Stronbo replied.

"And thy others?"

"Those whom are alive have retreated and safely behind our veiled walls," Eoin answered.

"And thy rest of thy kingdom?" Stronbo said.

"We have it sealed, Priestess."

"Show me my reflection," Vispera requested.

Stronbo made a circular motion with his hands in front of his body.

Vispera opened her tunic and turned her head from side to side and stared at her grayish colored skin. "'Tis growing."

"Yes, Priestess," Stronbo replied.

She cupped her hands together and dragged them apart. She then wrapped the silk scarf around her neck and reached for Stronbo's forearm. "Take me to him."

He helped her stand, and she wrapped her arm around his, and they walked down to the cells below the main fortress. They stepped across the hexagonal, glass floor and stood before a large pane of glass. Vispera waved her hand, and the smoke trapped within dissipated. Kieran was on his knees; with his arms chained behind his back and his ankles chained to the floor.

Kieran looked up when the smoke in one pain swirled and slowly dissipated, revealing Vispera and another warrior standing before him on the other side. "Vispera," he snarled.

"Kieran Acheron. Welcome to thy Gehenna of Shadows," she relayed telepathically.

"You look a little disheveled. Is there something wrong with your voice, Vispera? Did the dragon leave her mark?" he said in jest.

"'Tis thy power of thy cell. Thy only communication you have is with me telepathically, of course."

"What do you want?"

"Release him," she stated.

The chains fell from his wrists and ankles and disappeared through the floor as if being pulled by a cogwheel. He rose and stepped toward them. *"There is a reason I am standing here. I assume you need me, or you would have had me killed already?"*

"Your time is nigh. There is no escape. No one will feel your energy, nor will they hear you. It will be as if you do not exist."

When a large creature, on one side of his cell slammed its body against the thick pane, it created a large smoke ring within the panes, its center black as coal. Kieran didn't so much as flinch, but the strength of the glass was more than concerning. He glanced around and, upon first appearances, the cubed cell seemed to have been forged from glass. However, a thin layer of swirling smoke obscured all from view. Not even his keen sense of sight could penetrate it. *How the fuck and I going to get out of this?* He wondered, having cloaked his thoughts.

"Curious what they are?" she asked.

"Is that what happens to those who have slipped their cocks between your legs?" He chuckled.

Stronbo's eyes narrowed, he took one step forward, and pulled his sword.

Kieran smirked at Stronbo. *"Did I strike a nerve?"*

Vispera held up her hand and motioned for Stronbo to cease. *"Jest if you will. Soon you will know exactly what they are."*

He placed one arm behind his back and bowed in a mocking manner. *"I look forward to it."*

"I have something to show you." She slid one finger down the pane, and as she disappeared, a blurry image morphed and twisted and Kieran saw himself on the battlefield, along with Riordan and Nicolai. He watched as his doppelgänger ran toward Riordan, and just as he turned around, he shoved his sword into his brother's chest. The smoke consumed the image and filled the panes, and he could no longer see Vispera or her warrior.

Kieran stumbled back, consumed with rage and anguish. "What have you fucking done?" he bellowed. He turned and slammed his fists on the pane and dropped his head between his arms. *They will think I killed my brother. No—this can't be. Rio can't be dead! She cut off the image—which means he is alive. Had he died; she would have shown me?*

Once again, the creature on the other side slammed its body against the pane, and in response, Kieran's fist made contact multiple times in quick succession. "Come and fucking get me!" he bellowed. He then stepped back. *Think*, he said to himself. *Vispera is lying. If it can hear me, and I can hear it—there was no need for her to speak to me telepathically. She has to be keeping me alive for other reasons. The dragon? It had to have wounded Vispera?*

He looked down and the ambient, multi-colored light within the cell glimmering from the crystalline floor. *Find its weakness,* he told himself, as he knelt down and swept his hand over the floor. Although it appeared as if he was standing on crushed gems, there was not one imperfection to be felt. He rose and walked from corner to corner, and even though he could not see the other prisoners; he heard them. The grunting, groaning, and caterwauling were unfamiliar, and he had no idea what the creatures imprisoned all around him were or where they could have come from.

Sylvana jumped to her feet, ran down the path and stood at the edge of the river and a legion of warriors appeared. Nicolai and Tobias were carrying Rio, while other warriors were carrying the injured and the dead. They leapt across the river and Sylvana rushed to Nicolai. "Oh, my god—Rio!" She stared at the saturated material secured to his chest. "What the hell happened?" She then glanced around. "Where is Kieran?"

"Kieran is with us, but our immediate concern is for Rio. He needs your blood."

"Get him to the cave," Kundar said.

They laid him on his back and Sylvana kneeled on the bed next to him, slit her wrist, and Rio, who was barely conscious, placed his hand on her thigh.

She placed her wrist against his lips, and he cupped his mouth around the gash. "You are going to be okay, my love," she said, as she stroked his arm.

Nicolai stood at her side with his hands on her shoulders. Rio gently pushed her arm away, and she looked up at Nicolai. "Where is Kieran?"

Nicolai nodded to Kundar, who stood at the entrance. He stepped out of the cave and returned with Kieran who was escorted in by multiple guards, with his wrists bound behind his back.

"Why the hell do you have him tied up?" Just as she started to slide off the bed, Riordan squeezed her thigh.

"Stay away from Kieran," he mumbled telepathically.

"Why?" she asked.

"Syl, Kieran did this to Rio," Nicolai answered.

"What? No! He would never hurt either of you," she protested.

"He did it. We all witnessed him attack Rio."

"Nicolai, I don't understand? Why would he attack his brother?"

"There were three of you standing before us after you and Vispera disappeared. We believe they got to Kieran at the same time. Either he's a shifter or they fucked with his mind? We just don't know?" Nicolai answered.

She stared at Kieran, who smiled and winked. However, there was something peculiar behind his warm expression, and absent was the familiar gleam in his eyes. She looked back at Nicolai for reassurance. He again nodded to Kundar, who removed Kieran from the cave.

Tears ran down her face and Nicolai picked her up and she wrapped her arms and legs around his body and tucked her face into the crook of his neck.

"Your blood will heal Rio and we will find a way to get Kieran back. If it is a Faye Shifter, in order to keep his form, they need to keep him alive," he said, trying his best to comfort her.

Cathagne walked over to Kadric and whispered. "May I see Riordan's wound?"

"I suppose?" He then addressed Nicolai. "Milord, would you allow Cathagne to look at Riordan's wound?"

"Why?" he asked, as he set Sylvana down.

"Milord, I may know why he is not healing."

Nicolai nodded, and he and Sylvana stepped aside. Carefully, she undid the strap and pulled the material back.

Sylvana looked behind her at Nicolai. "It's barely healed?"

He wrapped his arms around her chest. "Thanks to you, it's better than it was."

Cathagne studied the wound and picked up on a subtle scent. She slid her fingers over the blood, rubbed them together, and smelt them; she then looked at Nicolai. "They have poisoned him with Ifyinpetta."

"What the hell is that?" Nicolai questioned.

"It is toxic to thy Faye. Why would they poison him with it? He is Nosferatu, yes?" she asked.

Nicolai looked at Tobias, who was leaning against the cave's wall near the bed. He pushed himself off and looked at Riordan before addressing Nicolai telepathically. *"The three of you carry the powers of the Faye."* Tobias then looked at Cathagne. "What will it do?"

"If he does not receive thy panacea, it will kill him."

"How do we acquire the cure?" Nicolai asked.

"I can make it. However, I need to gather enough sap from thy Azunpary flower."

"We will get whatever you need. Where is it?" Tobias asked.

"I need to go. It is a delicate plant, and you won't know how to extract its sap. It grow's only in thy Marsh of Savatham."

"How long does Rio have?" Sylvana asked.

"I have never seen thy would heal on one who has been poisoned with Ifyinpetta. I suppose as long as you feed him, he will survive until we return?"

"Well, that was reassuring," Sylvana mumbled under her breath.

"Cathagne, my men and I will take you, and I want to leave now," Tobias said.

"Very well. Let me gather my things." She walked over to a small chest and removed a few items. She then left to allow them a few moments of privacy. As she walked onto the ledge, she looked over and Kieran was sitting on his knees under guard. She tilted her head to the side and glared at him.

Kieran looked at her and furrowed his brow. *"Be a good little whore and keep your mouth shut, Cathagne, or I will have Vispera place your lover's head on a post,"* he threatened telepathically.

She walked over and the guards stepped forward. "May I? I need to see if he smells of thy poison."

Kundar, who was standing nearby, nodded, and she walked over and kneeled, and pretended to smell Kieran's neck. *"I don't believe these are tight enough,"* she whispered. She subtly clenched her hand around the binds, and they wrapped themselves tighter around his wrists and the heat from the liquid seeping from her palm seared them into his skin.

"You are in no position to threaten me, Diaspor." She let go, and as she walked away, he fell onto his side when the liquid seeped into his veins.

"What have you done to him?" Kundar asked threateningly.

"Not a thing. I can smell thy Ifyinpetta on him as well. I will gather enough of the plant for them both."

"Wise decision, Cathagne," Diaspor mumbled before losing consciousness.

Tobias walked over and placed his hand on Nicolai's shoulder. "I will take Rhazien with us. Kundar asked to remain behind to watch over Sylvana. We will be back as soon as we can."

"You know I would go with you—"

Tobias cut him off mid-sentence. "Your place is here with your brothers and Sylvana."

"Tobias, please be careful, and if you don't mind, can you hurry?" Sylvana asked.

Tobias smiled and pulled her in for a tight embrace. "Darling, I will get Cathagne back without haste."

She pulled away and placed her hand on his chest. "Thank you."

He looked at Riordan, one more time and then nodded at Nicolai. "We will be back."

Sylvana crawled onto the bed and laid down next to Riordan who wrapped one arm around her back. "I'm still with you, Sângele Nostru," he mumbled with a barely audible voice.

Nicolai walked out and motioned to Kundar to follow him; they walked down to the river and stared at the twin moons rising above the jagged mountain range.

Nicolai placed one hand on the hilt of his sword and the other on his hip. "We are trapped within the veil. Rio is in bad shape, Sylvana is beside herself and Kieran—I don't know what the fuck they have done to or with him?"

"We are all in this together, milord. However, the weight is now on your shoulders," Kundar replied.

Marius walked over and placed his hand on Nicolai's shoulder. "Heavy is the head that wears the crown."

"Now that you have returned, I assumed you would want it back?" Nicolai replied.

"Grandson, I have been incapacitated for far too long. I am as unfamiliar with the new kingdom as I am with this place. I have no interest in it. Until Riordan can stand on his own, it belongs to you."

"What are your thoughts where Kieran is concerned?"

"What does your gut tell you?" Marius asked.

"It's not our brother."

"My thoughts, exactly," Marius replied.

"What are your plans regarding Vispera and the Lycans?" Kundar asked.

Nicolai glanced at the unfamiliar surroundings and then patted Kundar on the shoulder. "Gather our warriors together. Marius and I will meet with the entire legion. It goes without saying the Faye are making preparations to either attack or defend themselves. Now would be the ideal time to strike, but we need to figure out what happened to Kieran. As for the Lycans, I can only assume they will not interfere after having turned on the Faye.

Marius nodded. "I agree. Running blindly into the situation is ill-advised. We need to figure out how to break their resistance without putting Kieran's life on the line."

"I will gather our warriors," Kundar said.

"I am going to check on our imposter, as well as Rio and Sylvana. And until we know what is up with Kieran, no one touches him," Nicolai said.

Kundar nodded in agreement and walked away, and Nicolai and Marius headed for Rio and Kieran.

To be continued in <u>Crowns of Darkness</u> Book 2
Coming Soon!

Glossary of Terms

Nosferatu – Vampire

Faye – Fairy's that have evolved over the centuries.

Lycans – Werewolves that have the ability to shape shift.

Shifter – Immortal humans that have the ability to shape shift, but do not have any other archaic powers.

Helot – i.e. half breed. Half Nosferatu, half Lycan – they do not have the power of either Nosferatu or Lycan and are seen as undesirable and lowest in class and status.

Inbreds- Inbred Lycans that are feral and wild, and do not carry the shape-shifting powers of the Lycans.

Gomorrah – a ghetto

Pudenda – Vagina

Panacea – a cure

Sirona – a healer

Governing bodies

The Guild of Entente – A council that consists of the highest ranking members from each purebred Nosferatu clan that reside in the Kingdom.

The Mercurial Guardians – A council that consists of the highest ranking Faye lords that reside in the kingdom

Barouqe Warriors – The highest ranking warriors who were appointed by the Acherons to guard the Nosferatu Lords as well as the Kingdom.

Black Moor – The large river that separates the Nosferatu Kingdom from the Lycans lands where they were sent after being banished.

The Veil – A barrier between the Faye kingdom and the rest of the world.

Kingdoms

Kroyidia – The Nosferatu kingdom – ruled by the Acherons

Estraxath – The Faye kingdom. – ruled by the Faye's High Lord Dronve and his mate Vispera, the Faye High Priestess.

Pronunciations

Acheron's Amulet: Sanguis Murielrum – Sang-wee Mar-eel-e-um

Sylvana's nick name: Sângele Nostru – Sang-lee Nos-true Meaning: Our blood

Clan Names

The Acheron Clan – Ash-her-on

Marius – Mar-e-us

Riordan Demidicus – Ree-or-dan Dah-mida-cus

Nicolai Theron – Nik–o-lye There-on

Kieran Malachi – Keery-un   Mal-a-ki

Tobias Severn – Toe-by-us Sev-run

Lenora Isadora Phelan - Len-or-a   Eza-dora Fey-lan

The Ascelin Clan – Ah-seal-e-on

Jarimor – Ya-uh-more

Lucinda – Lew-sin-duh

Cathagne Elsia Orendo-Ascelin – Ka-thag-knee E-lease-see-uh Or-end-o

Kadric Orfaedo – Kad-rik Or-fa-do

Phaidra Myrine – Fae-druh Mir-e-n

Alaric Kadric – Ala-rik Kad-rik

Calista Osada – Ka-list-a O-sad-uh

Sylvana Phaidra – Syl-van-uh Fae-druh

Miriam Pythia – Mere-re-um Pith-e-uh

The Marque Clan: Mar-keez

Cadell – Ka-dell

Enatta – N-natta

Laurent – Law-rent

The Cynfadel Clan – Sin-fa-del

Jorin – Yor-un

Orenda – Or-end-uh

Lycans

Bastan – Bah-stan – Rana's Grandfather

Ranan Lupine Kashgar – Ruh-nan Lew-pine Kush-gar

Lagar – Lay-gar **Cobium** – Ko-be-um

Cobium – Ko-be-um

Faye

Obernzel – O-ber-zeal

Dronve – Drone-vey

Vispera – Viz-pure-uh

Diaspor – Die-az-pour

Stronbo – Strone-bo

Mascuriel – Mask-cure-e-el

Ninbae – Nin-be

Eoin - E-on

Members of the Guild

Astaroth – As-tor-roth

Mordeci -Mor-deck-ee

Norix – Nor-ex

Rhazien – Ra-z-un

Leon – Lee-on

Kirnan – Ker-nun

Lucias - Lew-see-us

Phaone – Fae-own

Vestal – Ves-tall

Warriors

Barouqe – Bah-roke

Ilial -Ill-e-ale

Klyn – Klinn

Damascus – Duh-mask-us

Leodion -Lee-deon

Marius – Mare-e-us

Markus – Mar-cus

Cassius – Ka-c-us

Main characters

Muriel – Mir-e-l

Venthana Lynexia Mehira – Ven-than-un. Lynn-ex-e-uh Ma-here-uh

Florin – Flore-un

Others

Calantha – Ka-lan-tha

Aurelia – R-el-e-uh

Stefania – Steph-an-e-uh

Nora – Nor-uh

Latavia – La-tae-v-uh

Elsa – El-suh

Stallions and Mares

Skadi – Ska-dey

Kesaro – Ka-sorrow

Rana – Ra-nah

Rhone – Rone

Prada – Pra-duh

Shifter

Amarok - Am-ah-rock

CROWNS OF DARKNESS
FAMILY LINEAGE

Marius
Riordan Acheron

Emerande
Biju Scallion

Emilaï
Lysa Ascelin

Lucinda
Sabrione Ascelin

Anton
Roderick Orendo

Lyllith
Orenda Artemia

Viktor
Damascus Acheron

Phaidra
Myrine Ascelin

Kadric
Armond Orfaedo

Cathagne
Eldia Orendo-Ascelin

Riordan
Demidicus Acheron

Nicolai
Theron Acheron

Kieran
Malachi Acheron

Alaric
Kadric Orfaedo-Ascelin

Calista
Osana Orfaedo-Ascelin

Sylvana
Phaidra Orfaedo-Ascelin

Miriam
Pythia Orfaedo-Ascelin

Also By J.L. Weir

Crowns of Darkness

A Crown Without Mercy

Crowns of Darkness Book 2
Coming Soon!

The Legends of Mortem

I'd Rather Burn

Bound in Darkness

Beyond the Veil